Praise for

the
secrets
of primrose
square

'A **wonderful** read dealing with all of our human frailties through a prism of **warmth** and **compassion**. This is such an appealing story . . . **Funny**, **smart** and thoroughly **engaging**'

LIZ NUGENT

'A **wise**, **warm** and **witty** gem, that will make you weep as you uncover the truths of the residents of Primrose Square. This is a **special** novel and **I loved it**'

CARMEL HARRINGTON

'**Beautiful** . . . a **stunning** book full of **wonderful characters** that you grow to care about so deeply. The story is so perfectly paced and I loved the twist. It made me laugh and made me weep. It is layered, **tender**, **warm**, **funny** and **heart-breaking**. A truly **wonderful** book by an immensely talented writer'

SINEAD MORIARTY

Claudia was born in Dublin, where she still lives and works as an author and actress. She's a *Sunday Times* top ten-bestselling author in the UK and a number one bestselling author in Ireland, selling more than half a million copies in paperback alone.

To date, Claudia has published fourteen novels, four of which have been optioned, two for movies and two for TV. She's currently hassling producers for a walk-on role, and is hoping they might even let her keep the costumes for free.

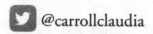 @carrollclaudia

 @claudiacarrollbooks

Claudia Carroll

the secrets of primrose square

ZAFFRE

First published in Great Britain in 2018 by
ZAFFRE PUBLISHING
80–81 Wimpole St, London W1G 9RE
www.zaffrebooks.co.uk

A CIP catalogue record for this book is available from the British Library.

Hardback ISBN: 978–1–78576–525–4
Trade Paperback ISBN: 978–1–78576–526–1

Also available as an ebook

1 3 5 7 9 10 8 6 4 2

Typeset by IDSUK (Data Connection) Ltd
Printed and bound in Great Britain by Clays Ltd, Elcograf S.p.A.

Zaffre Publishing is an imprint of Bonnier Zaffre,
a Bonnier Publishing company
www.bonnierzaffre.co.uk
www.bonnierpublishing.co.uk

A woman is like a tea bag.
You can't tell how strong she is until you put her in hot water

Attributed to Eleanor Roosevelt

This book celebrates female friendship, so very special thanks to my girlfriends, who've been like a life-support system to me over the years.
We're so much stronger together, ladies.
Always.

Winter

Susan

48 THE CRESCENT

Susan didn't used to be like this. To look at her now, soaked through to the skin on a dark, wintry night as she stood on the street outside an eighteen-year-old boy's home, staring, just staring up at his bedroom window, you'd think she was some kind of deranged stalker.

It's eight minutes past eight, she thought, glancing down at her watch. *I'll stay here as long as I can, no matter how bad the rain gets.* From bitter experience over the past few months, she knew that an hour was about as long as she could hold out safely for, before someone came out of the house to accost her. To tell her to cop herself on, that she'd a pre-teen daughter at home who needed her.

Haven't you better things to be doing with yourself, Susan? We know you're hurting, but hurting us isn't really going to change anything, now is it?

Worst-case scenario, someone from inside the house would call the Guards (again) and report her (yet again). Then if they weren't too busy, a squad car would generally arrive between thirty-four and forty-two minutes later, with flashing lights and full sirens blaring, if they really wanted to intimidate her.

Two cops would get out – it was always two – one usually a woman, who'd do a 'bad cop' routine with Susan, at least until they heard her side of the story. Then after a good talking to and maybe even the vague threat that she was running the risk of getting herself sectioned if she kept up this carry on, they'd take her back home to Primrose Square. There, they'd usually make her a strong cup of tea and give her the same 'you want to watch yourself' speech Susan had already sat through dozens of times.

Generally that's what would happen, as soon as they realised she wasn't an arsonist or a stalker or a deranged middle-aged woman in love with a minor. Just an ordinary woman dealing with the unimaginable the only way she knew how.

Time would pass, days, even weeks. Then sooner or later, the cops would try to wash their hands of the whole sorry mess (yet again) with the threat of a restraining order or a visit from a social worker 'just to check how you are', and a stern caution to 'try to be more careful in future, Susan. We know this can't be easy for you, but this kind of behaviour isn't doing you any favours. Next time you could end up in real trouble.'

Worth it, Susan thought, as a bus splashed past her, momentarily blocking out her view of the house she was fixated on. Well worth it. What real harm was she doing anyway? All she was doing was standing on a public pavement minding her own business, nothing more. Nothing she wasn't perfectly entitled to do. Besides, in this city, the cops should be out trying to catch warring drug barons, not hassling innocent women who weren't bothering anyone. At least, no one who hadn't bloody well asked for it in the first place.

I can't forget, she thought. *Never, as long as I draw breath, will I ever be able to forget. So why should he? Why should this fucker get to sleep soundly in his bed at night after what he's done?*

Tonight I'll give it exactly another fifty-seven minutes and forty-five seconds, she decided, squinting down at her watch through the icy cold darkness. Then, providing they didn't throw her into a prison cell overnight as a cautionary warning, she'd come back again tomorrow at precisely the same time and do it all over again.

Melissa

18 PRIMROSE SQUARE

At exactly 8:08 p.m., Melissa Hayes was at home, in the kitchen extension that once used to be her mother's pride and joy, heating up a beef stew that no one would touch, and taking care to leave the place spotless behind her, which no one would thank her for. Twelve years of age and desperately trying to keep up some semblance of normality.

Her dad had at least called her from abroad, she thought, picking at a tiny bit of stew. (It had tasted so delicious when she'd made it earlier in Miss Hogan's home economics class, but it was all dry and salty now, probably because she'd left it in the oven too long.) They'd only talked for a few minutes, but still, it didn't really matter. At least Melissa could silently thank her stars that her dad was one parent she needn't worry about.

He was in the army and on active service with peacekeeping troops out in Lebanon, where he worked in the Engineering Corps. It was to be a six-month tour of duty, which he'd signed up for last year, not long after everything that had happened. Escaping, Melissa had thought at the time, though, of course, she hadn't said a word out loud. Her dad had patiently explained that he had no choice; when you were a Lieutenant Captain in the army, you went wherever you were posted, without any say in the matter.

Still, though. It looked an awful lot like running away from where Melissa was standing.

'It's only for a few months, sweetheart,' he'd tried to reassure her before he left. 'That's all. And I'll call my little princess every single day – that's a promise.'

Melissa had swallowed back the tears and told him that she understood, even though she didn't really. It didn't make sense; her dad was like a rock to her, so why did he have to go and leave them at a time like this? Night after night, when she was meant to be in bed asleep, she'd overheard her parents rowing, and she knew how upset her mum was, so her job was to pretend not to be.

Ever since what happened, Melissa had got good at pretending. Really good. She'd got so good that she could act like she was fine all day long whenever grown-ups were around and save her crying for when she was all alone in her room. Silent tears that no one would ever hear. She could pretend she didn't mind a bit when her Auntie Betty ruffled her hair and said, 'You're to be a brave girl now, pet. Remember you're all your poor parents have left.'

Melissa even managed a big, bright smile that horrible morning when she waved her dad off, all dressed up in his full uniform. There was only Melissa to say goodbye to him; her mum hadn't even bothered to get out of bed. Probably because he was running away. She knew it, her mum knew it, they all did. Melissa didn't even blame him. Half of her even wished she were a bit older, so she could run away too.

'So where is your mum, then?' he'd asked down the crackling phone line earlier that evening. 'Can I talk to her?'

'She's just stepped out to do a bit of shopping,' Melissa said, hating that she had to lie. But then what was the point of worrying her dad when he was thousands of miles away? That was just mean. Better to act like everything was hunky dory at home and hope her mum wouldn't be gone for too much longer. Better to pretend. Better to keep the truth a tight little secret.

'And how is she?' her dad asked, worried.

'Mum? Oh, she . . . emm . . . she's cool. Fantastic. We both are. We just really miss you, Dad, that's all.'

'All right, princess,' he said after a long, doubtful pause, his voice wafting in and out of coverage all the way from the Middle East. 'Well, tell her I called and I'll call again tomorrow at the same time. And that I love you both very much.'

'Will do!' Melissa had forced herself to say cheerily before hanging up. At least he'd checked with her, though, she thought, making herself swallow down a bite of the horrible, chewy beef. Even if she'd just told him a big pack of lies.

The truth was it was almost a quarter to nine and there was still no sign of her mum. She wasn't answering her phone either; Melissa had been trying it all evening with no luck. So now she'd gone from being a little bit worried to feeling full-on sick, almost like she could throw up.

Unable to stomach the smell of the stew, she shoved it away and picked up her schoolbag from the kitchen floor, so she could at least make a start on tomorrow's homework. There was a towering pile of ironing and laundry still to be done, but that'd just have to wait till later, along with the rest of the housework.

The kitchen had been like a bombsite when Melissa had come home from school earlier and she'd already lost so much time cleaning it up – or at least trying her very best to. She'd emptied the dishwasher, filled it up again, taken out the bins – which by then were stinking – and wiped down all the kitchen surfaces. It wasn't much, but at least if the neighbours or social workers called to the house asking nosey questions again, the place looked okay.

Well, okay-ish. The bedrooms upstairs were a complete pigsty and Melissa couldn't remember the last time her sheets had been changed or the towels washed. But that would just have to wait till she had more time at the weekend, wouldn't it?

She was already dead late with an English essay on *Romeo and Juliet* and if she didn't hand something in tomorrow, there'd be big trouble. Sally Jenkins, the school counsellor, would take her aside and start probing her about how things were at home and how they were all coping. It was happening a lot these days and it was mortifying.

'I don't mean to put you on the spot with personal questions, Melissa,' Sally had said just a few days ago. 'But we do know things can't be easy for your family at present. I'm just saying, if you ever need to talk, you know my door is always open.'

Melissa knew Sally was a kind woman with a lovely office where there were little bowls of fresh fruit and Maltesers that you could help yourself to, and Sally never minded how many you took to have for later.

'Just make sure you don't ruin your appetite for dinner,' she'd said cheerily to Melissa only last week. 'Or else your mum will be angry with you!' Little did she know that the little fun-sized pack of Maltesers and the apple Melissa had stuffed into her schoolbag *were* her dinner.

Melissa couldn't remember the last time her mum actually shopped or cooked or did anything normal, like all the other mothers did. And she knew Sally only meant well, but still, how could she possibly tell her what was really going on? That she had to look after herself because her mum just didn't seem able to any more? How could she tell any adult the real truth, without the threat of being carted off into a foster home?

So Melissa did what she'd trained herself to do over the past few weeks and months: she put on her brightest, bravest face and assured Sally that everything at home was just fantastic, thanks very much.

'In fact, my mum is really looking forward to the cake sale this weekend.' She'd beamed, plastering on the biggest, fakest smile she could as she embellished the fib. 'She's been baking round the clock. Wait till you see the chocolate biscuit cake she's made, Sally, it's so cool!'

All lies, of course. Melissa's mother hadn't so much as cooked a single meal in months, never mind baked an actual cake. Chances were that if Melissa even bothered to tell her about the cake sale, her mum would just say something like, 'That's nice, love,' then go back to twiddling with strands of her hair and staring into space, like she did so much these days. But Melissa had to say something to keep up appearances. Someone in this family had to keep the show on the road, didn't they?

She sighed and looked around the empty kitchen table, which she'd automatically set for four, then felt sad when she remembered she'd never need to do that again. Time was when dinners around the table were full of chat about the day's news, just like any other normal family. Her mum and dad were always laughing at some private joke, while her big sister Ella held court, usually ranting on about politics or else whatever protest march she was planning on getting to next.

Ella always seemed to have her nose stuck in a book at the table and her mum would have to yank it off her every single time, saying that it was bad manners to read during family dinnertime. The two of them would often have rows, but only pretend-y little ones. Joke rows. Then Ella would sigh dramatically, saying something sarcastic like, 'Well, *excuse me* for trying to expand my mind, Mum'. But Ella would always shoot Melissa an exasperated eye roll, as if to say, 'parents, eh?', followed by a reassuring little grin to show she was cool about it really.

There was a time, not so long ago, when Melissa never had to tell any fibs about her mother's baking or about cake sales or about how her family was doing. There was a time when the Hayes were just happy and normal and Melissa never even considered having to set foot inside the school counsellor's office.

But that was then, she thought, putting the thought out of her mind as she whipped out her copybook, determined to make a fresh start on her essay. *And this is now.*

By 9 p.m., there was still no sign of her mum. With her schoolwork all but abandoned, the knot of tension in Melissa's stomach had got far, far worse. Still no reply to any of her texts, even though she'd sent about a dozen at this stage.

MUM, WHERE ARE YOU? PLEASE COME HOME, MUM. PLEASE.

Wherever you are, Melissa thought, rereading the message as she double-checked that it had gone through. That was a laugh. There was only one place her mother could possibly be, wasn't there?

There was no way she could concentrate on her homework any more, so instead she opened the hall door, went down the three stone steps that led onto Primrose Square and glanced fretfully up and down the street, just in case there was any sign of her mum's familiar little Nissan zipping around the corner. It was a dark, wintry night and it had started to rain, so she grabbed Ella's fleece jacket and threw the hood over her head to try and keep dry. It still smelled of Ella's good lemony perfume from Lush and somehow that was comforting.

If you can hear me, Melissa prayed to her big sister, *then send Mum home safe. Please, can she just be safe.*

She spent another half hour pacing restlessly up and down the square, praying her mum would come home soon, but it got to 9:30 p.m. and still there was nothing. The street was deadly quiet at this hour and the gates of Primrose Square Gardens were always locked early in wintertime, so it looked a bit scary and deserted. The wind howled through its towering, bare sycamores and the roundabout in the playground area squeaked, almost like there were ghosts riding it.

There were lots of lights on in the houses around the square, smoke coming out of chimneys, signs that there were normal families inside, doing normal family things, like dinner and homework and watching YouTube. Not pacing up and down the square in the icy cold looking for a mother who'd gone missing.

From the north side of the square opposite, Melissa could see Dr Khan clambering up into the huge jeep she drove, probably on her way to the maternity hospital where she worked crazy hours as an anesthesiologist. But Dr Khan looked busy and hassled and must have been on call, because she never even spotted Melissa out on her own in the rain; instead she leapt up into her car and zoomed off at top speed.

Melissa sighed and was just about to give up when she heard a faint squealing noise, then felt something warm and furry between her feet. It was Magic, her next-door neighbour Jayne's cat, crying to get back inside.

'Oh Magic, look at you, you're drenched,' said Melissa, scooping up the wriggling little bundle of damp fur and cuddling him into her fleece. 'Come on, Jayne must be going mad looking for you.'

She knocked on Jayne's door – number nineteen – where the poor old lady had the telly on so loud, you could hear the theme tune from *Agatha Christie's Marple* blasting onto the street outside. There was a long delay while Melissa patiently waited in the rain for the front door to be opened – probably Jayne fumbling around the place to find her door keys.

Jayne was a lovely neighbour, even though she was probably about a hundred years old. She was warm and friendly and seemed to 'get' when you needed to be on your own, unlike most other people. She never talked down to Melissa, or put on a sad voice and embarrassed her by asking, 'So, tell me, how are things at home?' like everyone else did.

She was almost like a granny to Melissa, yet she'd always treated her like a grown adult and Melissa loved her for it. Everyone on Primrose Square adored Jayne – she'd been there ever since she first got married back in the Dark Ages and was their oldest resident by a mile. Jayne had lived on her own after her husband Tom had died, but all the other residents made a point of keeping a special eye out for her.

It took ages, but eventually Melissa heard a slow, creaking noise from the other side of the hall door, as a light from inside was switched on.

'Oh, Melissa, love, it's you,' said Jayne, her face breaking into a big smile. 'What a lovely surprise. Come on in out of the rain, pet, you'll get your death. And you've brought Magic home to me too,' she added, as the cat leapt out of Melissa's arms and raced into the warmth inside. 'God only knows what that little monkey has been up to.'

'Sorry, Jayne, I didn't mean to disturb you,' Melissa said, shaking the worst of the rain off her jacket and stepping inside. Jayne's house was so homely, it was always toasty warm inside and spotlessly clean, even though it was cluttered with old lady china and books and vinyl records piled high. There was a permanent smell of baking wafting from the kitchen – it smelt of cinnamon and ginger tonight, which only made Melissa's hungry tummy grumble even more. She almost felt guilty for wishing she could just spend the night here, where she'd be safe and minded and maybe even fed.

'You didn't interrupt a thing,' said Jayne cheerfully. 'I was just messing about on the new laptop computer I got. Skyping, if you don't mind. It's all the go, I believe. I'm in the middle of a call right now – and it's not costing me a penny. Isn't that fantastic? And I'm on Facebook now too and I don't know myself. I'll have to send you a friend request one of these days, love.'

'Well . . . I'll leave you to it then,' said Melissa, slightly surprised that someone as ancient as Jayne knew all about Skype and Facebook. 'I really have to get going anyway.' She was half way down the stone steps again, reluctantly heading back out to the bitter cold, when Jayne stopped her in her tracks.

'Just one second, pet,' Jayne said, catching her arm and looking at her a bit suspiciously. 'What are you doing outside so late and on a wet night like this anyway? With no umbrella or anything?'

'Oh, nothing at all,' Melissa stammered. 'I just heard Magic squealing and thought she might need to get inside, that's all.'

'I don't see your mum's car,' said Jayne, stepping outside into the rain and peering up and down a line of parked cars. 'Where is Susan anyway, on an awful night like this?'

'Oh . . . just, you know, out . . .' Melissa's voice trailed off lamely.

'Don't tell me you've been on your own all evening?'

'No, not at all,' Melissa began to lie, from force of habit mainly, but Jayne's worried eyes quickly saw through her.

'You don't ever need to put on a brave face with me, pet, you know that,' she said, looking at Melissa keenly. 'This is me you're talking to. You can trust me, I won't say a word. I only want you to be safe, that's all.'

'Mum's . . . not here,' Melissa said in a wobbly little voice, hanging her head, glad to have that much off her chest.

'And do you know where she's gone?'

Silence. Just a little headshake from Melissa, that's as much as she could trust herself to do without crying.

'Right. Stay there, love. I'll grab my car keys and we'll go and find her.'

'But you're in the middle of a Skype call . . . '

'Never mind about that,' said Jayne firmly. 'You're far more important to me than some aul' phone call. I think we both know exactly where we can find your mother, so let's go and bring her back home, will we? And don't worry, sweetheart, I won't breathe a word to anyone else. This can stay our little secret, just between us.'

Jayne

19 PRIMROSE SQUARE

'Hello, Tom, love, it's me. Yet again,' Jayne said, pummeling at the bread dough she was making, as she chatted away to an empty kitchen.

'The thing is I really need someone to bounce this off or else I might lose my reason. Supposing you'd huge news to give your family and you didn't know how? I've tried my best to keep what's going on a secret for as long as I could, but it just doesn't feel right to keep this to myself any more. Jason needs to be told and told soon – it's the very least I can do for our only child. Fair is fair, and after all, this could end up changing his life just as much as mine.

'So I've just emailed him (I know . . . me, Tom, on the emails . . . Can you believe it? You were always on at me to get a computer and now there's no stopping me!) And I've invited him over later on this evening for a nice early dinner. The plan is, I'll do a few nice pork chops for Jason – his favourite – and if he brings Irene with him, then I suppose I'll just have to throw a head of lettuce at her till she gets over this whole 5:2 nonsense, or whatever fad diet she's on right now. Then I'll wait till the pair of them have eaten, because you know how Jason's always in miles better form with a big feed in him.

'Now, I know it might sound a bit rude of me, love,' she went on, spooning the dough onto her work surface and sprinkling it with flour, 'but the thing is, I'm secretly hoping they won't be able to get a babysitter, so Jason can't bring Irene with him in the first place. Granted, the woman has her good points and you were always at pains to remind me what a great wife she is to him and such a good mother to the twins too, but Mother of Divine, she really would try the patience of a saint.

'Do you remember the time Irene came around here not long after your funeral, and told me she could get the house professionally valued for free?

'"The estate agency I work for would only be delighted to look after it all for you," she said to me, brazen as you like. Then she spent the whole night going on about her own mother in a nursing home and how she'd initially dreaded it, yet blossomed the minute she got in. "Oh, they've taught Mummy to do flower arranging like a professional now and she's even learned to bake at the home," the little madam said to me, right here in my own kitchen, with you, sitting right there in your urn as a witness, Tom.

'"You really should consider it, you know," she said to me, smug as anything, with a big fake smile on her face. "None of us is getting any younger. And living on your own can't be easy, particularly since Tom passed away. We're the only family you have and we worry about you so much."

'Well, only good manners prevented me from giving Irene a good smack across that smug, pinched little face. I told her that I was going absolutely nowhere and that the only way I'd leave my home would be feet first in my coffin. "And as for flower arranging and baking," I said, "I'll have you know my Madeira sponge was third runner-up in the Primrose Square Bake Off this year."

'Then she started harping on about number twenty-four on the square, the house down the road that's had all the building work going on for ages. "My company will be letting it out very soon," she says to me, not taking the hint to shut up. "We're confident we can get at least two grand a month for it, and you know I'd only be delighted to do the same thing for you, Jayne. I pride myself on being able to rent *anything* – you want to see some of the tiny little shoeboxes that we charge premium rates for! You could let out this place, move in with us and we'd split the rental income between us. You'd never be on your own again – now wouldn't that be fantastic?"

'As if, Tom! As if I could ever bring myself to leave Primrose Square! With all the happy memories you and I made here? Remember how it nearly bankrupted us when we first bought it as newlyweds all those years ago? We'd hardly a bean to our name, and everyone said that a Victorian three-storey, with such big rooms and lovely high ceilings in a spot so close to town, was way out of our league.

'But we still did it, didn't we? You knew I'd fallen in love with Primrose Square; the way our bedroom looks right over it and how beautiful it is in springtime, when the cherry blossoms come out and the local kids have all manner of fun in the playground. God be good to you, Tom, you were always so determined that our own kids would grow up in a nice, safe area just like this, with lovely neighbours around us to play with.

'Granted, we were only ever blessed with the one child, who seemed happier spending most of his childhood cooped up in front of the telly rather than out on the square kicking a football around with his pals, but that wasn't our fault now, was it? Jason's long since moved out and you're not around any more, Tom, but I still keep the house exactly as it was when you were alive. Almost as if you could walk in through the front door any second, plonk down in the nice comfy, battered old armchair you loved so much and say, "What's for dinner, love?" Sure I've all your stuff piled up here from decades back, your old books and your vinyl record collection, which to this day I can't bring myself to take to the charity shop.

'Tom, you of all people know how my neighbours have been like a second family to me, especially since you passed away and I got so lonely. They were the ones who got me through the dark days when my whole world seemed to shrink without you and hell would freeze over before I'd ever leave them.

'You know how much I love every single neighbour here, and how I'd do anything for them. Sure, only last night, didn't that scrap of a thing from next door, Melissa Hayes, come knocking on my door, far too late at night for a young one like her to be out and about. No sign of the mother, of course, and I know that family have had more than their share of troubles, but honestly, how could anyone leave a young girl like that home alone in this day and age?

'Melissa is like another grandchild to me, you know that, so I did what anyone would do for one of their own – I jumped into the car and took Melissa off to bring her mother home. I was in the middle of a Skype call at the time with – well, you already know all about that, don't you, Tom? Suffice to say that I abandoned the call I was on, grabbed my car keys and away we went.

'Poor little Melissa, your heart would go out to her. I know she was only small when you passed over, love, but do you remember what a bright, bubbly, affectionate little thing she always used to be? "You're not my real granny," she used to say whenever she'd give me a hug, "but you're like my pretend-y granny."

'And I know if you were here, Tom, you'd be the first to tell me to mind my own beeswax, but honestly, leaving a young one on her own just isn't right. Susan Hayes should think herself very lucky it was me who found her last night and got her safely home, not some social worker who'd only have given her a hard time. The poor woman needs support right now and not an earbashing from social services. Still, though, she has responsibilities and a young daughter who needs her mammy.

'Course, it didn't take us long to find Susan. She was standing in full view right across the street from that kid's house, Josh what's-his-name, the one who everyone said was responsible for what happened. She was soaked through to the skin, shivering and blue with the cold, but I think she was glad it was me who'd found her and not anyone else. She got into the car for me easily enough, then just sat in silence the whole way home, twirling her hair around her fingers and staring out the window. Not a peep out of her. Didn't even thank me when we pulled up back at Primrose Square, not that I was looking for thanks.

'I'm worried, though, Tom. Susan Hayes has been through hell and back, and no one would blame her for acting out a bit. But it's poor Melissa I'm thinking of. Not even thirteen years of age and with her dad off on duty, there's only Susan to look after her. Of course I'll keep a special eye out for the little pet, but it just breaks my heart to think that's about all I can do.

'So anyway, back to Jason,' Jayne chatted away to the urn above her telly, as she continued pounding away on the dough she'd been kneading. 'God knows how he'll take my little bit of news, but I'm hoping he'll go easy on me. Say a prayer for me, will you, love? Put in a good word for me with the Man above. If I can get through this, I'll get through anything.

'Actually, now that I think of it, a nice Madeira sponge, wouldn't that be the very thing to put the lad in good humour? After all, as you always used to say, Tom, there's no trouble on this earth that can't be sweetened by my Madeira sponge, now is there?'

Nancy

FLAT 6B, SECOND FLOOR, CRAMPTON BUILDINGS

*P*lease let this be the one, Nancy thought, hauling herself up yet another flight of stairs on yet another day, her heart hammering from the mad dash she'd had to make to get to the appointment on time.

Haven't I been through enough already? Please Jesus/Buddha/ Santa – anyone up there who's listening to me - please, please, please just let this be The One.

'So over here we have the living area,' the letting agent said brightly with an authoritative sweep of her arm, indicating little more than an armchair and a tiny coffee table. And that was it.

'As you can see, the entire flat is lovely and cosy,' she chattered away to Nancy, with a big cheesy grin plastered across her face. 'Compact. Ideal for the single tenant, really. Absolutely perfect for a busy lady like you.'

Then, dropping her voice down low, she added, 'And just between ourselves, Ms Thompson, there's huge demand for flats at this price level, so in your shoes, I'd save myself a lot of time and bother and just sign on the dotted line. I've got three other prospective tenants all lined up to see this place directly after you and I know it'll be snapped up by the end of the day.

'But the good news is that I've taken a bit of a liking to you,' she added, with a patronising little smile. 'And I know that relocating to a new city can't be easy – particularly a city like Dublin, where property is at such a premium. So I'm just giving you a little heads up, that's all.'

'That's really kind of you.' Nancy smiled politely, spinning around on her heel, so she could really take in the tininess of the place. 'But can I just ask – where exactly did you say the living room was?'

Because she was seeing everything else except an actual living room in front of her. She noticed the drab, grey carpet that must have been standard issue on rental properties – she'd already seen its match in dozens of other Dublin flats to date. And the tiny Velux window overhead, which you'd need to stand on a stepladder to reach. The fact that it was almost noon, and yet so gloomy in the flat, you'd need to switch on lights to see properly.

And don't, she thought, *even get me started on the smell.* Oh dear God, the smell. Damp, mixed with fresh paint in a clear attempt by a desperate landlord to try and disguise it. Nancy had been flat-hunting in Dublin so aggressively by now, she'd have known that giveaway stench a mile off. As if that wasn't bad enough, the flat was situated directly beside an alleyway full of dumpsters, which wasn't exactly helping, pong-wise.

'No, no, no, lovey, I think you meant to say the living *area*,' said the letting agent, who was called Irene and who was bone-thin, over-bright and quite comfortable with calling Nancy 'lovey', even though they'd met exactly seven minutes ago. 'You're standing right in the middle of it, my darling. Fabulous, isn't it? Such a wonderful energy flow. Can't you just see yourself living here?'

'You mean this is it?' Nancy asked her, dumfounded. 'A chair and a coffee table?'

She badly wanted to add: 'Which you want nineteen hundred euro a month for?' but politeness prevailed. Plus the fact that her brand new job was due to start the following day, and she was officially homeless.

I bypassed 'desperate' about ten viewings ago, she thought, *and now I'm officially in a state of panic.* It was either settle for this kip, or else fork out a ridiculous amount of cash that she didn't have for yet another night in an exorbitantly priced 'budget' hotel. Yet again.

'Isn't it just to die for?' Irene said cheerily, with a big toothy grin. 'Oh, and yet another added bonus,' she enthused, 'look how handy the living area is for access to the kitchen!'

'The kitchen?' Nancy said a bit more hopefully, looking around and wondering if she'd somehow missed a room on the way in. 'Where's that?'

'You're already standing in it, my love.' Irene smiled back benignly.

'But I haven't budged an inch.'

'You see?' Irene practically beamed. 'Look how conveniently close it is to the living area! Can you think of anything handier? Who wants doors and hallways anyway in this day and age? Who needs 'em, eh? That's one of the main features I love about this flat: the fabulous, paired-back, Scandinavian minimalism. Stunning, isn't it?'

'Hang on a second, Irene,' Nancy asked, as her heart sank in utter disbelief. 'By "kitchen", do you mean that tiny microwave oven?'

'Well . . . yes, actually,' she said brightly.

'So just to be clear, the kitchen is actually a microwave perched on a windowsill approximately three inches from the sofa.'

'That's right!'

'The sofa, which you also describe as the living area.'

'Well, it's actually less of a kitchen, more of a food preparation area really,' Irene chattered away, undeterred by her client's total lack of enthusiasm. 'But just think,' she added, 'could a set-up like this be more ideal for a busy professional like yourself? Think of all the eating out you'll be doing in the evenings! The whole of Dublin will be like one giant restaurant for you. So why would you want the bother and hassle of a kitchen? More trouble than it's worth, if you ask me. A microwave and a kettle, that's as much as any hardworking, professional tenant needs, I always find. Perfect for you!'

'Irene,' Nancy said, 'I'm really sorry to have dragged you all the way out here, but I'm afraid—' She was about to say 'clearly we're both wasting our time', but Irene was having none of it.

'Oh! And did I draw your attention to the fabulous pano-ramic view?' she went on, indicating a tiny window beside the sofa in a clear attempt to distract, much the same way you'd distract a kitten by tossing a ball of wool in its direction. 'It's a massive USP of this particular flat and I really think you'll love it – it's super special!'

Gamely, Nancy peered out of the window, expecting some-thing – anything at all – to justify the staggering rent the place was asking, but no, there was absolutely nothing to see.

'Breathtaking, isn't it?' said Irene, hovering at her shoulder.

'I'm sorry, but what view are we meant to be looking at exactly?' Nancy asked her, mystified.

'The city!' Irene beamed, nudging her sharply in the ribs. 'Look, spread out like a glistening carpet beneath you. Out of this world, isn't it? Right up there with Manhattan, if you ask me. Or the Taj Mahal.'

'But we're overlooking a Lidl car park,' Nancy said. Granted, if you squinted closely enough, you could just about make out a roundabout with backed up traffic and a Tesco Metro, but that was pretty much it as far as the panoramic view went.

'You see?' Irene said, undeterred. 'Yet another plus to this flat! Proximity to a shopping centre. Very handy, I think you'll find. Single tenants are always looking for a convenience store close by. You are a single lady, aren't you, sweetheart?'

There was a tiny, giveaway pause before Nancy replied.

'Yes,' she answered, clearly and confidently. *Bugger it*, she thought, *better get used to saying it out loud and proud.*

'I knew it!' said Irene, with a snap of her fingers. 'I really do have a sixth sense for these things. My husband is always telling me it's a real gift. So just think of all that late-night shopping for microwavable dinners for one! Oh, you're going to be so happy here. I just know it.'

'And that's it?' Nancy sighed wearily, trying to ignore the whole clichéd, sad-saddo-with-a-microwave-dinner-in-a-plastic-tray image that had just been conjured up. 'That's the "spectacular view"?'

'Well, now, what did you expect from a top–flat window in Kilbarrack?' Irene replied, with a sharpness in her eyes that wasn't there before. 'The Spanish Steps? You've got to be reasonable here, sweetheart, don't you?'

'I know, I know.' Nancy sighed as a familiar wave of disappointment sank over her. 'And I know you're only doing your best, Irene. It's just that it's an awful lot to pay for a tiny one-bed flat without a living room.'

'Ahh, but you'll notice that I didn't say living *room*. I was actually very careful not to say living room. I clearly specified that this was a living *area*. There's a massive difference, you know. Like about a grand a month difference. And you get what you pay for, don't you? Particularly when you're . . . let's just say, on a more challenging budget. You're relocating from London, aren't you?'

'That's right, yes.'

'I thought I recognised the accent. Any particular reason why?'

Nancy braced herself. After all, it's not like she didn't expect lots of questions along those lines.

'I'm moving here for work,' she rattled off, almost like she was reading from a script. 'At the National Theatre,' she threw in, for good measure.

Now that wasn't so bad, she thought. *My first hurdle and I hope I handled it reasonably well, with minimal fuss.*

'So when did you leave London?' Irene probed, peering beadily over her clipboard at Nancy.

'Just over two weeks ago.'

'And when do you start at the National?'

'Tomorrow, as it happens,' Nancy answered, distractedly opening up the miniscule fridge door and burying her face in it, hoping against hope they could get off the bloody subject.

'Bit of a rush job, then, wasn't it?' Irene shrugged. 'You certainly haven't allowed yourself very much time to find somewhere to live before you start your new job, have you?'

'Emm . . . yes, well, you see the job offer came along very suddenly,' Nancy stammered, turning her face away from the fridge when the stink of gone-off eggs inside it got too much. 'It's not ideal, I know, but that's the theatre world for you. So here I am and I need somewhere to live, fast.'

'A theatre job. Wow.' Irene nodded. 'Onstage?' she added hopefully, her finger twitching at her mobile as if she was about to ask Nancy for a selfie, just in case she turned out to be some famous Brit import. Nancy could almost see Irene eyeing her up and down, then looking a bit disappointed at how utterly unlike a proper celebrity she was, with her total lack of contouring, skinny jeans and neatly tied back hair, with ne'er a beach wave in sight.

'Behind the scenes, I'm afraid,' Nancy said.

'Really? As what?' Irene fished, clearly far more interested in the job than in the flat she was supposed to be offloading.

'I'm about to start as an assistant director on a production of *Pride and Prejudice*,' Nancy told her, and even though it was only a short-term contract that had only come about because she was happy to be a last-minute replacement, she still swelled up a bit with the buzz you got from starting work on a new show. *Any* new show.

Particularly one that got her away from London as fast as she could.

'An assistant director at the National?' Irene whistled. 'Big job.'

'It's not really.' Nancy shrugged modestly. 'It's more like two hundred small jobs—'

'Well, now, you see?' Irene interrupted, as a fresh selling point seemed to strike her. 'So just think of all those long hours in rehearsal at the theatre! Not to mention all the after-show parties and functions that you'll be attending. Now just ask yourself – when will someone like you even be in the flat, other than to crash? Somewhere low-maintenance like this place couldn't be more perfect for you! Okay, I grant you, it mightn't exactly be Versailles . . . but you know it's available for immediate occupation . . .'

'I do appreciate that,' Nancy replied, locking eyes with Irene so she was forced to actually listen to her. 'And I'm sorry about this, but I really think you and I are done here. Trust me, this is not the kind of place I'd ever see myself living in.'

'But you're really not giving it a fair chance,' Irene sniffed. 'Tailoring the perfect property to an individual client is where my agency excels, and really, you'll go a long way to find a flat that suits you better. This flat is who you *are*. It makes a statement. And most of all, it's within your budget.'

'Look, there's no delicate way to say this to you. But sitting with a fridge at arm's length from me on a minuscule sofa that doubles up as a bed in a freezing, damp flat is actually not who I am. Not by a long shot.'

'Easy for you to say now,' Irene replied, with ice creeping into her voice as her smileyness quickly evaporated. 'But if you're expecting somewhere close to Dublin city centre on what you're prepared to pay, then dream on. If it's Dublin 4 you're looking for, then be prepared to pay D4 prices. Which, on the salary you gave us on your application form,' she added, with a quick, professional glance down to her notes, 'I'm afraid just isn't doable.'

'In that case, I'm really sorry for taking up your time,' Nancy said apologetically, even though Irene had practically strong-armed her into viewing the dive in the first place. Politeness prevented her from adding what she really wanted to, which was that she'd seen prison cells with more home comforts than this place. And that living like an extra from *Orange is the New Black* really wasn't her idea of how her new life in Dublin would be.

'Oh, but it's your own time you're wasting, Ms Thompson,' Irene said crisply, instantly downgrading Nancy from 'lovey' and 'darling'. 'I can guarantee you, this flat will be snapped up by the end of the day by a more, let's just say, street-savvy tenant than yourself.'

'Then all I can do is wish you well with it,' Nancy said as evenly as she could.

'Actually, no,' Irene snapped, making absolutely no attempt to hide how pissed off she was. 'I should really be the one to wish you luck.' Then, grabbing a fistful of keys, she added bitterly, 'After all, I've got a roof over my head and a home to go to. You're starting your big new job in the morning and you're the one who's homeless, aren't you?'

That horrible estate agent was right, Nancy thought miserably, being jolted this way and that on the packed train as she made her way back to the ridiculously priced hotel she'd pitched up in. *I am officially homeless. Ever since I arrived this city, I've traipsed my way in and out of dozens of rental flats, all with zero success.*

And it's not like I'm looking for the earth, she thought, her face pressed up against some total stranger's armpit as they both clung onto the overhead bars for dear life. After all, her new contact at the National Theatre was just a temporary one and, if the worst came to the worst, she'd be trudging back to London in a few months' time, as soon as the final curtain came down.

But at the very least, a few short months would give her what she so badly needed. Space. Time. A fresh chance to get away from London and, more importantly, everyone in it. Plenty of her colleagues in the UK would have regarded working in Dublin as a something of backwards step career-wise, and plenty more well-meaning pals said as much to her face. But Nancy's mind was firmly made up.

Because, just then, she needed three things and she needed them fast: to get away from the tight-knit, incestuous theatre scene in London where everyone *knew*; to start a brand new job with a fresh, clean slate; and, with any luck, to move on. And so what if this job wasn't at some flashy West End theatre with all its bells and whistles and career prestige? God knows, it couldn't have come along at a better time for Nancy and that, as far as she was concerned, was good enough.

Just then her phone pinged as a text came through and, out of habit, she jumped, just in case. Gingerly, she maneuvered her hand into her coat pocket to see who it was – and instantly her heart sank right back down to the ground again.

It was her mum.

> Your dad and I so worried about you, Nancy, love. Let us know you're OK, won't you? Come back to London to see us in the next few weeks – we miss you so much.

Nancy bit her lip and willed herself to stay strong. Of course she missed her parents and friends too, and there was nothing she'd have loved more than to hop on a cheapie Ryanair flight to zip home to see them all. But as she'd painstakingly explained to her nearest and dearest before she left, that was out of the question just now.

She'd already moved every stick belonging to her out of the gorgeous Islington flat she'd loved so much. She'd said a rushed, hasty goodbye to anyone and everyone she knew. She'd well and truly burned her bridges. She hoped they all understood, but if they didn't, then there wasn't a huge amount she could do about it, was there? So now, all she really needed in Dublin was to throw herself into work and find somewhere to live.

I'm thirty-three years old, she thought, as the train rattled on, becoming more and more packed and airless the closer it got to Connolly station in the centre of the city. *I'm too old to live in horrible hovels that stink of damp and cat wee. I'm not high-maintenance, but I've served my time crashing on friends' sofas and living in dives when I've toured with shows. And I didn't leave my lovely, warm, central little flat in London, just to end up living hand-to-mouth out of a suitcase.*

She was clinging onto an overhead bar to balance herself and the guy who was pressed right up against her was doing exactly the same. They were millimeters from each other and yet both stayed resolutely silent.

It was lonely and scary and intimidating pitching into any new job without having to relocate on top of that as well. *But then, you wanted this job, didn't you?* she reminded herself. She'd actively pursued it, never for a moment thinking she'd actually land it. It had been so last-minute too; all Nancy had been told was that the previous assistant director had dropped out of the gig because of 'artistic differences' with Diego Fernandez, her boss-to-be.

Granted, when the mighty Diego quizzed her about the logistics of relocating to Ireland and asked how she felt about that, Nancy just batted it away. Getting away from London was actually the main selling point of the gig, but that certainly wasn't something she was going to get into with a hotshot director she was trying to impress.

So instead, she stressed what a huge deal it would be to work at the National with someone like Diego, who was the most highly respected director, not just in his native Spain, but probably in the western world, with all the Tony and Olivier awards practically hanging out of his earlobes to prove it.

Anyway, the mighty Diego Fernandez must have seen something in her that he liked, but whether it was hunger or sheer desperation, it was hard to tell. Nancy was thrilled about the gig, though, and utterly determined to bring everything she possibly could to it. If she needed to work eighteen-hour days, then she was all for it. Weekends? Overtime? Not a problem. She was your gal.

Burying herself in work was good, she figured. After all, it was the one constant in her life that had never let her down. And so what if she was a bit lonely in a new city? Nancy would get over it in time. Quietly, and with minimal fuss, just like she did everything.

It was just that she'd really have welcomed having one single pal in Dublin; someone she could talk to, full stop. Someone who might steer her away from viewing flats in areas where you'd need pepper spray on you just to go out for the Sunday papers.

Nancy wasn't expecting to stroll into a Dublin 4 flat with a view over Dublin Bay for the rent she could afford; that bossy woman Irene had been quite wrong about that. But she did know this much: she couldn't and wouldn't haul herself on yet another gruelling rail and bus journey to a poky little flat no bigger than a prison cell, at a rental rate that would leave her foraging through the bins looking for food, only to be told, 'Well, this is Dublin, what did you expect?' Or worse, 'Our ad did clearly specify that fussy tenants need not apply.'

This girl, she thought, *has had quite enough.*

It was early evening and Nancy had just got off the train and was weaving her weary way back to her hotel on Pearce Street, when she happened to stroll past a gorgeous, residential-looking square, with Victorian villa-style terraced houses dotted all around it.

Most of the homes looked tidy and well maintained; each had scrubbed stone steps that led down onto the pavement below, and there were loads of well-kept window boxes and potted urns standing neatly beside gleaming hall doors. From where Nancy stood, she could see joggers wrapped up against the icy cold doing laps of the square, as kids kicked a football about and had a laugh in spite of the fading, wintry light. There was even the remains of a half-melted snowman right outside one of the houses, wearing an Ireland football jersey, with a half-eaten Twix for a nose, which made Nancy smile.

It was such a lovely scene, she paused to take it in. She even kicked the football back to the kids when it bounced her way, to loud shouts of 'Thanks very much, missus!' The square seemed neighbourly and yet so close to the city centre, you could walk everywhere. There was a warmth about it, a friendliness that radiated. She glanced up at the nameplate on one of the houses: Primrose Square.

Of course the houses along here were way out of her league, she thought, given the location. But still. Wouldn't it be absolutely wonderful to start afresh somewhere like this?

Susan

BERKELEY ST PHARMACY

9:28 a.m., Susan thought, glancing down at her watch. In exactly two minutes, the pharmacy she was parked across the road from was due to open.

Breathe, she told herself. *Just breathe*. Soon all would be well. She'd run out of pills, but she'd get her prescription topped up and somehow she'd be able to function again. Magical, lovely Xanax would help her with everything. Help her to start eating again, sleeping again, even help her cope with a husband serving in the army on the other side of the world, abandoning her at a time like this.

She proudly used to tell everyone that Frank was her soulmate and now she'd barely spoken to him for weeks. Months, even, unless you counted the odd, 'So how are you?' 'Fine. You?' 'Oh you know, fine,' Skype calls, where they'd swap mundane details and politely skirt around each other until Melissa came into the room and rescued them both. Last time they'd spoken, they'd managed to kill a whole ten minutes with a stupid, roundabout conversation about whether or not Susan had remembered to get their boiler serviced.

Jesus Christ, she thought, pulling her puffy anorak tighter around her. You could cut the tension between herself and Frank with a knife, but still. Polite small talk was better than the rows. Or the silences. Anything was better than that. Frank had been gone for six long months now; he'd fecked off not long after what had happened, but she could still recall with pin-sharp clarity some of the howlers they'd had before he'd left.

'Now? You really think now is a good time for you to run off to The Lebanon? After everything we've just been through?'

'Susan, please listen to me,' he'd said in that irritatingly reasonable tone he used whenever he was at his most angry. Frank had once done a course in hostage negotiation and Susan knew all too well that's how they trained you to speak in tense situations. 'I've got to work, you know that. I'm not running away, love, I've been posted abroad and I don't have any choice here. We've got to keep the roof over our heads and Melissa in a private school. You're still on a leave of absence from the bank, so there's only my salary coming in now—'

'You want to talk to me about money and salaries at a time like this?' she'd spluttered back at him. 'You don't think I've other things on my mind? Like trying to get justice for our own daughter?'

'What I'm trying to say is that we've already lost so much, we can't afford to lose any more.'

'So you're just going to leave me and Melissa here on our own?'

'I know the timing is shit,' he'd said so reasonably that she'd actually thought she might claw at his face. She wanted to draw blood. She wanted to hurt him physically just like he was hurting her. 'But come on, love, we have to face up to what's happened and keep on keeping on, don't we? We have to accept what the police are telling us. That's what Ella would have wanted.'

'Well, excuse me for not being able to face up to having a dead daughter cold in her grave as easily as you seem to be! And don't fucking DARE tell me what Ella would or wouldn't have wanted!'

Even Skype calls where they'd talk about crap like whether or not she'd watered the plants were better than that, Susan thought bitterly to herself. Besides, Melissa adored her dad; she needed him and, if nothing else, it was at least something that the two of them got to speak daily.

Melissa . . .

Oh Christ, Susan thought, actively trying to block out the image of her child's pale, worried face from the night before. Her heart cracked open with guilt when she thought of her daughter, her little girl, helping to shoo her away from that house, then bundle her into the back of Jayne Dawson's car, hoping she hadn't already been seen from inside the house and reported again.

'Now I need you to listen to me very carefully, love,' Jayne had calmly told her when they were safely back at Primrose Square, after Melissa had gone to bed. 'I know you're going through hell right now, and not for one minute would I blame you for doing what you were doing tonight. But there's Melissa to think of, isn't there?'

As if to stress the point, Jayne reached across the kitchen table to take a firm grip of Susan's thin, bony hand. 'You still have her, love. Remember she's struggling with all of this too and, more than anything else, she wants her mammy to be there for her. For God's sake, she's only twelve years old, and she's trying to process this too. Believe me, everything will be so much easier if you put that poor child first from now on.'

Coming from anyone else, Susan would have spat back at them, told them to piss off, stop interfering and just leave her alone. What the hell did anyone else know about what she was going through? How dare anyone tell her how to behave and how not to behave? How dare anyone tell her how to be a mother?

But Jayne wasn't like that. She'd never been one for fake sympathy and faux-sorrowful head shakes like everyone else.

Instead, throughout the past year she'd been nothing but kind, compassionate and calm. Always dropping in big bowls of healthy casserole for dinner, always there for a chat, always watching out for Melissa, particularly since Frank fecked off. So Susan sat in silence, holding her tongue at the kitchen table, while Jayne gently reminded her that she was playing with fire.

'Supposing it had been someone else who'd found you this evening, instead of me? What then?'

Susan didn't answer, she just sat there mutely, taking it, nodding whenever prompted and thanking Jayne mechanically when she eventually got up to leave, just before midnight.

'Now you will be more careful in future?' Jayne had asked as they said their goodbyes on the doorstep. 'No more going back to that boy's house. That Josh, what's his name.'

'Andrews,' Susan had said quietly. 'His name is Josh Andrews.'

'You'll stay away from him, though, won't you? Do you promise me?'

'Promise,' Susan said dully as she waved the older woman off, not even bothering to lock the front door behind her, as she peeled herself off to bed for yet another sleepless night.

But hours later, as she stared up at the ceiling through the darkness, she vowed to go back there and do exactly the same thing, all over again.

Fuck what everyone else said. To hell with what the police kept telling her and to hell with Frank too. Susan knew the real truth and hell would freeze over before she'd ever let the likes of Josh Andrews forget it.

'We're very sorry, Mrs Hayes, but this prescription has expired.'

'What did you say?' she asked, trying to ignore the sailor knot of tension in her stomach.

'I'm afraid this script was only good for three repeat prescriptions, and as you've already reached your limit, that means I can't help you today.'

Jesus Christ, Susan thought, sudden panic electrifying her. Who did this pharmacist one think she was, anyway? The girl looked about fifteen years old, not far off Melissa's age. And she was wearing a badge that said 'trainee'. Did she know what she was talking about? Was she even qualified?

'That's not possible,' Susan told her, unable to keep the rising note of panic out of her voice. 'You see, I need the Xanax now, urgently. Can you check your system again?'

'I already did, Mrs Hayes, several times,' the young pharmacist said nervously. 'And there's no mistake; this prescription is well out of date. But if you'll just make an appointment to see your GP, I'm sure they'll be happy to issue you with a fresh one.'

'No, no, no, no, no, you don't understand,' Susan insisted. 'You see, I can't do that. I need the tablets *now*. Immediately. If I go through my GP, it'll be tomorrow at the earliest before I can even get an appointment and I can't wait that long. It's out of the question. This really is an *emergency*. Do you understand?'

'I'm so sorry, Mrs Hayes, but I really can't help you – it's against all our regulations,' said the pharmacist, biting her bottom lip and glancing anxiously over her shoulder for someone to come along and rescue her. Susan Hayes was well known among the staff at this pharmacy – the woman was trouble, pure and simple.

'You're not exactly being very helpful,' Susan snapped, aware that she was raising her voice and that other customers were beginning to stare. 'So look – can you just go and get Simon for me? He'll sort me out, I know he will.'

Simon was the manager; he knew Susan personally. Surely he'd sidestep all their gobshite rules and regulations just this once and give her something to tide her over. He *had* to.

The queue behind her had started to swell and she could sense a lot of grumblings and dirty looks directed her way. Susan ignored them, though, because she had no other choice. Besides, she figured, most of these people were probably only queuing up for packets of Lemsip or a few pathetic paracetamol. None of their medications could possibly be as urgent as hers.

Finally Simon appeared from the back room, a gaunt, older man with a stoop, who looked stressed enough as it was, and whose face fell even further the minute he saw Susan.

'Ahh, it's you again, Mrs Hayes,' he said curtly. 'Can you take over from me in the back room?' he added to his young trainee. 'It's okay, I'll deal with this.'

At that, the young girl quickly grabbed her chance to get out of the line of fire, looking relieved.

'Simon, there you are,' Susan said determinedly. 'I'm so sorry to bother you, but you really have to help me. My prescription has expired and the thing is, I can't get through the day without a few Xanax . . . '

'I'm so sorry, Mrs Hayes, but as my assistant explained, there's nothing we can do for you until you've been to see your GP. Now I'm more than happy to make an appointment for you, if you'd like?'

'*No!*' Susan said, raising her voice, although she hadn't meant to. 'I don't have time for that – I need something right away, Simon. *Now*. Do you understand? I can't wait. I promise I'll get to see my doctor, but just for now, can't you give me one or two tablets to get me through the day? That's all I'm asking for. God knows, it's not much, is it?'

They knew exactly what she was trying to cope with. Surely they could spare her a few poxy Xanax?

'I'm so sorry, Mrs Hayes,' said Simon patiently, 'but you do understand that would be against practice rules. Now you wouldn't want me to get into trouble, would you?'

'Excuse me,' said a narky voice from behind. Susan turned around to see an elderly woman with a tartan shopping trolley at the front of the queue, looking deeply pissed off. 'Some of us do actually have valid prescriptions, you know, and you're taking all day.'

Tempers were getting frayed, but Susan still couldn't bring herself to budge. She couldn't face going back to that house again, back to look at *her* room, *her* things, *her* photos – everything – without at least some kind of medicinal back-up. Christ alone knew, the nights were bad enough, but the days were far, far worse and she didn't know what she could do to fill them. At least a good strong sedative numbed her for a while, so she could function on autopilot, if nothing else.

'Come on, Simon,' she pleaded, hating that she had to say this in front of an audience of strangers. 'You know what I'm coping with here. Don't make me ask you again. Don't make me beg.'

'While I have the greatest sympathy for you personally,' Simon answered calmly, 'I'm afraid I really need you to move aside now so I can deal with other customers.'

'You heard the man, love,' the elderly lady insisted. 'Move out of the way, would you? I've been here waiting for ages, and I need my blood pressure medication. At this rate, I'll miss my bus home.'

'Can't you see he's dealing with me?' Susan barked back at her.

'And he just told you he can't help you,' said the older woman, squaring up to her. 'What, are you deaf or something?'

'Come on now, Mrs Hayes,' said Simon, sounding exasperated. 'Come back to me with an up-to-date prescription and we'll sort you out then. That's a promise. Okay? Next, please.'

'No, it's *not* okay,' Susan snapped, really starting to lose it. 'Absolutely none of this is okay, Simon. I'm not leaving here without those pills. This is an emergency. I'll have your precious prescription for you later on this week – will that keep you happy?'

There was much tsk-tsk-ing from behind her but she was beyond caring by then.

'Mrs Hayes,' said Simon sternly, 'I'm afraid I won't ask you again. Now kindly step aside and let me help other customers.'

'Other customers who actually bothered to go to the doctor and get a proper prescription before they came here,' came another ratty voice from the back of the queue.

'Yeah . . . unlike your woman,' muttered another, to loud grumbles. 'Some people are so self-centered, aren't they? Think the whole world revolves around them.'

'*Please,* Mrs Hayes,' said Simon, trying to break the Mexican stand-off that had developed, 'if you don't move aside, then you'll leave me with no choice but to call security.'

'Excuse me, is that some kind of threat?' said Susan loudly. 'What are you going to do anyway? Have me dragged out of here in handcuffs? All I'm looking for is a few lousy sedatives – would that kill you? I'm a good customer, I've been coming here for years!'

'I'm a good customer too,' said the same elderly lady from behind, twitching her umbrella, like she was itching to clatter Susan with it. 'And let me tell you, Mrs Whatever-Your-Name-Is, you're being extremely selfish, delaying everyone else like this. Now come on, you've already been told three times to move out of the way.'

White-hot with rage, Susan turned around to face this woman full-on. 'Don't you dare,' she growled. 'Don't you dare speak to me like that.'

Jesus Christ, who were these people anyway? Had they the first clue why she was humiliating herself like this? Was there a single one of them who'd even understand?

'I'll speak to a rude woman like you any way I like,' came the sharp response. 'You don't deserve any better.'

'Oh really?' Susan snapped. 'You're standing there with nothing more to whinge about than coughs and colds and your bloody blood pressure medication. Have you any idea what some of us are dealing with? Have you a single ounce of compassion in you?'

'Sounds to me like it's a psychiatrist you need, love, not a pharmacist.'

'What did you just say?' Susan spat back, in danger of really losing it. She would have said more, might even have lunged at the woman, she was so dangerously close to the edge, only just then, she felt a hand clamp down on her shoulder. A man's hand, warm and sweaty.

She looked up to see a security guard, a giant brick wall of a man towering over her.

'Excuse me, madam.' He glowered down at her. 'I need you to step this way.'

Nancy

Nancy took a deep breath and tried to ignore the butterflies in her belly. The room fell silent as thirty pairs of eyes turned to look at her with anticipation. *Here we go,* she thought, as she smiled and addressed the room. *This is it,* she told herself. Her new start. Her new beginning.

Showtime.

'Good morning, everyone,' she said, hoping that she sounded a lot more confident than she felt. 'And welcome to our very first day of rehearsals.'

Just an hour earlier, she'd hovered uncertainly in the giant foyer at the National Theatre on Marlborough Street, when a woman about her own age came breezily up to meet her.

'New girl? Hi. I'm Mbeki, senior production assistant.' She'd beamed brightly, reaching out to shake hands.

Nancy would later learn that Mbeki, originally from Ethiopia, was now living in Dublin and was officially the coolest girl on the team. Just about everyone fancied her; men went absolutely gaga over her and most of the women seemed to fall under her spell too.

Two minutes in Mbeki's company and it was hard not to see why; she was warm, bubbly and probably the first person Nancy had met since she first moved to Dublin who'd actually given her the time of day. Even though it was lashing rain out on a grey, cold, February morning and everyone else was darting in and out of the building huddled up in warm winter coats and snug boots, Mbeki arrived to greet Nancy dressed in a vibrant yellow jumper with boyfriend jeans and chunky metallic shoes, which only made her stand out all the more.

'As soon as the cast read-through is over, I'll give you the whole tour.' She'd smiled warmly as Nancy followed her up a flight of stairs to a lift.

'Thanks, I'd really appreciate that.' Nancy grinned back, delighted that she'd met someone so lovely on her very first day. A good omen, she felt, for what lay ahead.

'So, your first proper day working here,' Mbeki chatted away, as the lift arrived and both women stepped inside. 'How are you feeling? Nervous? In dire need of a G&T?'

'You have no idea.' Nancy smiled back. 'It's just that this is a huge deal for me.' She couldn't explain it any better, though; her fear of messing up was too huge for her to even verbalise. *Just try to be calm, cool and professional,* she told herself. That's how she'd got the job in the first place and that's what would ultimately win the day.

'I hear you.' Mbeki nodded. 'This job would be a huge deal for anyone. But then, your reputation kind of precedes you – after all, you've worked on proper West End shows, haven't you?'

'You know about that?' Nancy asked.

'Some of the lads in production already googled you.' Mbeki grinned cheekily. 'In fact, I was dying to ask you something, if I'm not being too nosey, that is.'

'Ask away,' Nancy said, as the lift zoomed upwards.

Please don't ask, please don't ask.

'Well,' said Mbeki, 'you were an assistant director in the West End. You've worked on a lot of the biggies. *Matilda, Wicked,* huge shows . . . some of the biggest in the business.'

Nancy blushed a bit, but said nothing. Just watched the lift floors zoom past, steeling herself for what she knew with absolute certainty was coming next.

'So,' Mbeki went on, 'if you don't mind my asking, isn't this show a bit of a sideways step for you? Career-wise, that is. With your CV, I mean, you could probably be working in the Royal Court or the RSC, if you wanted to. It's cheeky of me to ask, I know, but I just wondered . . . '

'Why I took this job in Dublin?' Nancy politely finished the sentence for her. She'd expected questions along these lines, but at least she'd prepared her stock answer in advance.

'Well . . . yeah,' said Mbeki, with an apologetic little smile. 'We're so lucky to have someone like you on board, I know that, but we were . . . just curious to why . . . that's all,' she trailed off.

'Well,' Nancy said, smoothly slipping back into the response she'd already mentally dress-rehearsed. After all, fail to prepare, prepare to fail, as she always told herself. 'To work with someone like Diego Fernandez, for one thing. Plus,' she added, 'it's good to get out of London to do other things every now and then, you know how it is. Fresh challenges and all that.'

'Of course.' Mbeki smiled warmly. 'And if Rumpelstiltskin hired you in for this gig in the first place, then you're already half way to winning your first Olivier, if you ask me.'

'Ehh . . . did you say Rumpelstiltskin?' Nancy asked, puzzled.

'Oh, don't mind me,' Mbeki said, after a suspiciously long pause.

The lift pinged open onto the top floor and she followed Mbeki as they weaved their way down a long corridor covered in show posters and on towards the rehearsal room.

Nancy had only been to the National once before, and that was in the audience, so it was a first for her to even get up to this level. And although she'd hightailed it over to Dublin for her interview with Diego Fernandez, he'd insisted on meeting her for lunch at the intimidatingly posh, five-star Merrion Hotel, just beside Government Buildings.

'If I give you this job,' he'd said to her in the broken English of someone who's only recently started to master it, 'then you must have passion.'

'I do,' Nancy told him baldly.

'No, no, I mean real *passion*,' he stressed, making the word sound genuinely sexy in his Spanish accent, and beating his chest as he said it.

'Absolutely! I've so much passion – passion for the show, for the source material, for Jane Austen, for the National, for the theatre . . .'

'You no understand,' Diego had said, sadly shaking his head.

'No!' Nancy had insisted. 'I understand you entirely and if it's passion you're looking for, then trust me, I'm the assistant director for you.'

At that stage, she thought, she'd happily have said anything to get the gig. To get out of London for the fresh start she needed so badly. The thought of losing out, having come this far, would have killed her.

'No! You not listening to me,' Diego had insisted. 'You must have *passion* with my English.'

Oh, Nancy thought. *He means patience.* It was mortifying, yet not so mortifying that she wavered for even a second as soon as the job offer came through.

'So here we are then,' said Mbeki, waving around proudly as she showed Nancy inside the rehearsal room, 'the nerve centre of the whole operation. Pretty cool, isn't it?'

'That's putting it mildly.' Nancy grinned back, suitably impressed.

They were standing right in the middle of a huge room on the top floor, a bit like a dance studio, except with comfy chairs dotted around a giant table in the centre of the room, with dozens of chairs placed around it, all set for the first cast read-through. Huge glass windows dominated the room and what little sunlight there was on a grim, wintry day flooded in, so the view really was spectacular.

'Come on then,' Mbeki said, sliding open one of the glass doors and waving at Nancy to follow her onto the terrace outside. 'I know it's freezing today, but trust me, you have to check this out.'

Nancy did as she was told, stepping through the door and on out into the icy, bracing wind outside. *And oh dear God,* she thought a second later, *was it worth it or what?*

The National Theatre was situated just across the River Liffey from the Customs House, just beside the Rosie Hackett Bridge, and from where she and Mbeki stood, the view really took your breath away. It seemed like there was nothing you couldn't see from that vantage point, stretching right the way across from the National Conference Centre to the 3Arena and beyond. Mbeki was a tireless tour guide and helpfully picked out everything for Nancy, from the Pro-Cathedral right behind them, to the GPO on O'Connell Street, which seemed like it was barely a stone's throw away from that height.

'Worth getting a dose of double pneumonia for, isn't it?' Mbeki grinned cheerily.

'Well worth it.' Nancy smiled back as the sharpness of the wind started to numb her face.

'Smokers' terrace, we call this,' Mbeki went on. 'And even if you don't smoke, just coming out here is the greatest destresser there is in this building. Take it from me, when the going gets tough, here's where you need to be.'

'To regroup, I suppose,' Nancy said, thinking aloud. She'd certainly done more than her fair share of regrouping lately.

'Or throw yourself off, if the need arises. You're going to be working with Rumpelstiltskin himself. You'll find yourself spending a lot of time out here in the freezing cold, is my guess.'

'Why do you keep calling him Rumpelstiltskin?' Nancy asked, checking over her shoulder to make sure the rehearsal room behind them was still empty. If Diego Fernandez had been unusually short with a habit of sticking his foot through the floorboards, then she'd get it, but he wasn't. At least, not that she was aware of.

'You'll see, honey. You'll see.'

Moments later, the rehearsal room behind them started to fill up fast, as cast and production crew filed in together, all clutching freshly printed copies of their scripts along with take-out cups of tea and coffee from the coffee shop across the street.

Soon the whole room was buzzing, as actors who'd worked together before exchanged squeals and gossip, air kisses and hugs. Nancy and Mbeki stepped back inside and all you could hear was a chorus of: 'Hi, it's great to meet you, I've always wanted to work with you! No, *really*!'

One elderly diva, who was proper 'telly famous', was chatting to another equally well-known actress of about the same vintage.

'I saw your last play and it really was terribly good, you know,' she was saying, 'in spite of what everyone said. Shame it closed so early, darling. Bloody critics. What do those idiots know anyway? I hear you closed after – what was it – five perfor-mances, is that right?'

'Oh, never mind about me, what about you?' cooed the other, batting off the sting with a smile that didn't quite reach her eyes. 'It must be wonderful for you to actually be working again. I'd say it must make a lovely change for you, because it's been quite a while, hasn't it? You know we share an agent and she was telling me only the other day that it's been nigh on impossible to get you seen for extra work these days.'

'Oh Christ,' Mbeki hissed, 'that's our Lady Catherine de Bourgh and Mrs Bennet having a proper go at each other. And the day has hardly even begun.'

'Fireworks between actors,' Nancy whispered back, 'are best saved for the performance, I always find.'

The mighty Diego Fernandez was late, but Nancy had been reliably informed that was perfectly normal for him, as apparently he considered himself well above and beyond something as mundane as a humble call-sheet. So she grabbed her chance and got busy introducing herself to anyone she hadn't already met yet, welcoming everyone while the going was good.

Pride and Prejudice was probably Nancy's favourite book of all time. To say that she was honoured to even be in that room was an understatement. And that's before you even got started on the cast, who were a who's who of general hotness in the entertainment world.

Among the seventeen-strong cast and creative team standing around chatting and gossiping, there was a Tony award-winner, six IFTA winners and an actual, bona fide Academy Award nominee, for costume design. *Were this room to blow up right now,* Nancy thought, *the entertainment industry in this country would take a long time to recover.*

'Such a pleasure to meet you, my darling,' Mrs Bennet said, wafting over to Nancy and gracefully shaking her hand, a bit like the Queen on a state visit.

'And you too,' Nancy said warmly. 'I'm so looking forward to working with you.'

'And I with you, my dear. We have lots of people in common over the pond, you know. You worked at the Kensington Theatre for a time, didn't you? A few years ago?'

'Yes,' Nancy replied, hoping this conversation wasn't going where she feared it was.

'So you'd know Peter Wallace and all of his team over there, wouldn't you, my dear?'

Nancy kept breathing. She probably blinked. Outwardly, she stayed calm and professional and limited herself to saying, 'Yes. I have very happy memories of my time at the Kensington.'

And then – *There is a God,* she thought – she was rescued just in the nick of time.

'Hey, Nancy, great to see you again,' said Alan Vaughan, a guy about her own age, with bright copper-red hair, a faceful of freckles and a London accent. 'Last time we met was at my audition, and I was a such a bag of nerves, I was even trembling, do you remember?'

'Well, if it isn't our very own Mr Wickham.' She smiled back warmly, shaking his hand, her heart hammering at the near miss she'd just had. Mrs Bennet thankfully drifted off to air kiss someone else, so for the moment at least, Nancy had escaped. *For now,* she thought.

Of course she remembered Alan's audition well; it was the very day after she'd just been hired herself and he'd really been fantastic. He'd read the part so perfectly, it was like he was born to play it. In casting terms, he was what you called a CNB. A complete no-brainer.

'Anyway, thanks for going easy on me at the audition,' he chatted away casually.

'Great to see you again, Alan.'

'You too,' he said, with a big crinkly smile. 'You know, if you ask me, we Brits really need to stick together on this gig. I mean, look around you: we're well outnumbered by the Irish.'

'So how are you finding life in Dublin?'

'Scary,' he said, 'but amazing at the same time. This is a massive break for me and my agent was practically shoving me onto the flight.'

'Oh, come on now, you'll be fantastic,' she said warmly, really meaning it too. Nancy had seen Alan onstage before in several theatre productions over in London and he'd always been terrific. He'd got two of the rarest things going for him onstage, she thought: easy, lighthearted charm and effortless charisma. Perfect for a character like Wickham.

'Well, I'll certainly do my best.' He grinned. 'It really means so much to me just to make it as far as this room. There was no way in hell I was turning down a job like this.'

'Whereabouts are you staying?' she asked, her own homeless situation never far from her thoughts. 'Somewhere close by?'

'Are you kidding?' He laughed. 'Have you seen what they charge for rents in this town?'

'Don't remind me,' she groaned back at him.

'I'm actually staying with my brother and his partner out in Lucan. He fell in love with an Irish girl and moved over here years ago. Mind you, when I say "staying with", I actually mean that I'm sharing their box room with my three-year-old niece.

But hey, it's a roof over my head, it's not too far out and as long as I earn my keep in babysitting and can sing along to *Peppa Pig*, then all is good. For now.'

'Lucky you,' Nancy said enviously. 'I'm in the throes of trying to find somewhere and it's a complete disaster. If I decide to live centrally, then every penny I earn will go towards rent, and yet if I move out to somewhere that I can actually afford . . . '

'Then it's the equivalent of living in Brentwood, facing a three-hour commute in and out of London, day in and day out,' Alan finished the sentence for her, summing the whole sorry situation up.

'Which, when you work late nights in the theatre, is far from ideal.' She quickly bit the words back on her tongue, afraid that she might sound narky and a bit ungrateful, but then she was facing another two flat viewings later on that evening, with that awful woman Irene from the estate agency. One flat was in Celbridge and the other was in Maynooth. Both so far away from the theatre, Nancy thought, and both so extortionately expensive, she might as well have saved herself all the bother, stayed in London and just commuted back and forth every day on cheapie Ryanair flights.

'Hey, it's great to see you guys,' said Clara Devine, bouncing over for a chat. She was a doe-eyed young ingénue, who looked about seventeen and had the most translucent skin you ever saw. Clara was playing Lydia Bennet, Nancy reminded herself, the wild child youngest sister, and this was her first professional job.

Mind you, Nancy thought, the fact that Clara was straight out of drama school and stepping onto the stage of the National

Theatre hardly seemed to faze the girl at all, she was so brimming over with confidence and giddy high spirits. At the callback audition stages, she'd breezed in as a complete unknown and blew everyone in the room away with her lively, spirited reading of the part.

'Would you mind reading the part of Kitty Bennet for us as well?' Nancy had asked her, just to be perfectly thorough and to keep an open mind, casting-wise.

'Can't, I'm afraid.' Clara had shrugged, tossing her auburn curls over her shoulders. 'I don't know that part. I only bothered to read Lydia's bits.'

Ordinarily, that would immediately rule out an actor for a part; coming into any audition unprepared is such a no-no. But Diego Fernandez seemed to work to the beat of his own drum and the minute she'd left the room, he turned to Nancy and said triumphantly, '*Ahí va nuestra* Lydia Bennet. That is her, she is perfecto! Self-absorbed, as you say in Eeenglish. Only thinking of herself and no one else. That is my Lydia Bennet!'

'Did I interrupt you guys?' Clara asked brightly. 'You looked like you were talking about something *waaay* too serious for this ungodly hour of the morning.'

'Only about how hard it is to rent anywhere affordable in this town, I'm afraid.' Nancy smiled back. 'All deeply boring.'

'Oh, you should think about trying homesitter.com.' Clara beamed. 'Mummy and Daddy rent out their *pied à terre* on it all the time whenever they're in Barbados. You can land the most fabulous places in brilliant locations for, like, half nothing. You should totally check it out! After all, what have you got to lose?'

What indeed?

Susan

From the journal of Susan Hayes

Oh my darling girl.

It was your very first day in primary school, all those long years ago. Do you remember? My eldest girl Ella, my wild child, taking the huge leap to proper, big school.

'Family photo!' Frank had insisted, before we'd even left the house.

'But Dad, Melissa is only a baby in her pram and she's not even awake!' you had protested, stomping your little five-year-old feet impatiently. 'She's not going to school today – I am. It's MY day – like my birthday!'

'Still and all,' Frank had insisted, clustering us all together and waving his digital camera in the air, to squeeze all four of us in. 'This is a huge day for the Hayes family and I want us all in the photo. Trust me, Ella, love. You'll be glad when you're twenty-one and you look back on this happy day.'

When you're twenty-one.

Oh Christ, Ella . . .

At the school gates, my heart had gone out to other parents trying their best to cope with frightened little kids. Some of them were in tears and clinging on tightly to grown-up hands, terrified to make this seismic leap into the big, scary world of teachers and schoolbags and so many intimidating new faces.

Not you, though, my darling. You didn't even need to hold my hand as we wove our way through the crowd of other parents and kids in their brand new little uniforms, saying their teary goodbyes. Instead you kissed me goodbye, then skipped, actually skipped, towards the school gates.

'Hi,' you said, bouncing over to another little girl, a pale, delicate-looking thing, who seemed to be on the verge of tears. 'I'm Ella and I'll be your friend if you like.'

'This is Sophie,' her worried mum had said, clinging to her little girl's hand as the child seemed to be struck dumb with shyness.

'Don't be afraid,' you said, taking Sophie by the hand. 'Come into school with me – we can play together, if you like? Do you like Dora the Explorer? That's my favourite and I bet they have Dora in here!'

The smaller child's pale face burst into a big smile as you led her up to the school door, confident as you like.

'Goodbye, Ella, sweetheart,' I called out to you, furiously snapping photos on my camera. 'Be a good girl and have loads of fun!'

'It'll be brilliant, Mum!' You grinned back, that adorable cheeky, gap-toothed little grin that I miss so much. Then you tossed your wild, unruly mane of strawberry blonde curls and laughed. 'This is going to be so exciting, I can't wait!'

The two of you scooted inside, with you boisterously leading the way, as I watched you go, ready to burst with pride. You were so confident, so secure in yourself, such a happy, easy, outgoing child, and yet so considerate to everyone around you. A dream girl. My little angel.

'Is that your daughter?' the other mother said to me, wiping away a tiny tear.

'That's my girl, all right,' I said proudly.

'She's a very special child. You've done a great job with her. Did you see how kind she was to my Sophie?'

'That's Ella for you.' I smiled. 'And don't worry a bit about Sophie — Ella will look out for her. That's a promise.'

Oh Ella, Susan thought, reading back over what she'd just written. *How are we supposed to go on without you?*

Jayne

19 PRIMROSE SQUARE

In the end, Jayne heard them before she saw them. Jason and Irene were bickering on her doorstep in low voices, but still, loud enough for her to hear from down the narrow hallway as she fumbled about for the door keys.

'Honestly, Jason, did you have to park that monstrosity right outside?' Irene was saying. 'It's bad enough being driven around in it, but I don't want anyone on Primrose Square seeing me getting out of the bloody thing. For God's sake, we *know* people here.'

'Excuse me,' Jason retorted, ringing on the doorbell, 'I'll have you know "that monstrosity" is what's keeping our kids in fancy schools and you in all your Botox jabs.'

'Jason, please, will you shut up about Botox?' Irene snapped back, just as Jayne threw open the hall door, wondering what it was about them, that they always seemed to bring out the worst in each other.

At a glance she took the pair of them in: Jason sweaty and uncomfortable-looking in a suit and tie, and Irene as bony and pinched as ever. And there, right behind them, Jason's ice cream van was parked on the square, attracting attention from a gang of kids who were kicking a soccer ball around.

'Givvus a ninety-nine, will you, mister?' one of them yelled at Jason.

'Not now, I'm off duty,' Jason shouted back.

'Arsehole!'

'Piss off with yourself, so!' said Jason, waving two fingers back at him.

'Now, now, there's need for bad language, son,' Jayne chided him gently, pecking them both on the cheek. 'Come on in, won't you? Dinner is almost ready. Irene, you're looking lovely, as always.'

'This is for you, Ma,' said Jason, thrusting a warm bottle of white wine at her. 'Have you any tins of cider in the fridge? I had a really crappy day and I could do a proper drink.'

'You are categorically *not* drinking cider at the table, Jason,' Irene said. 'We have wine with dinner. How many times do you have to be told?'

'I hate that cat piss.'

'Well, too bad.'

'After the day I had,' Jason said sulkily, 'I'll drink what I like.'

'What happened to you today, son?' Jayne asked him, as they both followed her down the hallway and on through to her toasty warm, cosy kitchen, which smelt deliciously of garlic and sage. Comforting smells, or so she hoped.

'Let's not even go there,' Irene groaned, instantly taking charge and opening up the kitchen cupboards till she found wine glasses.

'I got turned down for a loan at the bank, didn't I?' Jason grumbled, easing himself into his usual seat at the top of the table and undoing his tie, which was knotted tight as a noose around his neck.

'Is that why you're all dressed up in your good suit?' Jayne asked, going back to stir her apple sauce over at the kitchen range. 'I don't think I've seen you wearing that since your dad's funeral.'

'I look like a right gobshite in this get-up,' said Jason, taking off the jacket, 'and it's itching me like fuck.'

'Language, please, Jason,' said Irene, fumbling around in a drawer for a corkscrew. 'I told you, if you want to be taken seriously, then you have to dress seriously.'

'Still didn't get the bleedin' loan, though, did I?'

'What did you need the loan for, love?' Jayne asked, anxious to diffuse the tension between them.

'Jason has decided to expand the business,' Irene said crisply, answering for him as she so often did. 'Because the mobile confectionary trade is so seasonal, you see.'

'I suppose by that you mean you only sell the ninety-nines in the summer?' Jayne asked, trying to hide a little smile, as she continued stirring the pot of sauce. Only an out-and-out snob like Irene would describe an ice cream van as being in 'the mobile confectionary trade'.

'And, you see, a mate of mine is getting out of the ice cream trade,' Jason explained, 'and he offered me his van at a great price. So my plan was to overhaul the van and turn it into a mobile catering unit.'

'Mobile catering unit?' Jayne said, mystified.

'You know, selling burgers and chips at soccer matches and big stadium gigs, that kind of thing.'

'So the cash he's looking to borrow,' said Irene briskly, 'is reflective of the amount of work that would have to be done to the back of the van.'

'I even had a name for my new business venture and all,' Jason added sorrowfully. "Munchies by Jason." But, of course, that scaldy-headed prick in the bank was having none of it. He just wished me luck with my bun burgers and ninety-nines and nearly shoved me out the door."

'Now, now, you were already told to watch the bad language,' Jayne said, trying to keep things nice and civil. 'Not in front of your father,' she added, with a respectful little glance up at the urn above the telly.

Jason rolled his eyes, but then he was well used to his mam chatting away to a big jar of ashes.

'But at least *you're* still working at the estate agency, Irene,' Jayne went on. 'That has to count for something, doesn't it?'

Why was it, she wondered for about the thousandth time, that *just about everything with this pair came back to money?* After all, they were both working and, as Irene never failed to moan about, she was run off her feet with viewings all over the city. And okay, so Jason made most of his money during the warm summer months when everyone wanted a Mr Whippy, but still. It was a cash business and he made more than enough to get by, didn't he? So why did the two of them spend most of their time giving out about being broke?

'We badly need a second income, you see,' Irene said patronisingly, as she took the tiniest sip of her wine. 'The twins are about to start secondary school – a private school, of course – and the cost of their school fees is absolute extortion. So it's particularly timely that you asked us around tonight, Jayne,' she went on, with a shifty look across the table at her husband. 'Because Jason and I actually have something we want to run by you.'

'And I've some news I'd like to tell both of you as well,' said Jayne quietly, serving up the pork chops with a big dollop of apple sauce on the side, just the way her son liked them.

'Jesus, this looks amazing, Ma,' Jason said as his wife glared hotly across the table at him. 'I'm bleeding starving. Let's eat first and talk business after, yeah? Grub first, the money chat can always wait.'

Dinner had come and gone and Jayne had still to get a word in edgeways, never mind gently easing the subject around to her Big News.

'The property market is really picking up now, you know,' Irene was chattering away.

Though she hardly ate at all, Jayne thought, clearing away Irene's still-full plate. *Would you look at that,* she said to herself, crossly. *All the woman really did was rearrange her food around the plate.* All on account of this ridiculous some-days-you-eat, some-days-you-fast thing she was doing, Jayne guessed. Jason, on the other hand, was still eating, horsing into the leftover mash like a man who hadn't seen a complex carbohydrate in months.

'Oh, we can barely keep up with demand these days,' Irene prattled on as Jayne cleared up the remains of dinner. 'I'm doing viewings morning, noon and night. In fact, I've got a very exciting rental property right here on Primrose Square that's just come on our books. It's number twenty-four, just down the road from you. Do you know the new owner, by any chance, Jayne? Apparently he's a businessman working in the Far East for at least a year, or so I've been told.'

'I've no idea who owns that house now,' Jayne said from the kitchen counter, where she was taking a Madeira sponge that she'd made earlier out of the fridge. 'Although I was glad to hear the house was finally sold after poor Emily Mathews died.'

Emily had been a lovely friend to Jayne and her biggest competition in the annual Primrose Square Bake Off, but she'd passed away not long after Tom and her family put the house on the market.

'Well, you must at least have noticed all the building work that's been done on the house recently,' Irene said condescendingly. 'There's been nothing but skips outside number twenty-four for months now. Mark my words, whoever the new owner is, he's certainly not short of money.'

'Is that right?' said Jayne flatly, dishing up the Madeira sponge and wondering how she could shut Irene up and steer the conversation around to her own announcement.

'Anyway, my instructions are to rent the house out on homesit-ter.com. You do know how Homesitter works, don't you, Jayne?'

'I've heard of it, yes,' Jayne said, trying to keep nice and cool. Mother of God, what did the woman think anyway? That she was a complete eejit, stuck in the last century? They knew she had an iPad and that she was online a lot. For God's sake, she and Jason had been the ones who insisted she get the iPad in the first place.

'From now on, Ma,' Jason had said to her at the time, 'you'll be able to order all your own groceries online and get them delivered right to the front door. Saves you all the hassle of supermarket trips.'

Jayne had said nothing, but thought to herself: *Jason, love, do you even realise how it is for me here on my own? And that sometimes going out to the supermarket and chatting to my neighbours is the only human company I get from day to day?*

'Course, the wonderful thing about Homesitter,' Irene was blathering on, 'is that you make an absolute fortune! Maybe it's something you might like to consider, down the line?'

'We'll see,' said Jayne as politely as she could.

'Oh, I'm so sorry, no dessert for me, please,' Irene said, waving hers away as though it was radioactive. 'I can't have dairy, I'm afraid. Blows me right out. I suffer terribly from trapped wind, you know. Okay if I just have tea instead, Jayne?'

'If that's what you want,' said Jayne quietly, putting the kettle on.

'Herbal tea, of course,' said Irene. 'I'm off caffeine at the moment and I don't know myself. You really should try it – does wonders for the bags under the eyes, I find.'

'Is that so?'

'Can I have your dessert, then?' said Jason, helping himself to Irene's, in between stuffing his face with oversized spoonfuls of his own. 'This is gorgeous, Ma. Don't suppose you've any Viennetta to go with it?'

'You're meant to be off sugar, Jason,' Irene said to him sternly.

'Ah, sure, he's grand, he's in his mammy's,' said Jayne, taking the ice cream she'd bought earlier out of the freezer and taking care to cut her son a good, hefty slice.

'Anyway, as I was saying,' Irene said briskly, shooting her husband a sharp glare, 'here's the dilemma: Jason and I need cash badly just now; meanwhile you're sitting on a property in a prime area that's not generating a single penny for you. But if you were to consider moving in with us, we'd make a killing renting out a fine family home like this. I wouldn't even charge you the full commission. We'd clean up!'

We? thought Jayne. Did the woman just say *we?* Was she for real?

'An area like Primrose Square is so ripe for gentrification,' Irene chattered away while Jason wolfed down the Viennetta like it was his last meal on earth. 'Or if you ever decided to sell up, I'd be happy to take care of that for you too. We'd get seven fifty for a house like this in the morning – easily! Plus there's lots of other things to consider too.'

'And what other things might they be?' Jayne asked, as politely as she could.

At that Irene shot Jason a significant look as he finished up dessert, wiped his mouth, then looked absolutely anywhere except at his mother, reddening in the face all the while.

Just like you used to do when you were a little boy, Jayne thought calmly. *When you'd done something naughty and knew you were in big, big trouble.*

'The thing is, Ma,' he began, speaking slowly and deliberately.

Most unlike you, Jayne thought, sitting back and folding her arms as she glanced from one of them to the other. *In fact, I think the pair of them have actually rehearsed this.*

'Irene and I love how independent you are,' Jason went on, 'but let's face it, you're not getting any younger, now are you?'

'No, indeed I'm not.' Jayne smiled.

'And living on your own can't be easy for you, particularly since Dad . . . you know . . . '

'What he means to say is that we're both so worried about you, Jayne, love,' Irene chipped in, reaching across the table and taking her husband's pudgy hand in hers. 'We're the only family you have and we're entitled to be worried. Here you are all alone, night after night. Suppose something happened to you? Suppose there was a break-in? You do read the most awful stories. Just the other day, there was an item on the news about an elderly woman your age who was held at knifepoint, in her own bed, and all for a paltry few euro she had lying around the house.'

Patiently, Jayne heard her daughter-in-law out, then took great care to take a very, very deep breath before replying. 'Well, in that case,' she said coolly, 'the good news is that neither of you need to worry about me any more. Because I'm not on my own, as it happens. At least, not any more I'm not.'

'No, Ma, course you're not,' Jason chimed in. 'Sure you have us and the kids. You have your family.'

'And you know, we could always install a lovely granny flat at our house, should the need arise,' said Irene.

'I'm afraid that isn't what I meant at all,' said Jayne, 'and while I'm deeply grateful to you both, I'm not on my own any more because . . . well, because, you see . . . things have changed for me. In quite a significant way, actually.'

'Changed?' said Jason, looking a bit puzzled as the colour slowly started to fade from his puffy, red cheeks. 'What do you mean, changed? Is something wrong? Is it your health?'

'I thought you hadn't been looking too well lately,' said Irene. 'Do you need to go into hospital?' she added hopefully.

'No, thank God, it's absolutely nothing like that,' said Jayne, astonished that their minds would even work that way.

'What is it then, Ma?'

'Well . . . the thing is . . . and there's no easy way to say this . . . '

'What, Ma? Tell me!'

'I've met someone,' said Jayne, delighted with herself for finally having the courage to get it out.

Stony silence as they both looked across the table at her, the horror on their faces almost comical.

'What did you say, Ma?' Jason began to splutter, while Irene looked on, not so much stunned as poleaxed. 'Do you mean, like . . . *met* someone met someone? As in . . . like . . . oh, for feck's sake . . . like . . . like . . . '

'Don't be so ridiculous, Jason,' Irene snapped, 'I'm sure that's not what she meant at all.'

'As a matter of fact, that's exactly what I meant,' said Jayne evenly. 'We met a few months ago on a website on the iPad you got me, and we've been in touch every single day since.'

'Like . . . as in . . . a *man*?' Jason stammered with an expression on his face that actually made Jayne want to smile in spite of herself. 'Like an actual *boy*friend?'

'Yes, that's exactly what I mean,' Jayne said calmly. 'And the good news is you'll get to meet him very soon.'

'*What?*' said Jason.

'Oh, didn't I say?' said Jayne nonchalantly as she began to clear away the dessert dishes. 'He's coming to Dublin. To visit me. To stay! This weekend, as it happens. You know, to see how we get on face-to-face. His name is Eric Butler, he's from Florida, if you don't mind, and I think we'll all get along famously. Another nice slice of Viennetta for you, Jason, love?'

Melissa

18 PRIMROSE SQUARE

'Would you like me to come into the house with you?' asked Annie Gibbons, the mother of Melissa's best friend, Hayley. 'Just to check that everything is okay?'

'No need, thanks,' Melissa said, clambering out of the back of Annie's swishy jeep, unaware that she was giving herself away by being just a degree too bright and bubbly. 'But thanks so much for the lift home!'

Annie had gone to pick up Hayley from the after-school drama class that the girls had once a week, but when she saw that Melissa Hayes, the poor little scrap of a thing, had been left to get the bus home on her own in the pitch darkness on a cold, wintry night – and not for the first time, either – Annie had insisted on driving her back to Primrose Square.

'I could just come in with you for a second,' Annie said worriedly, 'to see how your mum is, that's all.'

'Emm . . . well . . . the thing is, Mum won't be there this evening,' Melissa stammered, reddening in the face and hoping the lie wasn't too obvious. She hated lying. And she really hated that she'd got so good at it in the last few months. 'She's out . . . at . . . emm . . . yoga. She does it every Thursday night after work. Sorry about that.'

'But her car is there.'

'Emm . . . yeah . . . that's because she always parks here, then walks to her yoga class . . . ' Melissa improvised wildly. 'It's just . . . around the corner, you see.'

'Are you sure, Melissa?' said Annie, looking keenly at the child in the rearview mirror. 'You wouldn't like me just to come in and check that everything is okay?'

'No need, thanks. Honestly. I'm fine. We both are.'

'Come and stay with us tonight!' Hayley piped up. Hayley was lovely and bubbly. She and Melissa had been big pals ever since kindergarten. 'And maybe we can order in pizzas when we're home? Can we, Mum?'

Melissa felt a huge pang at that because ordinarily she'd have loved nothing more. Hanging out at Hayley's house was always such fun. It was a welcoming, happy house, full of chatter and laughter where there was always food in the fridge and a warm, indescribable feeling of security. Hayley's parents and her two older sisters were really cool – they actually talked to one another and went on family outings all the time. They'd even gone camping together once. Actual *camping*.

But she couldn't run off to Hayley's house for pizza, could she? With a sinking heart, Melissa instinctively knew that the minute she stepped through her own hall door, she'd see that her own house would be exactly as she'd left it that morning before school: the kitchen a mess, dishwasher stuffed with dirty dishes and a pile of laundry that she still had to get around to, if she didn't want to wear the same manky uniform to school the next day.

'Thanks so much, Hayley,' she said reluctantly, 'but I really better stay home tonight. I've tonnes of schoolwork to catch up on.'

'You know you're welcome to stay with us for a sleepover anytime,' called Annie kindly, as Melissa made her way up the three little stone steps to her front door. 'And will you tell your mum that I'll meet her for coffee whenever she's free?'

'Will do,' said Melissa, waving them off as she fumbled around the bottom of the schoolbag for her door key. 'And thanks so much again for the lift home. Bye, see you tomorrow!'

The house was in pitch darkness when she let herself in and, as Melissa knew right well, everything was exactly as she'd left it that morning. She hadn't eaten since lunchtime and her tummy was rumbling, but she couldn't even think about food until she saw her mum was okay.

'Mum?' she called up the stairs, then tip-toed softly up so as not to disturb her mother, in case she'd taken some of those purple pills that made her sleep for hours at a time.

'Mum? It's me. I'm home.'

'Melissa?' came a groggy voice from the main bedroom. 'I'm in here.'

In her bedroom, Melissa thought. *Again.* Like she was ever in any other room of the house these days.

Gingerly, she stepped into the main bedroom. Through the gloom, she could make out the mound of her mum lying on top of the duvet, still fully dressed. The air was stinky in there and Melissa was itching to open a window, but knew of old that was the kind of thing that might disturb her mother's nerves.

'How are you today, Mum?' she whispered through the darkness.

'Oh, don't worry about me, pet,' Susan half groaned, hauling herself up onto one elbow so she could read the time off the alarm clock on her bedside table. 'How are you? Isn't this late for you to get home? What time is it anyway?'

'It's half eight, Mum,' Melissa whispered. 'I stayed on after school for study club, because I'd drama class this evening, remember?'

'Oh God,' said Susan, slumping wearily back against the pillow. 'I must have slept through it, pet. I really am so sorry. I'll make it up to you, I promise.'

'So how do you feel?' said Melissa, perching on the edge of the bed and reaching out to squeeze her hand. 'How did you get on today?'

Maybe one of these days, Melissa hoped, her mum would say that she actually felt a little bit better. Maybe.

'Okay. I'm just a bit tired, that's all.'

Groggy and half-sedated as she was, Susan was still able to edit out what her day had really been like. The grilling she got from security and then from a policewoman who had to be called to the pharmacy, the almighty scene she'd caused – *oh dear God*, she thought, feeling sick at the memory, had she really shouted at an elderly lady? Had she really hammered on the counter and screamed the place down? Was this what she was turning into?

Jesus Christ, she'd only got out of there without getting arrested after her family GP, Dr Taylor, had been called. Dr Taylor had been fabulous, though; she'd taken great pains to explain Susan's situation to the staff at the pharmacy, not to mention the guard who had to be called, stressing that the whole incident was a one-off that wouldn't happen again.

'Everyone has huge sympathy for you, Susan,' had been her exact words, 'and we're all here to help you in any way we can. But no more causing scenes in public, okay? You're only asking for trouble.'

This was followed by a gentle but firm talking to about getting local social workers and a community care nurse to check in on her more often. Then the policewoman, who'd been perfectly nice in every other way, took Susan aside and cautioned her very firmly that in light of everything else she'd been up to lately, 'you can consider this your final warning, Mrs Hayes. You're wearing police patience very thin.'

But Susan chose to block that bit out. The main thing was that Dr Taylor had emailed over a prescription for more sedatives, with a strict warning only to take one a day. Which, of course, Susan completely ignored the minute she was alone again.

'I'm grand, thanks, pet.' She swallowed, forcing a tiny smile, as Melissa's pale, worried little face looked back at her from the side of the bed. 'My day was . . . well, I've had better days. Never mind me, though, I want to hear about you.'

'My day was . . . fine,' said Melissa flatly, also editing out highlights that she knew her mum was too fragile to deal with. How her class tutor, Miss Jenkins, had humiliated her in double maths class that morning, asking if they could have a 'little talk' afterwards, then pointedly asking how things were at home.

'It's not like you to be so late with your homework, Melissa,' Miss Jenkins had said worriedly. 'And such sloppy work too. We're all very concerned about how things are for you at home right now. I'm going to ask your mum to come in and see me, sooner rather than later.'

Melissa had been fifty shades of mortified, particularly as Abby Graham had been passing down the corridor where she and Miss Jenkins were talking, accidentally on purpose, no doubt, so she could overhear everything. Abby was already giving Melissa a hard time because her school uniform was starting to pong a bit and this could only add fuel to the fire.

'Whatever you do, don't put me sitting beside stinky-arse,' Abby had said loudly, to a chorus of titters in science class earlier. 'Her uniform's so manky, it could be a science project all on its own.'

So with Miss Jenkins, Melissa did what she always did: put on the biggest, brightest smile that she possibly could and reached for the most positive thing she could think of to say.

'Thanks so much, Miss Jenkins,' she said stoutly, 'but there's absolutely no need for Mum to come in and see you at all.

Honestly, we're doing fine at home. We're cool. Mum is just so busy right now with . . . emm . . . work.'

'I thought she wasn't working?' said Miss Jenkins, concerned. 'Not since . . . well, not since what happened. Last time I saw her she mentioned that she was still on a leave of absence. She has a job in the bank, doesn't she?'

'Yeah and she's doing loads of overtime too,' Melissa improvised. 'So she's really busy just now, you see. You're far better off just leaving her be.'

'Is that right?' said her teacher, biting her lip doubtfully.

'Honestly, Miss Jenkins.' Melissa said. 'Mum and I are fine – really. We're sad, of course, and we miss Ella every single day, but we're going to be okay.'

'Hmm,' Miss Jenkins said after a scarily long pause. 'Well, you know I'm always here if you need me, Melissa. My door is always open.'

'But we're fine, miss. All we really need is to be left alone.'

'Pay no attention to me, pet,' Susan said to Melissa, back upstairs in her stale, gloomy bedroom. 'I'm just having a bad day, that's all. But tomorrow will be better, wait and see. I'll take you to the park, if you like. Or the movies. Or we can go to the Dundrum town centre and do a bit of shopping together. '

'You just rest and get well, Mum,' Melissa said, as Susan's eyelids slowly grew heavier and heavier. 'And I'll see you in the morning, okay?'

'Did you have something to eat, pet?' her mum asked, just before she nodded off.

'I'm full to the brim, Mum,' Melissa lied, 'so you don't need to worry about me.'

It was only a little lie, she told herself. At lunchtime in school, she'd got away with telling everyone that she'd just forgotten her lunch again, so Hayley had very kindly shared some of her egg sandwich. Melissa didn't really like egg sandwiches, but it was better than nothing and it kept her going.

Susan didn't even answer her, though; she was already out for the count. And Melissa knew well enough to put all thoughts of the movies or a day's shopping right out of her head. Her mum was always promising stuff like that and it never came to anything.

Tip-toeing out of the room, she noticed a new jar of those funny-looking purple pills by the bedside table and wondered how many her mum had taken. But at least she was at home this evening, where she was supposed to be, and not standing in the lashing rain outside Josh Andrews' house. That was a step forwards, wasn't it? That had to count for something, even if it was only something little.

To this day, Melissa didn't understand why her mum hated Josh Andrews so much – almost like a vendetta, she overheard her dad saying once when they were fighting. Melissa wasn't sure what vendetta meant, but she'd googled it and she hadn't liked what she'd read one little bit. No one at home would tell her anything either because they were all trying to protect her. All she knew for certain was that Josh Andrews had somehow caused her family all this pain and no one would tell her why.

On her way back down to the kitchen, she hovered outside Ella's room, same as she always did. There was a huge KEEP OUT sign on the door, which Ella had put there years ago and no one could bring themselves to take away now. Gently, Melissa grasped the creaky door handle and let herself inside, something she often did whenever she needed to feel close to her sister.

Not that she could ever have done that when Ella was around. Not a chance. Back then, she was Ella's pesky kid sister, and on the rare occasions when she was allowed into the room, Ella would always say something like, 'Just stay at the door, kiddo. Don't even *think* about coming in any further. And don't dare go near my iPad or you're dead meat.' Then a load of stuff about respecting boundaries that had never meant anything to Melissa; most of the time she only wanted to hang out with Ella, her super-cool older sister. Her sister, with her wild head of curly hair that she used to chop off herself whenever it got too long. Ella, who dressed out of a charity shop and who was always in trouble and who never, ever seemed to care.

The room was exactly as Ella had left it, right down to all the stacks and stacks of books that she kept piling high, spilling out over the bookcase and onto the floor. Her mum even insisted Ella's laptop be left exactly where she always kept it, right bang in the middle of her desk, overlooking Primrose Square.

There was a time when their mum was always giving out to Ella over the state of her room, nagging her that it was like a bombsite and that if she didn't tackle it immediately, then everything was going straight into a binliner for the charity shop. Things were different now, though, Melissa thought sadly, perching herself on the edge of Ella's cosy single bed with its deep purple quilt the exact match of the deep purple painted walls that Ella had insisted on.

'Purple is the colour of wisdom and integrity,' she used to say, 'so therefore it's my signature colour.'

These days, her room was a sanctuary. It was quiet and peaceful, like the chapel in Melissa's school. Everything was exactly as if Ella had just stepped out for a bit and would be back home any minute.

Mum's not the only one who misses you, Melissa thought, feeling sad and lonely as she picked up a pink scarf that was lying on the floor and breathed in its scent. It smelt lemony, a bit like the good perfume from Lush that Ella always lashed on before she went out.

I do too.

Later on that night, her dad Skyped her, same as he always did.

'So how's my little princess this evening?' he asked, looking tanned and fit in his army combats, even through the grainy image on the computer screen.

'We're cool, thanks, Dad.' Melissa smiled brightly, instantly clicking into her 'on show' face. 'Mum and I are both doing great.'

'And where is she, love? Can I talk to her?'

'Oh . . . emm . . . she's just in the kitchen cooking dinner, Dad, so she can't really come to the phone. She's making . . . emm . . . a mushroom risotto and she says she has to keep on stirring it or else it'll end up like mush.'

Melissa's tummy rumbled just thinking about how much she'd have loved a mushroom risotto for dinner, but then she remembered there was an unopened packet of crackers in one of the kitchen cupboards. That would just have to do her.

'Sounds gorgeous, pet,' her dad said. 'So how was school today?'

'School was fine, Dad,' she told him, aware that he could see her face clearly and giving him a big smile. 'Hayley and me had drama afterwards and . . . emm . . . ' She broke off there, trying to grasp at another white lie, so her dad wouldn't be worried about her. 'And my new friend Abby Graham asked me to her birthday party this weekend. We're going to the movies, then a sleepover. So I'm cool, Dad. Mum and I both are. Honestly.'

Nancy

BEST BUDGET HOTEL, DUBLIN

Dear God, Nancy thought as she hunched alone over a dinner that consisted of a rock-hard baked potato with a plate of wilting lettuce leaves on the side. Another night sitting in the same featureless, poky little hotel bedroom she'd been holed up in for almost two weeks. What she wouldn't give for a normal chat with normal people when she came in from a hard day's work. But once time was called on each day's rehearsals, her new colleagues all scattered to the four winds, and Nancy was back to her sad little cube of a hotel room.

She thought mournfully of the little flat in Islington she'd loved so much, and how much she missed the friendliness and warmth of all her pals in London. Of course she'd been in touch with her parents and a few close friends since she'd moved to Dublin, but the chats were mostly along the lines of, 'You okay, hon? How are you holding up?' Plus there was the unmistakable feeling that a lot of once mutual friends were still listening to horrible gossip, talking about her behind her back and taking sides. As people did.

But it's best not to dwell on that, she thought, picking up her rehearsal script, determined to get ahead on some blocking and questions for a couple of the characters before the next morning.

Work, she thought. *Just work your way through this.* All she needed to do was keep her head down and keep working and, in time, all would surely be well. London was an ocean away and no one in Dublin need ever know what had gone down over there.

If there was one thing Nancy had got very good at lately, it was keeping secrets.

Jesus Christ, look at me, she thought, sitting back wearily and looking around her gloomy little room. *I'm too old for this. Too old and too tired.* And it wasn't like she was a high maintenance type either; Nancy had backpacked her way through India, Vietnam and Thailand in her twenties, staying in places where even a mattress was considered a luxury. But you bypass all that when you hit thirty, she thought, and sometimes when you're working your arse off, and you're emotionally bruised and battered to start with, you just need a few little home comforts around you, that's all.

Which is when Clara's words of advice came back to her. So picking up her laptop, she typed in 'Homesitter.com', thinking, *What the hell have I to lose?*

Total revelation – and the first time all evening that Nancy had actually smiled. She was in complete shock; some of the properties listed really were exquisite. She thought of Clara describing how 'Mummy and Daddy' occasionally rented out their town pad via the site, and offered up a silent little prayer that she might luck out and land such a miracle for herself.

Some of the homes available really took her breath away. She clicked on dozens and couldn't find a single one that was anything less than out-of-this-world gorgeous. Central, clean, cheap – the three Cs as far as Nancy was concerned.

I want living in this city to be a happy, healing experience for me, she thought firmly. *And to do that, I need somewhere to call home.*

And that's when she saw it. Right there, in glorious technicolour, buried away on page fifteen.

Primrose Square, Dublin 2 – terraced Victorian townhouse available for short to medium-term rental. Longer lease preferred.

Primrose Square? It sounded weirdly familiar to Nancy – hadn't she heard that name somewhere before? Immediately, she clicked on Google maps to check it out. And almost fell off the chair in shock. Because she recognised what she saw; she distinctly remembered walking past this beautiful, residential square only the other day.

Primrose Square was located just off Dublin's busy, bustling Pearce Street, right across the River Liffey from the National Theatre. Literally, all she'd have to do was stroll down the square, cross the Rosie Hackett Bridge and then she'd be in work. Unheard of luxury!

She read on, her attention well and truly caught, searching for the snag. Because of course there was going to be a snag. The property itself was a two-bedroom townhouse in a row of Victorian terraced houses, but you'd never guess it was an old house from the pictures. The photos were jaw-droppingly impressive and so slick-looking, you'd think Mario Testino had just signed off on them.

The house might have looked Victorian on the outside, with three granite stone steps leading up to a very grand-looking front door and immaculately painted wrought iron railings to the front. Inside, though, it was completely modernised, so now it was all black leather sofas, deep-pile cream rugs and an open-plan basement kitchen with the pièce de resistance – a master bedroom with an en suite and an actual walk-in wardrobe.

Greedily, Nancy zoomed in on every photo on offer, and each one was more stunning than the last; the whole place was beautifully, sympathetically refurbished, so the period features all seemed to be untouched. Tasteful artwork dotted the walls and there was even a proper working fireplace in the main living room with a giant plasma TV screen just above.

Well, the rent here has to be out of orbit, she thought, forcing herself to be realistic for a minute. Photos could be deceptive, she knew of old, but even if this place had been located on Assault Alley right beside Drug Drive in the middle of the city's most depressing slum, the rent would surely be in the region of a good four figures. Per night, that is.

'Price on application,' the site said, which was never a good sign. But figuring what the hell, and as an act of faith in the universe if nothing else, she clicked on the link for more information and punched in her details. There was even a comment box where you could elaborate a bit, so she did.

To sweeten the maximum rent she could afford, she threw in that she was happy to muck in with whatever the owner or landlord wanted while they're away. You want the plants watered, she wrote? I'm your girl. Dogs walked? Not a problem. You've left fifteen cats in the flat that need minding? For the chance to stay in a pad like this, they could sleep on top her head and use her bare limbs as a scratching post, for all she cared.

She clicked send, offered up a silent prayer, and waited for a reply.

At eight thirty the following morning, Nancy was hopping off the bus at Stephen's Green, unable to believe her luck that she was en route to an actual viewing in Primrose Square. Although it was relatively early, town was already humming and all she could think was how blessed she was to escape to a city as vibrant as this.

Maybe this is it, she hoped fervently. *Maybe after all the awfulness in London, now everything will start to go my way. Maybe.*

She took a shortcut down South King Street and spotted about a dozen places she really, seriously wanted to come back to explore properly when she had more time. Her head kept swivelling around – this time taking in the Gaiety Theatre, which was showing a brand new play by an up-and-coming female playwright, which she'd heard was unmissable.

Nancy strode past, terrified of being late for the viewing, but still making a mental list of all the upcoming shows around the city that she was dying to check out. There was the Gate Theatre, where a revival of a Bernard Shaw play was playing to rave reviews, a clatter of awards and packed-out houses. Then there were all the smaller theatres, like Smock Alley, the New Theatre and the Project, showing so many more productions, all of which Nancy had heard great things about and couldn't wait to see, to hone her craft, to watch and, with any luck, to learn.

How lucky am I? she thought, *to earn my living doing something I love so much, I'd willingly do it for free?*

The sun was just beginning to shine as she paced down the busy, bustling street towards Trinity College, then wound her way around the wrought iron gates at its perimeter till she found Pearce Street. And just a few minutes later there she was, at Primrose Square.

The whole square was so neatly laid out, it didn't take Nancy long to find the house she was looking for. From the outside, number twenty-four was so picture perfect, all she wanted to do was Instagram the shit out of it, to impress everyone she knew back in London . . . but then she remembered that the less contact she had with her old life back in London, the better.

A pang of regret, but it quickly passed as she tried to concentrate hard on what was in front of her.

Care has gone into this house, Nancy thought, rapping on the front door and peeking through the windows. Care and love. And good taste. And, of course, money. Lots and lots of cold, hard cash. The sash windows that looked out onto the street all seemed brand spanking new, with heavy, expensive-looking curtains visible on the inside. Two neat box hedge trees sat in twin pots on either side of the front door, and all Nancy wanted to do was hammer on the front door, screaming, 'Let me in . . . and don't show this house to anyone else . . . I'LL TAKE IT!'

No one answered the door, though. So she knocked again and waited.

Still nothing.

Anxiously, she kept glancing down to check the time on her phone; rehearsals started at 9:30 a.m. on the dot and the last thing she wanted to do was be late. Torn between the wrath of Diego Fernandez and not wanting to miss out on what could be the coolest home in the city, she settled for pacing up and down instead.

Then, sharply to her left, she heard a front door bang shut. Immediately Nancy looked over to see a sprightly, sixty-something lady dressed in a fleecy pink tracksuit, struggling down the steps of a house just a few doors down, dragging two stuffed bin bags behind her.

'Morning,' the stranger said with a big warm smile as soon as she spotted Nancy. She was struggling with the bin bags, so instinctively Nancy went to help her. Between the two of them, they lugged them down to a black wheelie bin on the pavement.

'Well, aren't you just an angel?' the older woman said gratefully. 'Thank you so much, love. I know young women your generation hate hearing anything remotely anti-feminist, but I have to say, I always think it's a man's job, dragging out the bins.'

'Delighted to help.' Nancy smiled back.

'It was always something my Tom took care of,' this friendly lady chatted away, in that freewheeling, stream-of-consciousness way Nancy noticed all Dubliners seemed to have. 'The bins, I mean. But the poor man's not able for it any more. So these days, I have to do it all by myself or else it won't get done. Simple as that.'

'Is Tom your husband?' Nancy asked her.

'He certainly is,' she said proudly, with a big pink beam on her face that instantly took years off her. Now that Nancy saw her close-up, this woman actually reminded her of a younger version of Mary Berry. Same neat, fair, bobbed hair, same twinkly eyes, same zest for life emanating from her.

'Are you married yourself, love?' she added.

'No, I'm single,' Nancy replied a bit over-brightly, with a smile that she hoped wasn't too fake-looking. 'Married to the job, you know how it is.'

'Well, if you ever do take the plunge,' the Mary Berry looka-like said, gently patting Nancy's arm, 'I hope you'll be as happy as me and my Tom.'

'Thank you.' Nancy smiled, really touched at her kindness. 'Where is Tom now?' Then she instantly bit her tongue back, thinking, *Hopefully not bedridden or in hospital.*

'In a grand big urn, just above the telly.'

'Oh. Okaaaay.'

'I hope you don't mind my asking,' the woman went on, folding her arms and changing the subject, 'but are you English? You sound English to me.'

'Yes, I'm from London,' Nancy told her, thinking, *what the hell.* If her dream came true and she were to end up living here, this lovely, chatty lady could end up being her neighbour. 'I'm trying to rent a place here and I've got an appointment to view number twenty-four.'

'Well, now, isn't that wonderful?' came the reply. 'That house has been empty for such a long time, you know.'

'Really?' Nancy asked, wondering how that was even possible, in a location as great as Primrose Square.

'Builders,' she said, with a knowing tap on her nose. 'Sure you know what they're like. My Tom always said that when you're young, you think love can break your heart, but when you get older you realise it's builders. I thought they were renovating the Taj Mahal, there was that much work going on. And the dust! Don't talk to me about the dust. None of us have a clue who owns the house, but whoever it is, they have to be a multi-millionaire, I'd say.'

'It's a stunning house,' Nancy said with feeling. 'You're so lucky to live here and I'm just praying that this all works out for me.'

'I'm sure it will, pet. I'm Jayne, by the way and I'll be sure to say a little prayer for you—' She broke off abruptly, though, as they both heard the sound of a car approaching from behind.

Nancy turned around, hoping it was the estate agent, but to her surprise, it was actually an ice cream van that pulled up neatly at the kerb, right where they were both standing.

'Strange time to sell ice cream, isn't it?' Nancy wondered out loud. 'On an icy cold day like this?'

Jayne, however, stayed tight-lipped. Then, seconds later, a familiar-looking woman in her early forties, with her hair neatly tied back into a chignon and wearing a pencil skirt, clambered inelegantly down from the driver's seat, laden down with a briefcase and a pile of plastic-covered folders.

'Irene, is that you?' Nancy asked in total disbelief. *God*, she thought, *of all the estate agents in Dublin, why is it that I always end up stuck with this one?* She'd lost count of the number of poky flats Irene tried to up-sell her in the last few weeks and how snooty and off-hand she'd be whenever Nancy would politely decline to live in whatever overpriced rabbit warren Irene was trying to pass off as the Times Square of Dublin. And now, the idea that the woman drove around in an incongruous looking ice-cream van was making Nancy want to giggle.

'Miss Thompson,' Irene said, banging the van door shut with as much dignity as she could muster. 'Here we go again, it seems. Will we get started?'

'Good morning, Irene,' Jayne calmly said to her, with a polite little smile.

These two know each other? Nancy thought. Was Dublin really that small?

Meanwhile, Irene bustled up the stone steps, scooped out a big bunch of keys and opened the hall door. Jayne stood benignly to one side, as the other woman pointedly ignored her, not a single hello, good morning, nothing.

Nancy definitely wasn't imagining it; the atmosphere, which had been warm and friendly before Madame Irene got there, had turned to antifreeze. Irene flung back the hall door and strode inside, then glared impatiently back at Nancy, as though to say, 'Well, come on then, what's keeping you?'

Nancy gave Jayne a puzzled look as Jayne gave her a tiny half-wink back.

'Long story, love,' was all she said. 'But if you do end up moving in, I'll tell you everything.'

'I'll most definitely drop in for a cuppa.' Nancy smiled back. 'I'd love that. I've missed having someone to talk to so much, you've no idea.'

'Oh, never mind your aul' cups of tea. A nice strong gin and tonic is much more what I had in mind.'

Susan

18 PRIMROSE SQUARE

Melissa. She had to think about Melissa. It's a new dawn, it's a new day and from now on, Susan decided, she was going to pull her socks up and start behaving like a normal mother around the child. No more forgetting to collect her from her after-school activities, no more letting the poor kid come home to a filthy house where she was expected to get her own dinner.

I still have my baby, my little Melissa, she thought to herself, staring up at her bedroom ceiling and vowing to start afresh. *I've been spared that much at least.*

From now on, Melissa would be her reason for getting out of bed in the morning and the sole focus of her day. Starting there and then.

Today will be a good day.

The grogginess from the Xanax she'd taken the night before was starting to wear off, but when Susan looked at the time on her bedside alarm clock, she realised with horror it was already past 11 a.m.

Oh Christ, she thought with a jolt, *I've been out for the count for over fourteen hours. Fourteen fucking hours. How the hell did that happen?* Which of course meant that, once again, Melissa would have had to get up by herself, get her own breakfast and get herself to school without even seeing her mother. Not a kind word for the poor kid as she started her day, not a goodbye hug, nothing.

Well, that carry-on ends here and now, Susan thought, forcing herself out of bed and into a scalding hot, reviving shower. No more feeling racked with guilt over the child, yet paralysed from doing anything about it. No more shutting herself away from the world and from all her neighbours on Primrose Square, who only had her best interests at heart. No more dodging Frank's calls when he rang, worried about his wife and only wanting to talk to her.

How long has it been since we even spoke? she wondered. Really spoke, that is, like they used to, back in the day. Hard to believe on days like this, she thought, but there really was a time when she'd quite literally have the minutes and hours counted till Frank would get back from a tour of duty. Time was when the two of them would have regular phone sex, when he'd call late in the evening and the girls were safely in bed and out of earshot. Time was when her whole day revolved around Frank's Skype calls; she'd even jot down funny stories and little things that happened during the day, just to make him smile. To make him feel less homesick, when they were so far apart.

And now, Susan wondered, did she even have a marriage at all? She felt lonely and angry and betrayed when she thought of Frank so far away, leaving her and Melissa to cope on their own. Did he get how bloody hard this was for her? Why couldn't he understand how vitally important it was for her to get justice for Ella? Why did he keep on at her to drop the whole Josh Andrews thing? How could he love her and ask that of her? How could any parent just move on, the way Frank seemed to?

'Mum, is everything okay between you and Dad?' Melissa had asked Susan out of the blue not so long ago. Which was a loud wake-up call, the fact that the child was picking up on every scrap of tension between them. She made a mental note there and then to keep the truth from Melissa, because the truth wasn't pretty. The hard, cold fact, however, was that Susan's marriage was very definitely not in a good place and the best outcome was that time apart would give both her and Frank space to think.

'Your dad and I are fine,' she'd rushed to reassure her baby with a tight little hug. 'We both love you so, so much. It's just that we're each dealing with things in our own way, that's all, love. There's nothing to worry about.'

'Whenever I hear "there's nothing to worry about",' Melissa had said quietly, frowning, 'it actually means there's loads for me to worry about. Loads.'

Jesus Christ, I have so much making up to do to that child, Susan thought, suddenly full of verve and new energy. *So now this is the new me.* Welcome to Susan 2.0. A better wife, a far better mother and a far better neighbour to everyone on the square, all those people who'd shown her nothing but kindness and tolerance ever since . . . well . . . Ever since.

And, above all, she decided, *absolutely no more pills.*

Her resolve lasted a good hour, during which she actually managed to clean the kitchen, start tackling the mountain of laundry that had built up, and even hoover the stairs. Her kitchen had once been her pride and joy; she and Frank had put in a huge, modern 'glass box' extension a few years ago and she used to love its clean lines and clear granite surfaces. It was all so 'architect-y' and bang on trend, and Susan had absolutely loved it. It was a pigsty now, though. *But from today on,* she thought, *that all changes.*

When she went upstairs, though, she barely got as far Ella's bedroom door, with the giant KEEP OUT sign still stuck to it, when she crumpled. Just doubled up in agony. The pain was too sharp, too overwhelming; it came in slow, sickening waves and she knew she'd never see the day through without a bit of medicinal back-up.

Did I really think today would be a good day? It seemed she'd spoken too soon.

Half a Xanax, she decided, going back to the bedside drawer where she'd stashed her fresh supply. *Just a half,* she thought. *Just to take the edge off.* Who'd even notice? Who was even to know, except her?

Later that afternoon, Susan managed to get as far as her car, parked just across the road on Primrose Square. She had a blurry memory of bumping into lovely Jayne, her old pal from next door, who was unloading the boot of her car with what looked like about a month's supply of groceries.

'Susan, how are you?' the older woman had asked her kindly, abandoning the huge pile of Tesco bags at her feet.

'Good. I'm good, thanks,' Susan replied, trying her best to sound cheery and upbeat. 'Isn't it a lovely day?'

'Yes, love, I suppose it is,' said Jayne, glancing uncertainly upwards at the grey, overcast, wintry sky.

'And how is everything with you?' Susan asked politely, all the while thinking, *Look at me! I'm actually doing it. I'm holding a normal conversation with another adult. Just passing the time of day in an ordinary, casual way. Like people do.* Things at the periphery of her vision were starting to get a little fuzzy, but still. Progress, she thought.

Jayne chatted about how she had a visitor coming at the weekend, hence the huge grocery shop.

'He's a friend,' she said, a bit coyly, 'just one that I haven't met properly yet, that's all. But we chat all the time, you know, on the Skype thingy, and he seems like a real dote. His name is Eric and he's coming all the way from Florida for a few weeks, just to see how we get on IRL. That's what you say when you mean *in real life*, you know. Gas, isn't it? Another world away from how you met fellas in my day.'

But Susan couldn't bring herself to answer or even register surprise at what she was hearing. She'd started to feel woozy and had the strangest sensation of her body standing stock still, while the rest of the world spun on its axis without her. She was dimly aware of an awkward pause in the chat, which kind old Jayne then filled with her usual conversational blather.

Then silence. Weird, awkward silence.

'Susan, love,' Jayne said, looking at her worriedly. 'Did you hear what I just asked you?'

'Emm . . . yeah,' Susan improvised. 'You've met this very nice new friend. Great. Fantastic. Well, I'd better get going now . . .'

'No, actually,' said Jayne evenly, 'that wasn't what I said at all. Eric is a bit more than just a friend, you see, and I was wondering if you and Melissa would like to come for dinner to meet him properly? He really seems like a dote and I think we'll all get along famously.'

'That's really nice of you,' said Susan as brightly as she could, given that she was by then seeing dots in front of her eyes. Actual bloody dots. 'But I have to get going now. I'm picking up Melissa from school,' she added, impressing herself, even though that was the kind of thing most mothers did in their sleep.

'Oh Susan, is that wise?' Jayne was saying, her voice coming in and out in waves. 'Should you really be driving? You don't really seem . . . like yourself.'

'Not like myself, how?' If Susan sounded defensive, she hadn't meant it to come out like that. At least, not with a good-hearted old soul like Jayne, who only meant well.

'Your words sound a bit slurred, pet. And if you don't mind me saying, you're swaying on your feet. How about I drive you to the school and we can pick up Melissa together?'

'I'm absolutely fine, thanks.'

'Are you?' said Jayne, taking a gentle hold of her arm. 'You can talk to me, you know that. I'm on your side.'

'I just told you, I'm okay. Now can you please let go of arm so I can get out of here?'

Shoving her off, Susan somehow got to her car, clambered inside and started the engine, aware all the time of Jayne standing right behind her, concern etched all over that big, warm face. Well, she needn't bother worrying, Susan thought groggily, driving off. All she was doing was collecting her daughter. Maybe even taking her for an after-school treat, like McDonalds. Or maybe even a movie. Like normal mothers did. Every day of the week.

Car horns were blaring at her. A lot more than usual. What the fuck was wrong with these drivers anyway? Susan was only trying to park at the school. Why was everyone in such a temper with her driving? She found a spot just adjacent to the school rugby pitch, switched off the engine, texted Melissa to tell her she was right outside the gates, then lay her head back on the car's headrest.

Tired. She was so, so tired. Her eyelids grew heavy, but she resisted the urge to nod off. Over at the school gates, she spotted a gaggle of the Yummy Mummy Brigade, chatting and laughing. Passing the time of day in a bit of harmless chat, as she herself had done so often before . . . well . . . before.

I'll join them, Susan thought. *I can do it. I can be like any other normal mum. I'll show everyone that I'm okay. That I'm actually fine. That it's business as usual for me and my family. I'll do it for Melissa.* It would make a change for the poor child to think her mum was actually having a good day.

Fuelled with fresh resolve, she got out of the car and walked over to where the other mothers were all gathered. She stumbled a bit on the way, then couldn't figure out why, since she was only wearing a pair of trainers, not even heels.

She was dimly aware of that horrible feeling she was interrupting something when the others saw her, because every swishy, blow-dried head instantly seemed to turn her way. Then a flushed, embarrassing silence, as though no one really knew what to say next. Susan hadn't seen most of this gang since the funeral and didn't even blame them for not knowing how to handle her. After all, what did you say to the mother of a dead seventeen-year-old girl?

Treat me normally, she thought. *For fuck's sake, that's all I'm asking here. Just talk to me like you would any other parent.* Couldn't they see that was all she needed here?

'Hi, Susan.'

'Hello.'

'Susan, hi there.'

Mortified, hushed hellos as Susan became aware of all the eyes drinking her in, clearly not having the first clue what was the right thing to say. Then, thank God, Annie Gibbons, Hayley's mother, bounced over, instantly shattering the awkward silence.

Hayley was in the same class as Melissa, and Susan had always been fond of both the mother and the daughter. Annie was one of the few school mums who was rock-solid and dependable, no matter what the circumstances. Susan still carried a vivid memory of her back at the house after the funeral, doling out big bowls of chicken curry and bossily taking complete charge in the kitchen, flashing Susan reassuring smiles whenever she could bring herself to look up from the floor.

'Hey, would you look who it is!' said Annie, in that loud, bellowing, hockey-mum voice. 'Susan Hayes, great to see you. Come here to me, love.'

With that she bear-hugged Susan, who couldn't have been more grateful the other woman had come along when she did.

'So how are you then?' Annie asked straight-up, as the other mums looked on. 'No plamasing me now – I want the truth.'

'I'm . . . well, I suppose I'm getting there.' Susan nodded, surprising herself by even forcing a smile. 'On a strict day-by-day basis, you know how it is.'

'I dropped Melissa home last night,' Annie went on, 'and she told me you were back at work already. A bit soon, don't you think? You need to take it easy on yourself.'

'She said . . . I'm sorry, Melissa told you what?' Susan answered, confused, as her thoughts trailed off. It wasn't entirely her fault; out of the corner of her eye, she caught a glimpse of the school's Senior Cup team weaving their way onto the rugby pitch for after-school training.

'Work. That you were back working at the bank,' said Annie as Susan's eyes scanned through the gang of lads, now all doing vigorous press-ups and burpees, or whatever you called them, on the side of the pitch.

Are you out there now? Susan wondered. *Are you about to train for some stupid match, like you hadn't a care in the world?*

'Susan?' said Annie, worried. 'You all right? You look like you've seen a ghost.'

And sure enough there he was, right in the centre of the players. Laughing, messing, even joshing with another guy roughly
the size of a tree trunk, larking about in horseplay. Josh Andrews
himself. Laughing. Actually bloody well laughing, the bare-faced
cheek of him.

How can you act like this? Susan thought, as a flash of something
beyond rage zipped through her. *How can you just live your life as
though you hadn't destroyed mine? How dare you?*

Frank's words came back to her, as clearly as if he were standing there beside her: 'Susan, you've got to let this go. You've got
to stop fixating. When are you going to accept what the inquest
told us and what the police are trying to tell us every single day?'

But Susan was done listening to voices in her head. Before
she knew what was happening, she had broken away from
Annie and the gang of mothers, and wasn't so much walking
as striding towards the pitch. She could feel all their eyes following her, but she didn't care. From behind her, she heard her
name being yelled out.

'Susan, get off the pitch! Come back, will you?' Annie was
hollering, but Susan ignored her. Her focus stayed rooted on that
one figure, now doing squat lunges, wearing a number thirteen
shirt in the school colours. Aware that Annie was hot on her
heels, Susan picked up her pace and broke into a run.

He couldn't even see her coming.

Good, she thought.

Because this fucking ends here.

Melissa

Melissa loved English class. Really loved it. But today she was daydreaming. *If I work really hard and am lucky enough to get to college*, she thought, *then I'm definitely going to study English Literature.*

The first years were doing *Pride and Prejudice* by Jane Austen and Melissa had already read ahead to the end – she literally couldn't sleep till she found out what happened to Lizzy Bennet and Mr Darcy, and that bold-as-brass Lydia when she ran off with Mr Wickham. The first time she'd smiled in ages was when she'd finally finished the book under the bedcovers late one night, then went right back to the very start to read it all over again. These days, Melissa wasn't sleeping too much anyway, so reading was the nicest way she could think of to keep all her worries far away.

Her dad had faithfully promised her that if she studied hard when he was away and got good grades, he'd take her to see the stage show of *Pride and Prejudice* that was coming to the National Theatre in Dublin. Melissa had read all about the play and its director, who was meant to be, like, really famous in Spain – Diego somebody – and she was determined to go.

'Then that's a deal,' her dad told her over a crackling Skype call late one night. 'We'll go to the play as soon as I'm home again. As a very special treat, for my very special princess.'

Melissa literally had the days counted till he was back (three months, two weeks and four days, to be exact) and had even checked out the theatre listings online to see exactly when the show was opening and how long it would be running for. For months, it seemed. Her dad would be back from Lebanon in loads of time to see it.

And her mum might even come too, of course, providing her nerves weren't at her. The night out would do her good, Melissa thought. It would do them all good. That was the problem with being home on Primrose Square day in and day out – there were memories at every turn, just waiting to creep up on you, even when you were trying to be brave and not cry and keep the whole show on the road.

It had been months and months now since what happened. But to this day Melissa still bumped into Ella's ghost in just about every corner of their house. She couldn't go into the TV room at the front of the house without seeing her big sister stretched the full length of the sofa, glued to Netflix, with a big bowl of popcorn balanced on her tummy.

'Don't even think about changing the channels,' Ella would say, barely looking up. 'We're watching *Thirteen Reasons Why* and that's the end of it.'

'But isn't that about teenage suicide?' Melissa had asked her innocently.

'Yeah,' Ella told her, 'there's a Darkness into Light march coming up next week and if the folks let me go to it, then I'm dragging you along with me. Do you good to see what life is like on the dark side.'

There were memories all over school too. Afterwards, it was like a ripple of shockwaves had gone through each and every classroom. Letters had gone out to all the parents. Bereavement counselling had been offered to anyone who wanted it.

Melissa had gone along to a few sessions, but instead of helping, she found they only made her sadder. And she couldn't afford to be sad; she needed to be bright and happy for her parents, now that it was just the three of them. She'd asked her mum if she could drop out, but her mum had just twiddled with her hair and said, 'Do whatever you want, love.' It was one of her Bad Days, and much as Melissa would have loved nothing more than a big warm hug from her mother and to be told that everything would be all right, she knew that wasn't going to happen.

For weeks back in school, though, all anyone could talk about was Ella Hayes, and Melissa would have a knot in her stomach every time she so much as walked down a busy corridor.

'You see her?' Everyone seemed to be pointing and whispering in her direction. 'That's Ella Hayes's little sister.'

Weirdest of all was that even kids who barely knew Ella turned her into a kind of saint – there was even an impromptu altar by the sixth-year lockers where people would put fresh flowers every day.

'But Ella wasn't a saint!' Melissa had wanted to scream at them all. 'She was just . . . normal. She was my big sister and half of you didn't even know her!'

That carry-on went on for weeks, till Sally Jenkins, the school counsellor, put a stop to it, on the grounds that it was 'causing unnecessary upset'. Worst of all, though, was all the talk about Josh Andrews. More letters had gone out to parents, but Melissa didn't really understand the ins and outs of it. All she knew was that her mum was getting worse instead of better. An awful lot worse.

No wonder Mum is the way she is, Melissa thought sadly. *If it's this horrible for me, then how much worse must it be for her?* Her dad was grieving too, she knew, in his own private way. But he was thousands of miles away, with the distraction of his busy job and life in the army to keep his mind off everything. Her mum had nothing to distract her, just horrible memories and those stupid purple pills that made her sleep for days.

I'll make her a nice dinner tonight, Melissa vowed to herself. She was supposed to have rehearsals at her drama class after school, and while she loved drama and hated missing out on it, wasn't her mum far more important?

I'll skip class and go to the supermarket instead, so I can buy everything I need.

Her dad had sent her over some pocket money, but instead of blowing it in Zara and H&M, like all the other girls in her class, she could always go to M&S and buy some of the chocolate profiteroles that her mum used to love so much. *And I'll make a big fuss of her and I'll mind her and talk to her,* she decided. Melissa had faithfully promised her dad she'd look after her mum when he was gone and, if it was the last thing she did, she was determined to keep to her word.

'So why would you say marrying well is so important to Jane Austen's heroines?' Miss Jenkins was saying sharply to the class, pulling Melissa's attention back to that stuffy, sleepy classroom. A weak, wintry sun was actually shining for once and the school's senior rugby team had just jogged out to the rugby pitch to warm up.

'Is it primarily for love, or for status and security?' Miss Jenkins said, briskly pacing up and down the classroom, her eagle-eyes out on stilts for anyone who wasn't paying attention.

Bony-bum, Ella used to call her behind her back, but then Ella had funny nicknames for all the teachers. 'The woman is basically Jeremy Paxman in drag,' Ella used to say, and

Melissa would giggle, even though she didn't know who Jeremy Paxman was.

'And in the world of *Pride and Prejudice*,' Miss Jenkins was saying, 'which of these would you say is most important for a woman? Would anyone care to discuss?'

In fairness, most of the class seemed far more absorbed by the fifth- and sixth-year lads doing squats and lunges than by the intrigues of the Regency marriage market. But then everyone at Melissa's school seemed to be completely obsessed with rugby. The team had got to the finals of the Senior Cup last year and the team captain was almost carried shoulder-high through the school, even though they'd been beaten out of sight. Melissa didn't really understand rugby – or any sport, come to that. She'd prefer to go to a play or read a lovely book by herself any day.

But the cheering from the pitch outside seemed a lot louder today, Melissa thought – or was she imagining it?

'Will you all please try to concentrate,' Miss Jenkins said sharply, beginning to sound narky. 'If you're finding rugby practice more interesting than English class, then I'll pull the blinds down so you can concentrate properly.'

'Fight, fight, fight, fight, fight, fight . . . ' a dull chant drifted from the pitch into the classroom. Just the lads doing their lad things, Melissa thought, focusing on the book in front of her. But the chanting grew louder and louder, and pretty soon most of her class were glued to the window, everyone itching to find out what the commotion was outside.

'Please! Will you all get back into your seats?' Miss Jenkins snapped.

'But look, miss,' said Abby Graham, 'there's murder going on out there!'

'What's happening? I can't see . . . '

'Aggro with the players?'

'No . . . I don't think so . . . '

'Jesus! It's one of the parents having a go at your man, the scrum half . . . what's his name . . . '

'It's one of the mums, I think.'

At that, Melissa's blood turned icy cold.

'Hard to see through the crowd that's gathered . . . '

'Get back to your desks!' Miss Jenkins yelled above the melee. 'Otherwise, I'm warning you, it'll be detention for the lot of you.'

'Would you look at her?'

'I don't believe it!'

'She's walloping the shit out of Josh Andrews!'

It was like shockwaves rippled through the class, just at the sound of his name. But then he was such a school star, everyone knew who Josh Andrews was.

'No way!'

'Josh Andrews? Are you kidding?'

'He's, like, six foot three. He'll murder anyone who has a go at him!'

No, no, no, no, no, thought Melissa, squirming in her seat, the only one in the whole class who wasn't looking. It couldn't be. It wasn't possible. *She never comes to the school any more . . . How could it possibly be her?*

Next thing, there was a discreet rapping at the classroom door and, as Miss Jenkins opened it, every head turned to see the school secretary standing there.

'Apologies for interrupting class,' she said in a voice loud enough so the whole class heard, 'but could Melissa Hayes please come with me right away?'

Stone-cold silence in the classroom as every head then swivelled Melissa's way. Melissa shrivelled up in her seat, hoping that if she could make herself very, very little, it might all just go away. She'd only ever felt fear like this once before in her whole life and just look what had happened then.

Jayne

'But you're a widow!' Jason was spluttering at his mother. 'So why can't you just act like one?'

'And how exactly is a widow supposed to act these days?' was Jayne's calm response, as she thumped away at the dough she was kneading to make tomato and fennel bread from scratch. 'Would you and Irene be happier if I took up knitting and just sat in front of the telly all day, watching daytime soaps until the day I die?'

'You know that's not what I meant at all, Ma,' Jason back-pedalled. 'But you have to understand I'm having a lot of problems getting my head around this.'

Jayne nodded, having figured as much the moment she saw his ice cream van trundle up outside her house, just a few minutes before. A good measure of how badly her son was reacting was the fact he'd even refused to sample one of the tiffin squares she'd just taken fresh out of the fridge.

'I do understand, son,' she said kindly. 'But at the same time, you want your old mother to be happy, don't you?'

'Yeah . . . course I do,' he said grudgingly, standing stock-still at the kitchen door, arms folded, refusing to budge one centimetre further if it meant sharing the same air space as her. 'But come on, Ma – this? There was me thinking that you were content enough pottering around with your bake sales and your flower arranging and your bit of chat with the neighbours, and the whole time you were trawling through these dating sites looking for fellas? I mean . . . online dating? Where did you even meet this gobshite anyway?'

'On the *Silver Dates* website, love. And I know, in a million years, that online dating lark was never something that would even have crossed my mind. It was Violet Dunne from across the square who put me onto it in the first place.'

'Violet Dunne?' Jason spluttered. 'You mean the Merry Widow?'

Everyone called Violet Dunne the Merry Widow. Violet had hair the colour of burgundy, wore Ugg boots with skinny jeans, and had gone through so many boyfriends since her husband passed away, the nickname had stuck.

'Well, of course I didn't particularly want to be a merry widow myself,' Jayne went on, 'but I did think how lovely it would be to just have a bit of company for myself. Someone to chat to at the end of day, to tell all my news to, and to hear his in return. So Violet helped me to sign up to the site and, before I knew it, sure wasn't I chatting away to fellas from all four corners of the world!'

'Jaysus, Ma, at your age? It's obscene, that's what it is!'

'I'm only sixty-six,' Jayne replied. 'That's not really old, now is it? Not by today's standards.'

'Ma, you're a pensioner!'

'Only just,' she said, reaching for a fistful of flour and sprinkling it lightly on her kneading board. 'And you know Eric was telling me that in some cultures, people are respected far more as they age. Apparently in Japan, the sixties and seventies are considered the prime of life.'

'*Eric?* Jesus, Ma, will you stop talking about him like this is actually happening?'

'Oh, but it is happening, love. Eric will be here at the weekend, so you can meet him for yourself. I think you'll like him, though – he really is a lovely man. I think we'll all get on famously.'

'How can you even think that, never mind say it?' he groaned, smacking his hand off his forehead in frustration. 'My da will be turning in his grave at this!'

'He won't, as it happens,' said Jayne, glancing fondly towards the jar of his ashes. 'Your dad always wanted me to be happy. Even on his deathbed he told me that I was still young and that my job was to live life for the two of us from that day on. So that's what I'm doing, plain and simple. I'm living life to the full for the two of us.'

'Ahh here, you're off your bleeding bikkies, you are,' Jason grumbled, shaking his head. 'For feck's sake, you still talk to a jar of Da's ashes! It's a psychiatrist you should be seeing, not some arsehole you picked up online!'

'Jason, you really need to cool down here,' his mother replied evenly. 'Now either you and I can talk about this like reasonable adults, or else I suggest you leave and come back when you've centred your chakras a bit.'

'Centred me what?'

'Your chakras, love. You know, energy centres through the whole body. Eric says apparently it's very important to keep them in alignment and yours are all out of kilter now.'

'Ma, can you hear yourself? You're talking complete shite! Chakras? What the fuck?'

'Jason,' she replied, a bit more sternly. 'I won't remind you again about the language. Not in front of your father.'

'Just listen to me, Ma, will you?' he pleaded, as his mother went back to pounding away at the bread mix. 'Me and Irene are the only family you have, and it's up to us to protect you from all these scam artists and chancers that your meet online. We're both worried sick about you. Irene's in bits and I hardly slept a wink last night.'

That much was true, although there was a whole other reason why Jason had a sleepless night. He knew that more demanding letters from a payday loan crowd he'd fallen foul of would arrive by post, and he was terrified Irene would get to them before he did. In the end, he'd got up at 6:30 a.m. to intercept the postman, but even at that, Irene had started asking all sorts of questions.

'You never get up early,' she'd said to him beadily that morning. 'What's going on?'

Jason had pleaded insomnia, feeling the final demand hidden in his pocket almost burn through his trousers as he lied to her face, telling her he just couldn't sleep so he got up and pottered around the house instead. *Jesus Christ*, he thought. When would this nightmare end? How much longer could he keep what was going on a secret?

'Eric isn't a scam artist at all,' said Jayne, sprinkling rock salt on the bread mix before carefully covering it with a tea towel, so the yeast could do its thing. 'You have to trust me. He really is a dote and if you'd only give him half a chance—'

'Oh, you needn't tell me about your new boyfriend,' said Jason with a sneer. 'Irene was up half the night googling this Eric bloke – we know all about him and his meditation retreat centre in the back arse of bleeding Florida.'

'He's a practising Dharma Buddhist and a very old soul, I think,' said Jayne, with a little smile. 'Although Eric makes me laugh, he firmly believes he and I knew each other in a past life. That we were slaves together in Ancient Roman times, can you believe it? Me? In Italy? And I don't even like pasta.'

'Ma!' said Jason, clamping his hands down over his ears, as if this conversation were physically hurting him. 'Will you stop?'

'Oh, but it is happening, love,' she replied softly. 'And the sooner you accept that, the better it'll be for all of us. I've been very lonely since your dad passed away, you know, and Eric has put the smile back on my face again.'

'But sure how can you be lonely when you've me and Irene? And the twins too? Your own granddaughters?'

Jayne looked at her son squarely in the eye.

How can I be lonely, you ask? Because I never really see you, unless you want something. You drop over here for about an hour once a week, and other than that, the only time I hear from you or Irene is if you need an unpaid babysitter. That's why I'm lonely. In fact, if it weren't for the good neighbours I have . . . there have been times when I honestly didn't know what I'd do.

She remembered fondly how Eric's profile had first caught her eye all those months ago. Because he hadn't written out all his hobbies, likes and dislikes, the way every other man seemed to. Instead, Eric had written the most beautiful poem for his late wife, Claire. And it was so heartfelt, it almost made Jayne want to cry.

After a time, I surprised myself with a smile
After a time, I found I could talk about you without tears
After a time, I could go a whole hour without you at the front
of my mind
After the longest time, I'm beginning to heal
I'll never forget you, my love, and I'll always keep my promise
to you
After a time, I'll learn to live life for both of us

Jayne had got teary reading it, it resonated with her so deeply. It was just exactly what Tom had said to her, before he went off to his big urn above the telly. So she got in touch with Eric to tell him how beautiful she'd thought his poem was. Turned out they'd both lost their spouses in the same year – another thing that really bonded them. Eric chatted to her all about the Healing House in Florida that he'd set up, and they'd spent hours talking late into the night about their 'journey through grief', and coming out on the other side.

And Jayne *knew*. Even though he was a total stranger from a whole different culture, in a whole other part of the world, she knew a good man when she found one. Just like when she'd first met Tom, all those decades ago.

She was spared from having to tell Jason any of this as, just then, her mobile started ringing. She could hear it getting louder and louder, so she fumbled around all her usual places looking for it, while Jason kept ranting on and on.

'Irene hit the nail on the head last night,' he was saying. 'She says it's up to us to protect you and to make sure that no money-grabbing chancer out to make a quick buck comes within six feet of you.'

'Ahh now, pet,' Jayne said. 'Of course I understand this has been a bit of a shock to you both, but in time you'll come around. Now, help me look for my phone, will you, love?'

'Oh, you'll think I'll come around, do you?' said Jason, pointedly ignoring the ringing noise.

'All I ask is that you keep an open mind till you meet Eric, that's all,' Jayne went on, rummaging around in her handbag, trying to trace the sound of the phone. 'He's flying in on Friday. We'd love it if you and Irene could join us for dinner. When you both calm down a bit, maybe you'll consider it?'

'I'd rather starve to death then eat with your scam artist new boyfriend,' he said proudly, to a frustrated 'tsk!' from Jayne as she finally located the phone, which had fallen deep behind a sofa cushion.

'Mrs Jayne Dawson?' came an unfamiliar voice as soon as she answered.

'Yes.'

'Good afternoon. This is the secretary from Kingsbay Secondary School speaking. Forgive my calling you, but you were on the contact sheet Mrs Susan Hayes provided the school with.'

'Is everything all right?' Jayne asked, as a cold clutch of panic instantly gripped at her heart.

Kingsbay was where Melissa Hayes went to school. Why were the school ringing her? They never rang; sure why would they? Then she remembered meeting Susan out on the square earlier and how strangely she'd been acting. Like the poor woman was on something.

'Is it Melissa . . . or is it Susan? Is she okay?' Jayne asked, dreading the answer.

'Mrs Hayes is meeting with our headmistress just now,' said the secretary in a clipped, enunciated voice. 'You're Melissa's nominated adult, we understand. I really am sorry to alarm you, but I'm afraid it's best if you come straight to the school so we can explain everything. As soon as you possibly can, please.'

Susan

ST MICHAEL'S WELLNESS CENTRE

'Now, Susan, you do know why you're here, don't you?'
Susan nodded, knowing it was less hassle all around to just play along and have done with it.

'So is there anything you'd like to talk to me about?'

Oh yeah, because it's that easy, isn't it? Susan thought, moving her head slowly around to face the considerably younger woman perched on the edge of a leather armchair opposite, notebook and pen poised in her thin, bony hands.

You think all I need do is lie here on your comfy, expensive-looking therapist's couch, open up my heart to you and that the pain will just magically go away? You really think you're that qualified? You think anyone on this planet could possibly make sense of all this?

'Susan?' her therapist gently prompted, a reminder that they were up against a ticking clock. 'I'm here and I'm listening.'

Dr Kennedy was this one's official title, but her first words had been, 'Call me Ciara.' She was one of those.

Silence from Susan as she lay back against the plush, cushioned sofa, resolutely saying nothing, just playing for time.

'Tell you what,' said call-me-Ciara, 'to get the ball rolling, why don't I fill you in on what your treatment here will involve?'

'Whatever,' Susan muttered.

'You'll be with us here at St Michael's for a minimum of four weeks, depending on your progress. Treatment here involves good food, lots of exercise, group therapy and, it goes without saying, no stimulants whatsoever. Our goal is to reduce your dependency on sedatives over time, but we do offer patients a low dosage of sleeping pills, at least till your body starts to readjust.'

'Pills,' Susan echoed dully. That word at least caught her attention. 'Well, that's something, I suppose.'

'I also encourage patients to write a journal,' Dr Ciara went on, 'as you'll find it can be a useful barometer to track your progress over time.'

'If you say so.'

'So how about we start with what happened yesterday at your daughter's school?' Dr Ciara said, clicking the pen in her hand. 'Would you like to tell me about it, in your own words?'

Just at the thought, Susan shuddered. No, she would most definitely not care to open up her heart to this total stranger, who looked late-twenties tops and far too ridiculously glamorous to ever be taken seriously as a head shrink. The woman was wearing leopard-print kitten heels, for feck's sake.

Besides, there was nothing to tell, really. All she'd done was react in the moment – that was all there was to it. Surely anyone who knew where she was coming from would understand? Even Andrea Johnson, the headmistress, had been at pains to stress to her yesterday, 'how much we all feel for what you're going through'.

'Susan?" call-me-Ciara persisted. 'I'm here and I'm listening. Remember that this is a non-judgmental environment. A safe place for you to talk.'

More uncooperative silence as the minutes ticked down. *Fuck it, I better come out with something*, Susan thought. *If not, I'll look like I'm not cooperating and then I'll end up in even more trouble.*

'Well . . . ' she said tentatively, taking great care to pick her words.

'Yes?' Dr Ciara said, pen twitching in her hand.

'I was waiting to collect Melissa from school – just sitting in the car, minding my own business, really.'

'Melissa. That's your younger daughter, right?'

Younger daughter, Susan thought, slumping her head wearily back against the soft cushions behind her. Like there was any need to distinguish between the two of them any more. Melissa was now her only child and that was the end of it.

'Melissa is my little girl, yes.'

'And I'm guessing that's when you spotted Josh Andrews?'

'That's right.' Susan nodded, as calmly as she could. 'He was out on the school pitch, training for a match. He plays for the school Senior Cup team.'

Looking every bit as smug and self-satisfied as ever, she'd wanted to add, but somehow managed to keep her mouth zipped. The mental image of that monster was still there, though – with his toothy grin, Kennedy-thick hair and even thicker neck, doing lunges and squats at the side of the pitch with-out a care in the world. Blithely messing about and *laughing*, actually having the barefaced cheek to laugh with his mates as the team warmed up.

It was all his larky high-spirits that had sent Susan over the edge. That someone like Josh Andrews could actually blank out the agonising pain that he'd caused all around him, then act like nothing had happened.

But that fucker had ruined four lives. Hers, Frank's, Melissa's and, of course, Ella's. Four human souls who'd never be the same again, all thanks to that hulking bully-boy, high-fiving his mates on the pitch as they all lined up to do squat thrusts. Looking at Josh Andrews yesterday, it was as if he'd drawn a neat line under Ella Hayes and her family, and was now moving on with his own life like nothing had happened. Like he had absolutely nothing to reproach himself for.

But something did happen, didn't it, Josh? You can act like you're blameless all you like, but you and I both know the truth, don't we?

Susan's breathing started to become short and shallow, and she began to claw at the woolly jumper she was wearing, suddenly boiling hot in that stifling little therapy room. Josh had got exactly what was coming to him yesterday, she thought, quietly getting more and more furious. And if there were even a gram of justice in this world, he'd have gotten far worse. He could act as blameless and innocent as he liked, but certainly not when she was around. She'd never forget what happened, and if it took her the rest of her life, she'd make bloody sure that Josh Andrews never forgot either.

'I reacted exactly the way any other parent would,' Susan blurted out. Dr Ciara was listening intently to every word. 'No one with a gram of compassion could possibly blame me for what I said or did.'

And no court in the land would convict me if they knew my side of the story.

Josh Andrews rightly belonged behind bars, so he couldn't put any other family through what he'd put Susan and her family through. So if this frankly useless therapist were to ask her how she felt, the answer, in a nutshell, was vindicated. She felt no regret, just a bitter satisfaction that she'd done what she did. God knows, it was little enough, late enough, but at least it was something.

She'd physically hurt Josh, she'd caused him pain, and it frightened her just how good that had felt. She'd been on fire when she assaulted him, a slender little woman like her taking on a strapping six-footer, but somehow that didn't matter. All that mattered was that she'd clawed back some sort of revenge for what he'd done, and Jesus Christ, she thought, that had made her feel euphoric.

'You know I'm here to help you work through this,' Dr Ciara said after a long and thoughtful pause. 'So how about you tell me exactly what happened?'

Susan twitched around uncomfortably on the sofa as snippets of conversation from the previous day came back to her. 'Verbal abuse,' was what the Garda from community relations had kept saying to her. He'd been a nice enough guy, although he looked about fourteen as far as Susan was concerned, with the pimples to go with it.

'You slandered and then physically assaulted Josh Andrews in a public place, Mrs Hayes. His parents feel they've been incredibly understanding, what with everything you've been going through, however I do have to caution you that there's a limit to their patience. As of now, I can tell you that the Andrews family have a right to sue you for assault causing harm under the 1997 Non-Fatal Offences Against the Person Act.'

'There's a whole other side to this story, you know,' Susan had snapped back at him in the windowless, airless Garda interview room that she'd been made to sit in for hours. 'You are aware that my daughter is cold in her grave?' she kept repeating. 'And that Josh Andrews might as well have put her in there with his own two hands?'

'Please understand, Mrs Hayes, that Josh Andrews has not been convicted of any wrongdoing. His family are naturally very upset by what's happened. They're considering their legal options just now and if they do proceed, court charges could follow. If found guilty, the penalty for assault is up to twelve months in prison.'

At that, Susan laughed bitterly. The very thought that Josh Andrews and his family could end up taking *her* to court beggared belief. For fuck's sake, what kind of an upside-down world was she living in?

'Good,' she replied, folding her arms. 'Let them.'

'And I'm afraid there's more, isn't there, Mrs Hayes?' the teenage guard had said, referring to a thickly stuffed folder on the desk beside him. 'I have reports on my desk claiming that you've been standing outside the Andrews' house for hours at a time on more than one occasion. Several times a week, in fact. For months now, it seems.'

'And so what if I did?' Susan had slurred back at him defensively, the Xanax she'd taken earlier still clouding up her system. 'There's no law against that, is there?'

'You do realise that too could be construed as threatening behaviour?'

'Oh, so now it's against the law to stand on a public pavement, is it? The prisons must be stuffed full to capacity, if that's the case.'

'No,' came the measured reply. 'But the Andrews family maintain that your behaviour has been intimidating and hostile ever since the inquest, almost a year ago. And now you've assaulted their son, which only makes matters worse.'

'Excuse me,' Susan interrupted, 'are you seriously saying that someone like Josh Andrews is accusing *me* of being hostile? After what he's put my family through? Can I remind you that waster gets to sleep peacefully at night with his whole life ahead of him? His Leaving Cert, his college years, a career, a family and then the rest of his life beyond that, the works. My daughter *doesn't*. Ella is gone and she's never coming back. Don't you understand?'

'Of course we understand, Mrs Hayes, and here at Community Relations we're only trying to help you to help yourself. The problem is that incidents such as yesterday aren't helping anyone, are they? We have a full account here from several eyewitnesses claiming you had to be dragged away from Josh, quite literally kicking and screaming. You've almost broken his nose, you clawed at his face and, by all accounts, you even drew blood. The Andrews family feel they've tolerated your behavior up until now, but enough is enough.'

'I only behaved the way any other parent would if they came face to face with the person responsible for their child's death,' Susan had told him straight up. 'Josh Andrews is responsible for what happened to my Ella,' she'd insisted. 'Jesus, have you even been listening to a single word I've been saying?'

'But, Mrs Hayes,' came the measured response, 'I know this is hard for you to hear, but your daughter's case was investigated thoroughly at the time. Police found that although Josh Andrews might not have behaved particularly well, that no possible charges could be brought. There is no evidence to link him to what happened to Ella.'

Oh yes, there bloody well is, Susan had thought furiously. There was plenty of evidence all right, just nothing strong enough to hold up in a court of law. But Josh Andrews still had to live with himself and with his own conscience, didn't he? And she, for one, would make sure that he never, ever was allowed to forget the consequences of what he'd done. Never could, never would.

The rest of that horrible, nightmarish evening was all a bit of a blur to Susan. There were some memories that comforted her and some that stung. And last night was one she never wanted to think about again. Stuck in that grey, depressing little back room at Pearce Street Station, not far from Primrose Square, as phone calls were made, so many bloody phone calls.

Community care workers were consulted, the police were in and out asking her questions non-stop, they even contacted Frank. *He must really be worried about me,* Susan had thought flatly, because he'd sent for a solicitor pal of his, Jack Evans, who came to the station the minute he got the call.

'Here's the bad news, Susan,' Jack insisted in his sing-song Cork accent. 'I think they're deadly serious about prosecution. And my advice to you now is to voluntarily present to a rehab clinic, for immediate treatment. If the worst comes to the worst and the Andrews family take us to court, at least it shows contrition on your part and a willingness to get well again. We've made a few calls, and there's a bed available at St Michael's, but you'd need to go immediately . . . Susan?' He looked worried. 'Are you even taking this in?'

She wasn't, as it happened. This was way too hard for her to deal with, it was too painful and she was bloody grateful that the fistful of sedatives she'd taken earlier still hadn't worn off properly. Jack had droned on and on as she stared out of the window at a neat line of squad cars parked just outside. A sulky-looking teenage lad in double denim was sitting on the bonnet of one of them, sucking on a cigarette and looking like he didn't give a shite if he got arrested.

Good on you, she remembered thinking. *As Ella used to say, 'Up the rebels.' And you know something else? I don't give a shite if they arrest me either.*

'Susan?' Jack persisted. 'Are you listening to me?'

But Susan might as well not have been there. She felt numb. Groggy. On the periphery of pain, with a dull expectation that it was yet to hit her.

She continued to feel that way until the moment they eventually took her home to Primrose Square to pick up her things, before driving her to St Michael's. The moment when she had to say goodbye to Melissa.

The child's pale, worried little face, the wobbly lower lip where she was trying desperately not to cry at the sight of her mother being bundled off to a rehab centre in the back of a police car . . . banging her fists on the windows of the car, screaming Melissa's name, desperate to hug her baby goodbye, only it was too late. The driver didn't see how distressed she was, and just zoomed off, taking her down the square and away.

Oh God, Susan thought. Pain as sharp as a punch to the stomach hit her hard. *Think of something else,* she told herself. Now. Quick. Something happy. A memory she could cope with.

A discreet cough pulled her attention back to Dr Ciara's therapy room, as her therapist crossed and uncrossed her legs, showing off those annoying leopard-print kitten heels.

'You're very quiet, Susan,' she eventually said. 'So how about this? Would you like to talk about Ella?'

Ella.

Susan slumped back against the sofa as her thoughts cast about for a good memory – a soothing, comforting one this time.

'Mummy? I have something to tell you and it's very important. I don't want hamburgers for dinner, not now and not ever!'
'But, Ella, love, hamburgers are your favourite.'

'No! I read that meat is murder and I don't want to be a murderer. I can't go to prison. I've got a hockey match on Saturday.'

'Now, sweetheart, don't be silly. You know perfectly well nobody goes to jail just for eating meat. You had chicken wings the other day and you ate every one of those, didn't you?'

'That was different,' Ella said firmly.

'How was it different?'

'Because that was before we went on the school trip. Remember I told you about the two Angus cows at the working farm? Well, one was called Mitch and the other was called Cam, like in Modern Family, and they're brothers as well as best friends. But the farmer told us they were farmed for beef, and that they tasted the best in the whole world because they're grass-fed. But I don't want to eat Mitch or Cam and you can't make me. It's mean. And yeukky.'

'It's just a phase she's going through,' Frank had said wisely, as I hastily threw on a pot of pasta and made up some pesto sauce, in the hope we could get Ella to eat something. 'Wait till you see. I guarantee you that if we take her to McDonald's at the weekend for a treat, all this will be forgotten.'

'I heard what you just said, Dad!' said Ella stubbornly from under that big mop of strawberry blonde hair. 'And you're wrong, you know. I'll never eat meat again, as long as I live.'

You were at the time, my darling Ella, all of eight years old. By the age of ten, your role model in life was Malala Yousafzai. By thirteen, when other girls in your class were pestering their parents for One Direction tickets, all you wanted was to go to a talk about feminism in the National Concert Hall. By fifteen, you'd read everything Caitlin Moran had ever written and you even got a white streak put in your hair, to match hers.

You were fearless, my darling. A trailblazer. More strong-minded than your dad and I put together. Rules meant nothing to you, and even when you were in trouble in school – which was every other day – part of me could only admire your strength and feistiness. You were the kind of girl who could have gone anywhere in life and achieved anything. '

She'll either end up in prison or else running the country,' your class tutor used to say.

But still. You made your dad and me so proud.

'Anything you'd care to share with me?' said Dr Ciara, interrupting Susan's thoughts. 'We still have some time.'

'No,' Susan said, turning her head away as the darkness descended again. 'Just get me some sleeping pills and leave me in peace. '

Melissa

'Do you see her?' Abby Graham said, at the very top of her voice. 'That Melissa, with the tatty hair that looks like it hasn't been combed in about a month now?'

'And she stinks,' replied one of the little coven who trailed everywhere after her. 'Don't sit beside Melissa or you might end up with nits.'

'Well, I heard her mum's a mental case. It's, like, totally official now.'

'That's not news; the dogs on the street already know that.'

'Yeah, but you hear the mother caused, like, the hugest fight out on the rugby pitch yesterday?' Abby bossily replied. 'She had a total melter and apparently it took the senior PE teacher and three of the players to haul her off Josh Andrews. At least, that's what I heard. My older brother's on the team and he says the Andrews' family are going to sue the arse off her. Dead right too. I mean, would you blame them? If someone had a go at me in public, I'd sue too.'

'I heard she called Josh a murderer. Is that, like, actually true?'

'Totally!' Abby said, delighted with herself now that she was the centre of attention. 'My dad's a lawyer and he says Josh Andrews has grounds to prosecute for assault. You can go to prison for that, you know. That's what Dad says.'

'If that happens, then I bet social services will come and take Melissa away.'

'And I bet she'll end up going mental too, just like her mum.'

Melissa bit down hard on her bottom lip and tried to act like she hadn't overheard a single word. She'd dreaded coming into school today. And it was every bit as horrible as she'd thought it would be.

'Don't mind them,' Hayley said kindly, as the two girls shuffled down a busy corridor on their way to First Year Science. The bell had just rung and the corridor was jammed with their classmates, nabbing books from lockers and scurrying off in all directions to the next class. 'Abby Graham is just a mean girl, everyone knows that,' Hayley went on. 'She and her bitch crew will be gossiping about something else by tomorrow and it'll all blow over. You know what that gang are like. They haven't a clue.'

'I'm okay, honestly,' Melissa said, forcing a weak little smile and hoping no one could tell she wasn't okay at all. She couldn't say any more, though, for fear her voice might start getting wobbly, the way it always did whenever she was about to cry. She was in school, in public, and that meant she had to act all cool and pretend she wasn't bothered. So she and Hayley inched their way through the throng side by side, making their way to the science labs, managing to find two seats together.

But Melissa knew all the talk about her was still going on behind her back, and she honestly didn't know which was worse: her having turned up for school in the first place, or else doing as Sally Jenkins, the school counsellor, had advised her, which was to think about taking some time off, 'because you've been through so much lately'.

'You're a wonderful student, Melissa,' Sally had kept saying, as Melissa sat on the sofa beside her the previous day. Sally's office was more like a playroom, really, with bright yellow cushy sofas and posters of Justin Bieber on the walls. Sally was so kind, though, all the pupils adored her, and she'd been lovely to Melissa after what happened. She'd plonked herself down on the sofa beside Melissa, given her some fizzy water and told her that she needn't bother doing her homework that night if she didn't feel like it.

'Thanks, Sally,' Melissa had said, unsure as to where this 'little chat' was going. She knew her mum had caused big, big trouble and now things were starting to get a bit scary.

'The thing is, Melissa,' Sally said warmly, 'I know you're staying with your guardian just now . . . Jayne Dawson, isn't it?'

Melissa just nodded, not really able to say much more.

'Okay, let me call Jayne and arrange for the three of us to have a little talk sometime soon, just so we can decide how best to help you here at school. We're so anxious to support you through this as best we can. Maybe we can talk about a nice safe place where you'd be happy to spend break times and lunchtime? Or we may even look at you taking the rest of the term off, then maybe repeating first year again in September? If you like, that is?'

'No!' Melissa had pleaded with her. 'Please, Sally, I really don't want to stay back a year. I'll work harder, I'll do better, I'll do anything, if I can only stay where I am.'

Melissa couldn't put into words what she was really feeling, though, which was that, more than anything else, she *needed* school. She needed routine, discipline, a reason to get out of bed every day, a purpose. Schoolwork kept her focused and stopped her remembering all sorts of things that she didn't want to remember. This was her lifeline and she couldn't possibly lose it – hadn't she lost enough already?

'Well, if that's really what you want,' Sally said doubtfully, peering across the squishy sofa at her and pulling one of three baggy cardigans she was wearing even tighter around her.

She'd been super-kind to Melissa, though. In fact, aside from Abby and her bitch crew, as Hayley referred to them, pretty much everyone was gentle and understanding. After school, when they were all gathered at the school gates, Hayley had even begged her mum to let Melissa come and stay for a sleepover.

'That sounds really lovely and maybe something the girls could do together at the weekend?' a familiar voice replied from right behind Melissa.

She turned around to see Jayne standing right behind her, smiling warmly, exactly like she had done yesterday. Immediately, Melissa felt like a heavy weight had been lifted off her chest as she gave her pretend-y granny a shy little smile.

Jayne had been such a guardian angel to her yesterday. It could have been one of the worst days of Melissa's short little life but, somehow, Jayne had minded her through the whole thing. She was the one who'd come to collect her from school, patiently talking to both Susan and the headmistress, Miss Johnson, then insisting on bringing Melissa back to her own house on Primrose Square, where she made her feel wanted and welcome. Then, when the police had taken Susan home to pack her bags before they took her away again, Jayne had been the one who protected her and minded her, a bit like a human shield.

'Now you can come outside and say goodbye to your mum if you like, pet,' she'd said, 'but you don't have to if you don't want to. It might be upsetting seeing your mum in the back of a police car, so if you prefer, you just stay here with me where you're nice and safe, love.'

But Melissa had run outside to try to hug her mum goodbye, only to find she was too late. Her mum was already in the back of the squad car and on her way off, so the only person Melissa saw was mean old Mr Murphy from number seventy-seven, who was always out pretending to walk his dogs, but really sticking his nose into everyone else's business.

'Nothing to see here, Mr Murphy,' Jayne had shouted across the road to him, crossly for her, before steering a sobbing Melissa back inside and slamming the hall door firmly shut behind them. For the whole rest of the evening, Jayne had been absolutely brilliant, never talking down to Melissa like some of the social workers who'd called to the house after Ella died, yet not making a huge big fuss of her either, the way everyone else did. The two of them just had a normal evening, with a delicious, home-cooked, normal dinner, chatting about normal things, like *Love Island* and whatever else happened to be on telly that night.

Last night could have been a horrible nightmare, like so many nights Melissa had had recently, but Jayne turned it into another regular, ordinary school night, and Melissa couldn't have been more grateful to her. Not only that, but when Melissa went to get dressed for school that morning, she saw that Jayne had washed and pressed her uniform, so it smelt fresh and lovely for the first time in weeks. And at break time, when she opened up her schoolbag, there was a neatly wrapped avocado sandwich, with a delicious cheese and tomato salad in a Tupperware container, with healthy nuts and a fruit juice to drink.

Melissa had to bite back the tears when she saw what Jayne had done for her, only this time, they were happy tears. It was the first time in months and months that she actually felt cared for. For an old, old lady, Melissa decided, Jayne was pretty cool.

'I won't even bother asking you how your day was,' Jayne said, as she and Melissa strapped themselves into her battered little Honda Civic. 'I just think you're very brave for going to school in the first place. Today was the worst; wait till you see now, tomorrow will be so much easier.'

But Melissa couldn't bring herself to answer. She was suddenly tired to her bones, wiped out with the huge effort of putting on a brave face all day. Just then her phone pinged and she looked down to see a big pile of texts and missed calls from her dad, which probably came through when her phone was switched off in school. Jayne glanced over at her from the driver's seat, correctly guessing what she was reading – and from who.

'Your dad?' she asked gently.

Melissa nodded silently.

'He's been calling me too, pet. All day, in fact. He's been so worried about you. He's stuck on deployment, he said, but he's trying to get home as fast as he can. Don't worry, though, I told him that you were more than welcome to stay with me, till your mum is well enough to come home again. Sure it's a pleasure having you; I'd love you to stay for as long as you like. Mind you, I think your dad wanted you to stay with your Auntie Betty for the next night or two till he can get back, but I put my foot down and told him you were miles better off with me. Primrose Square is nice and handy for school and you're still close enough to visit your mum.'

'Are you sure it's okay with you?' Melissa asked, in a small voice. 'I don't want to be a bother.'

'As if you could ever be a bother!' Jayne laughed. 'Besides,' she added kindly, 'you're the one doing me the favour, really; sure you keep me young.'

Melissa managed a watery smile, but deep down she felt utterly torn in two. Half of her desperately wanted to see her dad again. She missed him so much it felt like a stone in her chest whenever she thought about him so far away from home. But at the same time, they were an army family and she'd been brought up knowing that active service meant making sacrifices. Besides, her mum was only going to be in hospital for a little while, that was all.

There was a long silence while Melissa stared out the window, totally wrapped up in her thoughts. That was another great thing about Jayne: she never tried to make you talk whenever you were feeling a bit low, like a lot of other adults did.

Just then, Jayne's mobile started to ring, shattering the silence. You couldn't mistake it: her ringtone was the theme tune to *Coronation Street*.

'Oh, that phone hasn't stopped all day,' said Jayne, as her car rolled to a halt at a red light. 'Answer it for me, would you, love? Last thing I need is more penalty points on my license. Not after I was done for speeding when I was late for bingo last week.'

'Hello, Jayne's phone?' Melissa said, as soon as she managed to fish the mobile from the bottom of an overstuffed shopping bag in the back seat of the car, lying under a box of Brillo pads and a family-size pack of mini Mars bars.

'Hi there,' came a bossy-sounding woman's voice, as Melissa clicked her onto speakerphone. 'I'm calling from Salon Rouge to confirm your appointment for this afternoon. You're booked in for a haircut and colour at four p.m., with a spray tan and leg wax afterwards. Then our nail technician can take you for a mani/pedi, if you like?'

Melissa could have sworn she saw Jayne flush a little bit.

'Oh pet,' she said, 'would you please apologise to that nice lady for me, say that I won't be able to make the appointment after all? Tell her not to worry, though, I'll be sure to book in for another day.'

Melissa went back to the phone, all the while thinking: *Jayne?* Having a wax, a spray tan and a pedicure? It just didn't seem right, somehow; Jayne always went around in brown elastic-y-looking trousers, sensible brown leather shoes and brown woolly polo necks, even at the height of summer. Brown was her colour – like a bird who just wants to blend into the background. And no way on Earth was she the waxing type.

Although come to think of it, Jayne had been dressing a bit differently lately, only Melissa had been too caught up in her own family dramas to pay much attention. She'd started wearing colours a lot more, like the bright pink jacket she was wearing now, and she'd definitely started wearing make-up too.

Something was up. Melissa didn't know what, but she wasn't imagining it. Then, when they got back to Jayne's house on the square, she was even more puzzled to see bags and bags of shopping on the kitchen table, all waiting to be unpacked. A full-sized ham, two frozen chickens, mountains of fresh vegetables and, most surprising of all, two bottles of champagne.

Jayne? Drinking champagne? She always seemed like a mug-of-Horlicks type, not a secret champagne drinker at all. As well as that, there were fresh-cut flowers in vases dotted all around the living room and even scented candles on the fireplace, beside where her dead husband's ashes were.

Please don't let all this be for me, Melissa thought. *I'd be mortified if Jayne spent so much money, just on me.*

'I thought I might do a bit of baking later on,' Jayne said, as Melissa automatically started to unpack the groceries. 'Maybe you'd like to help me, pet? I could show you how to make a proper chocolate biscuit cake – I know that's your favourite.'

'Sounds cool,' Melissa said. 'Are you having people over for dinner? It's just you've bought so much food. It's almost like Christmas Day in here.'

'Well, as a matter of fact, love,' said Jayne, stuffing the freezer full with all the meat she'd bought, 'I've been meaning to tell you. I am having someone else come to visit for a little while. A friend. Well, a sort of friend. He's a sweetheart, though, and I think you'll really like him.'

'Where is your pal from?' Melissa asked, instantly picturing an elderly gent tottering around on a Zimmer frame, maybe a pal of Jayne's late husband.

'Eric is coming to see me all the way from Florida, can you believe it?' Jayne said, reddening a little bit. 'So, as you can imagine, I'm a bit nervous meeting him for the first time IRL. That's why it's so great that you're here, love. You'll give me moral support, I know you will.'

'What does IRL mean?' Melissa asked, getting more and more confused the longer this conversation went on.

'Oh, you know, love, in real life. That's what they all say on the website where Eric and I first met.'

'So do you mean . . . this Eric guy is like . . . a date? Except that you just haven't met him yet?' said Melissa, having to abandon unpacking groceries and take a seat at the kitchen table. Her head was swimming.

'Yes, pet. I've put you in the good spare bedroom and Eric can have the little box room at the back of the house. He's a spiritual healer, you know, and he works in a commune in Palm Springs, so sleeping on a little small bed should be no bother to him at all.'

'Jayne,' said Melissa slowly, 'are you telling me this guy is, like, someone you might end up dating? Like . . . a boyfriend?'

'Yes,' Jayne said, with a girlish little giggle. 'Yes, I suppose you could put it like that, pet.'

Melissa instantly started to worry. Was a total stranger about to move in on lovely, sweet, trusting Jayne? And in that case, wasn't it a kind of blessing that she herself would be there, to keep an eye out for her pretend-y-granny?

From the outside, she thought, *it might look like Jayne is the grown-up taking care of me but maybe, just maybe, it's the other way around.*

The following morning, just as she was getting dressed for school, there was a ring at the doorbell.

'I'll get it!' Melissa called out to Jayne, who was in the kitchen, still in her dressing gown, making what smelt like a big, delicious, greasy fry-up. It was probably Bill the postman, Melissa thought, rummaging for the right key and unbolting the door. He always called early and was so full of moans and gripes about the osteoarthritis in his knee, he often made her late for school.

Nothing, though, absolutely nothing prepared her for the sight that greeted her when she flung open the hall door.

Because it wasn't poor old Bill standing there at all. Instead, there was an elderly man about Jayne's age, with long, grey hair tied back in a scrunchie, dressed in a flowing white linen shirt and jeans with Jesus sandals, even though it was a cold, grey, rainy morning.

'Namaste,' he said, with a big smile on his tanned, friendly face as he gave a little half bow. 'I'm Eric. And I've come to meet a beautiful soul by the name of Jayne Dawson.'

Melissa

19 PRIMROSE SQUARE

Melissa sat in the late afternoon sunshine on the steps outside Jayne's house, with her hands clamped over her ears. She needed some time out – badly. It had been such a lovely day with Jayne and Eric too, cooking and baking and chatting as the three of them worked side by side. It had been so nice to get to know Eric, who seemed wise and kind and pretty cool, apart from the weird clothes and the long hair – in fact, he kind of reminded Melissa of Jayne's husband before he got sick.

Then something very, very bad happened. She left the grown-ups alone so they could chat in peace and slipped up to her room to try and call her mum at that hospital place they'd taken her to. But a nice-sounding lady told her that her mum wasn't allowed to speak to anyone for at least a week.

Please, you don't understand, Melissa had tried to say, only the words wouldn't come out properly. *She's my mum and I need her. I only want to know if she's getting better.* It was horrible not knowing. Couldn't they even let her talk to her mum for five little minutes? That's all she was asking for. But the lady she'd spoken to had been firm: no phone contact and no visitors for a minimum of seven days. Those were the rules, she said. No exceptions.

Melissa hugged her knees tightly, grateful that there was no one around to see her getting upset. She already had so much to worry about and now here was another thing. Then something weird happened: Ella's voice came back to her. 'Whenever I'm stressed about anything,' Ella used to say, 'I just get the hell out of the house and try to focus on how lovely Primrose Square is. Works a treat, any time of year. Trust me, kiddo, just looking out at the square will make any problem disappear. It's like that square has healing properties.'

So that's what Melissa was trying to do. It was well past 7 p.m., but it was almost spring now and still bright and sunny enough to sit out and enjoy the beautiful view over the treetops and the gorgeous flowers that were just beginning to come into their own. Begonias and azaleas – Ella had even taught her a few of their proper names. They had outdoor yoga on the square sometimes and there was a class in full swing now; she could see about twelve people of all shapes and sizes huffing and puffing, doing sideways planks right beside the playground.

A youngish woman came around the corner onto the square, breathless and panting as she lugged two stuffed suitcases behind her, with an overlarge backpack strapped to her back. She must be a tourist, Melissa thought. Maybe looking for a B&B, or a hostel for the night? Without a second thought, she'd scrambled up to her feet, with a shy little wave towards this stranger.

'You look like you could do with a bit of help,' Melissa said, instinctively going to take one of her wheelie bags. 'Are you looking for somewhere? A hotel, maybe?'

'Well, aren't you just a little sweetheart?' The stranger grinned back. 'The weight of those cases was killing me. I'm actually on my way to number twenty-four, which, as far as I remember, is just a little bit further down the square, is that right?'

'Number twenty-four?' said Melissa, puzzled. 'I didn't think anyone lived there. It's been empty for ages now. But come on, I'll show you where it is.'

'I'm going to be renting it for a while,' came the smiling reply. 'And if you're from around here too, then that'll make us neighbours. I'm Nancy, by the way.'

'Your accent is so posh! Are you English?'

'Londoner, born and bred. You ever been to London?'

'No,' said Melissa shyly, 'but I've always wanted to go. I keep on at my dad to take me over so we can see a few shows there. My friend Hayley went to London with her family and they saw *Matilda* in the West End, can you imagine? She said it was, like, the BEST night of her whole life.'

'Makes me very happy to hear that,' Nancy said with a little smile. 'I was the second assistant director on *Matilda*, as it happens.'

'Oh my actual God!' Melissa squealed. 'You're a director? In the theatre? Like . . . a real one?'

This woman certainly didn't look like a theatre director, but then Melissa had always thought that to be a director, you had to be flamboyant, larger than life – and more often than not, a man. This woman seemed way too young for a job like that. She seemed . . . *normal*. She was dressed in jeans, flat shoes and a jacket, with her neat light brown hair scooped up into a knot on top of her head. She looked arty and cool, like a photographer, maybe, but definitely not a real, live theatre director.

'Certainly am,' Nancy said. 'And thanks for the great feedback about *Matilda*, by the way.'

'Oh my God!' Melissa beamed, 'Hayley said it was just *fab*. She even said that Miss Trunchbull picked up one of the kids in the show, spun her around and around by the pigtails and flung her right out into the audience. Did that really happen?' she asked, goggle-eyed.

'You'll just have to come and see the show for yourself.' Nancy grinned down at her brand new fan. 'I'd be happy to sort you out with tickets anytime you like.'

'Wow, really?' said Melissa, grinning. 'That would be, like, the *best* thing ever! Wait till I tell my dad, he'll love that.'

'You never told me your name, by the way?' Nancy said, as the two of them made their way to number twenty-four, with the neat box hedges outside and the sparkling clean stone steps leading up to it.

'Oh, I'm Melissa – and here we are, number twenty-four. Come on,' she added, 'I'll help you with your bags up the front steps.'

'You're an angel,' Nancy said, as they both struggled to haul the wheelie bags up the steps.

'Wow . . . I've never been into this house before,' Melissa said, hovering cautiously on the doorstep. 'Imagine – I've lived on the square my whole life and this is the first time I've ever seen it from the inside. Pretty cool, isn't it?'

'In that case, come on in,' said Nancy. 'I'll give you the grand tour – you can be my first ever visitor.'

'Oh my God, that's, like, the biggest TV I've ever seen!' Melissa squealed as Nancy showed her into the living room and she set eyes on the giant plasma screen just above the fireplace. 'And look at the leather sofas – so posh!'

'I know,' Nancy said, shaking her head almost in disbelief. 'I can't really believe I'm going to be staying here. I keep thinking that the owner will soon discover it's all a horrible mistake and throw me out on my ear.'

'So who owns it?' Melissa asked, wide-eyed, as they walked in and out of every room, oohing and ahhing all the way. 'Whoever it is must be, like, the richest man in the country. Look at this!'

she added, as Nancy led her upstairs to see the master bedroom in all its glory. 'A walk-in closet! I thought only the Kardashians had them!'

'Isn't it incredible?' Nancy laughed. 'All owned by a guy called Sam Williams, I believe. Ever met him?'

Melissa wrinkled her nose, thinking for a second, then shook her head. 'No, sorry,' she said. 'I've never even heard of him.'

'That's the weird thing,' Nancy said, plonking exhaustedly down on the bed beside her new little pal. 'No one else seems to have either. Even the estate agent who showed me the house didn't know him. They'd only been in touch via phone calls and emails.'

'It's just been a building site here for ages,' Melissa said. 'My sister used to fancy one of the workmen and she was always hanging around here, trying to chat him up.'

'How old is your sister?' Nancy asked, as she led Melissa back downstairs and into the basement, to show her the kitchen.

Melissa went very quiet for a second.

'Seventeen. She would have been seventeen going on eighteen now.'

'I'm sorry . . . ?'

'She's dead,' Melissa said baldly. It was the first time she'd said that out loud to someone she didn't know and it felt very weird.

There was a long pause while Nancy looked keenly at her, but she didn't put on a sad face, like other grown-ups did. Melissa was glad of it; it was a big relief to meet someone who didn't come at her with sympathy. It was hard enough feeling sad herself, without having to deal with everyone else being sad for her as well.

'I see.' Nancy nodded, then, to Melissa's great relief, she instantly changed the subject. 'In that case, do you fancy a cuppa?' she asked brightly. 'You're my first ever visitor and if you'll just help me find a box of tea bags, I'd love you to stay and chat for a bit.'

'I'd really like that, thanks.' Melissa smiled, deeply grateful they were talking about something else.

'So no one has seen or heard of my mystery landlord, then?' Nancy said, putting the kettle on and rummaging about the bottom of one of her bags for a box of Typhoo.

'Which is bonkers when you think about it, isn't it?' said Melissa, perching up on a trendy stool at the breakfast bar and feeling incredibly grown-up. 'I mean, around here, everyone knows everything about everybody else's business. I've known most of the neighbours here since I was in nappies.'

Almost on cue, a text message pinged through to Nancy's phone and she immediately went to check it.

'Speak of the devil,' she said. 'It's from the man himself.'

HOPE MOVING DAY GOING WELL, ENJOY AND TRY NOT TO TRASH THE PLACE TOO MUCH IF YOU HAVE A HOUSEWARMING PARTY.

'He sounds pretty cool,' Melissa offered.

'Hmm,' said Nancy quietly, putting the phone back in her pocket and allowing her thoughts to drift a bit.

'You okay?' said Melissa after a pause. 'You've gone all quiet.'

'Sorry,' said Nancy. 'I was just thinking how much you can glean about a total stranger, purely from being in their space.'

'Yeah, but that Sam Williams has never actually lived here, though. Otherwise we'd know his whole life story. My dad always says that's what he loves most about Primrose Square. He says if you as much as sneeze in the morning, that night half the square will be asking you how your terrible dose of pneumonia is.'

'I know Sam has never officially lived here,' said Nancy thoughtfully. 'Yet the whole house is full of his stuff. And it's decorated entirely to his taste. So you know what? That tells us a lot about him already. I don't want you to think that I'm nosey or anything, but this is where being a theatre director comes in very handy.'

'How do you mean?'

'I've worked on a lot of classical theatre,' Nancy explained, stuffing tea bags into two mugs. 'And I'm well used to working on scripts with scant character detail. Which is where the fun really starts for us in the rehearsal room. In fact, directing a play can be a lot like detective work, you see.'

'How is that?' Melissa asked, puzzled.

'Well, you'd be astonished at the number of playwrights who give you very little, if any, information about a character to work off. Take Shakespeare, for instance. He just gives you the bare bones of any character and the rest is one hundred per cent down to interpretation. So that's when a director and actor really start to collaborate, comb through the script and put two and two together.'

'Wow.' Melissa beamed. 'Your job really sounds amazing. You get to be in the theatre all day every day and you even get paid for it. Talk about a dream job!'

She was really loving this chat; it was like a one-on-one English class and that was by a mile Melissa's very favourite subject. To her surprise, she felt better than she had for ages.

'So come on then,' said Nancy, handing Melissa a mug. 'What does this amazing living space tell us about its mysterious owner? Let's try to figure it out, shall we?'

'It tells us that he has bucketloads of money, for one thing,' Melissa replied. 'I think he must be, like, a gazillionaire.'

'He's working out in Shanghai at the moment,' said Nancy, 'so my guess is that he's in high finance or something similar. A hedge fund manager, maybe.'

'Maybe he's designed an app that's gone on to make an absolute fortune?' Melissa said helpfully. 'Just about everyone in my class wants to design an app from their garden shed and sell it for, like, two billion by the time they're twenty-one.'

'He must be sporty too, I think,' said Nancy, getting up and walking over to a bookshelf in the kitchen, which was dotted with photos. 'Judging by this shot of him windsurfing, at least.'

'Can I see?' Melissa asked, following her and peering at the photo over her shoulder. You couldn't see Sam's face, though, which was annoying.

'He's in great shape, I'll say that much for him,' said Nancy, staring pensively at the photo. 'Although I did notice a golf trophy in the hall on the way in. But let's try not to hold that against him.'

'You can see his face more clearly in this one,' said Melissa, picking up a photo of a guy in cap and gown, posing in a graduation photo and awkwardly holding up a scroll, as you do. She was really enjoying this impromptu game of detectives – Nancy had a way of making even mundane things seem really interesting. 'And look at this,' she added, spotting a framed certificate of a college degree, which was just behind the graduation pic.

'*This is so to certify that Sam Williams graduated cum laude with a Bachelor of Commerce degree, in the year of Our Lord two thousand and nine,*' Nancy read out loud. 'Which would make him roughly in his thirties, give or take.'

'Isn't he handsome?' said Melissa, staring down at the gradu-ation photo.

Nancy took a good long look at the picture over her shoulder, as if she were assessing a Tinder profile. 'Yes, I suppose he is,' she said thoughtfully.

'Isn't it funny that there aren't any wedding photos about the place?' Melissa added innocently.

'And I'll tell you something else,' said Nancy. 'I don't think this guy has kids either.'

'What makes you say that?'

'Well, just take a look around you,' said Nancy, waving her hand across the sun-drenched kitchen, with its sleek chrome table, high metallic stools and hard-as-nails flagstone tiled floor. 'Just look at all these sharp edges and pointy stools. Not very child-friendly, now is it? And there isn't a single photo of kids around the place either. The spare room upstairs certainly doesn't look like a bedroom for a child, now does it?'

'Do you want to know what I think?' Melissa said.

'What's that?'

'I think you're getting a bit of a crush on this Sam Williams, whoever he is,' she teased.

'Oh now, don't be daft,' Nancy said, batting it away.

But she blushed bright red when she said it, though, Melissa noticed. Just like she always noticed everything.

Spring

Susan

ST MICHAEL'S WELLNESS CENTRE

The sun shone brightly for the first time in months, and crocuses were beginning to stick their heads up from the rolling lawns Susan could clearly see from her bedroom window. St Michael's was a huge Victorian house close to the Dublin Mountains, surrounded by acres of soothing, calming parkland. Susan had come to learn that the whole ethos of rehab there was that patients would ultimately feel 'safe, healed and well again'.

Safe, she'd thought bitterly, when she initially signed the official registration forms. Is that all they thought was wrong with her? That she felt a bit unsafe? That all she needed were a few pills and a comforting hand to hold before she could be released back into the wild again?

After a few days at St Michael's, though, her opinion started to shift a bit. Because there really did seem to be a sense of security about the place, which somehow seeped inside your bones. You were trusted, for one thing. You could even lock the bathroom door behind you if you wanted to.

'That's a pretty huge thing for a place like this, you know,' as Emily, a recovering alcoholic, had told her. Emily was about Susan's own age and had been battling 'the demon drink', as she called it, for so long, she was a veteran of institutions like this.

'Last place I was in, they didn't even let you go to the loo on your own,' she'd confided to Susan in the semi-private room they were sharing. 'Can you imagine? Tying to pee with a nurse looking at you? Having a shower while you're being supervised? Just in case anyone I knew had smuggled in vodka and I was trying to drink it in the bathroom. The last place I was in, they didn't even allow me to have toiletries, just in case I'd suck the deodorant out of a bottle.'

'Why would you want to do that?' Susan asked, mystified.

'For the booze hit, you eejit.'

'Okaaay,' Susan said warily, not too sure what to make of her new roommate.

'So what are you in for anyway? You seem fairly sane. Compared to some of them around here, anyway. Mind you, that's not saying too much. I got talking to a guy yesterday who's in here because he has a fear of cockroaches. Katsaridaphobia, they call it. Can you believe that's actually a thing?'

'Is he the guy who had a jam jar with a cockroach trapped inside at the dinner table last night?' Susan asked.

She'd seen him all right. You couldn't fail to notice this long, lanky, wiry guy, who was like an edgy ball of tension, utterly fixated on a jam jar with a cockroach crawling around inside. Utterly gross.

'Apparently there's method in his madness,' Emily went on. 'Roach Boy was telling me that this way, at least he always knows where the cockroach is. He's harmless, though, really. Most of them in here are, you'll find. We all just need a bit of time out from the outside world, that's all.'

Susan had bonded with a few of the other patients too, most of whom were surprisingly open about their reasons for being in St Michael's in the first place. On her very first day there, Doctor Ciara had suggested she attend the group therapy session, which was held every day in a bright, warm sunny room, with tea, coffee and even plates of biscuits on the side. Susan went along purely because anything was better than being left alone in a two-bed room with nothing but her own memories and thoughts.

Some of the other patients' stories made her heart twist in her chest. There was a girl called Rose, who was just eighteen years of age and who was bravely battling bulimia.

She's exactly the same age that Ella would be now, Susan thought, as she listened to the poor girl, gaunt and grey-looking, talk about the 'urge to purge' she still felt after every single meal. Emily spoke in turn too, talking matter-of-factly about her lifelong battle with alcoholism.

'I'm fifty-two days sober now,' she told the circle, as the others, Susan included, gave her an encouraging little round of applause. 'But it's a huge struggle for me, every single hour of every day. Booze blanks out the dark days for me and I have to be honest – a cup of Nescafé and a Hobnob doesn't quite cut it in the same way. So I have to constantly remind myself that booze took everything from me. My husband, my home, my job, even any chance I might have had to have kids. Drink robbed me of the life that I should be living and I have to deal with that. It's not easy, but I think – I hope – that I'm getting there.'

Roach Boy was there too, jam jar firmly embedded in his lap with a fat-looking cockroach crawling around inside. Then there was a huge, burly guy, who everyone called Bungalow Bill, because he'd set fire to the bungalow he lived in, with his wife and mother-in-law inside. It was a miracle they survived – apparently he'd almost killed them. Bill spoke bravely about his depression and was candid and open about how just getting out of bed every day felt like climbing Kilimanjaro.

He gets it, Susan thought, as she listened quietly to his story. *This total stranger has just described how I feel every single hour of every single day.*

'And now let's give a warm welcome to Susan, our newest member,' said Dr Ciara, to a polite smattering of applause. 'Is there anything you'd like to share with us this evening, Susan? This is the circle of trust, and remember, no matter what you say, no one here will judge you.'

A long pause as every eye swivelled towards her.

They're all wondering why I'm here, Susan thought, suddenly feeling very alone and vulnerable and nervous. *This lot have probably all been here for weeks so they already know each other's stories inside out. They're so comfortable with each other that they can sit around in their dressing gowns and bare feet. And they're looking at me now, in my neat little Zara dress and sensible pumps, unable to fathom what someone like me is doing here.*

'I don't think you're a boozer,' Emily said, thinking aloud. 'You haven't got that red-faced, puffy, bloated look about you. Jammy bitch.'

'And she's like, what, a size twelve?' said Roach Boy, sitting in the corner. 'No eating disorder going on there either. No offence, love,' he added hastily.

'She seems too together for it to be depression,' said another voice.

'Nahh. She's all shaky and trembly. That's some class of an anxiety disorder, mark my words,' said Bungalow Bill sagely, folding one pudgy, tattooed arm over the other.

Anxiously, Susan looked to call-me-Ciara for support as the rest of the group openly speculated about her, but Ciara just gave her an encouraging nod back, as if to say, 'Come on, you can do it. Name it, claim it and tame it.'

Say it out straight, Susan thought, forcing herself to be strong. *If everyone else in this room can be open about what they're going through, then why can't I?*

'I'm Susan,' she eventually said in a wobbly voice, as the hum of chatter died down and it seemed every eye in the place was focused on her. 'And I'm here because I think I'm having a nervous breakdown.'

Silence, while they all digested this. Then a snort of derision as some wag sitting across from her said, 'Sure that's nothing. I have a nervous breakdown every morning before breakfast.'

'Just take a few Xanax and go on lie on a beach for two weeks,' said another dismissively. 'That'll sort you out.'

'There's people in here with far worse than that, love.'

'I almost burned my own wife and mother-in-law to death and the prison services sent me here instead of Mountjoy jail. Jaysus, I'd *kill* to have nothing worse wrong with me than a little nervous breakdown.'

'Yeah, what the hell are you doing in here anyway? Just about everyone I know has had a Nervy B.'

'Now come on, let Susan finish,' said Ciara sternly. 'Fair is fair, everyone gets their turn in our circle of trust.'

'But I didn't used to be like this, you know,' Susan said defensively, as attention swivelled back to her. 'I know you're all looking at me now, thinking that I don't have a right to be here. Not compared with what most of you are going through. After all, I'm just a normal, suburban wife and mum, and up until a year ago, I had it good. I had a lovely husband, who I loved very much, and two beautiful daughters, the light of our lives. I had a job I enjoyed and enough spare cash to be able to treat my two girls. Up till a year ago, my life was pretty good and – no offence or anything – but the thought of being in a place like this, opening up to a roomful of strangers, would have sent me screaming for the hills.'

'Thanks very much,' said Roach Boy dryly.

'Shhh!' Ciara said, cutting him short. 'Let the woman speak. Keep going, Susan, you're doing great.'

'But then, during the spring of last year,' Susan went on, surprising herself at how much easier it was to open up to people she barely knew than to some people she'd known for decades, 'my whole life as I knew it got flipped on its head.'

'What happened?' Emily prompted.

Susan really had to brace herself for this one. 'It was on a Friday,' she managed to get out, after several deep, soothing breaths. 'Just a normal, ordinary Friday afternoon. I was at the bank where I worked, and my daughters were in school – or so I thought. Frank – that's my husband – was at work too; he's in the army and he was on duty at the barracks in Rathmines, not far from where we live. Ella, my eldest, was in sixth year and was supposed to be studying for her Leaving Cert, but Ella was never much of a one for schoolwork. My youngest, Melissa, now she's a real A-student and works so hard I sometimes have to drag her away from her desk, but Ella just dances to the beat of her own drum. Sorry . . . ' she said, breaking off as a stab of pain that was so sudden and sharp almost winded her.

'I keep talking about her in the present tense,' she said quietly, looking directly at Ciara. 'Can't help it.'

'Keep going,' Ciara replied soothingly. 'You're doing great.'

'Anyway, I'd been bickering with Ella all week,' Susan went on. 'About how this was the biggest exam she'd ever have to face and that if she didn't want to end up working in Poundland, that she'd better knuckle down and start studying. But with Ella I might as well have been talking to the wall. She was such a wilful girl. She was bright and well able to get through her exams, if only she'd apply herself. She'd wanted to do politics and economics at college and what kills me is that she'd have been a born natural at both, if only she'd . . . well, if only she hadn't gone and . . . '

Susan had to break off there, as some kindly soul from the edge of the circle passed her down a cupful of water.

'My Ella was an activist, you see,' she went on, gratefully taking a sip of the water and picking up the threads of her story. 'And had been ever since she was a small child, really. She cared about things with such intensity. She was always going off to protest marches and was so passionate about the causes she stood for. Whereas other teenagers her age spend their Saturdays trawling about H&M and Topshop, Ella would be outside furriers' stores in town handing out flyers about how fur is murder.'

'She's not wrong there,' said Rose, the young girl who'd admitted to bulimia earlier. 'Fur is murder, isn't it?'

'Shh,' Bungalow Bill hissed. 'Let the woman finish, will you?'

'But even when I didn't agree with whatever stance Ella was taking on whatever issue,' Susan went on, slowly getting more comfortable the more she spoke 'she still made her dad and me so proud, every day. Mind you, dinnertime in our house could be like a battlefield at times. Ella would debate you to death about whatever was on the news that day. When Donald Trump got elected, the joke in our house was that we'd have to physically restrain her from protesting at the US embassy. She was smarting over Brexit for months and, as Frank used to say to me, "If she's like this now, can you imagine what she'll be like when she's old enough to vote?" Oh, she was the most wonderful, special girl,' Susan went on feelingly. 'I know every parent thinks their child is perfect in every way, but my Ella really was.'

'So what happened to her?' Emily asked warily.

'What happened,' Susan said, as the warm glow she got from talking about her perfect child started to ebb and instead the panic and darkness rose to constrict her throat, 'is that Ella . . . was taken from me . . . by someone who . . . he . . . his name was . . . is . . . and he . . . I can't. I'm sorry.'

Deal with facts, not emotions, she told herself, as her voice cracked and, in spite of herself, she began to shake uncontrollably. *It's easier. It's cleaner. And it's just about all I can handle right now.* She took a breath and tried again.

'On March twenty-ninth last year,' she forced herself to say, in a weak, trembling voice, 'my Ella, my angel, my perfect girl, my force of nature, died on a stretcher in the back of an ambulance with absolutely no one there to comfort her. No family, no friends, no one. She was just seventeen years of age and now . . . now I honestly think I'm going to lose my mind without her.'

Somehow, barely even knowing how, Susan managed to stand and stumble blindly from the room, to total silence from behind her.

Jayne

19 PRIMROSE SQUARE

Dear God above, Jayne thought. It wasn't if she'd asked for very much, was it? Her only hope was that Jason and Irene would sit at her dinner table having a friendly chat with Eric and sharing a nice, convivial evening – nothing more. The perfect way, she'd thought, for them to really get to know each other over a lovely, relaxed meal.

But everything was wrong.

Almost from the minute Jason and Irene barged through her front door, the tension was practically pinging off the four walls, all directed squarely at poor, patient Eric. Just about every comment that passed Irene's lips might as well have come with barbed wire wrapped around it. Nothing was right for her and all she did was snipe at everyone around her – even poor little Melissa, who was doing nothing more than sitting innocently in the crossfire.

And as for Jason? Honestly, there were times during that abysmal night when his behaviour bordered on downright rudeness and Jayne found herself staring at Tom's urn on top of the telly more than once, thinking, *Thank God you're not here to see this, love. You'd die all over again.*

From the minute Eric first greeted him, Jason eyed him up and down warily, drinking the other man in from head to foot. The way Eric towered over him, the long, silvery white hair, the flowing linen shirt, the fact that he was barefoot, and seemingly quite comfortable with it.

Jason pointedly didn't shake the hand Eric offered him, just snorted and said, 'Bare feet? In Ireland? In early March? Are you soft in the head or what? You're not in Florida now, you know.'

Jayne had wilted with embarrassment, but Eric just gave a benign little nod.

'It sure is great to meet you folks,' he said in that beautiful, deep, drawling accent, completely surfing over the jibe. 'I've heard a whole heap about you from your mom. I really hope we can all get along just fine.'

'We don't say "Mom" in this country,' Jason replied sniffily. 'It's "Ma", actually.'

'It sure seems I have a lot to learn,' Eric said, with a warm smile in Jayne's direction, as she served up a selection of antipasti for starters: bruschetta and mushrooms stuffed with pesto, and fresh-from-the-oven garlic bread on the side. Eric had prepared all this himself earlier on, and as much as Jayne prided herself on being a great cook, she had to admit they were absolutely gorgeous.

'Comfort food,' he'd said wisely, as he ground fresh garlic into unsalted butter for the bread, just before their visitors arrived. 'In case things get a little tense tonight, good, solid carbohydrates should keep your son and daughter-in-law grounded and nourished from within.'

'None for me, thanks,' Irene said, waving the dish away when Jayne tried to serve her. 'Mushrooms are very bad for my PH balance.'

Jayne said nothing, just served everyone else around the table and silently blessed Melissa for being there, even though the poor kid looked bored out of her head. Until Irene started picking on her, that is.

'So how is school coming along?' Irene asked her imperiously. 'Studying hard, I hope?'

'Melissa works so hard that I really want her to take a bit of time off,' Jayne answered for her, almost ready to burst with pride when she looked at her pretend-granddaughter. 'Honestly, you'd have to drag this young lady away from her books!'

'So how did we do in the Easter half-term exams?' Irene insisted.

Melissa glanced nervously around the table before answering. 'Emm . . . well, I did okay, I think,' she answered in a shy little voice.

'Define "okay"?' Irene demanded. 'Because Holly and Molly did exceptionally well, didn't they, Jason?' she added proudly. 'Holly even got a B2 in honours maths. We're thrilled with her! We think she might go on to do medicine, you know. She'd make such a wonderful doctor. And Molly got a B1 in English, so we're confident that she's a future little journalist or news presenter. I always think she'd be wonderful on television. She has just the right cheekbones for the six o'clock news.'

'Oh really?' said Melissa, trying her best to be polite.

'Come on, then, out with it. What sort of grades did you manage to get?'

'Oh, now, does it really matter?' Jayne interrupted. 'Melissa has had a lot on her plate lately, so the last thing I'd be thinking of is school grades. Isn't that right, pet?' She smiled across at her.

'Actually, I got six A1's and two B2's in the half-term exams,' Melissa said quietly, to a stunned silence from Irene. She looked so poleaxed, Jayne thought, she almost wished she could take a photo.

'And you're staying here for how long exactly?' Irene said, instantly changing the subject.

'Melissa will be here for just as long as she likes,' Jayne answered for her. 'Sure it's a pleasure to have her.'

'Jayne, may I be excused?' Melissa said, pushing away the half-eaten bruschetta in front of her. 'I'd really love to get some fresh air, if that's okay?'

The tension is getting to the poor girl, Jayne thought. And really, who could blame her?

'Of course, love,' she said. 'Why don't you go for a nice walk around the square and see if you can't find that useless cat of mine? Magic loves you and I know she'll come inside for you if you coax her enough.'

Melissa heaved a big sigh of relief, and didn't so much skip as bolt away from the table and straight out the hall door.

'Right then, now that it's just us adults . . . ' Jason said to Eric, easing himself back into his chair as his mother served up the main course – a lentil stew with chickpeas, cauliflower, and broccoli, and a green bean salad with toasted almonds on the side. 'I suppose it's time to talk about the elephant in the room.'

'Jason,' Jayne said warningly, but it was too late.

'You and my ma, then,' Jason went on.

'Of course I appreciate that this is the source of a lot of negative energy emanating from you.' Eric replied calmly. 'And I'd very much like to help you work through that, if I may.'

'Sorry, what did you just say?' Jason began, but Eric spoke over him.

'First, though, may I ask that we all join hands and just take a moment of mindfulness? I mean, come on, you guys. Look at this beautiful food that this beautiful soul has prepared for us. It's like a banquet! Isn't this the perfect moment to give thanks to your mom? Sorry . . . ' he added, catching the flint in Jason's eye, which in fairness was hard to miss. 'I mean, your "ma".'

Jayne flushed a bit at that, unused to being thanked. Unused to being complimented, for that matter. Then Eric locked his tanned hands with hers, in a warm, firm grip. He reached across the table to offer his spare hand to Irene, but she pointedly refused it.

'I'm so sorry,' she said crisply, 'but I'm afraid I can't possibly give thanks for food I'm allergic to. No offence or anything, Jayne, but I'm on a special low-fibre diet just now. The chickpeas in this would blow me right out for a full week. I already told you this, don't you remember?'

Jayne distinctly remembered her saying no such thing, but she let it pass. Meanwhile Eric went on, undeterred.

'Thank you, Gaia,' he said in that deep, sonorous Southern accent, 'for the bounty we're about to receive. Love and peace to all here.'

Jason snorted, then said with a grunt, 'Right then, Eric. Now that the new-age, hippie stuff is out of the way, you can answer a few questions that Irene and me have been dying to ask you.'

'Jason, please,' Jayne appealed, but Eric kept his hand cupped over hers, as if to reassure her it was absolutely okay.

'Please. Go right ahead,' he said to Jason soothingly. 'At the retreat where I worked, we had a saying: "Honesty is the first chapter in the book of wisdom".'

'Right then,' Jason replied, squaring his shoulders and adjusting the belt of his trousers, as if he was gearing up for a right good row. 'In that case, maybe it's time for you to start being honest with us, mate. So what's the deal with you, anyway?'

'Excuse me?' Eric said politely, looking puzzled.

'I mean, what's the story, sunshine?' said Jason. 'You beam in here in your white rig-out like an extra from *Jesus Christ,*

Superstar, you latch onto my mother, a poor, gullible widow, you dump your backpack in the corner and it looks to me like you've no intention of going anywhere anytime soon. So here's what I want to know,' he added, waving a fork threateningly in the air. *'What. Is. Going. On?'*

'Jason, that's quite enough out of you,' Jayne said firmly, putting her foot down and wishing she'd done it a lot sooner. 'Eric is my guest and either you welcome him warmly, or else you can leave. The choice is yours.'

'We don't mean to be offensive,' Irene chipped in, 'but you have to understand where we're coming from. Jayne is family and we have a duty to protect her from . . . well . . . let's just say from casual encounters that could end up causing a great deal of pain in the long-term. After all,' she added, speaking slowly as if she were choosing her words carefully, 'we know absolutely nothing about you, Eric. Other than the fact you're from Florida and you run some kind of mind/body/spirit centre that seems to charge a small fortune from elderly retirees looking for "inner wellness".'

'Posh way of describing a snake oil salesman,' Jason muttered under his breath. 'I checked you out online and that's what you sound like to me.'

'I'll thank you both to stop it right now,' said Jayne warningly, but Eric kept his hand squeezed tightly down over hers, his grip was warm and reassuring.

'It's okay,' he said evenly. 'I get it. Information is currency, so let me tell you guys a little bit more about myself. I'm exactly the same age as Jayne and, like her, I'm a widower.'

'You're sure you don't have five wives hidden away somewhere in Florida?' Jason asked petulantly. 'That you've conveniently forgotten about?'

'I sure don't.' Eric smiled. 'My late wife passed away five years ago now – she was a schoolteacher, you know – and I firmly believe that her spirit, along with Tom's,' he added with a respectful bow towards the urn on top of the TV, 'is what brought Jayne and I together.'

'Yes,' Jayne said thoughtfully, 'I think so too.'

'We met online, didn't we?' he went on, with a fond glance towards Jayne. 'But even though we were thousands of miles apart, the connection really felt immediate.'

'That's because of the whole past lives thing that you were telling me about.' Jayne smiled back at him.

'Oh, please, Ma,' Jason spluttered, 'are you hearing yourself? Past lives? For feck's sake!'

'But it's a very real thing,' Eric said evenly. 'When our spirit is ready to pass over, we often reconnect with souls we've known in a different incarnation. Be it a husband, wife or a child – believe it or not, we've all known each other before going back thousands of years, just in different guises until we've purged all our Karma. And that wonderful process goes on and on for generations, until we reach Transcendence.'

'Go on, Eric,' Jayne said fondly. 'Tell them about our past life, when I was a young slave girl in ancient Rome and you were out fighting for Mark Anthony. In forty degree heat, can you imagine?'

'Right, that's it,' Jason said, getting to his feet awkwardly, considering his belly was wedged in behind the table. 'Come on, Irene, we're out of here. There's only so much shite I can listen to and I've reached my limit. And as for you,' he threw back at Eric, 'if you've got any secret skeletons in your cupboard we should know about, then trust me, sunshine, we'll find out and send you packing so quick your head will spin – and that's no idle threat, mate. Now I mightn't be able to stop you staying here, but I sure as hell can watch you like a fecking hawk when you're under my roof.'

'Except that it's not technically "your roof" at all, now is it, love?' Jayne replied calmly. 'And there's no need to leave so abruptly. You still haven't had dessert. I made Eton mess especially – you like that.'

Jason wavered for a second as he hated refusing food, but Irene calmly took control. In one deft movement, she was on her feet, handbag clutched against her bony little frame.

'Thanks all the same, Jayne,' she said, crisply. 'but frankly, I think it would sicken us.'

'You know, I'm sensing a lot of energy imbalance in the room right now,' Eric said, rising to his feet and towering over everyone. Just like a gentle giant, Jayne thought, looking up at him with admiration. 'So what do you say we all just take a little time out, to sit together in silence and maybe burn a little sage to cleanse the atmosphere? As we say back at the Healing House, negative thoughts will never give you a positive mind.'

'We've a great saying where I come from too,' said Jason, who was something of a last-word merchant. 'Take your "energy imbalance" and shove it right up the high hole of your arse.'

Nancy

NATIONAL THEATRE

'Yes, of course I was offered your part first, dearest, but I just had to turn it down. I didn't feel it was quite challenging enough for me, you know.'

'I'm sorry,' came the astonished reply, 'did I actually hear you right? Do you really mean you didn't feel it sufficiently challenging to play one of the most comic matriarchal characters ever to grace a stage? What an extraordinary admission! Do you mind if I write that down, my darling? I might have to quote you in my memoirs.'

The cast of *Pride and Prejudice* were having a quick coffee break at the National and, to no one's surprise, Mrs Bennet and Lady Catherine de Bourgh were sitting side by side in the green room, tearing strips off each other, but with the politest of smiles plastered on their faces as they stuck the knives in.

Nancy was standing over by the coffee machine, well within earwigging distance and struggling to keep a straight face as Alan Vaughan, who was playing Mr Wickham, sidled up beside her, wanting to know what was so funny.

'You mean you're actually writing your memoirs?' Lady Catherine said cattily, wafting a prop fan in front of her face in mock horror. 'Goodness, is it really possible something that inflammatory could actually be published? Is there actually a market for that sort of thing?'

'Absolutely,' Mrs Bennet simpered back. 'I'm working on it as we speak. In fact, I'm quite confident that it'll be a bestseller. You'll have to come to my little book launch, dearest. Do you good to get out and about.'

'And will this be a tell-all autobiography?' Lady C sniped. 'By which I, of course, mean, will you include details of your private life? After all, that's what you're most famous for, isn't it, darling? That's really what everyone will want to read. You know, the dirty, salacious bits. Shall we say, the more tabloid side of your life.'

Mrs B faffed about with her prop reticule for a bit, trying to think of a suitable comeback, but in the heat of the moment, couldn't.

'It's certainly going to be a considerably long book, then, isn't it?' Lady Catherine said, getting up to refill her coffee. 'Volume one of three, I should think. Mind you, the bit about your actual career could probably be condensed into a single chapter at most.'

'Game, set and match to Lady Catherine,' Alan hissed to Nancy under his breath, as she hid a discreet little smile.

'Course, the challenge for me now,' she said, 'is to transfer all that combustible energy between them onto the stage.'

Truth be told, though, Nancy thought, aside from the bitchiness between the two elderly divas, rehearsals were whizzing along very nicely, thank you very much. The production was actually in pretty good shape and with six weeks and counting to the opening night, they even had the luxury of coffee breaks.

Working with Diego Fernandez was proving to be both gruel-ling and challenging, and there were days when she crawled out of the theatre so bone-tired that all she was really fit for was a quick Deliveroo meal for one before collapsing into bed. But so far, they'd already blocked out all of the first act and most of the second too, and were now really drilling down to some serious scene and character development work, which was the part of the process where Nancy really felt herself come alive.

She was fast learning that just sitting at the same table as Diego was like a masterclass. He cared so deeply about his work and once stayed on at the theatre till well past midnight, discussing the most authentic Regency patterns on china cups with the set designer, as an exhausted Nancy stood patiently beside him.

Diego's nickname may have been Rumpelstiltskin, she discovered, but only really because he cared about every tiny detail so passionately, and how could you possibly fault that? Plus, she'd noticed, he only ever really lost his cool whenever he was trying to communicate something vitally important, but his English deserted him. Which is when he'd start stomping at the floor in frustration and almost doing a little flamenco dance on the spot, until she calmed him down and did her best to interpret whatever it was he'd been trying to say in the first place. He seemed to trust her by now, though and as a result, everyone was benefitting.

By and large, though, Nancy was finding the whole process almost exhilarating and there really were times when she had to pinch herself and marvel at her sheer good fortune that she got to work with actors of this calibre all day every day. She'd taken the job in Dublin primarily because it *wasn't* in London, little knowing how much she'd end up enjoying the whole process and how quickly she'd settle in.

She, Alan and Mbeki had been having a lovely chat about the upcoming Dublin Film Festival, each of them earmarking movies that were definite 'must sees'. The three of them were fast becoming firm friends; again, something that made Nancy really look forward to getting to work every day.

'I've got a mate coming over from London to stay with me.' Mbeki was smiling. 'He's a huge film buff, so the film festival sounds perfect.'

Then Nancy noticed the time and gave everyone their five-minute call, before they began the rest of their rehearsal session.

'So how is the flat-hunting coming along then?' Alan asked her, as he pulled himself back into a too-tight looking Regency ruffled shirt, which messed up his head of bright coppery red hair so that it stood up on end.

'You'll regret asking me that.' She smiled back, trying not to laugh at the way his hair made him look like he'd just been electrocuted. 'You must be one of the few cast members who I haven't bored to tears about the absolute palace I've been lucky enough to land.'

'Have you got photos? Go on, then, let's see how the other half live.'

'Have I got photos?!' Nancy replied, dramatically whipping her phone out of her jeans pocket and instantly bringing up pics of twenty-four Primrose Square. 'Take a look at this, my friend, and prepare to weep.'

Alan peered over her shoulder as she scrolled down through every one of them, giving him a running commentary on each and every corner of the house, estate agent-style. Proudly, she bragged about every single feature, particularly dwelling on the walk-in closet, which really was so fabulous, it was a bit like a Pinterest board come to life.

'Even my own mother can't believe it,' Nancy said happily. 'She says she's coming over to Dublin just to make sure I'm not making the whole thing up.'

'So I take it the opening night party will be held *chez vous?*' he said cheekily, as Mbeki tried to coral everyone back into the rehearsal room to continue blocking Act Two.

'Not a bad idea,' Nancy said thoughtfully, taking her place at the director's table, with Diego on her right and Mbeki on her left. 'I'd love for you all to meet the neighbours. They really are salt of the earth Dubs and probably the nicest people you could ever come across.'

In fact, the very thing that Nancy had never experienced over in London was the very thing she'd been lucky enough to land bang slap in the middle of: good neighbours who actually gave each other the time of day, and that wonderful sense of warmth and friendship that you only get when you're really made to feel like you belong somewhere.

Jayne, for instance, from number nineteen, further down the square. Just the previous evening, she'd generously sent down a Tupperware container full of nourishing lentil stew, which Nancy had gratefully devoured, along with a few slices of home-made chocolate biscuit cake for dessert.

'Sure I know what all you career girls are like.' Jayne had smiled kindly when Nancy called around to her house the following morning to thank her and to return her Tupperware. 'Never enough time to eat. No wonder you're as skinny as you are, Nancy, love. You need a bit of fattening up while you're with us here in Ireland.'

'Nothing beats a proper home-cooked meal.' Nancy had grinned back. 'When I first came to Dublin, dinner for me meant siting in a horrible hotel room eating stale crisp sandwiches on the side of the bed. So this was like a Michelin-starred meal, by comparison.'

'I'm only delighted you enjoyed the bit of stew,' Jayne said. 'Least I could do after you were so good to Melissa.'

'She's a little sweetheart.' Nancy smiled, remembering her big chat with that adorable girl the day she'd first moved in.

'She loved meeting you . . . It was all "Nancy this and Nancy that". You've got a little fan there, let me tell you.'

'I thought maybe Melissa was your . . . '

'Granddaughter?' Jayne said, finishing the sentence. 'Oh, don't worry, everyone thinks that. But we're just as close as family any day of the week – I've been appointed her guardian, you know, and I'm only delighted about it. Melissa's parents live next door,' she added, indicating number eighteen just next door with her thumb. 'But things aren't so good there just at the moment, I'm afraid.' Then she dropped her voice and whispered, 'Long story, love. Her dad is away and he's trying to get home as soon as he can, but still, if you ask me, he's not trying hard enough. The man's place is here now with his family, not thousands of miles away in the middle of the desert.'

Of course, Nancy was dying to get to the bottom of this, intrigued to know what had or hadn't gone on in number eighteen. Just then, though, a tanned, good-looking man about Jayne's own age, with shoulder-length silvery hair tied back in a ponytail, wafted through the hallway behind. He was super tall, so tall that he almost had to stoop down a bit just to get out through the front door. He had two yoga mats tucked neatly under his arm, but instantly stopped in his tracks to say hi when he noticed Nancy standing there. Jayne flushed a bit, then introduced him as Eric.

'Now, you will excuse me for not asking you in,' she added apologetically, 'but the thing is, Eric and I were actually on our way out. To an Ayurveda yoga class in town, if you don't mind . . . Did you ever?'

'Forgive my ignorance,' Nancy said as the pair of them stepped out through the door, 'but what exactly is Ayurveda yoga?'

'You've never heard of it?' Eric asked, in a deep, soft-spoken accent that Nancy recognised. She'd once worked on a show that had toured to Florida and South Carolina, so she knew that lilting drawl a mile off. 'It's completely transformational – and truly humbling,' Eric went on. 'It's a whole other lifestyle choice, you know.'

'Eric got me started on it only just last week,' Jayne beamed, locking the hall door behind her, 'but already I feel ten years younger.'

'You're more than welcome to join us for today's class?' Eric said, politely extending the invitation to Nancy. 'It's all about finding balance within your three doshas. I've never met anyone who didn't find it hugely beneficial.'

'Excuse me . . . my three what?' Nancy asked, utterly mystified.

'Don't worry, it's not nearly as complicated as it sounds,' Jayne laughed as they walked companionably down Primrose Square together.

'They're energies that exist between all of us,' Eric went on to explain. 'First, you've got the vata, which is the space and air we all need. Then you've got your kapha, which is the water and earth we're all dependent on. And lastly, you've got pitta, which is the fire that exists within all of us.' Then he turned to look at Nancy, almost assessing her.

'I think she's more of a pitta type,' he eventually said, like a doctor pronouncing a diagnosis, as Jayne nodded along in agreement.

'Excuse me?' Nancy said, thinking that the only 'pitta' she'd heard of up till then was pitta bread.

'Oh, now, it's nothing to worry about,' Eric said, 'it's real common in the Western world.'

'It means you have an excess of fire, love,' Jayne explained patiently. 'Although not in the heartburn sense. More in the emotional sense, isn't that right, Eric?'

'I'm guessing you work in a high-stress environment?' Eric asked.

'That's putting it mildly,' Nancy replied, with a mock eye-roll.

'I'm sensing some pain too,' he added sagely. 'Maybe something from the past that you're still working through?'

There was a tiny, giveaway pause before Nancy answered. 'Something like that, yes,' she eventually said, and left it at that.

Eric and Jayne both seemed like real sweethearts, and completely trustworthy too, but still. That was as much as Nancy was prepared to give away. For the moment, at least. From the corner of her eye, she caught Jayne looking at her keenly, as if she was trying to second-guess at some deep-buried secret, but thankfully, she said nothing.

They said their goodbyes and Nancy watched as the two of them strolled happily off towards busy Pearce Street, marvelling at what a happy, contented couple they seemed to be. Life could be hard sometimes, she thought, cutting and cruel with unexpected curveballs that knocked you for six. And yet, occasionally, if you were very lucky and held the faith, every now and then miracles could and did happen. A sweet old soul like Jayne, for instance, meeting and finding happiness with someone lovely like Eric. A pair of dotes, as Dubliners were wont to say.

Nancy strolled on, admiring the springtime loveliness of the cherry blossoms on Primrose Square. No matter what age you are, she thought, and no matter what you've been through, you're never really too old for romance, are you?

And after everything she'd been though herself in that department, maybe, just maybe, there was light for her at the end of tunnel too.

Later that same day, after yet another gruelling rehearsal session, Nancy found Melissa sitting outside the steps of her house on Primrose Square in the watery evening sunshine, with a battered copy of *Pride and Prejudice* on her lap. Melissa absolutely lit up when she saw Nancy coming, and scrambled over to her like a puppy who's just happy their owner is home and wants to hang out.

'Hey, there you are! Look, I've been re-reading the book and I'm up to the bit where horrible Mr Collins proposes to Lizzie and it's still so funny every time I read it! How were rehearsals today?' she added, beaming brightly up at Nancy, adoration written all over her pale little face.

'Well, I'm afraid to say this out loud in case I jinx it,' Nancy smiled back, 'but I've got a feeling that we're getting there.'

'Wow,' Melissa said, almost with stardust in her eyes. 'Your job is just *so* cool. I was telling my friend Hayley all about you in school today and she was, like, seriously impressed.'

'Just don't speak too soon.' Nancy laughed at her innocence. 'The thing I find about any rehearsal process is just like that line from *Shakespeare in Love.*'

The kid looked up, mystified.

'"The natural condition of any show is one of insurmountable obstacles on the road to imminent disaster. But strangely enough, it all turns out well. No one knows why, it's a mystery."'

'*Shakespeare in Love*?' Melissa asked, puzzled, so at that point Nancy shut up, realising that the kid wasn't even born when that movie first came out.

'Melissa, you *have* to watch that film!' Nancy said. 'It should be required viewing for anyone with even a passing interest in theatre. Come over to me some evening and I'll download it for us. Would you like that?'

'Yes, please, I'd love it!' Melissa chatted away, skipping on the pavement as they reached the steps of Nancy's house. 'You know we're doing *Pride and Prejudice* in school? When I told my English teacher today that one of the directors of the stage show was my new neighbour, she couldn't believe it! She's taking our whole class to see the show, and I can't wait.'

'In that case,' Nancy smiled, 'you could get to see the show twice. Because I was kind of hoping you'd be my guest on opening night?'

'Are you kidding me?' Melissa squealed almost at warp level. 'That would just be the best thing *ever*!'

'I hope you still think so after you've seen the show,' Nancy laughed, delighted at her enthusiasm.

'So is it okay if I call to your house in about an hour or so?' Melissa asked, as they got to Nancy's front door and she began to fumble about in her bag for the keys. 'We can find out some more about your mystery landlord. I mean, can you just imagine how cool it would be if that Sam Williams guy did turn out to be single? And if he liked you and you liked him and you ended up dating and this was how you met and then maybe you ended up getting married and it was all because you housesat for him and I was your bridesmaid and you got married out here on the square and all the neighbours were invited and Eric did a weird kind of chant-y blessing and there was a party afterwards and even my best friend Hayley was invited? Wouldn't that just be the most amazing thing ever?' She looked up at Nancy with hopeful, shining eyes.

'Sounds like you've put an awful lot more thought into it than I have,' Nancy said, with a wry little smile. 'But please, swing by later if you'd like, when you've done all your homework. I don't think Jayne would be impressed otherwise.'

A text message pinged through and the two of them instinctively went to check their phones at exactly the same time.

'It's my phone, I think . . . Oh my God, that's my dad!' Said Melissa, brightening as she read the message on her phone. 'He says he'll Skype me in five minutes, so I better run. See you later, Nancy! And don't worry, between the two of us, we'll find out everything there is to know about Sam Williams!'

Sam Williams, Nancy thought, as Melissa skipped happily off and she let herself in through the hall door. In what little spare time she had, she'd been googling him to death, as you do, but he seemed to be one of those people who was pretty shrewd about their online privacy, because apart from page after page of boring company listings and details of various work functions he'd attended, she could find very little of a more personal nature about him.

According to all her trawling, it seemed that yes, indeed, Sam Williams was pretty senior at a large software development company and seemed to travel a helluva lot for his work. His company was vast, with tentacles in every major city going, stretching from New York to Frankfurt, and from London to Shanghai, where he was now. Every single thing he'd been telling Nancy about himself tallied and there was very little about him that wasn't calculated to impress the shite out of any woman.

As the line in *Pride and Prejudice* went, it is a truth universally acknowledged, that a single man in possession of a fortune, must be in want of a wife. Sam Williams seemed single, he acted single and there was certainly nothing about his living space to suggest that there was a wife, a lover, or any kind of a long-term partner on the scene.

Not only that, but Sam had been in touch with Nancy regularly. A lot. An awful lot. She didn't think she was imagining it, but far, far more frequently than seemed usual in a conventional landlord/housesitter relationship.

It had been almost two weeks since she'd moved in and they'd quickly graduated from emails flying back and forth about mundane things, like what the alarm code was, how to switch on the boiler or else when bin day was. The kind of queries Nancy knew she should have been onto the letting agency about, but somehow she couldn't bring herself to get in touch with that awful Irene again. Far easier, she thought, to just hear it directly from the horse's mouth. Anyway, in no time at all, Sam's messages to her quickly became far friendlier in nature.

Hey! How are you settling in? No complaints so far, I hope?

This came through just as Nancy was leaving Primrose Square to get to the National Theatre in time for rehearsals. She was crossing the road at Townsend Street, but still zipped him back a reply while she was waiting for the pedestrian lights to change.

Settling in so well, I may never leave. May also revise my rash decision not to have a cast party here. House too stunning, needs showing off.

Almost immediately, Sam was back to her.

Sighs reluctantly No vomit on the carpet, that's my only stipulation.

And like a tennis rally, she was back to him moments later.

Entirely your own fault for decorating house so beautifully.

There was a natural lull in all communication then, but at lunchtime Nancy checked her phone again, the minute she was out of the rehearsal room. And sure enough, there was yet another text waiting from him.

You've gone vv quiet on me, Nancy.

She was straight back onto him and the ensuing text marathon went thusly:

Ahem. Well excuse me for having to work for a living.

And his reply?

Am currently swimming in the South China Sea, if you're interested in knowing about my day.

Well, of course that was too big a bait for Nancy to resist.

Forgive me, Sam, am clearly labouring under a gross misapprehension here. Was under the impression you actually had a proper job. Or are you a trust fund boyo gallivanting out in the Far East while the rest of us slave away here in lashing rain and actual hailstones?

His response was instantaneous.

Boyo. Love it. It seems, Ms Thompson, that you're picking up on one or two Irish-isms during your stay in Dublin's fair city. P.S. Personal apologies about the hailstones. Now, if you'll excuse me, I need to reapply factor thirty sunblock – it's eighty-five degrees in the shade here, dontcha know.

By then, of course, Nancy was hooked. Yes, this was flirting between herself and a total stranger based somewhere out in the backarse of Shanghai. But it was all good, light, teasing fun, so what the hell, she thought.

Right, that's it, Mr Williams, you're well and truly rumbled. I've decided that you've got to be one of those Euromillions lottery winners who tells no one, just retires young and travels the world lounging around in 5 star hotels. Now, if you'll excuse me, sadly some of us have actual jobs to do.

He was back to her within minutes.

You are doubtless aware, Ms Thompson, that there is a time difference between Dublin and Shanghai? Seven hours ahead here, to be exact. So you will admit it's possible that I, too, have done a 12-hour day and am now chillaxing with a swim?

She was on her way back to rehearsals after lunch when that one pinged through. Although for 'lunch', the rest of the cast grabbed a snack in a coffee shop across the road, while Nancy stood on the pavement outside where there was a better Wi-Fi signal, on her phone the whole time.

She was racking her brains trying to think of a smart-arse comeback to that, but just then a breathless Mbeki caught up with her, all fresh-faced and clear-skinned and so brimming over with energy, Nancy was sorely tempted to ask her what health supplements she was on.

'Hey, Nancy,' she said brightly as they fell naturally into step together. 'You've been on your phone non-stop for the whole lunchbreak; you never even ate a scrap. Like a good production assistant,' she added teasingly, 'I notice everything.'

'Mbeki,' Nancy said, turning to her thoughtfully. 'Can I ask you something?'

'Fire away,' came the smiling reply.

'Have you ever used Homesitter.com before?'

'Yeah, loads of times.' Mbeki shrugged. 'I once landed a place right on Times Square in New York, for a complete song . . . Best holiday of my life! Why do you ask anyway?'

'Well . . . did you hear a lot from your landlord? Like . . . an awful lot? Texting back and forth pretty much non-stop?'

'No,' Mbeki said, without hesitation. 'Not at all. I mean, I had an email listing out a few house rules and all the dos and don'ts, but other than that . . . ' She trailed off as Nancy's phone pinged yet again.

May have to call you for a proper chat soon, Nancy.

You know neither the day nor the hour.

Interesting, Nancy thought, as she and Mbeki strolled back to the theatre. This guy was thousands of miles away; he couldn't do any real harm to her. So completely unlike what she'd just been through in London.

But in a good way.

Susan

From the journal of Susan Hayes

Dearest Ella,

It's your birthday soon and words can't say how much I'm dreading it. So here's what I'm journalling today instead. A happier memory of a far happier birthday. Do you remember, my darling? How could your old mum ever forget?

'So, sweetheart, it's your birthday very soon, and your dad and I were wondering what you'd like to do? Maybe a trip to the movies and then something to eat with your pals afterwards?'

'No offence, Mum,' you said, flicking back that mane of unruly strawberry blonde curls that I could never get to lie down straight, no matter how hard I tried. 'But most of the movies targeted at my age group are so juvenile. Just gross-out comedies or, even worse, chick flicks.'

'So I'll take that as a no, then?'

'A definite no!' you'd told me firmly. 'Chick flicks,' you'd added disparagingly, miming a gagging gesture at the very phrase. 'Who even thought up a term like that? Not a woman, anyway. Hollywood is so patriarchal and it's our duty not to support gross-out comedies. It's the principle of it, Mum.'

'Okay,' I said, 'well instead of that, how about a sleepover here for your girlfriends? We could order in pizzas and I could even get a chocolate fountain for you?'

'Mum, I'm not a child any more! What are you going to suggest next – getting a magician in to do party tricks for us?'

'Well . . . ' I said, racking my brains to come up with something else, 'at your friend Holly's party, there was a make-up artist who did all your make-up for you. You said it was great fun and you all had a lovely time. How about something like that?'

'I only said it was fun because I was being polite to Holly,' you said pointedly, abandoning the book you'd had your nose buried in. 'But the truth was, I came home looking like a panda bear with all the ridiculous eye make-up that had been plastered on me. I looked like I'd been in a fight.'

I nodded, remembering how loudly you'd complained when it took you a good hour to scrub away the 'smoky eye' look.

'Besides,' you went on, 'why should woman bother wearing make-up in the first place? To bolster their confidence? To impress boys? You shouldn't need a mascara wand to do that for you, should you? Confidence is something that should come from within, Mum.'

I shook my head and smiled quietly to myself. Because you were just so sure of yourself, my darling. So spirited and confident. You'd say things like that and it would almost make me burst with pride to think that you were my daughter. My perfect girl.

'The thing is, though,' you said, 'I've kind of already decided what I'd really like to do for my birthday. If it's okay with you and Dad, that is.'

'What's that, love?'

'Well, some of the members of Riot Grrrl are coming to Dublin soon, to give a talk about the third wave of feminism – you know they're my total heroines. The tickets are pricey, but I'd love nothing more than to see them and hear them speak. Please can I go, Mum? Please?'

I knew from other mums at the school that when it came to birthdays, their daughters only ever wanted hard, cold cash to spend in the Dundrum town centre, to splash out on clothes/ make-up/nails/spray-tan before they hit whatever disco or party the gang were all heading to.

But no, not you, my darling. Instead, what you wanted was to see and hear your inspirational role models speak live. I must have done something good in a past life to deserve a daughter like you, I remember thinking, looking at you with such love and pride.

You were, at the time, all of thirteen years old.

So what happened, love? My innocent, brave little fighter. What happened to you?

Susan

'The one advantage of being off the sauce,' Emily said, as she got dressed on her side of the twin room she and Susan were sharing at St. Michael's, 'is the sheer amount of weight you lose.'

'Is that right?' Susan said flatly, hauling herself out of her own bed and facing into the day. Not just any old day, either; this of all days. The day that she'd dreaded so much was finally on top of her and now somehow she had to find a way to struggle through it.

'Are you kidding me? Take a look at this and weep, baby!' said Emily, oblivious to her roommate's mood as she twirled around, holding out the too-big waistband on her jeans. 'When I first checked in here, these actually used to fit. Now look at me – I'm practically a waif.'

'Oh yeah, Kate Middleton, eat your heart out,' Susan managed to respond, pulling on the same warm jumper she'd been wearing for days. *What does it matter what I wear*, she thought. *Who even gives a shite what I look like?*

She'd known today's date would come around eventually. She'd been anticipating it for weeks, and now that the day had actually dawned, the best she could hope for was just to get through it.

Keep putting one foot in front of the other, she told herself. *Before you know it, it'll all be over and time for blissful sleep again.*

That was the one good thing about being in a place like St Michael's: they were generous to a fault with sleeping tablets – strictly the non-addictive kind, of course – so for at least seven hours every night, Susan could park the thoughts that haunted her during the day. The memories that twisted her over in pain, the deep wells of fucking longing that everyone seemed to think would magically percolate away, just by being in here.

'Keep talking,' they said to her. 'Joining in with group therapy is the route to healing. You'll only get out of this process what you put into it.' True enough, it seemed to be working for everyone else, but Susan's grief was different and she knew it. This wasn't just raw pain she was feeling, this was something else entirely – this was hell. Unbearable, searing hell.

'You want know something else?' Emily said, as both women made their way down to the canteen on the ground floor, Emily chatting away while Susan stayed resolutely silent. 'I think my skin is starting to look a little bit clearer too. Honestly, they should stress these things far more at AA meetings. It's torture giving up the booze, but I will say this much: you do come out of a place like this looking like you've been at a luxury health spa. Don't get me wrong, I'd still strangle my own granny for a bottle of vodka if I could get my paws on one, but on the plus side, my zits are gone and I'm down to a size ten. Every cloud, is all I'm saying.'

Sadly, there's no silver lining when you lose your eldest child, Susan thought, as the two of them tripped down a lino-clad staircase that stank of Dettol. You were just expected to keep on keeping on, in spite of the fact that your insides felt like they'd been ripped out and splattered up against a brick wall. One minute you'd thought you were fine, that you were coping, that you were actually functioning like a normal human being in the world again. But then a day like today came around and suddenly you were right back to square one. If you'd asked Susan how she felt just then, the answer was like a raw, walking mound of open flesh, which some sadistic bastard kept throwing fistfuls of salt over. When, she thought in despair, would she fucking well start to feel better? Wasn't that the whole point of being in a place like this? So when would her so-called 'treatment' actually begin to work?

God, she missed her family so much it hurt. She couldn't even bring herself to think about Melissa, her little princess, the one good thing in her life that hadn't been ripped away from her. And the crippling fear that she didn't know how to reach her any more. That she'd forgotten how to be a mum.

No, Susan thought firmly, shoving the thought away. *Can't go there today.*

She desperately missed the comfort of Frank's face on the pillow every night, holding her tight and kissing away her tears as they both talked about Ella, remembering. But then a sudden wave of hot fury came over her, at the thought of him so far away at a time like this.

The fucking Lebanon, she thought. *Right now, Frank is in the desert heat, distracted with work and his army buddies and his job as an engineer. He'll probably have a beer after work this evening with the lads. He's probably sleeping at night and eating three square meals a day. He's probably getting a fucking suntan. He's just drawn a line under this and buggered off, when we needed him most.* Worst of all, before he left, he begged her to let the whole Josh Andrews thing drop. Fixation, that was the exact word he'd used. As if Susan would – as if any mother ever could.

Emily babbled away and Susan let her. Not talking suited her. Besides, she'd talked enough at that meeting the other day to last her for a while. One tiny blessing, though: ever since she'd tried to open up a bit to the rest of the residents at St Michael's, they were certainly all being a lot nicer to her.

Bungalow Bill, for one, and that big, blowsy older woman who described herself as a survivor of 'three daughters, two suicide attempts, and one alcoholic ex-husband'. Everyone called her Bunny, she was a true-blue salt-of-the-earth Dub and Susan was starting to warm to her. Bunny had a motherly way about her and was constantly at Susan to try eating more.

'You need to keep your strength up, love. The food in here mightn't exactly be Michelin-starred, but it's not the worst.'

Susan's own parents were long since retired and now living in Toronto with her younger brother, so apart from Skype calls and the odd flying visit, that was as much as she got to see of her own family, really. Yet as the days passed at St Michael's, slowly but surely she was starting to feel like a part of a sort-of family, albeit a highly dysfunctional one.

But could anyone really help her on a day like this?

Side-by-side, she and Emily walked into the canteen and found two free places at a long, rectangular table, beside Bunny and the huge, hulking frame of Bungalow Bill. What passed for breakfast was plonked down in front of them as Susan slid into a seat, hoping that no one would notice her or the fact that she could barely even look at food, never mind eat it. All she asked for was just to sit there, untroubled and in peace.

No such luck, though.

'So, Susan, love,' said Bunny, talking with her mouth full as she horsed into the remains of a sausage roll. 'You still haven't really told us why you're in here. It's not good for you to keep it to yourself, you know.'

Susan looked blankly back at her.

'Yes she did!' said Emily stoutly. 'You just weren't listening properly.' Then she dropped her voice and mouthed, 'Because of the daughter who died.'

'Ella,' said Bungalow Bill gruffly. 'That was her name, wasn't it? You see? At least I was paying attention.'

All three heads turned to face Susan, but she didn't answer them. Instead, she just fiddled with the black coffee on the tray she'd been given and stared blankly at a dry-looking piece of wholewheat brown bread.

'Oh yeah, now I remember,' said Bunny warmly. 'So what happened to your Ella, love? You can tell us, you know. You can say anything you like in here. We're unshockable.'

'"At the circle of trust, we all come together to form a secure place,"' Emily chirruped, doing a reasonably passable impression of Dr Ciara.

Susan shook her head and kept her eyes down, praying they'd take the hint and just leave her be. *Pity there's no polite way to tell people to fuck off*, she thought. Tomorrow, maybe tomorrow she'd be able for all this. But today was different.

'If the woman doesn't want to talk, then she doesn't want to talk,' growled Bungalow Bill defensively, the only one of them who seemed to sense her mood. 'And by the way,' he said to her, 'if you're not eating your breakfast, love, can I have it? This cereal tastes like crappy birdseed and the portions they give you in here wouldn't feed a fly.'

Susan nodded and shoved her food his way, but Bunny still wouldn't let the subject drop. 'Oh, now come on,' she insisted, 'I'm not taking no for an answer. There's nothing you can say to me or to anyone else at this table that we haven't heard before, you know.'

'We're only trying to help you,' Emily said encouragingly. 'It's all part of the ethos here. Be open about everything and it'll heal that bit quicker.'

A long pause as all eyes turned to her and Susan knew she'd have to come out with something. Anything. Just to get them off her back, if nothing else.

'Look, I do appreciate your concern,' she sighed, 'but I just . . . I just can't. Maybe another time, but not now. I'm sorry.'

'Ahh, go on out of that!' said Bunny. 'You couldn't possibly tell us anything new. Sure, look at me,' she said, thumping her pudgy hand on her chest. 'In here, it may seem like I'm fine and functioning and everything, but the trouble starts when I get home and the Black Dog starts at me again.'

'Depression?' Emily asked her matter-of-factly.

'Oh, don't talk to me. Like you wouldn't believe, Emily, love. There are plenty of days when I just can't get out of bed, while my three girls are downstairs tearing strips off each other. And back when my husband was drinking . . . '

'You needn't tell me about drinking,' Emily said sympathetically, rolling her eyes. 'I always say I drank half a house.'

'How can you drink half a house?' Bunny asked, and Susan looked up, intrigued in spite of herself.

'Well, when my marriage first broke up, my ex and I sold the house,' Emily said bluntly. 'We split the money fifty-fifty, as per our separation agreement, but when I got my cut of it, I went on the bender to end all benders.'

'Jesus,' said Bunny. 'You mean you drank your way through *all* of it?'

'Why do you think I'm in here?' Emily replied with a shrug. 'I'm almost two months sober now, but none of you wouldn't have liked me when I was boozing. Trust me. I'm working on myself now, but back then, I wasn't a nice person to be around.'

'And as for poor old Bill there,' said Bunny, nodding in Bungalow Bill's direction, and talking about him like he wasn't there. 'What can I say? Bill's been in here the longest and he's probably the least shockable of any of us. You can tell him anything that's going on with you, Susan. There's no judgment at this table, trust me.'

Bill looked up, aware that the focus was on him now, abandoning the dry brown bread he'd been wolfing back. Then, almost like it was a ritual, he held out the palms of both his hands facing upwards, so Susan could see them for herself up close. The burn tissue on both was so severe and the scarring so vicious that she winced at the sight of it.

'See that?' he said matter-of-factly. 'The doctors didn't think I'd ever be able to use either one of my hands ever again, not after what happened. They thought they'd have to amputate and that all I'd be left with would be two stumps where my hands used to be.'

Susan was momentarily shocked out of her own pain, hoping it didn't show on her face how horrified she was at his poor, mutilated hands. Instead, she nodded in sympathy, remembering that she'd heard Bill had set fire to his house, with his wife and mother-in-law inside.

'They thought I'd be upset about losing limbs, but do you know what?' Bill told her, shoving away the food on the tray in front of him. 'Actually, I would have welcomed it. Physical pain would have been nothing to me, compared with the mental torment I had to deal with. And that I have to deal with for the rest of my life.'

'Your wife?' Susan asked him as gently as she could, putting aside her own troubles for the minute. 'And your mother-in-law? Were they okay?'

Please say yes, she thought. *Please tell me they made it.*

'She's now my ex-wife,' he grunted, 'and she now has first-degree burns and scar tissue that no amount of treatment seems to be able to shift. But at least she and her mam got out alive. No thanks to me, though.'

'Jesus,' Susan said under her breath. 'If it's not too cheeky of me . . . can I ask you what happened?'

'I just snapped,' Bill told her bluntly. 'I was going through a separation from my ex, and she was barring me from seeing the kids. So one day I lost it, simple as that. We had a vicious row and, well . . . I hardly have to spell the rest out to you. So now, I've got two daughters living with their mother, on record as saying that they'll never talk to me again as long as they live.

'Meanwhile,' he went on, 'I'm in here with not much chance of getting out. I'm a diagnosed manic depressive and it'll take me a lifetime to try and build bridges with a family that wants nothing to do with me. Last Christmas was sheer hell, it nearly drove me over a cliff edge. So I checked in here and I'm not leaving till I can function again. I'll never get over it, but if I can at least get well enough to make it up to my family, then that's as much as I can hope for.'

'I'm so sorry,' Susan said quietly, sliding both her hands into his. 'There really are no words to say how very sorry I am.'

'So how old was your Ella when she died?' he asked her, with kindness in his eyes, as he gripped her thin, white hands in his.

Susan could feel all the lumps and bumps of his scar tissue and willed herself not to wince.

But she couldn't answer that one. Instead she just massaged Bill's poor swollen, puffy hands and kept her head down.

'Had she been sick, love?' Bunny asked her gently, from across the table.

They were all looking at Susan, but instead she kept her focus on Bill's big, gnarled, knotted hands, fighting back the urge to cry.

Don't start, she thought. *Because once I start, I might never stop.*

'You mentioned someone in our group session the other night,' Bill said quietly.

Susan looked up at him.

'Did he have something to do with what happened to your girl?'

She looked into his blood-red eyes that looked like they'd been through a hundred lifetimes.

'He had everything to do with it.'

She could trust these people, she instinctively felt. They all got it – they'd been through as bad, if not worse. Could she maybe bring herself to say more?

Next thing: an announcement came over the hospital tannoy.

'Paging Susan Hayes. Will Susan Hayes please make her way to the day room on the ground floor.'

'Oh, a visitor!' said Bunny, brightening up as the quiet, intimate mood around the table instantly shattered. 'Well, now, that'll cheer you up, won't it, love?'

'I wish someone would come and visit me,' said Emily morosely. 'If only so they could smuggle me in a few bars of chocolate.'

Susan scrambled to her feet, mystified as to who this could possibly be, and anxious that she wasn't really able to face anyone, today of all days. Lovely, sainted Jayne was bringing Melissa to see her at the weekend – but Saturday was still three whole days away. She couldn't think of another soul who'd make the trek all the way out to St Michael's, just to see her. She'd long since cut herself off from her old pals at the bank and apart from Hayley's mum at the school, none of the other parents had the first clue what to say to her.

It was the uniform she saw first, as he stood tall and erect by the window overlooking the grounds, like he was surveying them, looking lean and tanned and vigorous. He heard the door and immediately turned around.

'Frank!' Susan said, stunned.

'Hey,' he said simply, striding across the room to where she stood rooted to the spot.

'You're *here*,' Susan kept saying, over and over, as he hugged her so tightly her ribs hurt. 'You're really here. You came home. You came back!'

'I couldn't stay away,' he said. 'Today of all days? On Ella's anniversary?'

'Frank, oh God, Frank,' was all she could answer, nestling into his chest, her safe place, feeling warm and comforted for the first time in an age. 'I've dreaded today so much. And now it's here and you're here and . . . '

'Shhhh, love,' he said, placing a finger over her lips. 'Just know that I love you, and I'm sorry. I'm so, so sorry, Susan. But I'm here for you. So let's just remember our girl. Our little Ella. And let's somehow get through today together.'

Unknown to Susan, she had a silent audience. At that exact moment, Dr Ciara happened to be walking past the visitor's room. She stopped, then quietly and tactfully closed the door as two heartbroken parents held each other, cried softly and remembered.

Jason

SANDYMOUNT STRAND

Jason had parked his ice cream van on Sandymount Strand, which normally was a great aul' spot for business. It was a grim, overcast afternoon, though, one of those days in spring when it feels more like November, and there was nothing doing, no matter how loudly he played the tinkling Mr Softee jingle. There wasn't a customer in sight and the music was slowly starting to do his head in.

All in all, it was a pretty shit time in the life of Jason Hayes. Financial stresses were keeping him up at night and every time the postman came, he just wanted to pull the duvet over his head and blank out the sound of the letterbox snapping shut. There was never anything in the post but bills and more bills, all with 'outstanding' writ large across them in bold red lettering.

'I haven't got the dosh to pay any of you!' Jason wanted to scream at the TV cable company, the gas board and the Inland Revenue, who were sending him demands on a weekly basis by then. 'You shower of tossers have already robbed me of my peace of mind; what the feck more do you want from me? Blood?'

Not only that, but Holly and Molly had started at him now because their class were all going off on some fancy skiing trip to Verbier, but at almost two thousand euro for the pair of them, there wasn't a snot's chance of them going. There was just about enough dosh for their school fees, but as he firmly told them,

'Youse can't go and that's the bleeding end of it. Right? Put it out of your heads and, as the song says, let it go.'

Which, of course, led to nothing but a load of door-slamming and sulking for days afterwards. From Irene, as well as the girls.

'I just don't understand it,' she kept saying over and over, wrecking Jason's head, which was already pounding with worry over interest payments on loans he'd taken out behind her back and didn't have a hope of paying back. 'Holly and Molly are the only two girls in their whole class not going on the ski trip,' Irene went on, sounding more and more suspicious. 'Which makes us look like a right pair of cheapskates in front of the other parents. So what are we going to do?'

Irene herself came from a family of ten, and they'd never had a bean to spare for any kind of luxuries when she was growing up. The result was that, come hell or high water, she was determined that her own two daughters would want for nothing. Only the best was good enough for Holly and Molly – whatever the cost and with absolutely no expense spared.

Women, Jason thought glumly. *I'm surrounded by nothing but women making my life a misery.* With his own mother causing him more problems than the rest of them put together.

Eric. Fecking Eric Butler, the root of all his woes. If it weren't for that new-age hippie, who had to be seventy if he was a day, weaselling in on his ma, sure he and Irene would have been grand, thanks very much. Jason knew that, given time, he could easily have persuaded his ma to sign the Primrose Square house over to him, and move in with himself and Irene. Then it was happy fecking days, as far as he was concerned. He could pay off everyone he knew, nice and quietly under the radar, and sure no one would be any the wiser.

But his ma had changed, there were no two ways about it. Even Jason grudgingly had to admit, she was looking an awful lot younger these days. Gone were all her old housecoats and sensible slacks from M&S, and now she went around in gym gear the whole time. Hoodies, leggings, trainers, the works. What Irene called 'athleisure', whatever the feck that was, Jason wasn't quite sure. Her hair used to be a kind of gunmetal grey, but now, his ma was a full-on bottle blonde. Trying to have a phone conversation with her these days was a total waste of time, too; it was all 'Eric this' and 'Eric that'. That was all you ever heard.

During one phone call the previous week, Jason had the temerity to say, 'For the love of God, can we please stop talking about that git Eric – isn't it bad enough he's living in our house?'

And his ma's response?

'Jason, love,' she'd told him firmly, 'you need to stop being such a ball of negativity. Aside from everything else, it's bad for your health, you know. Eric is here beside me and he's suggesting that you should start up a gratitude journal. Now isn't that a great idea?'

'A what?' Jason had asked.

'It's sort of like a diary,' his ma explained, 'where you write down all the things in your life you're thankful for. Eric and I do it every single day now and I really do find it wonderful. It makes you appreciate all the little things that we're inclined to take for granted.'

'There'll be no one more grateful than me,' Jason told her huffily, 'on the happy day when Eric gets a taxi to Dublin airport and flies back to the arse end of Florida. When he finds some other old lady to scab off, I'll certainly start a gratitude diary then!'

His one and only consolation, he thought miserably, gazing out over the deserted beach road, was that little Melissa Hayes was staying in the house too. Just till the mother got out of whatever nuthouse they'd carted her off to. Melissa was a grand kid, quiet as a mouse, and at least when she was around, there was a sort of chaperone in the house. Although the thought that his ma and Eric had anything physical going nearly made his stomach want to heave.

The Hayes were a nice family, Jason had to admit. He'd always been fond of them and he knew they were very good to his ma when he wasn't around. Jesus, Jason thought, momentarily forgetting his own woes, that was a rough hand that family had been dealt.

Ella Hayes had always been a bit wild, all right – outspoken, never caring what she said or did, striding up and down the square, usually dressed in black with a big pair of Doc Martins on her. When she was a kid, she was always pestering Jason for free ice cream, then when she got older, she started shoving pamphlets under his nose and giving him lectures about the evils of dairy.

'Just make sure to keep the twins as far from that Ella Hayes as possible,' Irene often used to caution. 'She's a terrible influence, mark my words.'

But no one could have predicted what would happen next and it was no wonder poor aul' Susan had gone off the rails a bit. According to his ma, 'Susan's just taking a little time out, to regroup. So all we can do is love and support her at every turn.'

Jesus, Jason thought, as his hands involuntarily clenched into two tight fists. If that gobshite Josh Andrews, or whatever his name was, as much as looked twice at either of his own girls, he'd have to be physically tied back from whacking him one. That would put a good, quick end to his rugby playing days, wouldn't it? If the fecker couldn't walk straight for the rest of his life?

Next thing, Jason's phone rang – Irene.

'I can't really talk, love,' he said, surveying the empty beach in front of him. 'I'm up to me knackers here in work.'

'Just a quick call,' she said briskly, 'as I'm in the middle of a viewing right now. The thing is, I've had a good think about the whole . . . *situation* with your mother. And I think I may have hit on a way out of it.'

'Oh yeah?' said Jason, perking up a bit.

'As we know, Holly and Molly are wonderful,' Irene went on, 'but you know how . . . let's just say *challenging* . . . it can be, when you're dealing with the two of them at the same time. You know how *stressful* your mum can find it.'

Irene was picking her words carefully, but Jason knew exactly what she meant. There were times in his own house when it was like living in a warzone. Frequently, he'd take the paper and go and sit in the ice cream van parked in the front driveway, till whatever strop that was going on blew over.

'So starting from today,' Irene said, 'I'm going to tell Jayne I'm working late for the next few weeks and that the twins will be going around to her house every single evening after school. And you know something else?'

'What's that, love?'

'The later we are to collect the pair of them, the better. So let's see how Mr Eric Butler likes that! What harm in giving Mr Butler a good, firm, unsubtle nudge towards the front door?' Irene added, before clicking off the call.

What harm indeed?

Melissa

M elissa and Hayley were just coming out of the school gates together, when suddenly Hayley let out a shriek.

'Oh my *actual* Gawd!' she squealed. 'I think you've got a visitor, Melissa . . . Look who's here for you!'

Melissa had been engrossed in her phone, but immediately glanced up to see what her friend was getting so excited about.

'*Dad!*' she squealed, the minute she saw his long, lean, familiar figure waiting at the car park for her. 'I don't believe it . . . it's my dad!'

She dumped her schoolbag and ran straight into his arms, as he scooped her up into a huge, tight hug.

'I told you I had a little surprise for you, didn't I, princess?' he laughed as she clung to his arm and looked adoringly up at him.

'Dad . . . ' was all she could say over and over again. 'You're home, you're really here! I'm in total shock!'

Her dad looked so well too, so fit and strong. He was out of his army uniform and dressed in his 'civvies', as he called them – jeans and a warm jumper – but still, you'd know a mile off this was an army officer. There was something about her dad that just made people respect him, from his straight posture, like a ramrod, as her mum always said, to the air of calm authority that radiated from him.

'I'm not home for too long, I'm afraid,' he said, keeping his arm tightly locked around Melissa, 'but you know me. I'd cross oceans to see my princess, for no matter how short a time.'

'Does Mum know you're here?' Melissa asked excitedly.

'Of course, pet.' Her dad smiled back. 'I've just been to visit her and I thought we could both go back together and see her later, if you like?'

She didn't get a chance to answer, though, as just then Hayley bounced over to say hello. 'Mr Hayes, welcome home!' She beamed, before clamping her hand down over her mouth. 'Oops! Sorry, I meant to say Captain Hayes.'

'Frank is good enough for me, Hayley.' He grinned back. 'And I believe I owe you a big thank you. I know from my lovely daughter here how good a friend you've been to her while I was away.'

'Hayley's not just a good friend,' Melissa giggled, 'she's like . . . my *best* friend, for life. For always.'

'Just as well I brought little gifts for you both then, isn't it?' said Frank, dipping into his jacket pocket and producing two beautifully wrapped tiny jewellery boxes, which both girls gasped at, then ripped open, approximately two seconds later. Inside were two identical friendship rings, plain, simple silver bands with little raised knots sitting prettily in the dead centre.

'Wow!' squealed Hayley, 'that's like the coolest thing ever! Thanks so much, Captain . . . sorry, I mean Frank . . . I'll never take mine off . . . like, ever!'

'Thank you, Dad,' Melissa said a bit more quietly, but with a beam on her face that spread from ear to ear. 'They're . . . they're just perfect.'

She couldn't remember the last time she'd felt this good, even though she knew her dad was really only home because her mum was in that hospital, where Abby Graham said they only sent you if you were mental. But, of course, the main reason her dad was home was because of that day's anniversary. Melissa had been dreading it for weeks and now it was here, all she wanted was to just get through it, like any other ordinary day. She didn't breathe a single word about it in school and she'd promised herself that she wouldn't cry, not even in front of Jayne, who'd been so lovely to her all that morning.

'Now you can stay home today if you like, pet?' Jayne had said to her earlier. 'Whatever you want is fine by me.' But all Melissa really wanted was for the day to be over so they could put it behind them for another year.

I won't cry, she told herself. *I. Will. Not. Cry. I'll just act like everything is normal and it'll be tomorrow in no time.*

It was weird, but the only time she'd got a bit wobbly wasn't over Ella at all. At breaktime when she'd opened up her bag, there was a gorgeous homemade triple decker club sandwich waiting for her, with healthy nuts and fruit juice on the side. Jayne had been making yummy lunches for Melissa every single day since she'd moved in, but today was special as there was a tiny little note stuck to her lunchbox.

Always remember that a very special angel is watching over you from above, the note read, in Jayne's scribbly handwriting.

I'm a lucky girl, Melissa thought, tearing up as she read it in the packed, noisy school canteen. *I have Ella watching me from above and Jayne minding me down here.* And now that her dad was home, somehow the thought of this horrible day became a bit more bearable. *Even though there's only three of us left,* Melissa thought hopefully, *we're still a family. We still have each other.*

As soon as they got home from school, she and her dad moved straight back into their own house on Primrose Square. Before they did, though, they called around to see Jayne, and Melissa gave her a huge, grateful hug, locking onto her waist and thinking she might never let go.

'There really are no words for me to thank you properly,' Frank said, handing Jayne a bouquet so magnificent, she almost gasped when she saw it. 'I'll never forget what you've done. Never.'

'Go on out of that.' Jayne had blushed. 'Sure it was an absolute joy to have you here, Melissa. You're like family to me, you know that, love. And I hope you'll come back to stay with me in a few days, when your dad's gone back to army duty, pet? Eric and I would so love to have you again.'

'I'd love that, thanks.' Melissa smiled shyly at her pretend-granny.

'Who's Eric?' her dad asked, as they drove off, on their way to St Michael's. It was her third visit, ever since her mum had been allowed to have visitors, but for the other visits, her mother had been quiet and sat playing with her hair and staring out the window, and didn't say much apart from telling Melissa to be a good girl for Jayne. Melissa had left feeling hurt and confused – her mum was supposed to be in that place to get better, so why was she still acting the exact same?

Her second visit was even worse; her mum had burst into tears and a nice doctor called Ciara had to take her away. Melissa had tried her best not to cry, but as soon as she got back to Jayne's, she'd had to spend ages in her bedroom, sobbing quietly, so no one could overhear. But today would be different, she hoped. Easier, because her dad was here.

'Eric is Jayne's new friend,' Melissa told him. 'Look – he gave me this,' she said, producing a rose quartz stone Eric had given her from her pocket, 'and he told me it would help me heal.

And it is helping, Dad, it really is. And you know what else? Eric told me to look for signs from Ella too. Things like white feathers just floating down in front of me, that kind of thing. I thought it sounded a bit mad at first, but now I'm seeing literally dozens of white feathers everywhere I go, so it doesn't seem so mad to me after all. I still miss Ella so much but . . . somehow it's not as bad as it used to be.'

'We'll get there, princess,' her dad said quietly, his jaw tightening a bit. 'Together, we'll get there. There's not a single moment of the day when Ella isn't on my mind, but then I think of you, and I know that I'm a very lucky man.'

Melissa squeezed her dad's hand and looked out the car window, so he wouldn't see her tearing up. Normally they were super strict about visiting times in St Michael's, but because of the anniversary, Dr Ciara said that they could stay as long as they liked. So together, Susan, Frank and Melissa went to a private little memorial service in the tiny hospital meditation room.

Melissa couldn't remember the last time the three of them had been in the same room at the same time. She had to go right back to not long after Ella died, back to the really bad days, the days when her mum and dad didn't even talk to each other except to row when they thought she was asleep in her room. The horrible days when she used to fret herself sick that on top of everything else she had to worry about, now there was the very real worry that her parents might break up.

And yet, as the sun tried its best to shine through the huge windows in the meditation room, somehow things seemed . . . okay. Her mum and dad were being nice to each other, not pretend-y, over-polite nice, but genuinely caring and comforting. Her dad kept asking her mum how she was feeling, was she warm enough, was she tired, would she like something to eat afterwards? And her mum was being kind to him too, for the first time in ages. She kept saying she couldn't believe he was really there and holding his hand. They were only little things, but still. It did Melissa good to see them both at peace with each other.

Apart from the three of them, there was hardly anyone else there, just two other patients. One was a big, busty older lady called Bunny, who hugged Melissa tight and smelt like fags.

'Your mam is going to be fine, love, don't you worry a bit,' she'd said to Melissa, almost smothering her with the hug she was giving. 'She'll be home in no time, good as new, wait and see. She just needs a bit of time out to herself, that's all.'

'I know,' Melissa said quietly.

'So you behave yourself while she's in here,' Bunny cautioned, 'and maybe next time you're coming, you might bring me a pack of Marlboro Lights, would you, love? There's a good girl.'

There was another lady called Emily there too, tall and skinny with purple-y streaks in her hair. She held Melissa's hand and told her that she knew exactly how she felt. Melissa thought she was telling fibs, though. Unless you had a seventeen-year-old sister who died, how could you possibly know how it felt? She knew Emily meant well, though, so she just smiled back at her and said nothing.

'The first year is the worst,' Emily told her, 'but from here on in, it will get easier. Trust me.'

Her mum still wasn't feeling well enough for them to go out afterwards, but that was cool, Melissa thought. It would have felt wrong for the three of them to go for dinner in a fancy restaurant somewhere, like you did after a confirmation or a birthday. It was a fine, sunny spring evening, so instead the three of them strolled outside the hospital around the park grounds that surrounded St Michael's. They found a quiet spot, as Melissa sat on the grass in between her parents, just like she used to when she was little.

And between her mum, her dad and herself, they remembered Ella. Their lovely, precious, complex, feisty Ella, who they had to say goodbye to exactly a year ago to the day.

'The time she hacked all her hair off with scissors, because she wanted to look like Katy Perry . . . do you remember?' her mum blurted, out of nowhere.

'Or that time on her twelfth birthday, how she gave away all her presents to the Oxfam shop in town, because she said she couldn't enjoy nice things when kids in Africa had nothing?'

'Or when Mr Mendoza from across the square started dressing up as a woman, and all the kids were laughing at him, do you remember? How Ella gave out yards to them for being so intolerant, then organised a Primrose Square Pride Day?'

'Not only that,' Susan said with a small smile, 'but she gave Mr Mendoza a bagload of my clothes to wear. I hadn't a clue till I met him in Tesco's one day and he was dressed in my good Karen Millen suit!'

Then silence fell, but it was an easy, peaceful silence. Melissa was looking out at the view over the Dublin Mountains, when she felt her mum's arms slip around her shoulders.

'My baby,' Susan said, squeezing her. 'My amazing little Melissa. You've been through even more than the rest of us, because on top of everything, you were so worried about me. How, my little pet,' she said warmly, 'will I ever begin to make it up to you?'

Then her dad spoke. 'You're the best daughter anyone could ask for, Melissa,' he said, sitting forwards to look her in the eye. 'Do you know that? You make me proud every single day. And from now on, I promise you, things are going to get better for you. Your mum and I have so much making up to do with you and that starts right now.'

'Do you remember that song Ella used to love?' Susan asked. 'It went like this: *On the day that you were born the sun came out to shine . . .*'

Melissa's dad nodded and smiled and joined in the song.

'*But for your Daddy and Mum, you're the sun, moon and the stars too . . .*'

She and her dad were holding hands as they both hummed the tune, Melissa noticed. Which made her feel good. So she smiled along with her parents. Smiled and sometimes laughed, letting the sadness roll in too. And then she thought back to what that woman Emily had told her.

Maybe Emily is right, Melissa thought. *Maybe from here on in, it can only get better.*

Jayne

19 PRIMROSE SQUARE

Jayne pulled on her walking shoes and a warm fleece, and made her way into Primrose Square to her favourite bench. It was in just about the quietest part of the square, far away from all the traffic noise on Pearce Street, a place where the only sound you could hear was birdsong and the happy giggling of a few kids in the playground area, not far from where she sat.

She often came out there, particularly when she needed a bit of 'time out from the world', as Eric would say. Just a snatched half hour here, on this gorgeously sunny bench surrounded by beech trees and magnolia, was always enough to recharge her batteries, so she could cope with the stresses and strains of whatever was going on in her life.

When Tom first got sick and went from bad to worse so shockingly fast, Jayne would often slip quietly over onto the square by herself, to breathe deep, fresh air until she 'regrouped'. Then and only then was she was able to face back into illness and chemo and the whole roundabout of carers who were in and out of the house non-stop, with news that was never, ever good.

Just listen to yourself, Jayne thought with a wry little smile. *Did I really use the word 'regroup'? Did I ever even know such a word existed till Eric Butler first strolled into my life?*

It wasn't Eric who was on her mind just then, though. In fact, Eric was such a support to her, she didn't know how she'd ever managed without him. The two of them had spent the afternoon happily cooking and baking side by side, and Jayne almost burst with pride when Eric told her that the mousse she'd conjured up was 'real restaurant quality. You've got a gift, Jayne, a real gift. I know what I'm talking about too – I started out grafting in restaurant kitchens. You gotta think about writing a cookbook some time in the future.'

She'd beamed delightedly back at him, as he helped her to clean up, marvelling at the deep feeling of peace and happiness she felt when it was just the two of them together, alone.

'We make a good team,' he'd said to her, handing her a mug of tea just the way she liked it, when their work was finally done. And Jayne could only agree. So why was it so hard for her family to be just a bit happy for her? Was she really asking for the sun, earth, moon and stars?

Jason, Irene and the twins had been nothing but vile to Eric from day one, and all she could do was be awed by his patience in the face of such unrelenting rudeness. To date, Eric had met every insult with a smile, and every jibe with nothing but tolerance and understanding.

The latest batch of trouble had started earlier that evening, when without so much as a phone call to warn her, Jason's ice cream van had trundled onto the square and out he hopped with Holly and Molly in tow. With two big sulky faces plastered on them, like this was absolutely the last place either of the twins wanted to be.

'Great news, Ma,' Jason said cheerily, when she opened the front door to the three of them. 'The girls are coming to stay with you for the night. Isn't that a lovely surprise for you, now?'

He never even mentioned Eric's name, which immediately alerted Jayne to the fact that something was up. She said nothing, though, and went to greet her two granddaughters with a big hug for each of them.

'What's your Wi-Fi password, Gran?' Holly asked, barely looking up from her phone. 'The signal is total crap.'

'And is there anything to eat?' said Molly, brushing past her and heading for the kitchen. 'I'm starving.'

'Go on inside, girls, and make yourselves at home,' Jayne called back to them, 'I just need to have a quick word with your dad.'

She stepped outside into the warm evening sunshine, taking care to close the door gently behind her, so she wouldn't be overheard.

'Now, Jason, love,' she said, looking keenly at him. 'I'm thrilled to see the twins, you know that, they're welcome any time. But would you mind telling me what's really going on here, please?'

She stopped herself from adding, 'Could it possibly have something to do with the fact that I have a houseguest here, who you don't really approve of?'

'Nothing's going on.' Jason sniffed, looking anywhere except at her. A sure sign that he had a guilty conscience, Jayne knew of old. 'Me and Irene just fancied a bit of a night out, that's all.'

'A night out?' she said, raising her eyebrows in surprise. Jason and Irene never went out, ever. It was something he was forever moaning about, the fact that he was so cash-strapped; even a Saturday night in his local was beyond him. 'Oh really? Where to?'

'Ehh . . . a show in town.'

'A show?' Jayne said, folding her arms, her suspicions well and truly roused by then. 'Do you mean, as in an actual *play*, love? With actors in it?'

'Ehh . . . yeah,' Jason said, reddening a bit.

'But Jason, love, you hate the theatre,' she reminded him. 'Remember when you and Irene went to New York for your honeymoon and she took you to see *The Cherry Orchard* on Broadway? You said it was nothing, only moany woman looking out windows whinging about Moscow, and that you'd rather stay home and watch paint dry in future. You swore blind you'd never go to a play again as long as you were alive.'

'Ah yeah, well, you know yourself,' Jason said shiftily. 'A freebie is a freebie. Jaysus, is that the time?' he stammered, already half-way down the steps in his haste to get away. 'I better get going. And by the way, I'm assuming it's okay to leave the girls here with you overnight? And that you'll take them to school in the morning? Sure you already have Melissa Hayes staying with you anyway, so it's hardly any extra trouble for you. Melissa is only a neighbour, after all, the twins are your own flesh and blood.'

Jayne didn't have Melissa staying that night, as it happened, but she said nothing. *More's the pity*, she thought ruefully, as Jason hopped up into his ice cream van and drove off with the tinkly music playing. For all that Melissa was three years younger than the twins, she could easily have taught them a thing or two about good manners.

The entire evening had been horrible, long and gruelling and awful, Jayne thought, sitting on her private little park bench and massaging out the knots of tension in her neck.

'There's nothing to do in this shithole,' Molly had moaned. 'There isn't even Sky on the telly, which means I can't watch the Kardashians tonight.'

'You think that's bad?' Holly whinged. 'How am I supposed to post on Intragram with no signal?'

'What are you going to post anyway?' Molly sniped back at her twin, oblivious to the fact that Jayne was just in the kitchen and could overhear every word. 'How mind-numbingly bored off your head you are?'

'Shh! She'll hear you.'

God Almighty, Jayne thought, did the pair of them get away with this kind of behaviour at home? Did Jason and Irene actually tolerate all their rudeness?

'This is all on purpose, you know,' she whispered to Eric, closing the kitchen door for privacy. 'Leaving the twins here is Jason and Irene's not-so-subtle way of driving a wedge between you and me.'

She knew it without being told, but was determined not to let it get to her. After all, she thought ruefully, you can't start imposing discipline on someone else's kids, no matter how much you might want to.

Eric was over at the Aga, stirring the most delicious smelling sauce over a slow heat.

'Hey, come on now, they're your grandchildren.' He smiled softly across the kitchen at her. 'Family is real important to me and I only pray that they'll all come to accept me, in time.'

'Do you know something?' Jayne said warmly. 'You have the patience of a saint, you really do.'

'Oh now, come on,' Eric said, abandoning the pot and coming over to rub her shoulders. 'Don't stress it out; nothing is worth that. Remember that people who get under out skin in this life are really our teachers. We're here to learn from them about coping with life's challenges. In this case, how to be compassionate with teens, who are acting out a little. So let's ask ourselves why they're behaving this way and let's help them work through it with kindness and understanding. Sound good to you?'

'Sounds good.' Jayne smiled, letting his strong, expert fingers massage their way into the knots at her neck and spine, marvelling at how wonderful it was to have a bit of physical contact with another human being, especially after all this time.

Not that there was much else going on physically between herself and Eric; he'd behaved like a perfect gentleman ever since he came to stay. His very first night there could have been so strange, she thought. After all, this was a man she'd never met before, sleeping just down the landing from her. But Eric was just such an easygoing houseguest, he'd made it all seem perfectly normal and natural. He was only delighted when she showed him into the tiny little box room that no one else wanted and claimed he'd had the best night's sleep there he'd had in ages.

'It's that view over the square that makes that room real special,' he'd told her the next morning over a healthy egg-white omelette breakfast. 'Being so close to nature is magical. That's rare in the big cities back home, you know.'

And apart from the odd, lovely, soothing shoulder massage, he'd never as much as attempted to lay a single finger on Jayne. Which was something she was grateful for, in a strange way. It had been so long for her – she hadn't been intimate with poor old Tom since long before he'd first got sick. The thought of actually getting into bed with someone new was still a lot for her to get her head around. Maybe it would happen, she reasoned, and maybe it wouldn't. Time would tell.

In the meantime, though, what she was really enjoying most with Eric was the companionship side of things. The fact that she had someone to share the ins and outs of her day with, and to chat to over dinner in the evenings. That's why she was so glad to have someone as gentle and kind as him in her life.

But could Eric possibly say the same thing about her, she wondered, as she sat on her favourite park bench, particularly in light of how her family was determined to treat the poor man? Tonight being a case in point. It broke her heart to see Eric trying his level best with the twins for the entire evening, and getting absolutely nowhere for his trouble.

'So ladies,' he'd suggested over the dinner they all shared, which he'd spent hours putting together. 'How about you both put away your digital devices while we eat together?'

The twins looked up at him with horrified stares.

'What did you say?' said Holly, disgusted.

'Did I hear you right?' said Molly at exactly the same time.

'I think that's a great idea,' said Jayne, backing Eric up, and thinking that a bit of tough love wouldn't do either of the twins any harm. 'Come on, girls, hand over the phones and let's all have a nice chat instead. Don't you want to get to know Eric a little? He's come all the way over here from Florida, you know.'

'Yeah, but only so he can sponge off you,' Holly muttered under her breath as Molly erupted into fits of giggles. 'At least that's what Mum and Dad say.'

'Do they indeed,' said Jayne thoughtfully, catching Eric's eye. He gave her a half wink and she knew he didn't mind the jibe too much. 'Well, now, isn't that interesting. I wonder how much thought your mum and dad have given to the other side of the argument?'

'There is no other side,' said Holly bossily, looking exactly like Irene as she said it. Same tight, pinched mouth, everything. 'No offence or anything, Eric, you seem perfectly nice and everything. But as Mum says, we have to protect our granny from gold-diggers.'

'Woah, hold your horses,' said Eric calmly. 'That's a pretty big assumption you just made there, young lady.'

'She's right, though, isn't she?' Molly chipped in, backing up her twin as she always did. 'I mean, come *on*. You went online, met my granny, then moved over here to be with her? Who does that? She's a pensioner, for God's sake, and you're an old man!'

'Okay, you know what?' said Jayne, throwing her napkin down and speaking quite sternly, for her. 'That's it. That's quite enough out of the pair of you. Eric is my guest here and I won't tolerate any more rudeness at my kitchen table.'

There was silence as both twins glared hotly over at Eric. Then Holly, always the braver of the two, spoke out.

'We're only saying what everyone else is thinking, Gran.'

At that, Jayne sat forwards at the table, almost grateful that it was all out in the open at last. 'Girls, I'm sure you know the phrase that there are two sides to every story?'

'Yeah,' said Holly, moodily playing with her hair. 'So?'

'Let it go, Jayne,' said Eric kindly from across the table. 'We don't need to get into this right now.'

'The girls need to know the truth,' she said to him. 'As you always say, the truth is powerful.'

'What are you both on about?' said Holly, trying to keep up with the thread of the conversation.

'You're all assuming that Eric only came here to move in on a lonely old widow,' Jayne went on, 'and . . . oh, I can't imagine what else they supposed, Eric . . . that what? That I'd lose all control of my faculties and sign the house over to you? Is that really what they think?'

She and Eric shared a conspiratorial little smile about that.

'As if,' he said.

'So will you tell them, or will I?' she asked him.

'I think it's probably better coming from you,' he twinkled back.

'All right then, girls, listen to this,' said Jayne. 'Suppose I were to tell you that Eric is actually independently wealthy – extremely wealthy, as it happens – in his own right? And that before he set up the Healing House, he owned many valuable properties throughout Florida, including restaurants and hotels? And still does?'

'But you know, I started out sweeping floors in restaurant kitchens, ladies,' Eric explained to the twins as they both gaped back at him. 'And I worked my way up from there. Real estate was my trade for decades. Did kinda well out of it, too, I have to say.'

'He's far too modest,' said Jayne for him. 'But the truth is that Eric's net worth is considerably more than mine, and you know something else? That means absolutely nothing to me at all. We found each other, we're happy and that's all there is to it.'

'It's probably the biggest life lesson that I ever learned,' Eric said, with a little smile in Jayne's direction. 'You may think that money solves problems but it doesn't at all. All it does is bring in a whole heap of new problems. There I was, rich as Croesus, but I wasn't happy.'

'And neither was I,' said Jayne, gazing back at him.

'I was lonely. Real lonely after my wife passed.'

'Sure I was the very same after my Tom died.'

'Then somehow we found each other,' Eric said, reaching out to take Jayne's hand. 'And now it's like the world has gone from black and white to glorious technicolour.'

'Couldn't have put it better myself.' Jayne beamed back at him. 'Now come on, girls, eat up. And we'll have no more rudeness around this table for the rest of the evening, thanks very much. If you can't say something nice, then I strongly suggest you say nothing at all.'

Melissa

DUBLIN AIRPORT

Everyone kept telling Melissa that things would get better after Ella's anniversary, and so far, they were certainly right. Her dad had gone off to Lebanon again and she'd moved back into Jayne's. Thankfully, though, her dad had applied for a transfer back to Dublin, so this time he'd only be gone for a few weeks at the most. And Jayne's horrible twin granddaughters, Holly and Molly, had gone back to their own house, which was one less thing to worry about.

Melissa knew the twins vaguely from school, although they were fourth years and a good bit ahead of her. But even in school everyone said they were a pair of holy terrors, who someone had nicknamed The Bitches of Eastwick.

Melissa moved back into the spare room, relieved that they'd both gone, and even Eric, who never said a bad word about anyone, mentioned that the energy in the house seemed 'so much lighter now'.

Her dad's flight back to Lebanon was early on Saturday morning and Melissa waved him goodbye at the airport, trying her very best not to let him see her cry. Then something *very* weird happened. It turned out that Jayne, who'd insisted on getting out of bed extra early to drive them all there, had a little surprise up her sleeve.

'We're not going home after all.' She'd smiled, as she and Melissa zoomed out of the airport car park. 'I'm taking you somewhere a little bit special today instead.'

Jayne wouldn't say another word, though, no matter how hard Melissa tried to guess what was going on. Then, to her complete astonishment, Jayne pulled up at the National Theatre, right in the city centre.

Melissa glanced out the window, where a bunch of actors were drifting into the building, looking a bit bleary-eyed and all carrying take-out cups of coffee. Just then, though, a familiar face came smiling through the main door of the theatre, rushing over to open the car door with a huge big grin on her face.

'Well, here's my VIP guest for the day!' said Nancy, looking as cool as she always did, in skinny jeans, flats and a chunky warm jumper. 'Come on, Melissa. Lots of people here are dying to meet you; they've heard all about you.'

'Nancy!' said Melissa, looking from her to Jayne and back again, not having a clue what the two of them had cooked up between them. 'What's going on?'

'It's our very first full run-through this morning.' Nancy grinned. 'So Jayne and I thought that, as a little treat, you might like to see the show for yourself, first hand. A bit like your own private viewing, really. A very special showing, for a very special VIP guest. So what do you think? Are you game?'

Melissa was so overwhelmed she could barely bring herself to answer. 'Thank you,' was all she could keep whispering to Jayne and Nancy as she clambered eagerly out of the car. 'I thought this would be such a sad day, with Dad gone and everything, but now it's turned into, like, the best day ever.'

She looked down to see a single white feather floating down onto the pavement. And she smiled.

Nancy

NATIONAL THEATRE

It really was astonishing, Nancy thought, to see your own job, career and colleagues filtered through the prism of someone else's eyes. But given that the cast of *Pride and Prejudice* were about to perform an adaptation of Jane Austen's most beloved novel to an audience of exactly one, no one could possibly have asked for that audience to be as enthusiastic and encouraging as Melissa.

Once Melissa had got over the initial shock and awe of actually being in the National, Nancy took her by the hand and gently guided her upstairs to the backstage area, which impressed the kid no end.

'Wow, you've got an actual rehearsal room!' she squealed, as Nancy led her inside and showed her around the huge, wide open space, with its balcony view that almost seemed to overlook the whole city.

'This is incredible!' she kept saying, over and over again. 'I almost feel like I can see my house from here!'

'Now, be well warned,' Nancy explained, 'what you're about to see is really just a "stagger-through", which means that for the very first time the whole cast will perform the entire show, off-book and hopefully with as few stumbles as possible.'

'What does "off-book" mean?' Melissa asked, wide-eyed as Nancy steered her around the rehearsal room and on through to the green room, where the cast were all clustered around the coffee machine, eagerly looking for a good, strong caffeine hit to kickstart the morning.

'It's when you know all your lines off by heart,' Nancy explained. 'But I'm expecting a lot of hiccups along the way this morning, so it's not the end of the world if any actor dries on us. The main thing is that everyone, myself included, can just pull through it. The fine tuning can come later.'

'Hey, this must be our VIP guest for the day,' said Alan, leaping up out of his seat and abandoning a half-eaten croissant, as he bounded over to say hi. Nancy introduced him to Melissa, who shook his hand with a shy little blush.

'It's great to meet you, Melissa,' he said, with an exaggerated little half-bow, as he wiped crumbs from his face, 'and I'm only hoping that we don't mess up too much during the stagger-through this morning.'

'Mistakes will happen.' Nancy smiled. 'I'm allowing for that.'

'Well, now, isn't that very interesting?' he said with a cheeky grin. 'It's good to know that the assistant director doesn't mind any of us making a pig's ear of the show. I might well end up quoting that back at you before the day is out.'

'I was about to say, mistakes will happen *today*,' Nancy teased right back. 'But just as long as you're word perfect on the big night, that's all that matters.'

Melissa looked way too overwhelmed to join in the chat, though. Instead she just stared up at Alan, almost like she was seeing some kind of a religious vision.

'I *know* you,' she stammered. 'I mean, I know your face really well . . . from telly and movies, I mean . . . You're, like . . . famous. I mean, really famous . . . '

'Well,' Alan said modestly, 'I did do one or two films, but only bit parts, you know how it is.'

'OMG, now I remember!' Melissa squealed excitedly. 'You were in . . . one of the Harry Potter movies, weren't you?'

'All thanks to my red hair, yes, I did have a cough and a spit in one of them.' Alan grinned cheekily. 'You're a fan of Harry Potter, then?'

'Are you kidding me?' Melissa said. 'I've, like . . . read all the books and seen the movies so many times, I almost know them off by heart!'

'Well, in that case, when we get a lunchbreak today, how about I tell you a few tales from behind the scenes?' Alan very kindly offered, and Nancy had to smile at the look on Melissa's little face. The child actually looked like she was about to expire on the spot.

Mbeki came over to say hi too, immediately bonding with Melissa when she admired the pink spangly top the kid was wearing.

'Atomic pink.' Mbeki grinned that gorgeous wide smile of hers. 'My favourite colour ever. I always think there just isn't enough atomic pink in the world.'

Then Mbeki caught Nancy's eye and something very weird happened. Her whole expression seemed to change, and she looked at Nancy almost like she was seeing her for the very first time.

'Maybe you and me can have a little talk after work?' was all she said quietly.

Did I just imagine that, Nancy wondered, *or has something happened?*

'Of course,' she answered immediately, wondering what was up. 'Did you need to have a chat about the production?'

'No,' Mbeki said quietly. 'As a matter of fact, it's not about work at all. It's, well . . . actually, it's personal.'

Suddenly concerned, Nancy was just about to ask her pal if she was okay. Man trouble, maybe? Or maybe Diego was giving Mbeki a tough time and she needed to let off a bit of steam? She didn't get a chance to ask any more, though, because next thing they were interrupted by Lady Catherine, who'd ambled over to say hello, as graciously as the Queen greeting a line-up at a Buckingham Palace tea party.

'Well, now, this must be the famous Melissa I've been hearing so much about.' Lady Catherine beamed, as Melissa gaped up at her, utterly mesmerised. 'It's so wonderful to meet you. And you must forgive us if there are one or two stumbles in performance today. Some of us,' she added, raising her voice pointedly in the direction of Mrs Bennet, who was sitting within earshot, 'decided it would be a wonderful idea to go out on the town last night. The evening before a full run-through – can you imagine anything less professional?'

'I heard that!' Mrs Bennet growled back in a voice that sounded like she'd had about an hour's sleep. 'And I'll have you know I had a grand total of two drinks last night and then went home to bed.'

'You'd sound an awful lot more convincing, dearie,' Lady Catherine retorted, 'if you didn't have a large pack of Solpadeine in her hand, you know. I really think we should consider awarding you some sort of nickname. Solpacheina is what I'd suggest.'

'Oh my God, do those two really hate each other?' Melissa hissed up at Nancy with big saucery eyes, looking utterly horrified.

'Don't you worry a bit,' Nancy told her reassuringly, 'wait till you see the two of them onstage. The fireworks between them are extraordinary. If they can keep it up right through to opening night, I'll be one happy assistant director.'

Then Nancy steered Melissa towards a seat just behind her own desk in the rehearsal room, where the stage management crew were already setting up for the first scene of the play.

'This is just incredible!' Melissa whispered to her. 'I'm so crazy excited.'

'Let's hope you still think that when you've seen the play,' Nancy replied, just as a text message pinged through on her phone.

'So you and our Nancy are neighbours then, I hear?' Alan chatted away to Melissa, pulling on a Regency frock coat, which looked so incongruous with his jeans, it was laughable.

'Oh, she's just the coolest neighbour you could ever ask for,' Melissa answered loyally, as Nancy quickly scanned down through her phone.

'And have you ever heard of this mysterious landlord of hers, this Sam, what's his name?' Alan probed. 'Filthy wealthy with a high-spec townhouse in the centre of town . . . Now I wonder what she could possibly see in him?' he added with a cheeky smile in Nancy's direction.

The text was from him, from Sam, which came as absolutely no surprise to Nancy. But then again, just about ninety per cent of all the messages she was getting on a daily basis seemed to be from him.

Good morning all the way from sunny Shanghai, Nancy. How's your Saturday shaping up? Like you, I'm working today, but it's evening time here and the corporation HQ offices are deserted and I'm the only one here. I need distractions . . . Text me back!

Which, of course, Nancy did. Straightaway, before rehearsals started.

Oh poor you, on your six-figure salary. Tough at the top, is it?

'She's gone dangerously quiet on us,' Alan said teasingly. 'That means she's in the middle of another text marathon with Mr Wonderful.'

'Well, whoever he is, I wish he'd come back to Ireland soon.' Melissa smiled happily. 'We're all *so* dying to meet him. Nancy and I have had great fun playing detectives and trying to guess what he's like, from all the photos of him back at his house.'

'Is that so?' said Alan, looking right at Nancy, as she blushed bright red and clicked send on her text. But Sam's next one came through so fast, their messages must have crossed in mid-air.

I can see the setting sun from my office, Nancy. And I wish, I genuinely wish you were here to see it with me. Then we could maybe have a drink in a great little bar I know – am I tempting you? Then dinner in a restaurant near my hotel, where I happen to know they serve the best dim sum in town. Sound good to you? What do you think? I know you're over there and I'm over here, but hey. You can't blame a man for dreaming, can you?

She read it. Then re-read it to make sure she wasn't seeing things. Then yet another text from him.

On second thoughts, maybe we'll just have to settle for dim sum back in Dublin, when I'm home? What do you say?

She flushed but didn't have time to reply as, just then, Diego Fernandez barged in with a curt 'Hello, good morning,' to the room, before reminding Nancy in his gruff, broken English, 'We start showing of play when you are ready. Please to everyone can you prepare up for Act One, Scene One?'

Immediately, Nancy switched the phone off, as Diego took his place beside her at the director's table with Mbeki to her left and Melissa directly behind, as excited as a little puppy.

There was a brief little kerfuffle as everyone took a moment to settle down, and in the melee, Mbeki took the chance to grab Nancy's attention discreetly.

'Can you and me can grab a drink after work?' she whispered, so only Nancy could hear her.

'Of course,' Nancy hissed back. 'I just hope everything is all right with you, honey? Nothing wrong, I hope?'

'Not with me,' Mbeki said quietly. She looked right at Nancy unflinchingly.

In that moment, Nancy's blood ran cold.

She knows. Someone's told her. There's no doubt about it, she knows.

'What do you mean?' Nancy managed to stammer.

'I think that you've been keeping a secret,' Mbeki said calmly. 'And I think it's time we talked.'

Nancy didn't have time to react or think or even answer, though, because next thing, Diego grunted at her.

'When you are prepared, Nancy,' he said, in that heavy Spanish accent, getting lots of words wrong as per usual, 'you can initiate the performance.'

Nancy froze. *Jesus Christ,* she thought. Was this really happening? Now? Of all times? Just when she was expected to conduct a full run-through of the show for the very first time? And with Melissa there too?

It was like every eye in the room turned her way and she knew she'd have to sink or swim. *Come on,* she willed herself. *You're a pro, so act like one. Put on your work face now and you can collapse later.*

'Okay, everyone,' Nancy said, standing up on wobbly legs and addressing the room, aware of Mbeki's eyes boring into her. 'Welcome to our very first cast stagger-through, and a particularly warm welcome to our very special guest, Miss Melissa Hayes, who's joining us for the day.'

There was a generous ripple of applause and one or two whoops, led by Alan, which made Melissa beam broadly and squirm in her seat at the same time.

'Now we're not expecting perfection here, far from it,' Nancy went on, feeling more and more self-assured the more she spoke. 'All we ask is that you try and get through the show, scene by scene, without referring to your scripts and working to performance level. We'll be timing you, so if you need a line, just call for it. And if things go wrong – which they inevitably will – just bear in mind we have a very distinguished audience of one here,' she added, with a respectful little nod in Melissa's direction, 'so keep going and remember, that's what rehearsals are for. Like I always say, we're here to fail, but let's try our best not to.

'So when you're ready, Act One, Scene One . . . *Action!*'

Susan

ST MICHAEL'S WELLNESS CENTRE

From the journal of Susan Hayes

Oh my darling Ella, my perfect girl. If you only knew how much we missed you. If you knew how much you're missed on Primrose Square too. Before I was admitted here to St Michael's, I bumped into Dr Khan across the road and she described you as 'the life and soul of the square.' And you were, Ella. You really were.

Susan broke off from writing there and instead focused on looking out the bedroom window onto the park below. The spring daffodils were out in force and, with a sudden pang, she realised how much she missed Primrose Square, which was always particularly beautiful at this time of year.

Will I ever get home? she wondered, suddenly homesick for her own lovely house, for Frank and, most of all, for Melissa. *Will they ever let me out of here?*

It had been cold and drizzly earlier, but it had cleared up now and she could have gone outside for a bit of fresh air if she'd wanted to. She could have done a whole load of things if she'd wanted to, but somehow she just couldn't be arsed.

That was the thing about places like St Michael's, she was beginning to learn: they sapped your energy until it felt like quite enough of an effort just to stare out the window and spend the afternoon talking complete shite with Emily. Time passed so slowly here, even just a bare hour felt like a whole day when you'd absolutely nothing to do and no way of filling in the time. Surely there was only so much introspection and navel-gazing anyone could take, before you ended up even more off your head than you were before you were admitted?

Before this, Susan had really only ever been in hospital twice in her whole life. In a maternity hospital, as it happened, where she'd had Ella first and then Melissa five years later. She'd been well looked after and everything, but still. Having a baby didn't really count as being sick, per se, and she'd only been too delighted when she was allowed go home after both deliveries. All she'd really wanted to do was to start her life with each of her precious little bundles, to bond with them, to love them, to watch them grow with Frank at her side.

She was itching to get home again now too, for Melissa. It had almost cracked Susan's heart in two, seeing her with Frank at their little anniversary service. Her youngest, her baby, putting a brave face on things as she always did, seemingly happy just to have her parents together and the three of them in the same room after such a long time. Never moaning, never complaining, just living in hope that all would be well again.

Susan knew Jayne was taking great care of Melissa, but even so. All she really wanted was to be well enough to go home again and to start life anew, with Melissa to look after, to make a fuss of, and to spoil rotten. Her little one deserved a mother, a good mother, the very best mother Susan could possibly be. God knows, the kid deserved it, given everything she'd been through.

On the plus side, though, Susan was doing reasonably well, physically at least. She was one hundred per cent off sedation and was down to just a half a sleeping pill a night. Progress. Not a lot, but still.

'I still feel that you're blocked emotionally,' Dr Ciara had said to her. 'But don't you worry, we'll get there.'

Not only that, but she'd had a call from Jack Evans, their family solicitor, just the previous day.

'Some good news,' he'd said to Susan in that sing-song Cork accent.

'Tell me,' she'd said. 'I could do with some good news.'

'It's about Josh Andrews,' Jack said.

What possible good news could there be about that arsehole? Susan wondered. That he'd been moved down by a truck, maybe?

'His family have decided not to prosecute,' Jack said. 'They're dropping the charges against you, of course on the strict condition that an incident such as what happened at the school some weeks back is never repeated.'

'Oh,' Susan said dully. 'I see.'

'This is pretty big for you,' Jack had tried to impress on her. 'You don't sound exactly overjoyed.'

Overjoyed? Susan said to herself. What did he expect, that she'd start dancing from the rooftops? Yes, it was certainly one less thing to worry about, but as far as she was concerned, no more than that.

Her thoughts were interrupted when Emily, who'd been using the shower in the tiny en suite they shared, burst back into the room, towel-drying her hair and keeping up her usual one-way monologue. So Susan sighed, put her pen down and resigned herself to listening.

'I'm so glad I got to meet your husband the other day,' Emily was saying, as she vigorously lashed about a half a can of mousse into her wet hair. 'He's really lovely, isn't he? You know, the strong, silent, reliable type. Looks good in a uniform too. I've always thought I'd love to end up with a fella like that, except for some reason, I always seem to repel them. Mind you, that's what two bottles of vodka a day will do for you.'

There was a tiny pause and Susan knew she'd be expected to reply.

'Frank's more than that,' Susan said, staring blankly out the window in front of her. 'He's a *good* man. Good father, good husband. Sometimes I take for granted just what a gem he is.'

Only the truth, she thought. Frank was rock solid, reliable and dependable. All the things you looked for in a partner. Of course she was still furious with him for taking a posting abroad at the worst possible time. For letting her deal with Josh Andrews all alone; for single-handedly leaving her to get justice for Ella.

But now that he'd been home again, now that they'd reconnected – maybe bridges could be built. It had felt so right to sit holding hands with him the other day. Maybe there was hope.

It's spring on Primrose Square, she reminded herself. Spring always brought fresh hope.

'Bet he's the kind of fella who'll record your favourite shows on telly for you,' Emily said, 'without you even having to ask. And I bet he puts out bins for you and checks the tyre pressure on your car without you having to nag him the whole time. The perfect man, in other words.'

'And that's it?' Susan asked, shoving her journal away. 'That's your criteria for male perfection? A guy who puts out bins and knows how to use Sky Plus?'

'Given that the last fella I dated ended up in jail for embezzlement,' Emily replied coolly, 'yes, I'll take whatever I can get. And I'm telling you, missus, your Frank seems like a rarity. One of the few good guys left out there, trust me.'

'Well, he's certainly put up with a lot from me, that's for certain,' Susan sighed.

'He's stuck by you, though, hasn't he? That's a great sign. Shows hope for the future. No offence or anything, but most fellas I know would have run screaming by now, after everything your family has been through. Or else run off with the nearest twenty-seven-year-old and blamed it all on a mid-life crisis. But not your Frank. You're very lucky to have a man like that, Susan. You just don't know how lucky. At least, not yet you don't.'

'I suppose you're right,' Susan said in a small voice, as a pang of loneliness hit her. She was always left feeling low when Frank had to go back to Lebanon, but with her in St Michael's now, kept apart from her little Melissa, somehow this separation felt fifty times worse. 'You'll just have to forgive me if I don't feel very lucky right now,' she added wearily.

'Oh, sorry, love,' said Emily, hastily covering her mouth with her hand. 'I didn't mean to cause any offense, I only meant . . . Oh, don't mind me. Come on, let's change the subject. What are you writing in that journal of yours anyway? You're always scribbling away in it. Are you keeping a diary?'

'Sort of,' Susan said. 'Dr Ciara suggested I write down all my memories of Ella, as if I were talking directly to her.'

Absently, she flicked through the pages and pages she'd already written out. So many memories of her perfect child. Yet now . . . somehow she'd run out of 'perfect Ella' stories and she was beginning to remember a whole lot of other stuff that she'd kept buried for the longest time.

The not-so-good memories. The bad days with Ella, the rows, the vicious fights they'd had, particularly during that last, hellish year of her short little life.

Everything that Susan had struggled so hard to actively block out.

Because no matter how hard she battled against it, all the secrets she'd been keeping so tight to her chest were slowly beginning to surface.

Nancy

24 PRIMROSE SQUARE

'Wow, that was just *incredible*,' Melissa said to Nancy, as the two of them strolled back to Primrose Square together much later that afternoon, when the run-through was over. That was to say, Nancy strolled as Melissa almost danced around her, she was so beside herself with excitement.

Nancy didn't answer her, though; she was too wrapped up in a cloud of worry.

Mbeki, she thought, as an anxiety knot tightened in her stomach. *Mbeki knows. I don't know how she found out, but somehow she did.* Mbeki had wanted to meet for a drink after work, but Nancy had to put her off – for the moment, at least.

'I need to get Melissa home safely,' she said quietly to Mbeki after the run-through. 'How about I call you later and we can arrange to meet then?'

Mbeki had nodded, but gave absolutely nothing away. So, for better or for worse, Nancy would just have to wait it out till the two of them got to chat privately.

I have to compartmentalise that particular worry, she told herself sternly. *I have to focus on Melissa now and on making her day a good one. I have to put whatever Mbeki knows or doesn't know right out of my mind.*

Which shouldn't have been too difficult. After all, wasn't that what she'd been doing ever since she got the hell out of London?

'Nancy?' Melissa said, puncturing the silence. 'You've gone so quiet! If I were you, I'd be dancing down the street, like in *La La Land* right now. The show is amazing!'

'It wasn't a bad effort by any means,' Nancy replied, walking with her hands shoved into her coat pockets, lost in her own worries. 'Though there's still a pile of work to be done. A stagger-through like this one, though, is incredibly useful to us'.

'Why do you keep calling it a stagger-through?' Melissa asked, mystified. 'It was so good, you could have charged people to see it.'

'Well, put it this way,' Nancy said, 'it highlights the areas of the show that really need fine-tuning versus the ones that are ticking over very nicely. Which are very few and far between, according to Diego.'

'He did seem a bit grumpy, didn't he?' Melissa said, as they both crossed over the Rosie Hackett bridge on their way home. 'If I was the director, I'd be over the moon. Everyone knew their lines and no one walked into the furniture.'

'Diego lives his life in a perpetual state of grumpiness,' Nancy explained patiently. 'I think in his entire career, the man has only got about one smile on record. And that was for a show that went on to win a shelf-load of Olivier awards, so that'll tell you how high the man's standards are.'

But even though Diego wasn't exactly dancing in the aisles after the run-through, for her own part, she certainly thought the show held up pretty well overall.

'Scenes in the ballroom are bad . . . *baaad*!' Diego had decreed to her afterwards, as she frantically scribbled down page upon page of endless notes. 'I do not believe that these cast people are really, truly living in the nineteenth century. They must *live* it, *feel* it, make me believe these are women who boxed into big hole by society if they are not married by age of twenty. It must be *real* or else is just big pile of *popo de perro.*'

She'd googled it later. It translated as 'dog poo'.

So it was a great distraction for Nancy to have had Melissa there; the child's infectious enthusiasm was like the perfect antidote to Diego's unrelenting criticism.

It's going to be okay, she kept telling herself, over and over again. *It might even be better than okay, it might actually even be good.*

'That guy Alan is fantastic as Mr Wickham, isn't he?' Melissa chatted away, still on an absolute high and talking nineteen to the dozen. 'I mean, he's such a good actor. I still can't believe I actually met someone who was in *Harry Potter*! Wait till I tell them all in school on Monday – no one will believe me! He seems so nice and friendly offstage, but as Mr Wickham he was so sleazy and awful – I wanted to scream at him when he ran off with Lydia.'

'Which is exactly the kind of reaction you're supposed to have,' Nancy said, with a little smile. 'So at least we must be doing something right.'

They continued nattering away the whole walk home, about Darcy and Lizzy's onstage romance and about how vile Lady Catherine and Mrs Bennet could be to each other offstage, while being all sweetness and light to everyone else.

'Mind you,' Nancy said, thinking aloud, 'I think on some level deep down, the pair of them actually do have a sort of irritated fondness for each other. I don't know how else they'd put up with all the sniping and bitching otherwise.'

'You know what I've just decided?' Melissa announced, as they finally reached Pearce Street, and strolled on down towards the square. 'When I leave school, I think I want to be a director too. You really do have the best job in the whole world, Nancy. You get days like today every single day – and you even get paid for it!'

'You might not say that when it's production week.' Nancy smiled. 'And I'm living at the theatre twenty-four/seven with just days to go to opening night, tearing my hair out. Believe me, you won't envy me then.'

'Today was so perfect, though,' Melissa said feelingly. Then, after a pause, she said, 'You want to know something else?'

'What's that?' Nancy said, suddenly aware that her little friend's mood seemed to have shifted a bit.

'Well . . . I thought I'd be all sad and upset about my dad leaving today to go back to Lebanon. And, you know, with my mum still not well enough to come home just yet. But instead, I had one of the happiest days I can remember ever since . . . well, you know what I mean.'

She trailed off there as Nancy squeezed her hand supportively. She knew exactly what Melissa meant, as it happened. She'd bumped into Jayne on the square a few nights ago, and Jayne had taken care to fill her in properly. Nancy was only too glad that she had. It was good for her to know that, just at that particular time, the kid needed that bit more care and attention.

'I know, love,' Nancy said simply. 'Of course, this of all weeks must have been especially tough for you. And I'm so glad you had a good distraction today. The cast all loved having you there, you know, and you're so welcome to come back to see us again. Mind you,' she added lightly, 'Diego might just shove a script in your hand and put you to work next time.'

They walked on in companionable silence. It was a mild spring evening and there were kids still out playing five-a-side soccer in the square, shouting and cheering each other on.

'Ella, that was her name,' Melissa blurted out, after a long, long pause.

'Yes, I know,' Nancy said.

'She would have been eighteen now,' Melissa went on. 'She'd probably have been in college and, knowing Ella, she'd have been out organising all kinds of protests against the Eighth Amendment or Donald Trump . . . oh, that's just what she was like. My dad used to say that you could land Ella in a five-star hotel on a tropical paradise island and she'd still find some cause to protest about. Workers' rights or the way chambermaids work for minimum wage. That's Ella for you. I mean — that *was* Ella.'

'She sounds like a very special person,' Nancy said gently. 'A crusader. A fighter. It's the Ellas of this world who drive great change, you know.'

'Mum misses her so much, it's like something is broken inside her,' Melissa said, sounding so wise and grown-up, it made Nancy love her all the more. 'Except it's not like a broken bone that just needs time to heal, like the time I broke my arm playing hockey years ago. This is hurting my mum so much that it's driven her to a hospital, and now she has to stay there until she's better again. And Dad is away working hard and everything, but I know the real reason why he's away. It's because he just can't be here right now. With all the memories, I mean.'

'And what about you?' Nancy asked as they reached the door of number twenty-four.

There was a tellingly long pause before Melissa could answer.

'I miss Ella too,' she said simply, looking so lost that Nancy wanted to hug her. 'So, so much. I miss the way she'd make me watch *Mean Girls* and *Suits* and listen to Macklemore and Beyonce. I wanted them to play *Run the World* by Beyonce at her funeral, because it was her favourite song ever, but the priest said no. That it wouldn't be respectful.'

'Did he now?'

'You know, when Ella was alive, she used to kill me whenever I tried to borrow any of her clothes?'

'Perfectly normal behavior for any sister.' Nancy nodded.

'Now, though,' Melissa went on, 'sometimes I slip into her room and take one of her tops and wear it, even though most of them hardly even fit me and every single one of them is black. But it's just comforting, if that makes any sense. Like I'm inside Ella's skin.'

She was beginning to speak openly, and somehow Nancy got the sense that this was the first time Melissa had really talked about this to anyone outside of her parents. *What the girl really needs now*, Nancy told herself, *is a listener.* Someone who didn't know Ella, so the kid could tell all her stories, and share all her memories afresh.

'Tell you what,' she suggested, opening up her hall door and beckoning Melissa to follow her inside, 'it's been a long day and you must be starving by now. How about if we order in a takeaway? We could always call Jayne and tell her that you're safely here with me and that you'll stay here for a bite to eat? Does that sound like a plan?'

Melissa's pale, serious little face lit up.

'I'd really love that, Nancy.' She smiled gratefully.

'I just need to send a quick text message first,' Nancy said, peeling off her warm winter coat and steering Melissa towards the living room.

'Of course,' Melissa said, plonking herself down on the leather couch then bouncing up and down on it.

Can't meet you tonight, Mbeki. Am so sorry, but I need to be with Melissa just now. It's important. How's tomorrow for you?

The reply came through fast. Frighteningly, worryingly fast.

The sooner the better.

Susan

ST MICHAEL'S WELLNESS CENTRE

One of the staff nurses barged into Susan's room without knocking, as was the norm in St Michael's. But then, as Emily was quick to point out, they weren't exactly in the Four Seasons and trained medical staff couldn't be expected to act like room service.

'Visitor for you, Mrs Hayes,' this one barked, with a curt little nod in Susan's direction. 'Waiting downstairs in the recreation room.'

'Jesus,' Emily said enviously. 'It's like Grand Central Station here, with all the visitors. Except you'll notice they're always for you, and never, ever for me.'

'Why is that, do you think?' Susan asked, genuinely puzzled as she hauled herself off her bed.

'Simple.' Emily shrugged, staring up at the bedroom ceiling. 'Because I wasn't a very nice person when I was drinking. Everyone that I could drive away, I did. The fact that you've got a steady stream of people from the outside world coming to see you shows that there's hope for you when you get out of here.'

'If there's hope for me, then there's hope for all of us,' Susan said kindly.

'Oh, feck off, would you?' Emily said, swatting her away. 'And if there's any chocolate Hobnobs downstairs, bring me up as many as you can. Stuff them under your jumper, that way no one will see.'

'Do you know, I've absolutely no idea who this could be,' Susan said, dragging a comb through her hair before she went downstairs.

'Does it even matter? The fact is that someone, somewhere took time out on a Saturday afternoon to drive all the way out here to see you. People from your old life have kept faith with you, so like I'm always telling you, you're a very lucky woman. Your tragedy is you just don't know it yet.'

'Jayne, is it really you?' Susan said, as soon as she saw who was waiting for her downstairs in the recreation room. 'What a fabulous surprise! I can't believe you're really here.'

'Hello, lovey,' Jayne said, with a big, warm smile. 'Oh, it does me good to see you. And looking so well too!'

'I can't believe you came all the way out here,' Susan said, giving her a huge hug, overwhelmed with gratitude.

'Sure how could I stay away, pet?' said Jayne, tightly hugging her back. 'I thought you might be able to do with a bit of cheering up, especially today, with Frank gone back to his army duty. Oh and I've another little surprise for you,' she added, handing over a tray covered in a gingham tea towel. 'I baked these for you. Red velvet cupcakes, your favourite.'

'Oh Jayne, thank you,' Susan said feelingly. 'Do you know I sometimes think I'll spend the rest of my life trying to pay you back for everything you've done for me and my family. You've been a rock to me over the past year – I hope you know that. And if I ever seemed rude to you or offhand in any way, it was only because . . . well, because.'

'Go on out of that,' said Jayne, dismissing the compliment with a wave of her hand. 'Sure I'm only doing what any good neighbour would, that's all. I'm so glad to see you; I thought it would be so lovely if you and me could have a little chat, just the two of us. So what do you say to a stroll outside in the garden? I noticed a lovely rhododendron bush on my way in, and I know Eric would love it if I took a little snippet of it home for him.'

It was early evening, but still mild enough to stroll outside as the two women walked through the beautifully kept parkland that surrounded St Michael's. Jayne had a real spring in her step these days, Susan couldn't help but notice. She was looking so much younger, for one thing; she'd had her hair cut into a choppy, blonde, Judi Dench-style pixie crop, and she was dressed in white linen trousers and a floaty linen shirt and jacket. Exactly the kind of thing that Ms Dench had worn in *The Best Exotic Marigold Hotel*. More than that, though, Jayne seemed so much happier in herself than she had been for years – ever since her husband passed away, now that Susan came to think of it.

'You know, I may be cooped up out here in the middle of nowhere,' Susan said to her old friend, putting out little feelers, 'with no mobile signal or Wi-Fi or anything, but still, I do hear things. Bits of gossip and news, you know yourself.'

'Is that right now?' Jayne smiled, correctly guessing where this was going.

'So would I be a million miles out if I asked about this new man of yours?'

'I'm guessing Melissa's told you about Eric, then?' Jayne twinkled back.

'She's very fond of him,' Susan said. 'And you know my Melissa, she's a particularly good judge of character.'

Jayne thought for a moment before she could speak.

'Before Eric came along, you know,' she eventually said, as they strolled past a little herb garden that gave off a delicious smell of fresh basil, 'the only man I'd ever looked twice at in my whole life was Tom. We were so happy together and he was such a wonderful husband for almost forty years.'

'I know,' Susan said, 'and I know how much you missed him.'

'Oh lovey, after he passed away, I never thought I'd meet another man again. Never mind actually go on the internet, on all those strange new websites actually *looking* for one. There'll never be another like Tom, I thought. But then loneliness and missing someone can do funny things to you.'

'You needn't tell me about missing someone,' said Susan quietly. 'I know all about it.'

'Not for two minutes, mind you,' Jayne chatted away, as they came to an empty park bench overlooking the herb garden and sat down side by side, 'did I ever think the whole thing with Eric would actually turn into something like a proper relationship or anything. At most, I thought, Eric will stay for a few days, and if we drive each other crazy, then isn't he well able to hop on the next plane back to Florida again? But, he and I had been getting on so well online beforehand, I sort of had a feeling that this might just have legs, as Melissa is always saying.'

Susan smiled at the mention of her wise little Melissa's name.

'In fact, I have some news for you,' Jayne announced. 'Big news, really.'

'Tell me.' Susan smiled.

'Well, the funny thing is, now that Eric is here and settling in so well,' she went on, 'there's no question of his going back to the States. He's such a lovely companion for me, you see. And things do shift as you get older, you know. I see young ones now and they only want mad, passionate affairs with all the bells and whistles, but as you get older, you find that companionship is more important than anything else, really.'

'I know,' said Susan softly, suddenly missing Frank so much it hurt. Which was ridiculous, really; the life of an army partner meant you quickly got used to your other half being away from home more often than not.

Was I even nice to him while he was here? she wondered. *Was I kind enough? I want so much to be a better mother, but could I be a better wife too?*

'Eric runs a healing house over in Florida, I believe?' Susan said politely.

'Oh yes, and it's a great success too.' Jayne beamed proudly. 'All funded by him too – isn't that very kind and giving of him? Eric has made his few quid in the world, and he always says those with abundance have a sacred duty to help out anyone who is struggling. He's dying to meet you, you know. He says he can give you a lovely healing, if you'd like? The sort that helps us to close one chapter in life and get ready to embrace another. He says to tell you he's here to help you in love and peace.'

Susan glanced fondly across at Jayne, wondering for a split second if this really was the same Jayne she'd known before. The Jayne she knew wore sensible pantsuits like Hilary Clinton, and went to Mass, and seemed to spend most of her day glued to her soaps. So who was this glamorous, active, glowing woman who was talking about love and abundance and the new man in her life?

It's nothing short of inspirational, that's what it is, Susan decided. Proof that life has a funny way of going on, no matter how hard you struggle against it.

'So can I ask you something more personal?' she asked tentatively. 'Girl to girl? Come on, tell me the truth. Have you and Eric . . . ?'

'Sealed the deal, as all the young ones are saying now, I believe?' Jayne replied primly, looking very much like the old Jayne again. 'Oh no, love, nothing like that at all! In fact, if anything, Eric has been a perfect model of a gentleman. Staying in the little box room and everything, and not a word of complaint out of him, even though there isn't room to swing a cat in there.'

'Forgive my nosiness,' Susan added hastily. 'It was none of my business anyway.'

'Oh, that's okay, pet. As Eric says, though, real tantric love can only come from a deep and spiritual knowledge of each other and, right now, we're still very much at that lovely, getting-to-know-you phase.'

Tantric love, Susan thought to herself, suddenly getting a mental picture of Jayne and this Eric guy going at it like Sting and Trudie Styler, and fighting the urge to smile. She said nothing out loud, though, just let the companionable silence that fell between them sit. The sun was setting now over the Dublin Mountains, and it was so beautiful to watch.

'Eric always says,' Jayne began after a long pause, 'that when there's a natural pause in the chat, it's because an angel is passing right over our heads.'

Susan didn't answer, just thought what a lovely image that was. She was looking forward to meeting this Eric guy, who'd made her old friend so happy. Every time she tried to form a mental image of him, she kept seeing either Tim Robbins in *The Shawshank Redemption* or else a besandalled Jesus.

'As you can imagine, though, love,' Jayne said softly, 'I didn't come here to talk about Eric. I came here to talk about someone else entirely.'

Susan looked over at her. 'I thought as much.'

'We want you home,' Jayne said, gently taking her hand. 'Do you think you'll be well enough to come back to us soon?'

Susan sat back and sighed deeply. 'I don't know, is the honest answer,' she said. 'Everyone here keeps telling me to talk and talk and talk, and yet every time I try to, I stumble. So instead, I keep remembering and writing down all the lovely memories I have of Ella . . . I've been so focused on how perfect she was. And yet . . . yet . . . '

'None of us are perfect now, are we?' Jayne prompted. 'Ella was a wonderful girl, but she was human, just like the rest of us, wasn't she?'

'You know, only today,' Susan said, 'I started to relive some of the bad stuff. And you know how bad things got with her, Jayne. Especially towards the end. I like to think of Ella as my perfect little girl . . . but it wasn't always like that, was it?'

'I remember well,' Jayne said quietly. 'And I do know one thing. As Eric always says, three things can never be hidden: the sun, the moon and the truth.'

'The truth . . . ' Susan repeated. Jesus, had she been so blinded by grief that she'd completely blanked out the truth, the whole truth and nothing but? Had she been using denial as a coping mechanism to deal with her loss?

She felt the warmth of Jayne's hand squeezing hers.

'I know how deep your grief is, love,' Jayne said. 'And I know the pain will always be with you because, as Eric says, pain is the price we pay for love. But Melissa loves and needs you. Your beautiful Ella will always be with you, but she'd want you to move on. You're still young, Susan, and you have so much to live for. And it's time now, love. Don't you think it's time?'

Abruptly, Susan stood up.

In that one single moment, she knew exactly what she had to do.

She saw Jayne off, then rushed back into the main house, running, actually running down the corridor to Dr Ciara's private office, she was so anxious to talk.

Thank you, God, Susan thought. Dr Ciara was on night duty and was all alone at the computer at her desk – the perfect time to catch her.

'Susan?' Dr Ciara asked, looking up at her, surprised at the intrusion. 'Are you okay?'

'I'm sorry for barging in,' Susan said breathlessly. 'But the thing is . . . I'd really like to start again. I want to try to tell you the truth. The truth about my family, and the real truth about my Ella . . . I'm ready, Ciara. It's taken me a very long time to get here, but I think I'm finally ready.'

Melissa

24 PRIMROSE SQUARE

'His name was . . . I mean is . . . Josh Andrews,' Melissa said, as Nancy listened intently. The two of them were sitting side by side in the huge big TV room back at Nancy's house on Primrose Square, with a half-eaten pizza on the coffee table in front of them, and an abandoned episode of some reality TV show on that giant-sized plasma screen telly.

Most of the time, Melissa did her very best to keep all her private thoughts and feelings to herself. She missed Ella every single day, but at the same time, she knew it would only have made her mum sad if they were to talk about what happened. Really talk, that is.

But now, though, it actually felt good to open up about it, after keeping everything bottled up all this time. Especially to someone like Nancy, who was a really brilliant listener and who didn't know anyone involved, so it was like telling someone completely neutral, who didn't rush to judge or to point out that there were two sides to everything, like everyone else usually did. Nancy was chill, she'd get it, she of all people would understand.

Nancy just sat there the whole time and listened and asked all the right questions. She treated Melissa like a grown-up, instead of talking down to her and telling her useless things like, 'Now you just be a good girl for your mum and dad. You're all they have left now.'

Melissa's Auntie Betty was always saying that, and Melissa had wanted to scream back at her, 'I'm not a child, so stop treating me like one – I'm almost thirteen!'

'So what's he like then, this Josh Andrews?' Nancy asked, turning down the sound on the TV, just as some *X Factor* contestant was in the middle of bawling at Simon Cowell, 'But you don't understand, this is my *dream*!'

Melissa stayed quiet for a minute, not sure how to answer that one.

'It's funny,' she said, after a thoughtful little pause. 'Half the kids in my school love Josh and look up to him, and the other half say he's just a big eejit with an even bigger head to go with it. They say just because he can play rugby doesn't mean he gets to run the world. I used to think that too,' she added, not that someone like Josh would have cared tuppence what a lowly first year like her would have thought either way.

'So he's a bit of a school star then?' Nancy asked.

'Oh, you should see him!' Melissa said. 'Josh struts around the school like he owns the place, and he always seems to be in the middle of a gang who are messing or else laughing at something he just said. My pal Hayley says that Josh Andrews treats the school corridors like the catwalks at Tom Ford. And before Ella got friendly with him, she used to say that if an empty-headed halfwit like him ever gained political influence, then she'd emigrate on the first one-way ticket out of here.'

'Okay.' Nancy nodded. 'I'm starting to see the type of character we're dealing with here. Entitled. Gifted, but possibly arrogant along with it. And I bet you he's good-looking too.'

'Like he just flew in from Hollywood,' Melissa replied. 'Like Liam Hemsworth in *The Hunger Games*. Half the girls in school fancy him, and Abby Graham, this mean girl in my year, says anyone who doesn't fancy him is definitely gay.'

'Abby Graham sounds horrible and you should stay well away from her.'

'Believe me, I try to,' Melissa said, with a little eye roll. 'Anyway, Josh is in sixth year now, and Ella was in his class.'

'So what you do think of Josh?' Nancy asked gently.

Melissa hugged her knees up to her chest for comfort before she answered. This was harder than she thought it would be. Talking about Josh Andrews was kind of like talking about the Big Bad Wolf.

Then a sudden memory popped into her head.

Ella's funeral. A cold, wet, grey day when the heavens had opened, just as the cortege were leaving the church for the crematorium. The place was packed out and Ella's classmates had formed a sort of guard of honour at the church door, just as the coffin passed by.

Melissa walked in between her mum and dad, clinging onto both of their hands for dear life. She felt numb, overwhelmed and frightened as her mum's icy cold hand trembled in hers. She was trying her best, but couldn't understand that her only sister lay in the wooden box four feet above her head. White and cold and still. Wearing a dress she'd have hated if she were alive, but she wasn't, was she? She was really, actually dead.

But Ella couldn't be dead, Melissa kept telling herself, over and over again. 'Ella dies' just doesn't sound like the kind of thing she'd do. 'Ella goes to a protest at government buildings because of the homeless situation.' That sounds much more like her. 'Ella organises collections to help Syrian refugees.' That's the kind of thing she does. But Ella lying up there in that horrible mahogany coffin covered in flowers? No, no, no! There must be a mistake. Nothing about this felt right.

Just then Josh Andrews, all six foot four of him, stepped out from the crowd milling outside the church and went to help the pallbearers carry her coffin. He was so big and tall and strong, he could easily have helped the undertakers, even just for a little bit of the way. But that was way too much for Melissa's mum, who lost it. Just completely exploded.

'Get your filthy hands away from my daughter!' she cried out in a terrifying voice that was halfway between a wail and a screech.

'Come on, love, not here, not now,' Melissa's dad said, his arm tightly around her mum's waist, almost like he was half holding her back.

'How dare you even show your face here?' her mum kept on shouting and shouting at Josh, not caring that she was making a big scene and that everyone was staring at her in shock. 'After everything you've done? This is your doing and don't you think for one moment I'll ever forget it! Why are you even here anyway? To ease your guilty conscience?'

Melissa remembered looking around her and seeing the deep, white-faced expressions on mourners' faces. They were all so upset about Ella anyway, Melissa thought, and now they're shocked by the way Mum is behaving. Then the priest who'd done the service, Father Sean, stepped forwards and put his hand on Josh's shoulder and gently spoke to him. Melissa was passing right by them and could hear every word.

'Now, son, I know you mean well,' Father Sean had said, 'but sure the lads here don't really need help. Go on back to your friends, there's a good lad. Leave the family be, okay? This is not the time or the place.'

'I was only trying to help,' Josh said, just as Melissa caught his eye.

He's in bits, she thought. He looks just as upset as we do. For a split second, somehow, she blanked out the horrible pain that was cutting her like a knife and, instead, she was left feeling puzzled.

Don't do drugs, her parents were always telling her. Just say no. Never get involved with anyone who's trying to get you to try out some cool new drug, even if everyone else you know is doing it – just come to us instead.

And above all, her mum was always saying, you must have absolutely nothing to do with Josh Andrews or anyone who knows him. If Ella had only stayed away from him, she might still be alive today.

'But I don't understand!' Melissa kept wanting to say, only no one was listening to her. 'Ella was smart and sassy and she never did stupid things. Why did this happen to her?'

But no one, not even her parents, would give her a proper, grown-up answer. 'Melissa's just a child,' everyone kept saying, 'we have to protect her.'

'Ella made a terrible mistake,' her Auntie Betty told her. 'She fell in with that eejit Josh Andrews and that awful gang of his. They were the ones who did this to her and look at the price the poor girl paid! So you have to promise always to be a good girl for your mum and dad. They're broken-hearted and you're all they have now.'

But what on earth had Josh done to make her mum hate him so much? Was he really responsible for what happened to Ella?

I know Mum and Dad are only trying to protect me, Melissa thought sadly, *but don't they realise that I'd much prefer it if they told me the truth?*

DUBLIN AIRPORT

As Nancy and Melissa talked on the sofa, a portly, fifty-something businessman was striding through Arrivals at Dublin Airport's busy Terminal Two. His flight had been delayed on the transfer from Abu Dhabi and he was feeling exhausted, grumpy and jetlagged.

First-class service on long-haul routes, this gentleman thought sniffily, simply wasn't what it used to be. Time was it used to be quite a chic affair, with a welcoming glass of champagne and a soothing, cold towel to cool down with on boarding. The in-flight menu would be the kind of cuisine you'd expect at one of the Michelin-starred restaurants this gentleman so regularly entertained clients in. All on expenses, naturally.

But lately, he had noticed an alarming number of what could only be described as 'the backpacker brigade' disturbing the haven of his first-class cabin and behaving like a bunch of lager louts en route to some kind of stag do. Not only that, but there had been a marked rise in the number of small children travelling in first class too, whose parents seemed to think it the air crew's sole responsibility to babysit for the duration of the nine-hour journey.

He himself had needed to catch up on work during the flight, before the markets in Tokyo closed trading for the day, but how the hell was he supposed to concentrate with toddlers screaming raucously, running up and down the aisles and banging off his seat?

It was an utter disgrace, this particular gentleman thought, collecting his neat, black leather suit bag and matching case from the luggage carousel. When his own children were small, he would never have dreamt of inflicting them on other first-class travellers. No one paying premium prices to sit up front undisturbed deserved to have that inflicted on them. Instead, his own children travelled in economy with their mother, naturally, while he sat up in first, able to focus on his work undistracted.

Mind you, Ingrid had made such a fuss about this during their divorce, and had the cheek to cite this as an example of his so-called meanness. What kind of man, she'd asked, via the plethora of lawyers she'd gone through, travels in first class and lumps his wife and family back into steerage?

But I have to work, had been his response, again, via the medium of a bloody extortionate solicitor, who'd charged thousands for the privilege of writing a letter, when a simple text message between the warring couple would have served perfectly well. You know how demanding my job is, he'd stressed. And you certainly never complained when you were enjoying the lifestyle of a pampered, corporate wife all those years, did you?

But you barely know your own children, had been Ingrid's tart comeback. They're grown adults now and you have virtually no relationship with either of them. Utter nonsense, he thought. Hadn't he paid upfront Junior's college fees? Hadn't he bought him a brand new car for his twenty-first birthday? Hadn't he bailed his son out of just about every entrepreneurial start-up he'd tried and failed at? And now that Charlotte was getting married, she'd doubtless come banging on his door in the full expectation that he'd fork out for the lavish wedding she was planning.

It's not about money, Ingrid had retorted. That's the mistake you've made throughout your whole life and it'll be the rock you perish on when you live out your days alone. Mark my words, that's the road you're headed down and it's a lonely, miserable one if you've no family to share it with.

Delightful, he'd thought then, and continued to think now. Hell hath no fury, etc.

Ingrid. Now that he was back in Ireland, his thoughts filtered back to her. She'd bought herself a mews house in upmarket Foxrock since the divorce, with his money, of course, but apparently she was thriving and happy in her new life without him. At least, that's what his son and daughter had told him the last time he'd seen them, which seemed like almost a year ago now. Since long before this last business trip, which had extended far longer than he'd intended.

'Welcome back to Ireland, sir,' said the friendly Garda at passport control. 'Bet it feels good to be home, doesn't it?'

Did it feel good to be back, this gentleman asked himself, thanking the guard and putting his passport carefully back into his jacket pocket as he made his way out of the arrivals hall and on towards the taxi rank. Would anyone actually be glad now that he was back? Happy to see him, even? *I doubt it very much*, he thought, walking past a few little kids waiting at arrivals with a big banner that read, 'Welcome Home, Dad! We Missed You!'

What must it feel like, he wondered, to come through the arrivals hall and see a huge big banner with your name on it, written by your kids for no other reason than that they loved you and had driven all the way out to the airport to greet you?

How would I possibly know? he shrugged.

Anyway, this brief little Dublin stopover was just a flying visit, nothing more. He wouldn't have time for any of his golfing buddies, and would be hard pressed to squeeze in what was laughably called 'quality time' with either Junior or Charlotte during his brief stay. Junior had long since made it perfectly clear that his loyalties lay with his mother and, on the rare occasions when the two of them did meet up, he more or less ignored his father and spent most of his time glued to his phone.

And Charlotte? All she could chat about these days was her upcoming wedding, and frankly it was starting to give him a headache. Three thousand euros just for bridesmaids' flowers? Did she honestly think that he'd just pay up, shut up and have done with it? If so, she most certainly had another think coming.

He had a busy few days ahead of him, with conference calls from the Dublin offices, and the last thing he needed were family headaches. Then, by the end of the week, he'd be off on another work trip, this time jetting to New York to crack the whip at his US office.

But right now it was late, he was bone-tired, and frankly, all he wanted to do was crawl back to the pied à terre he'd bought before he went away, run a hot bath, then catch up on the day's closing figures with a comforting glass of whiskey before bed.

'Where to?' the taxi driver asked him, obligingly loading up the boot with the luggage.

'City centre, please,' the gentleman answered, climbing into the back seat in the hope that would discourage all conversation. Nothing worse than a chatty Dublin taxi driver when you were exhausted after a trip, and all they wanted to yak on about was the latest results from the Premiership.

'Yeah, but whereabouts in the city centre?' asked the driver. 'I need an address for me sat-nav.'

'Primrose Square,' he answered curtly. 'Number twenty-four Primrose Square, please.'

Nancy

24 PRIMROSE SQUARE

'Would you like to see a photo of Ella?' Melissa asked, and of course Nancy automatically said yes, she'd love to. Because sitting there, on Sam Williams' plush leather sofa, it really felt like a privilege to hear Melissa slowly open up to her.

'I always carry Ella's phone with me everywhere I go,' Melissa said, taking out an iPhone and scrolling down through it till she found just what she was looking for. 'So I can look at all her photos, that's all. I've backed them all up,' she went on, 'and I'll never, ever delete them. This is Ella . . . look! Doesn't she look funny?'

She shoved the phone under Nancy's nose and there, right enough, was a photo of a teenage girl of about sixteen standing at a kitchen table, painting a placard with bright pink paint that said, 'HANDS OFF MY OVARIES!' In the photo, Ella had somehow managed to get most of the paint on herself and it was everywhere: in her hair, on her face, and all over the denim dungarees she was wearing. But she was roaring with laughter, throwing her head back and guffawing right into the camera.

'It's a glorious shot,' Nancy told Melissa, as she looked fondly down at the photo. 'Ella looks so vibrant. I swear, I can almost hear her laughing from here.'

'She was on her way to a rally in town that day,' Melissa explained, 'to repeal the Eighth Amendment. She wanted to take me along with her, but Mum said I wasn't old enough. I hadn't a clue what the Eighth Amendment even meant, but Ella explained it all to me. Ella was so great like that – she never treated me like a child, she never talked down to me. She told me that it was about abortion rights and that it was a woman's right to choose.'

'Ella sounds like such a fighter,' Nancy said, as Melissa smiled in agreement.

'Oh, you've no idea! Look – here she is out on Primrose Square, when she was meant to be studying, but she was really sunbathing instead.'

Another photo was shoved under Nancy's nose, this time of Ella stretched out on the square, all long limbs and shorts, with cropped strawberry blonde hair that looked like she'd taken scissors to it herself, and wearing a black T-shirt that said 'Fuck the Patriarchy'. There was even a copy of *The Female Eunuch* lying on the ground beside her, which made Nancy smile.

'Ella looks so cool,' she said to Melissa, who nodded along. 'She looks like the kind of girl you'd want to be your friend.'

'She really was,' said Melissa sadly. 'I never used to have girlie conversations with Ella, like about hair or clothes or make-up, the way my pal Hayley has with her older sisters. But Ella would talk to me for ages about what was happening in North Korea or else about how women had no rights under the Taliban. She *cared* about things like that so much, she really did.'

'She was politically motivated,' Nancy said. 'I love it.'

'Hanging out with her was my favourite thing ever.' Melissa beamed, looking happy just to be able to talk about her sister and resuscitate happy memories. 'Even sitting in the back of the car with Ella on a long journey always felt like an adventure.'

Nancy noticed her pal glowing a bit, remembering.

'You must miss her so much,' she said, after a brief pause.

At that, Melissa's pale, serious little face screwed up.

'Well, the thing is . . . I miss the *old* Ella,' she eventually said, hugging a cushion close to her. 'I miss that Ella every single day. The big sister who'd scream at the TV every time Donald Trump came on, or who'd lecture me about why Starbucks was all well and good, but that it was a global corporation, so we needed to support small, independent coffee shops to keep them in business. That's the Ella I like to remember whenever I'm a bit sad.'

'Why do you say "the old Ella"?' Nancy asked.

'Because she changed.' Melissa frowned, playing distractedly with a strand of her hair. 'Everyone said so. In the last year of her life, she got . . . different, somehow, if that makes sense. Mum and Dad were both so worried about her. That's around the same time she started, to fall in with Josh Andrews and his gang, so Mum blamed him for what happened. She still does – every single day.'

'If you don't mind my saying,' Nancy began, picking and choosing her words very, very carefully, 'Ella sounds like a very special girl. Conscientious and driven, and just one of life's good people. But the way you describe Josh . . . well, he sounds more the laddish type, doesn't he?'

Melissa nodded quietly and stared into the fireplace, but said nothing.

'So what I'm trying to say is that someone like Ella and Josh Andrews seem like the unlikeliest of friends. Don't they?'

Nancy broke off as a text pinged through from her own phone, which she completely ignored.

'I know,' Melissa said. 'That's what I thought too. I mean, that's what surprised everyone so much.'

'Josh sounds so sporty and rugby-obsessed,' Nancy went on, 'and that doesn't quite fit with the picture I have of Ella as this fearless, brave, warrior princess.'

'It was all because of the school social science club,' Melissa said, hugging the overstuffed cushion even closer to her, and looking so little, Nancy had the strongest maternal urge to keep her there forever.

'Social science?'

'Yeah.' She nodded. 'Ella was auditor of the social science club and she took it really seriously. Just like she took every-thing seriously.'

'And I'm guessing that Josh joined up too, and that's how they became friends in the first place?'

'Well, he was made to do it, apparently. His grades were really low, but you got extra credits if you volunteered to help out with a charity. And at the time, Ella was working on a project to help the homeless. She couldn't believe it when Josh turned up at one of their meetings – they'd next to nothing in common and she didn't know what to do with him in the beginning. But then she changed her mind.'

'Why was that, would you say?'

'Well, back then, Ella was organising this big charity drive where volunteers from her class would spend a night on the streets and get sponsorship money to do it. It was coming up to Christmas and they were hoping to make lots of money for Help the Homeless. I remember Ella saying that at least Josh would be useful there. "He's so physically big and intimidating," she told me, "if any druggies come threatening us, then at least he'll be useful for protection".'

'If you're going to spend a night on the street,' Nancy said wisely, 'then no harm to do it with a strapping six-footer close to hand.'

Annoyingly, her phone pinged again with another text message, which yet again, Nancy ignored.

'Do you need to get that?' Melissa asked her. 'It could be important. It might be work?'

'You're far more important to me than any annoying text messages,' Nancy replied firmly. 'So go on, love. I'm guessing that once Josh got involved with the social science club, he and Ella became buddies?'

'Me and my mum thought maybe he might be her boyfriend in the beginning. Turned out we were both wrong, though. Ella and Josh started spending so much time together that my mum asked her if there was something going on. But Ella just snapped at both of us and told us to mind our own beeswax.'

'I see.' Nancy nodded along.

'Except Ella used ruder words than that. And the f-word too. A lot.'

'Oh-kaaay.'

'Mum used to go bananas whenever Ella used the f-word, but she still did it anyway.'

'I can imagine.'

'But then, out of nowhere . . . '

Melissa broke off there, though, as, infuriatingly, yet another text pinged through on Nancy's phone.

'Right, that's it, I'm turning the bloody thing off,' she said, picking up the phone from where she'd left it on the coffee table between them. Automatically, she went to punch in her password and realised that all the missed texts were from Sam. Again. She was just switching her phone off when she caught a glimpse of one of them.

Hello from Shanghai, where it's the wee small hours of the morning and I can't sleep. Any chance you're awake back in Dublin and fancy a chat? Am feeling jetlagged. Lonely. Plus now that I've got

the idea you and me might meet up for dinner when I'm home, I
can't get it out of my head.

'Him again?' Melissa asked, looking up at Nancy with big round
eyes. 'Sam?'

'Yes, but this time the phone stays off,' she replied. 'Sorry for
all the interruptions – please go on with your story.'

'Gosh, he's a bit keen, isn't he?' Melissa said, just as the front
doorbell rang. For a second, they looked blankly at each other.

'Who could that be?' Nancy asked. 'We didn't order any more
food, did we?'

'No,' said Melissa, getting to her feet. 'Unless it's Jayne, come
to collect me?'

'I hope not,' Nancy said. 'I'm enjoying our chat so much.'

She headed out into the tiny hallway, with Melissa hot on
her heels, but just as she switched on the lights, she heard the
scratchy, metallic sound of someone trying to put a key into the
lock. Then whoever was outside tried twisting the door handle
over and over, but they still couldn't get in. More fumbling about
with the key from the outside, but it was no use. Whoever this
was, their key wouldn't work. Someone with the wrong address,
Nancy wondered?

'Who's there?' she called through the door, fumbling around
the hall table for her own key. 'Who is it?'

No answer, though, and this time whoever was outside began
to push heavily against the door and hammer against it, almost
like they were trying to force it open.

'Whoever this is, it's definitely not Jayne,' Nancy said to
Melissa, starting to get a bit scared now. After all, she reasoned,
who tries to barge their way into your house at 9 p.m. on a
Saturday night?

'Maybe grab my phone from the living room,' she hissed, 'just in case we need to call the cops.'

Obediently, Melissa did as she was told, as whoever was outside started to wallop angrily on the door. Then there was a man's voice, sounding gruff and irritated.

'Whoever is there, can you open up, please?' he said crisply, in well-spoken, middle-class tones.

Nancy took the precaution of putting the chain latch on, before gingerly opening the door half an inch and peering through the darkness onto the gloomy, half-lit street outside.

Standing there was a man, in his late-fifties, at a guess, portly and red-faced, wearing a suit and an overcoat, with a pile of expensive-looking suitcases scattered all around his feet. Meanwhile a taxi in the square was doing a U-turn, as if it had just dropped him off.

'Who are you?' he said, eyeing Nancy up and down distastefully.

'Can I help you?' she asked at exactly the same time.

'What are you doing here?' he demanded crossly.

'Excuse me?' she replied, baffled. 'I might ask you exactly the same thing. Is there a particular address you're looking for? Because I don't think this is it.'

'No,' he contradicted her, checking the brass number plate on the door. 'I definitely have the right house.'

'Then who are you?' she insisted, mystified at his rudeness.

'This is my house,' the stranger said, 'and I'd very much like to know what you're doing in it.'

Susan

ST MICHAEL'S WELLNESS CENTRE

'First of all, thank you all so much for convening here at short notice,' Dr Ciara said, addressing the people seated in a circle in the meditation room. They were all looking from her to Susan and back again, dying to know what this emergency meeting was all about.

'As you know,' she went on, 'we're all here to support each other, and right now, I think that Susan has something she'd like to share with us. Something important.' She gave an encouraging little wave in Susan's direction, as if to say 'The floor yours. Away you go.'

Then there was curious silence and Susan felt all eyes on her. She cleared her throat, took a deep breath and went for it.

'I'm sorry,' she began to say. 'I'm so sorry for yanking you all in here so late in the evening, when I'm sure you all had miles better things to be doing.'

'No problem at all, love,' said Bungalow Bill, folding one chunky, tattooed arm over the other. 'Sure that's what we're here for.'

'And there was shag all on telly tonight anyway,' said Emily, with an encouraging little half-wink in Susan's direction.

'So what is it, pet?' Bunny asked, her big, blowsy, red face looking worried. 'What's the emergency?'

'I've . . . well, the thing is . . . ' Susan began tentatively, formulating her thoughts as she went along, 'I feel I haven't been entirely honest with you. With any of you. Least of all with myself.'

'How do you mean?' Dr Ciara prompted. 'Can you explain that further?'

Susan twitched nervously before she could answer.

'I've sat here for weeks now,' she eventually told the room. 'And I've listened to all of your stories. Sometimes I've laughed with you and sometimes I've cried for you, and you've all been an inspiration. Because every one of us here has a battle on our hands and it's only by being honest with that we can really move on, isn't that right?' she said, looking at Dr Ciara, who nodded in agreement.

'But, you see, I wasn't ready to face the truth,' Susan went on, finding her confidence as she spoke. 'Not until now. It was like a coping mechanism with me – sitting here and telling you all about my perfect daughter who was taken from me. Beautiful, flawless Ella. It's like I couldn't face up to how things really were between Ella and me, so I glossed over everything and made her out to be some kind of saint. She was a wonderful girl, of course she was, but the honest truth is, the last year of her life was sheer hell for her, for me, for her dad and for my little girl, Melissa.'

'You never talked about this before,' Emily said gently.

'Because I was never ready to,' Susan answered. 'Not really. Not before now.'

'This is all good work, Susan,' Dr Ciara said. 'So why don't you tell us what happened during Ella's last year? We're all here for you and we're listening.'

'What happened . . . ' Susan said tentatively, 'was that Ella started to change. To the point where I was worried sick about her. I know every mother worries about her kids, especially daughters, but the thing was that ever since she'd gone into sixth year, I started to notice a difference in her.'

'Changed how?' asked Emily.

'She was always such a robust, outgoing girl,' Susan replied, 'a real force of nature, people used to tell me. But then she started to change physically. Slowly, at first, but then over time, it became something I couldn't ignore. Up till then, Ella had never given a shite what she looked like; she went around in jeans and warm jumpers and always said people could take her as they found her. But that year she underwent a kind of metamorphosis. In the space of a few months, she'd got thin as a pin and had become so moody at home, it was like treading on eggshells being around her.'

'Ah, that's totally normal for teenagers,' said Bunny practically. 'Trust me, love. I've three of them at home and girls are by far the worst. Complete bitches from the age of sixteen till they hit twenty or so. Then it's like you get your daughter back again. I always think it's Mother Nature's way of preparing both of you for them to flee the nest. You're so delighted to get shot of them that you hardly miss them at all.'

Susan nodded politely, but all the time was thinking to herself, *You're wrong. It wasn't like that with Ella at all. It was so, so much more.*

'With Ella it was a different,' she said. 'I tried to help her, I really did. Frank and I reached out to her time and again. We talked to her as often as she'd allow us to, although most of the time, all we got were grunts in return. What was going on with her? We were baffled, both of us. I was watching her like a hawk, so I knew it wasn't an eating disorder. Was it that she was being bullied online, maybe? Frank talked to her teachers in school and pretty much got nowhere, while I limited her screen time, in the hope she'd engage with her family a bit more.'

'You tried to take a mobile phone off a teenager?' said Bunny. 'Jaysus, you're a braver woman than I am.'

'Keep going, Susan,' Ciara said encouragingly. 'You're doing really well.'

'But it was like Ella had completely cut herself off from us,' Susan said, in a weak, watery voice as she forced herself to be truthful. 'And there was worse to come, I'm afraid. Much worse. You see, there was – is – a guy in her year and Ella had fallen in with him and his gang. His name is Josh Andrews and I never liked him; he's a rugby star on the school team and a real jockstrap as far as I was concerned. His friends are every bit as bad; they're an arrogant, entitled bunch of spoilt brats and I knew without being told that they were bad news. Ella was hanging out with him far more than I liked, and it was like the more time she spent with Josh and his cohorts, the worse her behaviour got. It got to the stage where every single conversation with her descended into a blazing shouting match.'

She broke off there, as a memory bubbled to the surface, jagged and unwelcome.

'Where did my daughter go? My beautiful daughter who used to care about global warming and migrant workers and animal rights? Who used to be such a good big sister to Melissa? Why are you behaving like this, Ella? What is wrong with you?'

'Jesus, Mum, can't you give me one minute of peace? You're at me morning, noon and night, and I'm sick of it! Have you any idea what I'm going through?'

'No! Ella, how can I possibly know what you're going through unless you tell me? I'm not a mind reader! Your dad and I are here for you and we're worried sick about you. We want to help, but first you have to tell us what's going on!'

'Tell you what's going on? That's a laugh! All you do is nag at me and take my phone off me and go behind my back to check up on me with my teachers in school. Just back off, Mum, and leave me in peace. You haven't a clue!'

To this day, Susan could still hear the sound of the front door being slammed in her face as Ella thundered off. Then she felt a little pair of arms slip around her waist, as she stood silently in the hallway, trembling with rage.

'Why is Ella so cross all the time?' Melissa asked. 'All she ever does is shout at us. She never used to be like this. She used to be so much nicer.'

'I don't know, pet,' Susan said, hugging her back tightly. 'But you can be sure of this: your dad and I will certainly find out.'

'I still love you, Mum. No matter how mean Ella is, remember you still have me.'

There was a long silence as Susan opened her eyes and realised that everyone in the entire circle was staring at her, waiting on her to finish.

'You mentioned a name,' Ciara prompted softly, 'Josh Andrews. Would you like to tell us what happened between him and Ella?'

'Was he connected with your daughter's death?' Emily asked, looking transfixed.

'The truth,' Dr Ciara said, eyeing Susan.

'Yes.' Susan nodded. 'I'm here and I'm finally ready to tell you all the truth.'

'Good woman,' said Bungalow Bill.

'I want you to remember this moment, Susan,' Dr Ciara said. 'Because this is what we call a breakthrough.'

From the journal of Susan Hayes

My darling Ella,

From here on in, sweetheart, you'll find my memories far more realistic. It hurts me to even write this but, as Jayne said to me, there are three things that cannot be long hidden: the sun, the moon and the truth.

So here goes, Ella. How it actually was for us that nightmarish last year. Do you remember? Could either of us ever forget?

'Bloody Josh Andrews.' That's what you said, my darling, the first time I heard his name. Those exact words. A vivid memory for me, to this day. You were upstairs in your room, and from the kitchen downstairs, all I could hear was the sound of you effing and blinding as you threw half the contents of your wardrobe onto the floor, then tried to figure out what to take with you and what to leave behind.

So I went upstairs to see if I could help, but you were in a foul humour and in no form to be civil.

'He's an arsehole, Mum!' you said. 'A total tool. The charity sleepover tonight is my gig that I organised for the Help the Homeless, everyone knows that. And now I have to put up with that roaring eejit?'

'I know, love . . . ' I tried to soothe you, sitting down on the edge of your bed, just like I used to when you were little and upset over what global warming was doing to the polar bears, or something. This time, however, you were in no mood to be talked off the ledge.

'And now my social science class is letting anyone and everyone in, just because some gobshite Mr Johnson has decreed from on high that they can all score higher grades if they bunk into what they think is a doss subject.'

'I know, Ella, love, you already told me.' About two hundred times since you'd come home that day, I could have added, but didn't. I knew of old that when you were in one of your righteous tempers, the best your dad and I could do was sit, listen and wait patiently for the storm to pass.

Oh darling, I wish I'd known to ask more about him back then. I wish I could have protected you. But I didn't and I couldn't and now I'm paying the price in full.

'But Josh Andrews and his cohorts don't care, Mum!' you insisted, flinging warm jumpers and the thickest pair of socks you could find into your backpack. 'Not like I care. I invested blood, sweat and tears into tonight's sleepover and all that gang care about is getting wasted and how many bottles of WKD they can swig on a night out sleeping rough. We're meant to be raising money and awareness of the homeless, and this lot are acting like they're off to a cocktail party. You should have heard that idiot Josh in school today – he was wondering what to wear tonight, for fuck's sake! His gobshite best friend Marc asked me if there was somewhere we could all go for smashed avocado on toast for breakfast in the morning. Wankers, both of them!'

'Don't let your dad hear you using language like that, love.'

'Come on, Mum! This is a huge deal for me, and Josh and his gang are acting as if we're going to some kind of night on the piss. I bit the face off the lot of them in the school canteen earlier.'

'I can only imagine,' I said with a little smile, picking up some of the discarded clothes that you'd strewn all over the floor.

'And what's more I don't even care. Shower of twat heads.'

'So you said.'

'You should have heard me, Mum. I told Josh and his entourage that some people had lost everything and were now forced *onto the streets in the freezing cold with nothing to sustain them, only blankets and soup from Help the Homeless, and the odd few coppers that passersby might throw at them. You'd have been proud of me, Mum, I went straight for the ringleader. I told Josh to his face that if he took the piss or treated these people with anything less than respect and compassion, that I'd personally set fire to his hair and rip his teeth out.'*

'You didn't, did you?' I asked, wondering if I'd get another call from the school pleading with me to rein you in a bit. I was getting calls from the school about you so often, my darling, I used to wonder if the school secretary had my number on permanent speed dial.

'Course I did,' you said, with a defiant smile and a shake of your head, stuffing a thick woolly jumper into your backpack. 'And what's more, I meant it too. Just watch me, Mum. Josh fecking Andrews better not cross me tonight or I'm not kidding, he'll rue the day.'

I wasn't a bit worried when I dropped you off in town for the charity sleep-out. Not even a bit. There were two teachers supervising the students at all times, and besides, as Frank said, if any rough characters tried it on with you, my darling, then God help them.

As you clambered out of my car with your backpack strapped to you, I saw Josh in front, getting out of his mother's expensive-looking SUV. He turned around and waved at you, but you pretended not to see. I did see, though, and God help me, I even waved back. I may even have smiled at him.

A frighteningly short amount of time later, I certainly wasn't smiling.

Nancy

24 PRIMROSE SQUARE

'But . . . but you can't be Sam Williams,' Nancy kept spluttering, over and over again, as shock began to make her head spin. 'It's not possible. It's not making any sense!'

'I'm only too aware of who I am, madam,' came the clipped response. 'Far more to the point, who are you? And if it's not too personal a question, what exactly are you doing in my house?'

'I don't understand . . . Sam . . . Sam Williams is in Shanghai! He's been texting me for weeks now from the Far East . . . '

'While it's perfectly correct to state that I was in Shanghai,' said the middle-aged imposter standing on Nancy's doorstep, brazen as you like, 'as you can see, clearly I've returned. And if it's not too much to ask, I'd very much like my house to myself, please. Who exactly are you, anyway? Some kind of squatter?'

'Don't be so ridiculous!' Nancy blurted out, coming over all proprietorial about her beautiful, gorgeous home, which she'd put so much of her own stamp onto over the previous few weeks. 'I'm not a squatter – look!' she added, casting wildly around her for proof. 'I bought potpourri . . . and scented candles from L'Occitane! Now is that really the kind of thing a squatter would do?'

Next thing, Melissa burst out from the living room, with the good sense of taking Nancy's mobile with her.

'Just show him all the texts you've been getting, Nancy,' she said bravely, shoving the phone at her. 'Prove to him that Sam Williams really is in Shanghai right now.'

'Yes, fabulous idea!' Nancy said, delighted at least one of them was thinking straight, as she grabbed the phone and fumbled around to scroll up all the incessant messages she'd been getting around the clock from Sam. The *real* Sam.

'Look . . . here's a good one!' she said, pointing her phone at this total stranger on her doorstep, who was looking more and more pissed off by the second. For dramatic effect, she even read the text out loud. '"Hi Nancy, how were rehearsals today? Bloody hot here in Shanghai – almost need a Jacuzzi to cool down!" And may I point out that particular beaut only came through ten minutes ago. So what have you got to say to that, then?'

'You're an intruder in my home, madam,' came the sharp reply, 'and if you're not gone in precisely five minutes, I'm calling the police—'

'You needn't bother,' Nancy interrupted him. 'Because I'm calling them first. Right now.'

'Good!' came the cool reply. 'That's the first sensible thing I've heard you say. Let's see what the police have to say when I tell them that you're trespassing in my home.'

With her phone clamped to her ear, Nancy dialed 999. It was answered almost immediately.

'Hi there,' she said briskly. 'I'm at number twenty-four Primrose Square and I'm afraid I've got an urgent problem. There's a strange man standing on my doorstep claiming that the house I'm renting is actually his. Can you please come around to get rid of him? This is most intimidating.'

'Well?' said the gentleman caller.

'Cops will be here in five minutes,' Nancy said, folding her arms and resolutely not budging. A tense stand-off followed, with no one prepared to move an inch, till Melissa piped up.

'What about all these photos lying around the house?' she asked innocently, picking up one of the many framed pictures that were dotted on the hall table. 'This is the real Sam Williams, mister, and you're definitely not him! You don't look a bit like him at all.'

'Well done, Melissa!' Nancy said, trying to sound as calm and cool as she could, even though her heart was hammering. 'This here,' she added, waving a photo of a windsurfing Sam, 'is my landlord, Sam Williams.' She gave a quick nod to Melissa, who instantly took the hint, rushing around the hall to scoop up even more photographic evidence.

'Now there's no offence intended here,' Nancy said, 'but as you can see from this and many other photos he's left behind, Sam Williams is quite obviously a considerably younger man than you. Who kayaks and windsurfs, for God's sake. And has a master's degree from UCD – that he told me he got roughly about ten years ago, so I'd put him at thirty-one or thirty-two tops. So come on, whoever you are. You're not seriously suggesting that you can pass yourself off as a thirty-two-year-old, are you?'

'You're, like . . . waaaay older,' Melissa said, looking at him, boggle-eyed. 'Like . . . even older than my dad.'

The gentleman caller merely gave the photos a quick, cursory glance and nodded, as if something was slowly beginning to dawn on him. But Nancy was on a roll by then and there was no shutting her up.

'And may I just add,' she added defiantly, slipping a protective arm around Melissa, who'd folded her arms and stuck her chin out in solidarity, 'I rented this house in good faith. And what's more, I can prove it.'

'I don't doubt it, madam,' the stranger replied, wearily rubbing his eyes, as if exhaustion had got the better of him and the fight had gone out of him.

'Via the Homesitter website, if you'd care to verify it. And since then, I've been paying rent weekly into a bank account held by one Sam Williams. I've been here for about . . . five weeks now . . .'

'And I'm a witness to that,' Melissa said, loyally backing her up. 'Because you and me met the day you moved in, Nancy, didn't we?'

'Absolutely.'

Then, with theatrically perfect timing, yet another text pinged through to Nancy's phone.

'Now, look at this! Here's another one!' she said triumphantly, reading it out loud. 'Apparently it's five a.m. in Shanghai and Sam Williams is on his way to do a dawn gym workout before he goes to a breakfast meeting in the Mandarin Oriental – or should I say,' she added, aware that it sounded melodramatic, 'that's where the *real* Sam Williams is right now!'

She waved the phone under the gentleman caller's nose and he looked at it for a moment, then gave a derisive snort when he saw the number, as if he'd just got confirmation of something he'd already begun to suspect.

'Now look here, madam.' He sighed wearily. 'Clearly you're labouring under a gross misapprehension and if you'd just allow me, I think I can put you straight—'

By then, though, Nancy was full of righteous indignation and determined to give this total stranger a good flea in his ear before the cops arrived to turf him off her doorstep.

'So if you think,' she finger-wagged, 'that you can just barge in here on a Saturday night, claim to be someone who you're visibly not, and expect me to believe that this is your home, then you have another think coming.'

'If I could just—' the gentleman caller began to say, but she barrelled right over him.

'So what's it to be?' Nancy asked, with her hand on the door, as she readied herself to slam it in his face. 'Are you going to leave us in peace, or do the police have to deal with you?'

'Neither, as it happens.'

Finally, there was a silence.

'I'm sorry, what did you say?'

'If you'd allow me to speak for one minute,' the stranger said, 'I think I can clear this up pretty quickly.'

They both glared hotly at the gentleman caller, but instead of skulking off, or putting up a fight, or doing anything that they'd been expecting him to do, he just gave a deep, world-weary sigh, took his phone out of his jacket pocket and dialled a number.

'Who are you calling?' Nancy demanded.

'You think the person in the photos who's been texting is your landlord?' the gentleman caller said, holding the phone to his ear as he waited patiently for a reply.

'Of course I do. The point is . . . who are you?'

'Allow me to introduce myself,' he said. 'I'm also called Sam Williams and the person whose photo you're looking at happens to be my son.'

'Your son?' Nancy repeated stupidly.

'What did you just say?' Melissa said at exactly the same time.

'Yes, that's quite correct, my son. Sam Junior, as he's known in the family. I can understand your mistake, but I'm afraid that's what it is. A big mistake.'

'Your son?' Nancy kept saying.

'Correct. My son Sam, who lives here in Dublin and not Shanghai, and whom, at this point in time, is in a not inconsiderable amount of trouble with his father.'

He broke off there, as his phone was answered, then groaned and muttered, 'Oh God, bloody voicemail. Sam? Sam it's your father here. Yes, I'm home. And I'd very much like to know what the hell you've been up to while I was away. Kindly return this phone call as soon as possible, please.'

Susan

From the journal of Susan Hayes

My darling Ella,

You came home, sweetheart, the evening after the infamous Help the Homeless sleep-out, moody, distracted and wired. Do you remember? I'd expected you to be exhausted and starving, so had a lovely dinner waiting for you, with loads of hot water on standby so you could scrub yourself clean. Instead, though, you snapped the face off Melissa and I when we had the temerity to ask you how it had all gone.

'What's wrong with Ella?' Melissa asked me, upset at how rudely you'd barked at the poor kid.

'She's probably just tired, that's all,' I said, giving her a little wink, as you stormed out of the kitchen, slamming every door you possibly could on your way upstairs. 'Wait till you see, though. She'll be back to her old self after a good night's sleep.'

But you weren't, though, were you? Not many parents can put an exact date on when a teenager began breaking bad. But I can. From the day of that infamous sleep-out, my lovely Ella started to fade from view, leaving this rude, waspish, surly young woman in her place, who none of us could say or do the right thing around. To the point that trying to have a normal conversation with you felt like walking through broken glass. All day, all night, around the clock. Exhausting.

I don't think I'll ever forget the first major alarm bell that I really sat up and took notice of. It was barely a week afterwards, on a regular, normal Saturday afternoon, when I'd just come in from ferrying Melissa to and from her drama class she loves so much.

There you were, my love, but instead of having your nose stuck in a book, as you usually did, instead you were in the bathroom in front of the mirror, plastering on eye make-up belonging to me, which you never, ever wore. In fact, you used to give out to me for wearing make-up, on the grounds that a lot of it is tested on animals and that most women look miles better fresh-faced and natural anyway.

'Ella?' I asked you, peering around the bathroom door. 'What are you doing?'

'Just experimenting,' you said, faux-casually, messing around with a mascara wand and putting it on skew-ways.

'Am I seeing things?' I said in total surprise. 'Are you really wearing make-up?'

'Why shouldn't I?' You shrugged. You were just about to close the bathroom door for privacy when you thought the better of it.

'Oh, and by the way, Mum? I'm going out tonight.'

'Oh?' I said. 'Where to?' A movie with some of your pals in town, I figured. Or maybe to a talk somewhere, like in the Writer's Museum you loved going to so much. That was normal for you, that wouldn't have surprised me.

'To a party,' you said coolly. 'In Josh's house.'

But that did surprise me.

I stopped in my tracks, turning slowly around to face you, but you avoided my gaze and just stayed focused on your own reflection in the mirror.

'Josh's house? You mean, like, as in . . . Josh *Josh?*'

'Hmmm,' was all I got in reply.

'Josh, who you said was the greatest moron on the face of the planet? Josh, who you said was a total waste of space? I just want to double-check that this is one and the same person we're talking about here?'

'Yes, Mum, I only know the one Josh. Now just back off and leave me alone, will you?'

'But Ella, love, you said that—'

'Never mind what I said or didn't say,' you snapped. 'Come on, Mum, you're the one who's always preaching to me that I should have an open mind. So just keep an open mind about Josh. Because maybe you're wrong about him. Did it ever cross your mind that it's actually possible for you to be wrong?'

Jayne

'Pay it forwards.' That's what Eric was always saying and it was such a lovely thought, Jayne always felt. 'Wouldn't this world be a far better place,' he said, 'if we all carried out random acts of kindness for absolutely no reason whatsoever, other than it is the right thing to do?'

Quite right too, Jayne thought, letting herself into Susan's house at number eighteen with her spare key. Melissa was with Nancy, so she had plenty of time to spare. Not only that, but Eric had agreed to help her with what she was secretly planning. Ordinarily, Jayne would have felt a bit guilty for just letting herself into a neighbour's house, barring that the place was on fire, but on this very special occasion, she hoped she'd be forgiven.

Susan had mentioned that there was a chance she might be home from St Michael's soon. 'Just to see how I get on,' as she herself put it.

'You'll be just fine,' Jayne had told her gently. 'It's time, love. You know deep down in your heart of hearts that it's time. Because if I've learned one big life lesson, it's this: moving forwards doesn't mean that you love the one you lost any less. It just means that, from now on, you're going to live your life for the two of you.'

For the first time in a long time, Jayne really felt genuine hope for her old friend and neighbour.

'She'll need all the help we can give, though,' she'd said to Eric. 'The poor woman has been in total freefall for the last year, but her new life begins here and now.'

'Okay, then let's help,' Eric said firmly and without a moment's hesitation. 'How about we start by getting her house ready for her? It's been empty for some time now – dontcha think it could use a little spring cleaning?'

'Oh, now there's a wonderful idea!' Jayne had beamed, delighted at his incredibly thoughtful suggestion. 'Sure the place must be like a bomb site. Wouldn't it be a lovely surprise for Susan to come home to it shining and spotless?'

So, in short, that's how she and Eric had spent the entire afternoon. Working together, side by side, chatting companionably, giggling occasionally at silly, shared jokes, and making sure to leave the house exactly as they'd have liked to have found it themselves. Eric did all the heavy lifting, and even a light bit of DIY when he found dripping taps in the upstairs bathroom. Not only that, but then he borrowed Jayne's hedge trimmers and started to attack the overgrown wilderness that Susan's back garden had become, filling one compostable bin bag after another with weeds, working tirelessly for hours and never once complaining.

All this, Jayne thought, fondly looking down on him from an upstairs window, for a woman he'd never even met and for a family he barely knew. How many men, she wondered, would put themselves out for you like that? Not many that she could think of – and, she was very sorry to say, she had to include her own son in that.

Meanwhile, she herself hoovered, scrubbed and polished room after room till the place shone. She threw open the windows to let in fresh air, put clean bed linen on each bed and even made sure to arrange cut flowers in a big vase in the living room. Beautiful, bright orange tiger lilies. She'd chosen them with extra care because, according to Eric, lilies symbolised a mother's love, while the colour orange symbolised feminine strength.

'Hey, you know what this place needs now?' he'd asked, just as the two of them were finishing up, delighted at the transformation they'd brought to the house between them. The place really did look shiny and sparkling.

'What's that, Eric, love?' Jayne asked, packing up a bag she'd taken from her own house with Mr Sheen, Cif, window cleaner and enough bleach to fell a charging rhino. 'Is there something we forgot?'

'No . . . I don't think we forgot a single thing,' he replied, with that slow, lazy smile that Jayne was actually starting to find so deeply sexy, it was all she could focus on. 'But here's a thought: wouldn't it be really neat if your friend Susan came home to some good old comfort food in the freezer? So how about if I take myself into town and stock up for her? Sure as hell would save her a whole heap of trouble when she gets home tomorrow, right?'

'That's a fantastic idea,' Jayne said, and if she was a bit distracted at how muscly Eric's arms looked in the T-shirt he was wearing, she hoped he didn't notice. The *suntan* on him, she kept thinking. Like something out of a travel supplement.

'I'm only raging I didn't think of it myself,' was what she said aloud, though. 'Why don't you take my car, love? You'll be so much faster.'

'You know what?' he twinkled at her. 'I'm real happy just to stroll – it's kinda like a little meditation for me. Besides,' he added mysteriously, 'I gotta little errand to run en route.'

'Oh?' Jayne said, her interest piqued. 'And what errand might that be?'

'Well, you're just gonna have to wait and see, aren't you?' he said mysteriously, tapping his finger to his nose, as if to say, 'Never you mind'.

So Jayne finished up in Susan's, really delighted with how fabulous the place was looking once again. *Just like it used to when Ella was still with us*, she thought, remembering the *old* Susan, the one who was always so house proud, forever making jams and chutneys, and swapping recipes with Jayne whenever they bumped into each other at the front door or out on the square.

But the Susan of old had been in hibernation for some time, Jayne knew, as she locked up the front door and made her way back to her own house. That Susan needed time out to heal, and if not to mend exactly, then at least to try and process what had happened. The universe was asking a lot of poor Susan Hayes, she thought, pausing for a minute to look out over the square, where the cherry blossoms had just begun to bloom. To lose a child on the cusp of adulthood was unthinkable, by any standards. But under circumstances like that? How was any parent supposed to 'get over it', as all the young ones said nowadays?

Of course, Jayne knew the rough ins and outs of what had happened to Ella Hayes, and her heart just cracked in two whenever she thought about it. The waste, the useless waste of a young human life. Thrown away like that, and all for what? Drugs? To 'get high', as young ones said these days? And Ella Hayes, of all people, as everyone said at the time. Such a smart, bright, motivated girl. A bit wild, yes, but still, though – Jayne knew that under it all, there really was a true heart of gold.

Then her thoughts filtered back to that young kid, Josh whatever his name was. The boy who everyone said was really responsible. She thought of Susan and her fixation on him, how she'd stand for hours outside his house, staring, just staring up at his bedroom window in a sort of vigil for her lost little girl.

Of course Jayne had heard all the gossip that circulated around the time that Ella had passed away, concerning that fella Josh and how he may or may not have had something to do with what happened. But Jayne wouldn't countenance it then and certainly had no truck with rumours and idle speculation. Because it was hardly going to change anything for the Hayes family, now was it? No matter who or what was responsible for what happened to Ella, nothing would bring her back and the best Susan could do now was help ease her family onto a 'new chapter of life', as Eric put it.

Love and forgive, that was another thing Eric was always saying. Turn the other cheek. It was a hard call, Jayne knew, but still. It was time to move forwards now and the best thing she herself could do was welcome Susan back home with open arms and help her navigate the way forwards together.

Like good neighbours did.

With Melissa happily spending the evening at Nancy's, Jayne was greatly looking forward to a quiet night in with Eric – just the two of them. Nice cuppa tea, bit of telly and maybe a packet of Jaffa cakes – that was about the height of a Saturday night, as far as she was concerned. But, when Eric got back later on, it seemed he had a little surprise up his sleeve.

'Alrighty,' he said cheekily, bursting into the living room, stooping down low so as not to wallop his head off the door-frame. 'Get your coat on, lovely lady,' he added, with a big grin on his broad, tanned face. 'High time you and I had a date night, don't you think?'

'A what?' Jayne asked, looking at him mystified.

'Sweetie,' he said, gently giving her a hand to get up off her comfy armchair, where she'd just started to catch up on an episode of *Britain's Got Talent*, 'this is what people do, where I come from. Now I've been a guest in your beautiful home for a few weeks, and in all that time, you and me have never once had a single date night out together. So grab your coat, honey, because tonight that all changes.'

Susan

From the journal of Susan Hayes

My beautiful girl,

The signs were all there, my darling, only I refused to believe them. In the weeks and months that followed your newfound friendship with Josh and his gang, you gradually stopped eating. You'd pretend to eat, but I later learned that you'd actually stuff chunks of food into your napkin and throw it out when you thought I wouldn't notice.

Do you remember that Christmas? It was busy and hectic in our house as my own family were home from Canada for the holidays and I barely had time to draw breath. But come the New Year, I really had a chance to have a good, long look at you and, my darling, I didn't like what I saw. Not one bit.

Even your body language changed; gone was my languid girl, who'd lie for hours out on Primrose Square, trying to get a tan with a feminist book propped up against your nose. Instead you grew wiry, edgy and constantly distracted. Living under the same roof as you became intolerable, and my patience snapped when I caught you barking at poor Melissa to feck off and leave you alone, when all the kid wanted was to hang out with you.

She adored you so much, Ella. She looked up to you and wanted to be like you. The hurt in her eyes is something that made me see red, so then, of course, you and I started rowing, constantly. So much so that I was half afraid lovely Jayne next door might call the Guards.

Even Frank noticed. You were always your daddy's girl and in his eyes you could do no wrong. 'She'd be great in the military,' he used to boast about you. 'Providing she never had to use a gun. Could you imagine the lecture the enemy would get about the power of peaceful resistance?'

But when he came home on his next leave-of-absence, even he couldn't reach you. By then, things had deteriorated to the point where family life had become intolerable whenever you were around, and our dinner table a battlefield – on the rare occasions when we could get you to eat, that is. Or rather, when you'd pretend to eat.

'We have to do something,' Frank said, making an immediate appointment with our family GP. I had no choice but to agree with him. Up till then, I'd been in a sort of denial. This is just typical, moody teenage stuff, I tried to tell myself. It's hormones kicking in – it's normal. She'll grow out of it in time.

But you didn't, my darling, did you? Instead things grew worse, like you were stuck in a never-ending vicious circle. We took you to the local medical clinic, but it was a waste of time. Your blood and urine results all came back clear as crystal. Later, I found out exactly how you engineered this, but back then, I was as green as the grass and couldn't comprehend the level of deception you were operating at.

'Ella will be fine,' our GP told us. 'She's just stressed and under pressure with her Leaving Cert looming. Just cut her a bit of slack and she'll be grand.'

So I did, but things weren't fine, far from it. After a time, things started to go missing from the house. Little things at first, knick-knacks that Frank had brought back from his army postings, but over time it got worse. Diamond stud earrings that my mother had given me for my fortieth birthday mysteri- ously went missing, and then a brooch that your dad had given me when I had Melissa. Cash too, small amounts at first, like the odd tenner I'd suddenly miss from my purse, but over time, the amounts became bigger and bigger.

It got to the stage where I had to keep my purse under lock and key at home, in my own home. I asked you straight out about it. I even offered you a kind of amnesty. Just come clean, I told you, and we'll forget about everything that's happened and we'll start afresh. But you did what all addicts do, didn't you? You denied, denied and denied again. Right to my face.

And throughout all this, the one constant in your life was Josh Andrews and his gang. Going back months now, ever since that infamous charity sleep-out.

There's so much I should have done differently. But then, don't we all have twenty-twenty vision in hindsight? I should have listened to other . . . let's just say, 'concerned parents'. Like Marc Casey's mum, who I bumped into at the supermarket, not long after all of this started.

Marc had been a nice, quiet kid in your class, who'd fallen in with Josh and his gang. I wasn't sure of the ins and out of it; all I knew is that at around the same time, his parents had announced they were yanking him out of the school and placing him in a neighbouring all boys school instead.

'A word to the wise,' Marc's mum said, collaring me in the vegetable aisle, in a well-meaning way. 'I'd be super careful of your Ella these days. That gang she's started to hang around with . . . ' She sucked her teeth in and trailed off there, so I had to prompt her for more.

'What do you mean?' I asked, genuinely mystified. Back then, as far as I knew, Josh and his mates were spoilt and entitled, but other than that, the worst accusation I could make against any of them was they were a bunch of over-privileged idiots out for a good time. Not a hanging offence, surely? Besides, I kept telling myself, Ella has so little in common with that gang, she'll see them for what they really are soon enough. I was surprised at this newfound friendship, but it would soon run its course, I was certain. This, I told myself, was one of those challenging times as a parent, when you just had to step back and allow a strong-minded teenager to make her own mistakes, without ever resorting to the 'I told you so's.'

'Oh, come on now,' Marc's mum said, shaking her head at me. 'Surely you've heard all the rumours?'

'Rumours about what?' I asked, puzzled.

'Jesus, Susan, what planet are you on? Josh and his gang are into everything. I've had so many rows with Marc about it over the past year. And it's a waste of time going to the headmistress to complain – she just kept telling us that without proof, she couldn't make accusations. So now, we're just taking Marc out of the school, full stop. Anything to get him away from those horrible kids before things get worse. I've already found para-phernalia at home and, as my husband says, this ends now.'

'Paraphernalia . . . ?'

She looked at me like I was an idiot.

'Oh Susan, how can you be so naïve? I'm talking about drugs. Josh's gang have been shoving God knows what up their noses for years. Marc admitted as much to me, when his dad and I caught him out. It all starts with smoking a bit of weed, but that's noth-ing more than a gateway drug. Things got worse for us – fast.'

'Worse . . . how?'

To this day, I can still remember my shock at what she was saying, followed by a whooshing sensation of the ground sweeping up to meet me, as an annoying automated voice announced that there were 'unexpected items in the bagging area'.

'Ketamine,' she said coolly. 'And MDMA. Angel dust, as all the kids call it. Why do you think Marc wasn't around all summer? Because his dad and I got him checked into a rehab clinic, to get our boy clean again. He's okay now – as far as we know – but we're taking no chances. So we've taken him out of the school, and as far away from Josh Andrews and his cronies as possible.

'And if you take my advice, Susan, you'll do exactly the same with your Ella. Now, for God's sake, before it's too late.'

Jayne

TROCADERO RESTAURANT, DUBLIN

Jayne couldn't actually remember the last time she'd been taken out to dinner. A proper dinner, in the evening time, in a posh, fancy restaurant like the one she and Eric were in now. Of course Jason had taken her out to gastropub lunches with Irene and the kids for birthdays, confirmations and communions, but it was never like this. It had been years, if not decades, since Jayne had got all dressed up in her good suit from M&S and been whisked off to a restaurant like this one. It was the famous Trocadero, right in the centre of town, and Eric had chosen it himself with particular care.

'I hear this place is a Dublin legend.' He smiled across the table at her. 'Only the best will do for my girl.'

'It's absolutely perfect.' Jayne grinned happily.

They ordered: a risotto for Eric and a delicious-sounding cannelloni for herself. Then an easy, natural silence fell.

'An angel must be passing,' Eric said, after a thoughtful pause. 'Although right now, I feel like I'm sitting across the table from a real earth angel. You look beautiful tonight, honey, by the way. You don't get told enough how beautiful you are – inside and out.'

Jayne beamed, utterly unused to being complimented.

'Ahh, would you go on out of that . . . ' She blushed furiously, but Eric wasn't done.

'I see what you did today for Susan,' he went on, 'and I see every day what you do for Melissa. I look at you and think, there goes Jayne, minding everyone all around her, but who's minding her?'

'You do, Eric,' she told him, reaching her hand across the table to take his giant, tanned hand. He gripped hers back, in a warm, affectionate squeeze.

There was so much more she wanted to say, but somehow couldn't bring herself to articulate. She thought of Tom, her lovely, kind-hearted husband, and how much she'd missed him. The huge, gaping void that had been in her life after he died. How her whole world shrank so drastically that days would go by when the only people she'd interact with were her neighbours on Primrose Square

'I'm so happy we met,' she told Eric simply.

'And I am too,' came the warm reply. 'I can't tell you how much I've enjoyed staying with you over the past few weeks and really getting to know you properly. It's been – as we say back home – awesome.'

'We're so lucky that there's only one fly in the ointment for us,' Jayne said, straight out.

'I'm guessing by that you mean your delightful son?'

'Who else?' she said wryly.

'Jason seems . . . all blocked up to me,' Eric said, after a pause.

'Do you mean constipated?'

'No, honey.' He smiled. 'I mean emotionally. The thing is, I love spending time with you, Jayne. You've been everything I hoped for and more. I was so lonely after Clare died and it's like you filled that gap for me. I thought I'd never smile again, or laugh again. Then I come to Ireland and *whoomph* – there you were.'

Then he closed his eyes, the way he did whenever he was thinking deeply, so Jayne pretended to be glancing down through the menu, all the while thinking, *Don't leave. Don't let my son and his family come between the little bit of happiness we've managed to forge for ourselves here.*

'Here's a thought,' Eric eventually said, sitting back against the plush red velvet banquette and running his fingers through his long, silvery hair. 'Maybe there's something I can do to help. So . . .'

'So?'

'So if it's not too cheeky of me, Jayne, can I ask you to just trust me?'

Nancy

24 PRIMROSE SQUARE (FOR NOW, AT LEAST)

Nancy woke up after approximately fifteen minutes' sleep, to the living nightmare she now found herself in. Just the previous night, the police had arrived and Sam Williams Senior had told them in no uncertain terms that he had categorically never rented out his house on any website of any description, that Nancy had no right to be there, and that as far as he was concerned, she could pack her bags and be gone by the end of the day.

'This is my home,' he'd told the cops crisply and clearly. 'I have absolutely no idea what my son has been up to in my absence, but I can assure you, madam, you're only here by fraudulent means.'

'Excuse me!' Nancy interrupted hotly, petrified at the thought of being turfed out. The house, her house, that she'd come to love so much and had started to feel so proprietorial over. The house had been like a sanctuary to her, after everything she'd run away from in London. Her neighbours around Primrose Square had come to mean so much to her. Who did this total stranger think he was anyway, telling her to clear off and vacate the property ASAP?

'I rented here in good faith,' she said curtly. 'All I knew is that my landlord was called Sam Williams – how was I supposed to know that this was some messer pretending to be you? You can't just barge in here and tell me to leave – I have rights too, you know.'

'And look how clean and tidy she's kept the place for you,' Melissa had said, stoutly defending her friend. 'If you ask me, mister, you should be thanking her, not giving out to her like this.'

'So where's your contract?' said this particularly unpleasant incarnation of Sam Williams. 'Where's your lease agreement? With my signature on it? That I would very much like to see, please. I'm quite sure my legal representatives would be interested to see that document too.'

That shut both Melissa and Nancy up.

'Hey, come on now, take it easy, all right?' said the Garda who'd been called to the scene, as he tried to referee between the warring parties. Though it was hard to take the guy seriously, given that he looked not much older than Melissa. 'Now you both say you've a claim to this house,' he went on, scribbling away in a notebook, 'yet neither of you have any proof of occupancy?'

'Well, what do you expect?' Sam Williams went on. 'I hardly travel around the place with the deeds to all my properties on my person, now do I?'

'As for me,' Nancy began to explain to the Garda, 'I rented this place fair and square via the Homesitter website . . . '

But Sam Williams was in absolutely no mood to listen.

'Now look here,' he sighed wearily, addressing the Garda. 'It seems we're going round and round in circles and we're getting absolutely nowhere. I've been travelling for eighteen hours, non-stop. I'm tired, jetlagged and badly in need of a good night's sleep.'

'Yeah,' said the Garda nervously, 'but I still have to report this, don't I?'

'Never mind your report,' Sam Williams said authoritatively. 'So here's what I propose. I'll make one concession to this total stranger in my house and one only. For tonight, I'll check into a hotel and hopefully get a good night's rest there. Then tomorrow, I'll be in touch with Sam Junior to sort this unholy mess out once and for all. In the meantime,' he added, swivelling back to Nancy, 'you can consider this your official notice to quit. And I can promise you, madam, you'll be hearing from my solicitors.'

Nancy tossed restlessly around in Sam Williams' huge double bed and remembered a Shakespeare play she'd worked on at the Globe years ago. *When sorrows come, they come not single spies, but in battalions.* She'd already been sick to her stomach worrying about Mbeki and whatever she knew or didn't know. And now on top of everything – this.

Serves me right, she thought. *That's what I get for thinking I could have a happy ending. Did I really think that I could just leave the past behind me, up sticks to Dublin and live happily ever after in a beautiful home? Didn't I know that one day it would all blow up in my face?*

Melissa, brave little soul that she was, had been fabulous the previous night – she'd even asked if she could stay over, 'to keep you safe, Nancy. In case that horrible man comes back to threaten you.' Turned out Jayne was out on what sounded like a date night, so of course Nancy was delighted to have her little pal sleep over in Sam Williams' luxurious spare room. Which only meant, of course, that it would be much later that morning at the earliest before she finally got to sit down with Mbeki.

Oh God, she thought, her stomach twisting at the conversation that lay ahead. If her worst fears were confirmed and if Mbeki had heard what the whole of London seemed to be chattering about . . .

Her thoughts were interrupted by a text pinging through on her phone.

Him. Sam.

Not that Sam, she thought, reaching out for her phone, not the actual owner of the house. The other one, the son. Or the 'gobshite', as they said in Dublin, who'd been stringing her along for weeks now.

> Hi Nancy, so how was your Saturday night? Sadly for me, I had to attend the most boring work dinner known to man with business clients over from Frankfurt.

Then, as if to hammer the point home, came a load of sleepy face emojis.

> But it's not all bad, because at least dinner was a) held in one of Shanghai's Michelin-starred restaurants and b) entirely on expenses. Ever eaten dog liver or chicken feet? Quite the delicacy in this neck of the woods. Believe me, Nancy, you haven't lived till you've tried.

Then another text, hot on its heels. This one the length of a short story.

> The one upshot is that at least I get to swim in the South China Sea in the evenings and really marvel at the view. Wish you were here to see it too – it's breathtaking. Beach, azure blue sea and

a skyline to rival Manhattan's overlooking it all. So here's a late-night thought for you, Nancy. If you fancy dinner in Dublin when I'm home, we've got to do a walk on the beach afterwards – that's my condition!

And yet another one – sent just moments later.

Seriously, when I do get back, there's so much about my home city I want to show you and tell you about and introduce you to. You haven't lived till I've taken you for a pint of Guinness in the Storehouse, or till you've done a lap of Stephen's Green in a horse-drawn carriage, with a snipe of champagne to mark the moment. So what do you say, Nancy? You in? Can I be your Dublin tour guide?

At that, Nancy was suddenly boiling with fury, fingers hovering over the phone, poised to ping off some cutting, smart-alecky reply, to let this psycho know that his sick little game was up. But then she paused, wondering what would she say to him anyway? *Your dad turned up on my doorstep last night and if you bothered to check your voicemail, you'd realise that the shit has well and truly hit the fan?*

So instead she resisted, put the phone back on the bedside table and tried to compose herself.

After all, she reminded herself, she'd worked on a lot of Jacobean dramas in the past and if there was one thing she'd learned, it was this:

Revenge was a dish that people of taste preferred to eat cold.

From the journal of Susan Hayes

My dearest daughter,

If you were still here this might make you laugh, or roll your eyes at me at least.

To think that it all came about because of a block in the U-bend in the upstairs bathroom. Did you ever hear of anything so mundane, my darling? But that's the truth, pure and simple.

The loo in the family bathroom had been blocked for days and we were all at our wit's end. I moved heaven and earth trying to get a plumber, and in the end I could only find a guy covered in tattoos called Martin who charged me the earth just to 'take a look, love, not promising you nothing, mind'.

Anyway, Martin told me in no uncertain terms that the only time he was free was in exactly one hour's time – 4 p.m. one particular Thursday afternoon. Useless my protesting to him that I was stuck in work at the bank at the time; that, as far as Martin was concerned, was his final offer and I could take it or leave it.

So I took it. I left work early and came home, unexpectedly early. I thought you'd still be at school; you usually were at that time. Melissa, I knew, was getting a lift home from her pal Hayley's mother after her drama class, so I fully expected to come home to an empty house.

But I didn't, did I? Instead I opened the front door and Melissa came running out of the kitchen to meet me.

'Mum! Thank God you're home, I was so worried,' she said, the ghostly white face looking up at me.

'Why, sweetheart?' I asked, hugging her. 'What happened? Why are you home so early?'

'Drama got cancelled today,' she said. 'Because our teacher is off sick. So I came home and . . . oh Mum, I don't know what's going on with Ella, but whatever it is, it's really weird.'

'Darling,' I said, gripping her thin shoulders, 'tell me. I'm here now and I'll fix everything, okay? Just tell me what's going on.'

'I'm worried about Ella,' she said, in that quiet way she has when I know the poor pet is out of her mind with stress.

'What about Ella?' I said, thinking that if you'd upset Melissa in any way, then I really would kill you.

'I don't know, Mum. All I know is that she's upstairs in her room now with Josh Andrews.'

'With Josh?'

Before hearing another word, I felt my stomach start to shrivel.

'And when I knocked on her door, she told me to go away,' Melissa said.

'Did she now?'

'Except she didn't say go away, Mum, she said the f-word. And there's something else.'

'What's that, pet?'

I was already halfway upstairs to your room by then. But I stopped dead in my tracks and turned to face Melissa, who was still standing in the hall, her little white hand on the bannister rail.

'They're smoking something really funny, Mum. And it stinks too.'

I took a deep inhale and thought . . . bloody hell. Herbal cigarettes? Weed? Marijuana? Whatever it was, I started *taking the stairs two at a time till I got to your bedroom door and hammered on it.*

'They're both acting really weird too, Mum,' Melissa called up after me. 'All stupid and giggly and . . . like a pair of eejits, really.'

I didn't even wait for you to say 'come in'. Instead, I opened the bedroom door to find you and Josh sitting side by side on the floor, smoking what I later came to wish was hash. But it wasn't, though, was it, my darling?

It's hard to put into words the deep, visceral anger I felt. I remember roaring, shouting, yelling at Josh to get out of my house and warning him never to cross my doorstep again.

'Please stop overreacting, Mum,' you yelled right back, terrifying me with that glassy look in your eyes, you were so completely out of it. 'It's just a bit of PCP, that's all. It's harmless, really.'

'Harmless? Did you just say harmless?'

'Please, Mum!' you said, 'you're embarrassing me in front of Josh.'

'It's okay, Mrs H,' a woozy, stoned Josh tried to explain, getting up from where he'd been sitting cross-legged on the floor and towering over me. 'I promise you, PCP is totally safe – and virtually non-addictive.'

Course I threw Josh out of the house without a second thought and the row you and I had was legendary. PCP? I'd never heard of it. But I bloody well took care to find out exactly what it was. A gateway drug, Google told me. More commonly known as 'angel dust'. A hallucinogen that almost had the effect of an anesthetic. The very thing that Marc's mother had warned me about.

Jesus Christ, I thought. No, not this, not you, my darling.

'Everyone is doing it,' you tried to defend yourself. 'Josh got a hold of some and . . .'

'Josh this, Josh that,' I snapped back at you. 'You never used to be like this, Ella, until you started hanging around with that bloody user! Do you give me your word that you'll never do anything as stupid as that again? Your solemn word?'

'Never again, Mum,' you said.

'You're seventeen years old,' I told you. 'You're almost an adult, so I have to trust you. Do you understand?'

'You can trust me, Mum,' you said. 'And it'll never happen again.'

So I did trust you.

But you lied to me.

And now I can never forgive myself.

Nancy

AVOCA RESTAURANT, DUBLIN

'So,' Mbeki said, sitting across the table from Nancy and looking over at her, genuinely concerned.

'So,' Nancy replied flatly, shoving away a half-eaten bowl of rolled porridge oats and honey that she couldn't face. She and Mbeki had arranged to meet for Sunday brunch, but after the conversation they'd just had, her appetite had wilted like a dead lettuce leaf.

'Thank you for being so honest with me,' Mbeki said. She had hardly touched her food either. She was normally the healthiest eater going; she was forever the one in the rehearsal room who brought in her own lunches of avocado and tofu, snacking on nuts and seeds while everyone else horsed into packets of cheese and onion crisps. Yet now she was just playing with the egg white omelette she'd ordered.

She's worried, Nancy thought. *In her shoes, I'd be worried too.*

'You've been more than kind,' Nancy said, really meaning it too. Mbeki was cool, she was sound, Nancy liked her – she'd even hoped they might remain pals after the final curtain came down. 'And I appreciate you reaching out to me like this.'

Mbeki sighed and sat back, tugging at the sleeve of the electric blue fleece jumper she was snuggled into. On anyone else, Nancy thought distractedly, that jumper would look ridiculous; only Mbeki could carry it off.

'It's horrible, Nancy,' she eventually said. 'What I'm hearing is vile. Unthinkable. The question is, what are you going to do?'

Nancy ran her hand across her temples, which by then were pounding.

'I don't know,' she said honestly. 'I thought coming here to Dublin, getting away from London and from everything that happened there . . . '

'You were running away,' Mbeki said. 'But that's not going to fix this, now is it?'

Nancy shook her head. No, of course not. How could it possibly? All she'd wanted to do was work, do the best work she could possibly do, and put it all behind her.

And now this.

'Look,' Mbeki said, shoving away the green tea she'd been sipping at and locking eyes with Nancy. 'I like you. I respect you. And I just happened to hear about it from a pal who was over visiting from London. But you can't contain this for very much longer. Now you're a smart woman, you know that.'

'I hear you,' Nancy said quietly, remembering London and everything that had gone down there. In a flash, all the frustration and despair she'd felt came back to her. Pain and white hot anger. A lousy combination.

'Of course, it's your story to tell, and not mine,' Mbeki said. 'But if you take my advice, you'll stop running away and tackle this head on.'

'But . . . please, Mbeki . . . ' Nancy tried to say, but she stumbled over her words. 'I just need time. We're so close to opening night and I need to think clearly.'

'Don't worry,' Mbeki said calmly, 'your secret is safe with me. For now at least. But you're going to have to come clean, Nancy. You can't keep running for very much longer.'

Susan

From the journal of Susan Hayes

Dearest Ella,

I'll never forget it, my darling. It was a sunny Friday afternoon and I had come to a decision. It was weeks after I'd caught you smoking with Josh and you could have cut the tension between you and me with a knife. You swore blind to me that you hadn't touched any drugs since that awful day, but still – I was watching you like a hawk, still suspicious as hell. Which of course meant you and I only argued all the more.

'I'm sick of all the constant rows,' I said to your dad, who was home on leave at the time, as good luck would have it. 'It's wearing me down and I've had enough of being bad cop. So just for tonight,' I told him, 'as far as Ella is concerned, I'll try being good cop. Let's see how far that gets me.'

I had another motivation for this sudden about-turn, though. There was a big party on that night and you'd been at me for weeks to go but, of course, I'd been saying no to you all along.

'You're meant to be studying for your Leaving Cert!' I'd been hammering home to you for days. 'And instead you're upstairs in your room on the phone to your new best friend Josh and messing about on Facebook and Twitter and Instagram – and now you want to skive off to go to a party? Ella, when are you going to start taking responsibility for your own future?'

'It's my life!' you yelled back at me at our kitchen table. 'So I'll do as I like. And you know the first thing I'll be doing as soon as I leave school? Getting as far away from you and your

constant nagging as possible . . . I fucking hate you, do you hear me? Get off my back and just leave me alone!'

I think those words broke my heart, my darling. All I ever wanted was what was best for you, and it stabbed at me to see you, day in and day out, growing ever thinner and moodier, and distancing yourself from your family more and more.

Well, this ends here, I thought, that sunny Friday afternoon, as I walked back home to Primrose Square after work. I'd change tack, I told myself. Show you that I did trust you to behave like a responsible adult, even though I was far from convinced of it myself.

What you didn't realise, though, was this: I'd had help to come to this decision. I'd taken advice. Worried out of my mind, I'd arranged to see one of the staff at Narcotics Anonymous earlier that same day. I'd even been to one of their meetings, held above a coffee shop on Gardiner Street, not far from where I worked.

There I met with a lovely woman in her late twenties called Lucy, who, she openly told me, had been through hell and back with her own addiction. But Lucy wasn't the type, I remember thinking. She seemed middle-class, well-spoken and obviously well-educated too. How could someone like her have ended up on drugs? She looked more like the airhostess type, rather than a hardcore user. Then came the more frightening, tacked-on thought. If it could happen to someone like Lucy, it could happen to you too, my darling. All too easily.

'I've got no rock-solid proof that my daughter is still using,' I told Lucy, pouring out my heart over a lukewarm, watery cup of coffee, dizzy with the relief of finally talking to someone who'd actually get it.

'Parents of users seldom do,' Lucy said, with a wry smile.

'But I'm as close to being sure as I can be,' I went on. 'It's the crowd that Ella has taken to hanging around with, you see,' I added defensively. 'Before my daughter fell in with this gang, she'd have been the last person alive to get involved with drugs. She never even drank, for God's sake. But I know for a fact that the crowd she's in with are all users. I caught Ella in the act once, and she swore to me she'd never do it again.

'But I know she's lying to me, the way a mother just knows. We're rowing constantly and it's slowly tearing my family apart. So I'm here in desperation, really, and my question is: what should I do?'

'In my experience,' Lucy said, shaking her pretty head of blonde hair, 'drug use is rarely because of the crowd you happen to be hanging around with. People don't fall into drugs just because all their friends are doing it. They start doing drugs for one reason and for one reason only. Because they want to.'

I had to pause and really give thought to that one. Lucy, however, was completely practical and gave me great advice. Or certainly what I thought at the time was great advice.

'Look,' she said, 'I've been there, done that, got the T-shirt. I fought with my parents bitterly too, till in the end I ran as far away from them as I could. I ended up in a squat in London, begging during the day, to scrounge together enough to go out and score that night. I've got myself clean now, but it took every gram of strength I have to get me out of the vicious circle.'

'Ella is clean at the moment,' I told her.

'How can you be so sure?' Lucy asked.

'Because her dad and I took her to our family GP, who ran all sorts of urine tests on her. Everything came back clear as crystal.'

It had been a huge relief at the time – one less thing Frank and I had to worry about.

'Oh please!' Lucy snorted into her coffee. 'And you seriously believe that? You do know that's the first trick any self-respecting user will learn? How to fake a test.'

'What did you say?' I asked, slowly beginning to grow frightened.

'Susan, a committed drug user quickly learns how to pass someone else's blood and urine samples off as their own. There's quite a roaring trade online in clean samples. You'd be amazed.'

'So . . . what should I do?' I asked, in a very small voice, kicking myself for being so bloody stupid. So willing to believe what I wanted to.

'Show your Ella that you trust her,' Lucy said out straight. 'Believe me, if you start treating her like an adult, she'll respond accordingly. You say you row all the time? So let that end here and now. Cut her some slack and let her start taking a bit of responsibility for her own actions. The constant fights with my own family drove me away and, from then on, it was a downward spiral till I almost drove myself to an early grave. So don't repeat my family's mistakes, Susan, do you hear me? Because remember – you don't have to.'

You were sitting out on the square when I got back, pretending to study, as you so often did, but really on your phone to Josh Andrews, who you seemed so inseparable from back then.

'Oh hold on,' you said, putting down the phone as you saw me approach. 'Here comes trouble.'

But I was determined to do as Lucy advised, so I stuck to my guns.

'I come in peace,' I said, holding up my hands in mock surrender. 'Just to say that I've thought about it, and I've decided *that you can go to your party tonight. So go, Ella. Get all dressed up. Enjoy yourself. Have fun. You're old enough and I can trust you and I only hope in return you'll trust me?'*

You looked at me, scanning my face up and down, waiting for the catch. But there was none.

'Go back to your phone call,' I said. 'And tell Josh he's very welcome to call to the house beforehand to collect you. It would be nice for your dad and I to get to know him properly. Think about it, honey, and I'll see you back at the house, okay?'

You went back to your phone as I walked away, but I heard what you said, heard you loud and clear.

'Jesus,' you said. 'Did you hear that? Has to be early onset menopause. There's no other reason for the mothership's mood swings.'

That stung like merry hell, but I didn't let it show. I even bit my tongue when you came downstairs, ready to go out, dressed like an over-made-up scanger, in too-big jeans and a bra top that the Ella of old would have set fire to and laughed at while it burned.

'Now your dad will be outside the party to pick you up at midnight,' I told you. 'That's the deal, all right?'

You looked right through me, trying to figure out this about-turn in my attitude towards you.

'Ella, love, do we have a deal?'

'Whatever,' you said with a dismissive shrug, as you turned on your heels and went out the door.

I let you go, thinking, from here on in, I'd turn over a new leaf with you. I'd have a lovely, healthy breakfast waiting for you in the morning. Then maybe you and I could go for a walk in the square, or else I'd whisk you off to a movie – whatever you wanted. I was losing my daughter, but I was determined to fight with every gram of strength in me to win her back.

But it wasn't to be, my darling, was it?

Because those were the last words you ever spoke to me.

And we never even got to say goodbye.

Nancy

KELLY BURKE SOLICITORS, DUBLIN

My solicitor's office address is below. Appointment is for tomorrow evening. Your presence is urgently required. Sam Junior will be there too.

Thus ran the snotty text message Nancy received from Sam Williams Senior. So straight after work that day, she didn't so much walk to the address she'd been given as march there. Fuelled by silent fury, she mentally dress-rehearsed every cutting remark she planned on saying to Sam Williams, the younger, whatever his lame excuses were. She was still reeling from her conversation with Mbeki the previous day and now Sam arsehole Williams would be on the receiving end of all her wrath and frustration. *Serves him bloody well right, too*, Nancy thought crossly.

She hadn't discussed this with anyone in work, mainly because it was almost too embarrassing to admit why this was such a blow. But the hard, cold truth was she had almost come to feel like she was in a sort of virtual relationship. And who knew? Maybe even that Sam would get back from Shanghai and they'd eventually meet and the spark between them might lead to something.

And instead, what did she get?

A chancer, out to fleece his own father for a few paltry quid in rent, all the while stringing along a vulnerable woman, new to the city and new to the whole concept of online, short-term rentals.

Bastard, she thought, suddenly fuming all over again and wanting to kick a lamppost on the street, she felt so frustrated. *You unimaginable bastard.*

She eventually found the solicitor's office, which was right in the heart of Temple Bar, near the famous hotel that U2 owned, The Clarence. The street was completely buzzing with after-work boozers who'd spilled out onto the pavements and who all looked like they were out for the night, the twenty-four-hour party people. Such a sharp contrast to how Nancy herself felt.

She tried her best to cool down a bit as she rang the office doorbell and was immediately buzzed inside. A polite, smiley receptionist showed her to a waiting room with comfy leather sofas and impressively up-to-date magazines dotted about on a coffee table in front.

'Mr Burke will be with you shortly.' She smiled. 'And in the meantime, can I offer you some tea or coffee?'

Nancy said no thank you and the receptionist drifted away, when the office buzzer went again and in walked a guy in his early-thirties, tops, tall and wiry with a hipster beard, a woolly beanie hat and a granddad-style cardigan that looked like it had been foraged out of a charity shop.

'You must be Nancy,' he said, dumping a heavy-looking back-pack beside her and plonking himself down on the sofa opposite her, putting his feet up on the shiny glass coffee table, which only infuriated her even more.

'So you're Sam Williams, I take it?' she said, pointedly not reaching out to shake his hand. She didn't even bother to be polite, not after what the git had done to her.

'Yeah dude,' he said, making himself at home on the sofa. 'Ahh . . . well, thanks for meeting me and the old man, I suppose.'

And there it was, that voice. The same voice that she'd chatted to and laughed with and, God help her, even bonded with over the past few weeks.

Now that she took a closer look at him, though, she had to admit that yes, indeed, this was the guy whose photos and college graduation pictures were dotted all over the house at Primrose Square.

Idiot that I was, Nancy thought, suddenly angry with herself as much as with him, forever thinking those bloody photos had been of the homeowner. *I've been such a trusting, gullible moron, it's almost laughable,* she thought.

'Do you want to know something?' she said icily. 'I was actually glad when your father suggested meeting at his solicitor's office. If this is going to get legal, then be well warned that I'm prepared for a fight. Right now, though, I want to find out exactly what the hell is going on. Why, Sam? Why did you do what you did? Why put me through that?'

She glared hotly across the table at him, but Sam just shrugged like he'd heard it all before, like he was actually used to conversations like this. As if being hauled over the coals was absolutely nothing new to him. He pointedly ignored Nancy's question, then took out a packet of chewing gum from his jeans pocket, popped two in his gob and began to chew annoyingly.

'Sam,' Nancy said in a low, threatening tone, 'I'm entitled to an explanation here and I'm not leaving until I get one.'

He didn't respond, though, so she kept on talking.

'You illegally let out a property belonging to your dad without his knowledge,' she said, rattling off her carefully pre-prepared speech. 'You took my money, then you went and invented this whole fantasy life for yourself – that you were some kind of hotshot businessman working out in Shanghai. So come on, Sam. What kind of a sick person does all that?'

He laughed. Nancy couldn't believe it, but the guy actually sat back and *laughed.* Then he looked her up and down, as if he was assessing her.

'Had you fooled, though, didn't I?' he replied, squinting at her from the other side of the table.

'That's not the point!' she barked back.

'You have to admit, though, it was a good scam while I had it going.' He shrugged. 'But then single women generally are an easy target. You take everything at face value. God, I really had you!'

Now she looked at him in mute shock, stunned at his rudeness.

'Think of it like this, Nancy,' he went on, sitting forwards and cracking his knuckles annoyingly. 'I really did you a favour. If nothing else, I showed you to be a little bit less trusting from now on. Less gullible. Plus, you did get to stay in a great house for a few weeks for half nothing. I made a few quid and pissed the old man off at the same time. You won and so did I. Result.'

'I do not believe what I'm hearing,' she said, shaking her head in shock. 'You're actually proud of yourself! Do you know, I'm glad we're seeing a solicitor now – they'll throw the book at you.'

'If you knew the old man like I do,' Sam said, 'then you'd have done the same, believe me. And just so you know, I won't be meeting with any solicitor today – are you kidding me?'

'Then what are you even doing here?' Nancy spluttered. 'Why bother even coming in the first place?'

Sam Junior just sat back, put his hands behind his head and looked up at the ceiling.

'To give the old man a piece of my mind, I guess,' he said eventually. 'It's either see him here, or not see him at all. That's the way the miserable bastard operates. He's around for about two weeks of the year and that's it.'

'That's your father you're talking about!'

'My dad?' He snorted. 'That's a laugh. He shafted my mum and, after the divorce, she ended up with a paltry settlement, while he jets around the world and only stays in five-star hotels. Meanwhile, my mother is left in a one-bedroom apartment in the back arse of nowhere, with barely enough dosh to eke out from one end of the month to the other.'

'That still doesn't justify what you did to me!' Nancy screamed at the git, furious at his total lack of remorse.

'Oh doesn't it?' Sam replied coolly. 'Our family went from living in a huge house in Foxrock, with a swimming pool and a tennis court, to having virtually next to nothing as soon as the folks broke up. Because that's my dad for you: the most tight-fisted arsehole this side of a Charles Dickens novel. So I learned to shaft him every way I could and every chance I could get. That arsehole can consider it payback for breaking up our family and shitting on us from a height. Good enough for him, if you ask me.'

Nancy shook her head in disbelief, too shocked to even answer. Turned out she didn't need to, though, because just then the door buzzed again, and Sam Senior himself was ushered in, all red-faced and puffing, laden down with a briefcase and files.

'Miss Thompson,' he said, with a curt nod at Nancy, pointedly ignoring his son, who just glared up at him.

'Mr Kelly is still in court and is slightly delayed,' the receptionist came over to say, all apologies, and kowtowing so much to Sam Senior that Nancy guessed he was a much favoured client.

'Well, I don't have a huge amount of time for this,' Sam Senior replied, 'as I have a business dinner later, so hopefully we won't be delayed for much longer.'

'Typical,' his son muttered under his breath. 'Do you hear that? That's fucking typical.'

'I do hope that my son has apologised to you?' the dad asked Nancy, sitting down as briskly as if he was chairing a business meeting.

'No,' she answered truthfully, 'as a matter of fact, he hasn't.'

'Sam,' father said sternly to son. 'What did I tell you? You've behaved abominably to this young lady and the least you can do is say that you're sorry, while yet again, I'm forced to clean up another mess of your making.'

'Oh, just listen to yourself,' Junior replied, picking up his backpack and getting up to leave. 'You sanctimonious git. So I tried to make a bit of money on the side for myself. Ever ask yourself why? And if this would have anything to do with the fact that it was this, or else starve? Besides,' he added, 'this was a victimless crime. I made some cash out of a house you left empty, Nancy got somewhere to stay, and you were none the wiser. Now get over yourself, Dad. If you really cared about your family, maybe you'd provide for us so that I didn't have to do shit like this to get by.'

With that, he stood up, stormed out of the office and took good care to slam the door firmly behind him. He left his dad so puce in the face, Nancy actually worried the man would have a stroke.

'So now you see, Miss Thompson,' Sam Senior said, fingering at the collar of his shirt and sweating profusely, 'exactly what I've been putting up with for years now. May I just point out that Sam Junior is twenty-nine years of age and, since he left college, he has yet to hold down a single job? He talks about being an entrepreneur and yet refuses to do any actual work to achieve this goal. Instead, I'm an ATM machine to that young man, I regret to say. I've backed his more harebrained schemes time and again, and inevitably I end up bailing him out.'

'Ooo-kaay,' Nancy said, feeling like she'd somehow got caught in something with roots that went scarily deep. *The two of them should be telling this to a family therapist*, she thought, *not to me.*

'Oh, you name it,' Sam Senior said wearily, pulling away at his collar again to loosen it, 'and my son has tried and failed at it. His bespoke cupcake business? Cost me a fortune in the debts he ran up. Same with his online business to deliver vegan, gluten-free, sugar-free food. No matter what I do, it's always the wrong thing. My son would have you believe that he lives the life of a pauper, whereas in actual fact, I give both my children a very generous monthly allowance.

'Anyway,' he added briskly. 'I'm sure none of my family squabbles are of any interest to you, Miss Thompson.'

Nancy didn't get a chance to answer him, though, as next thing, the receptionist was politely telling them 'Mr Kelly is ready to see you now.'

They both stood up and were ushered into a dark wood panelled office, with legal tomes groaning down from every available bit of shelf space. The solicitor was bald and bloated, introduced himself as Eugene Kelly, shook Nancy's hand politely and appeared to be on the best terms imaginable with Sam Senior, as the pair of them chatted away about golf handicaps.

'So,' Nancy said, taking a seat and taking control, utterly determined not to let anyone lose sight of why they were there in the first place. 'We have a big problem here, gentlemen. And my question is, what do we do to resolve this?'

A pause as both men sat down and Sam Senior opened up his briefcase, shuffling about inside.

'If I may be so bold,' he said, 'I have a possible solution.'

'Fire away,' Eugene Kelly said, with a wave of his hand.

'Here's what I propose. With your approval, Ms Thompson,' he said with a little nod at Nancy, 'I'll give you another week at the Primrose Square property to gather up your things. Then, as recompense for the inconvenience, I'd like you to accept this.'

With that, he made a big deal of fishing around in his brief-case, before producing a crisp brown envelope.

'It's the rent you've paid since you moved in,' he explained, as Nancy looked at him, dumbfounded. 'I thought seeing as how you leased the property under false pretences, the least I could do was to make sure you weren't left out of pocket as a result.'

'If you think this is about money,' Nancy replied calmly and clearly, 'then you'd be quite wrong. False representation is a serious offence and I'm sorry, but I'm afraid I won't be bought out of this.'

'My client,' Eugene Kelly said to her, 'is making you a gener-ous and fair offer here. You'd do well to consider it, madam. He is the legal owner of the property, after all – I myself can vouch for that.'

'But you can't just throw money at the problem and hope it'll go away,' Nancy spluttered at them both. 'It's not good enough. You need to think about what your son did to me. And ask yourself why.'

'So how do you suggest we resolve this?' Sam Senior asked.

'There's a cash offer on the table for you right now, Ms Thomp-son,' Eugene said. 'If money won't fix this for you, then what will?'

Nancy sat back and folded her arms, refusing to be intimi-dated by the pair of them and their chummy, Tweedle-Dum, Tweedle-Dee act.

'I'll tell you exactly what I want, gentleman,' she replied coolly, to stony silence around the room as both men just looked at her.

Susan

From the journal of Susan Hayes

Oh my darling, where do I begin to write this?

I'll start with a Friday night. Just like any other Friday night in our house, when your dad was home. Except that I'd let you go to that infamous party, on the strict condition that you were waiting outside on the stroke of midnight for us to pick you up. But you rowed bitterly with me over even that small condition, didn't you?

'I'm almost eighteen, Mum! When are you going to stop treating me like a bloody child?'

'I'll start treating you like an eighteen-year-old when you start acting like one!' was my retort, and round you and I went over and over again.

But that Friday evening, with you safely off at the party, ended up being a perfectly peaceful, normal night. Frank and I let Melissa stay up to watch The Late Late Show, *we'd lit the fire in the living room and we even ordered in a takeaway, as a special treat because he was home.*

I'd got a bottle of wine to have with dinner, but your dad would only drink water, as he'd volunteered to go and pick you up on the dot of midnight, as pre-arranged – and you know what a stickler he always is for punctuality. Meanwhile, I'd had a glass of wine and was dozing away on the sofa, with Melissa cuddled tight into me.

Just your common or garden, regular weekend night.

Until my mobile rang on the sofa beside me, that is, instantly shattering the peace. I was half asleep, so your dad got to the phone before I did.

'It's after eleven at night,' he said, as he went to answer. 'Who calls at this hour on a Friday evening?'

My blood froze. And in that moment, I knew, the way a mother just knows. Something had happened. Something very, very bad had happened.

Oh Ella. So much after that is a blur.

I remember the frantic scramble to the hospital, where the ambulance had taken you. Melissa's terrified little voice, as I took her to Jayne's and begged her to babysit for me.

'But Mummy, what's wrong? If something has happened to Ella, why can't I come with you? I could help!'

Not being able to park at the hospital. Cursing and swearing at Frank as he drove around and around looking for a stupid free parking space, then jumping out of the car and running inside, abandoning him.

The A & E, so packed and crowded that night the poor staff were almost operating under World War One field hospital conditions. Demanding to see you, insisting on it. Then a frazzled, concerned-looking nurse telling me they were so sorry. They'd done everything they could for you, but it was over. You were gone.

And that's when I started screaming no. No, no, no, no, no.

I cried out, ran at them, took a hold of your chest myself and almost broke your ribcage, trying to force your heart to beat again.

'Come back to me, Ella,' I kept yelling. 'Come back. It doesn't matter what you did or didn't do – I'm here and I love you and I always will.'

You never heard me, though, did you, my darling?

The rest is all jumbled up in my mind, jagged and incoherent. Your dad and I being brought into a small, private room away from the busy A &E. Being told the worst. The very worst any parent can hope to hear.

MDMA. A small enough dose and you'd probably have been fine. But you never did anything by halves, did you, my baby? You'd taken a lorry-load of the shit, it seemed, and what made it fatal was that it appeared to have been cut with toxins too horrible to contemplate.

'We'll send her samples off to the lab for tests,' an exhausted-looking junior doctor was saying. 'It could have been cut with anything. Rat poison, anything. We see this kind of thing far too frequently. But please know that we did everything we possibly could.'

Your dad, stoic and stiff upper-lipped – the way he always is when faced with bad news. Army training dies hard.

But I was different. I stormed, raged, almost had to be restrained.

'No, you didn't do everything you could!' I kept screaming, again and again. 'Because if you did, she'd be sitting up in bed now, with a headache and a pumped stomach and story to tell. And instead she's . . . she's . . . ' I couldn't say the words, though, so I just roared and shouted at anyone till everything went dark. It was only afterwards I learned they'd had to sedate me.

The rest was chaos, then and now. They wouldn't even let me take your poor, broken little body home; instead there had to be a full post-mortem before the funeral. Your funeral! Oh Ella, I could barely stand, I was so lost and out of it by then. I remember the house on Primrose Square being stuffed to the gills with neighbours and friends and family from all over and being barely able to make eye contact with any one of them.

Then an inquest followed — more days of torture as we sat in a family courtroom and the full details came out. Everything you'd put into your poor little body that night — and who'd given it to you in the first place. Josh Andrews' name was mentioned time and again. He swore he had nothing to do with it, but I knew better, didn't I, my love? So I pressed charges, in spite of everyone telling me that I was wasting my time. Somehow, the inquest let him walk free, but still I wouldn't let it drop. Not until I got justice for you, in your name, my darling.

I started going to the police, time and again, till they told me there was nothing more they could do. 'Your daughter's case has been thoroughly investigated, Mrs Hayes,' they kept telling me, 'and we've been completely open with you about the findings.'

'It's time to let go,' your dad said to me, and I swore, the row we had as soon as the words were out of his mouth must have terrified the neighbours. But I was incandescent by then, incoherent with rage and grief. So I took the fight right to Josh Andrews' doorstep. It was like a mantra with me; I can never forget what that murdering bastard got you into, I kept saying. And so neither will he.

'You're ripping our family apart!' your dad said, just before he took his posting off to Lebanon. 'And this has to stop — we have Melissa to think of.'

But I wasn't even in a place where I could listen. The only comfort I could draw was in keeping my little silent vigil outside the Andrews' house night after night.

I like to think I've started to move on since those dark, black days. And I like to think that's because of you, gently helping me from wherever you are now. Because wherever you are, my darling, I know that you can hear me.

Susan

ST MICHAEL'S WELLNESS CENTRE

Days later, Emily was hugging Susan her final goodbye on the steps outside St Michael's.

'You won't forget me, now, sure you won't?' Emily said to Susan.

'How could I?' Susan smiled as she gathered up the last of her things and stuffed them into the same suitcase she'd arrived at St Michael's with. 'You're the one who kept me together while I was in here.'

'I'll miss you,' Emily said sadly. 'You were the normal one in here by a mile. Which I know isn't saying much, considering the rest of us are certifiable.'

'You know how you said you never got visitors?' Susan said, before snapping her suitcase shut and hauling it off the bed, so she could wheel it downstairs. 'Well, that ends here and now. I'll be back to visit you, and that's a promise.'

'I'd love that,' Emily said, brightening a bit. 'And if you were to bring very large quantities of chocolate, I'd love it even more. Seriously, though,' she added, 'I'm so happy for you, that you're going home to Primrose Square. From what you've told me, it sounds like the best place in Dublin to live – with the best gang of neighbours you could ask for.'

'You have *no* idea.' Susan smiled back. 'The community there really helped me through some very dark times, let me tell you.'

'Well,' Emily added cheekily, 'if you ever hear of a nice, cheap rental there going a-begging, give me a shout, won't you?'

'Will do,' Susan said, delighted with the suggestion, 'and that's a promise.'

Bunny and Bungalow Bill had gathered on the steps outside to bid her a genuinely fond farewell too.

'Don't be a stranger to us now, love,' Bunny said, hugging her warmly as Susan found herself choking back tears. 'Just get out there and live the life that your daughter would have wanted you to live. That's as much as you can do.'

'Take my advice, Susan,' Bungalow Bill said, lugging Susan's case into the boot of her car for her. 'And just take it one day at a time. Whenever anyone says to me, "Have a nice day", I want to vomit all over them. Fuck that for a game of soldiers, I always say. Never mind having a nice day, you just try to have *a day*. That's all. Then wait till you see, in no time, a week will have passed, then a month and then a year. Because that's really the only way to heal, love, trust me. One day at a time. One foot in front of the other. And you will heal, trust me. You have it in you.'

'Thank you,' Susan said simply, hugging him tightly and squeezing his scarred, mottled hands in hers. 'You've been such a good friend to me in here – all of you. I don't think I'll ever forget how kind you've all been.'

'Come back and see us very soon,' Emily said, as Susan clambered into the driver's seat of her car and switched on the ignition.

'With fags!' Bunny yelled, as they waved her off.

It was a quiet Sunday afternoon and by slipping away early, Susan had hoped she might get back to Primrose Square without any fuss and drawing minimal attention to herself. She'd even insisted on driving herself home, all by herself. A small act of independence, but one that was important to her.

Melissa was safely at Jayne's, she knew, so her plan was to pick her up, then spend the evening quietly and peacefully at the house, just the two of them.

She pulled up outside her own house. So far so good. Then she fished out her door key and let herself in, but nothing could have prepared her for the sight that greeted her.

For a start, the whole house was completely spotless and shining, just like it used to be – a million miles from the pigsty she'd left behind her. *How the hell did that happen?* Susan wondered. Not only that, but there was a bright neon pink banner with sparkly cut-out lettering dangling across the hallway that spelled out simply: WELCOME HOME, MUM!

She was just trying to digest this when, from behind her, there was a gentle tap on the half-open hall door, and in came Melissa, her little princess, with a beaming Jayne not far behind her.

'Mum!' Melissa grinned happily, running over to grip her in a huge, tight hug. 'We saw your car and . . . oh Mum, you're here, you're really home! It's so good to have you back . . . I missed you so, so much . . . And Mum, I've got millions to tell you!'

'My darling,' Susan kept saying over and over, burying her face in Melissa's thick head of hair, trying not to let the child see the tears that sprang to her eyes. 'It's wonderful to be home again. Just us, baby.'

'Just us.' Melissa smiled.

'Forgive me letting myself in here when you were away,' Jayne interrupted softly, from where she stood at the hall door. 'But I figured the last thing you'd want to face when you got home was a load of aul' housework.'

'Oh Jayne,' said Susan feelingly, breaking away from Melissa and going to give her old pal a warm hug. 'There never was nor never will be a neighbour like you. You're one in a million, do you know that? I'm hoarse singing your praises to all the gang at St Michael's.'

'Mum,' Melissa said, tugging at her arm and bursting to talk to her. 'So much has happened here on the square since you were in that place! You have to meet Jayne's new "friend",' she added, stressing the word 'friend' and giving Jayne a sideways, teasing look. 'Eric is absolutely lovely and so kind and he's knickers-mad about Jayne . . . I just know. I can tell.'

'Oh, would you go on out of that.' Jayne flushed red all the way down to her neck. 'Eric is dying to meet you, though, Susan. He's heard so much about you.'

'I can't wait to meet him either,' Susan said, intrigued and really dying to get a look at the famous Eric, who did healings and gave crystals to her daughter, and who seemed to slot in so well with Jayne's life.

'He did your hedges for you when you were away, Mum,' said Melissa. 'But that's not the main news I have to tell you. You know Nancy?'

'Your new pal from down the road who has the fancy job at the National?' Susan asked. Of course, she already knew all about Nancy from Melissa. It had been nothing but Nancy this and Nancy that for ages now.

'Yeah, but did I tell you what happened to her, Mum? Nancy says there's been more drama on Primrose Square than there is at the theatre.'

'What happened?' Susan asked, mystified.

'Well, Nancy's landlord turned up on the doorstep when I was having a sleepover with her, and it turns out he's not who she thought he was at all, and now he's threatening to throw her out on the street and none of this is Nancy's fault at all and now she's really upset, because she loves it here on the square and it took her ages to find anywhere to live—'

'Nonsense,' Jayne interrupted firmly. 'Nancy is a lovely young one and she'll always have a bed in my house. Especially with you moving back home with your mum, Melissa, love. Sure I don't know what I'm going to do without you.'

Melissa looked delighted at that, as Susan took a moment to squeeze her daughter's hand and take a good look around her.

Last time I was here, she thought, *I was a different woman. There was a stone in my chest where my heart should have been. I was out of my mind with grief and my brain was toasted with all the sedatives I could find. I was a lousy mother to the daughter I had left, the one thing God had spared me, and I was an even worse wife to a decent, loving husband who couldn't handle me or my breakdown.*

But all that ends here and now, today, Susan vowed silently. *Ella is no longer here, so now all I can do is try to live out the rest of my life for the two of us. Ella would have expected no less.*

'You even got tiger lilies,' she said, taking a moment to smell the delicious fresh fragrance from the huge bunch in the vase at her hall doorway. 'I've always loved that flower and I never knew why.'

'Oh, I can't take credit for that.' Jayne smiled. 'It was Eric's idea. He says they symbolise feminine strength.'

'Feminine strength,' Susan repeated softly to herself. 'What's not to like about feminine strength?'

It was an unseasonably warm, almost hot afternoon, and after 'a grand, strong pot of tea', as Jayne put it, with a few sticky buns and a big chat, all three ladies – Susan, Melissa and Jayne – decided to go for a stroll across the road in the square. They chatted companionably and found a deserted park bench under a mimosa tree, where they could all spread out to enjoy the late afternoon rays.

This feels good, Susan thought, training herself to enjoy the little things, as everyone in St Michael's had urged her to do. *Melissa is happily chattering away beside me, Jayne is acting like the rock that she is and the sunshine is on my face. This is okay,* she thought. *With women like this around me, maybe I can come through this.*

'So then Eric got me started on the Bikram yoga a few weeks ago,' Jayne was saying, 'and at first I nearly died. Forty-degree heat in the studio, if you don't mind . . . Unbearable! And the poor man in front of me farted every time he had to do a downward dog. We giggled about it so much afterwards, Eric and I.'

'When do I get to meet the famous Eric?' Susan asked. 'Is he at your house now?'

'He's actually not at the minute,' Jayne said, a bit mysteriously.

'Oh? Where is he, then?'

'He's . . . well, let's just say, he's trying to mend fences with Jason,' came the considered reply. 'And let's say a little prayer that it all resolves itself beautifully. As Eric always says, there's nothing as draining on the human soul as negativity.'

Susan smiled to herself, just at the way Jayne was speaking. God, she was almost like a new person these days. Gone was the Jayne of old, who seldom went out her front door, unless it was to Mass or else to sit quietly with her own thoughts under a tree in the square. In her place here was this bundle of still-youthful vitality, dressed like a teenager in 'athleisure' gear, leggings and a fleece jumper, chatting freely and openly about life, the universe and the man who farts in her Bikram yoga class.

Everyone had written Jayne off, Susan thought. But everyone was wrong. Because she bounced back and there she was, a new woman, unrecognisable from the Jayne of old. Bloody hell, no wonder Jason was having a tough time dealing with this new incarnation of his mother, not that Susan had much sympathy for him or that awful Irene.

Just then, a figure came striding down a pathway towards the three ladies, earbuds in her ears, looking distracted and miles away.

'Nancy!' Melissa squealed. 'Look, Mum, that's her, that's Nancy!'

'Oh, bring her over, will you, love?' Susan said. 'I'm absolutely dying to meet her.'

Like a bolt, Melissa leapt up from the park bench and raced towards Nancy, almost knocking the girl over in her eagerness to give her a hug.

'This,' she said proudly, showing off her new pal, as she dragged a smiling Nancy back across the lawn with her, 'is her! It's Nancy, Mum. Isn't she fab?'

Nancy took out her earbuds and gave Jayne a quick peck on the cheek, before shaking hands warmly with Susan.

'It's so wonderful to finally meet you,' Nancy said, 'and if it's not too cheeky of me, can I just say welcome back?'

'That's lovely of you.' Susan smiled gratefully. 'It's fab to finally meet you too. I know how good a friend you've been to Melissa – all I hear about is the production of *Pride and Prejudice* that you're working on and how amazing it's going to be.'

'She's a little star,' Nancy said, with a sideways wink at Melissa. 'She's like the best neighbour you could ever ask for.'

'Listen to her accent, Mum,' Melissa said. 'Doesn't Nancy sound so posh?'

'Speaking of neighbours,' Jayne interrupted gently, 'Nancy, love, I was horrified to hear what happened to you with that Sam what's-his-name turning out not to be your real landlord at all. I can tell you this, if the father comes to live here permanently, he'll get a right lash of my tongue, that's for certain.'

'It's rotten, isn't it?' Nancy said with a grimace, as she plonked herself down on the ground in between the other ladies. 'But the worst thought of all is that I'll have to move away from neighbours like you. What you have here on the square is so special. I've lived all over the place and don't think I've ever experienced anything like it.'

'I won't hear a word of your nonsense about moving,' said Jayne, with great finality. 'You always have a room at my house, Nancy. Anytime you like, you just say the word and Eric will help you move all your bags into my spare room.'

At that, Susan caught a quick, hopeful glance from Melissa. She needed no further prompting, immediately taking the hint.

'No,' she said firmly. 'Nancy has to stay with us.'

'Really, Mum?' said Melissa, beaming up at her. 'I'd love that so much. That would be like the best thing ever!'

'You could always take . . . ' Susan broke off there, though. God knows, she needed all her resolve to get to the end of her next sentence.

You can do it, she told herself. *Deep breath. Go for it.*

Three pairs of eyes looked expectantly at her.

'You're more than welcome to have Ella's room,' Susan said quietly. 'It would be so lovely to have someone in there again.'

There was a little silence, then Jayne slipped her arm supportively around Susan's thin shoulders.

'Good woman,' she said. 'You know it's the right thing to do.'

'Do you really mean it?' Nancy asked, stunned by her generosity.

'Of course she does!' Melissa squealed. 'In fact, let's move you in right now . . . The sooner the better, right, Mum?'

'I don't know what to say,' Nancy said. 'There really are no words for me to thank you.'

'OMG, this is going to be, like, sooooo amazing!' said Melissa happily, unable to contain herself. 'We'll be like the best flat-mates ever . . . like sisters!'

The words were out there before she could claw them back, and anxiously she glanced up at her mum to gauge her reaction. Her mum said nothing, but seemed . . . pretty okay with it all.

'If I've learned one thing,' Jayne said, after a thoughtful little pause, 'it's that we ladies are all stronger together.'

At that, she held her hand out and clasped Susan's. Then Melissa instinctively piled her hand on top of theirs. Lastly, a smiling Nancy placed her hand on top, so all four women were linked.

'Stronger together,' Nancy said. 'I love it.'

'We're tiger lilies,' said Susan.

'Exactly like tiger lilies.'

Later on that day, as Susan and Melissa made their way back to their own home, and just before Melissa went upstairs to her spotless bedroom in a house so tidy she barely recognised it, she went to give her mum a big hug goodnight.

'It's really wonderful to have you back home again, Mum,' she said simply. 'I missed you so much.'

'Not half as much as I missed you, babes.' Susan smiled, tucking Melissa under the chin, just like she used to when she was little.

But then Melissa paused midway up the stairs, as if she'd something on her mind and wasn't quite sure how to say it, or whether to say it at all.

'What's wrong, love?' Susan asked, sensing it.

Melissa bit her lip. 'Well . . . it's good to know you won't do what you used to, before you got sick, Mum.'

'What do you mean?' Susan said, her eyebrows knitting downwards.

'I mean . . . ' Melissa stammered, 'that you won't go back to *his* house again tonight. You know who I mean, Mum. Josh Andrews' house. Because they've cured you now, haven't they?' she added hopefully. 'So there won't be any more of that, will there? Please tell me no, Mum. Please.'

The plaintive look in her eyes almost cracked Susan's heart in two, and she knew the child needed an answer more than anything.

'No, love, I won't,' she said firmly. 'I can promise you.'

'So . . . you forgive Josh, then?'

Susan looked at her, weighing up whether in this instance honesty really was the best policy. And decided that it was, actually. After all, in St Michael's they were always being hit with mantras like: 'the truth will set you free'.

'No, my darling,' she said, after a thoughtful pause. 'To be honest, I don't think I ever could or ever will forgive Josh Andrews for what he did. Ever. But you know what? He has to live with himself and the knowledge of his involvement in Ella's death for the rest of his life, so good enough for him. And my having a go at him in public and trying to shame him by parking myself outside of his house isn't going to do anyone much good now, is it?

'So rest assured, pet,' she went on, 'I'm not going anywhere tonight or any night. I'll try to forget what that guy put us through, and I'll try to remember that Ella had some responsibility for what happened too. But I don't think I'll ever forgive him. Maybe when you're a mother one day yourself, then you'll understand.'

'Oh,' said Melissa flatly, staring down at the floor. 'I see.'

'So you just put all of that nonsense about Josh Andrews right out of your head, okay, love?' Susan said, a bit more brightly. 'Now up you go to bed and I'll come in to check on you shortly. And sleep sound, pet. You've no idea how much your old mum loves you.'

'Love you too, Mum,' Melissa replied automatically, as she turned on her heel and made her way slowly upstairs.

Shit, shit, shit, Susan thought, as a dark cloud fell over her day. The poor child had seemed so happy and upbeat all day, so glad to have her mother back home again.

But now, somehow, the old worried look was back on that pale little twelve-year-old face. And it was all Susan's own doing, just for being honest.

I've made progress, she thought sadly. *But it's scary how much work I still have to do.*

Jason

O'DONOGHUE'S PUB

Jason had always liked O'Donoghue's. It was a real, proper Irish pub, with a decent pint of Guinness on tap and none of your fancy 'alcopops' or any of that gastropub shit that drove him up the walls. *Jaysus*, he thought, making his way inside, if you were gobshite enough to ask for a smashed avocado on toast here, you'd be laughed out of the place. Besides, he figured, if that eejit Eric insisted on meeting him, it might as well be somewhere Jason was comfortable in.

To his surprise, Eric was already there ahead of him, sitting at a quiet little table in the snug.

'There you are, now,' Jason said, tossing his keys and phone down onto the table in greeting.

'Hey, Jason, my man.' Eric smiled, standing up to greet him like a long-lost friend. 'Thanks for meeting with me at short notice. Say, what's with the sunglasses?'

'Oh, them?' Jason stammered, patting the side of the wrap-around black shades he had on. 'Ehh . . . nothing. Bit of . . . retina damage, that's all.'

Mind your own fucking business, he'd wanted to say, but didn't. Part of him was too intrigued to know why Eric had wanted to meet him in the first place. What was going on, anyway? All gobshite Eric had said on the phone was that it was important they have a face-to-face, 'sooner rather than later'.

'What can I get for you?' Eric asked, waving over one of the bar staff.

'Pint of Guinness,' said Jason. 'And you could order me a cheese and ham toastie, while you're at it. I'm bleeding starving.'

Fuck this, he thought. *If I have to spend my afternoon listening to this eejit, then I might as well cash in. He's paying for it, not me.*

Eric ordered from one of the lounge staff, almost making Jason laugh in his face when he added, 'And for me? A cup of your finest peppermint tea, if you'd be so kind.'

Peppermint tea, he thought furiously. *In a Dublin pub. Jaysus, they'll think he's gay and I'm his boyfriend.*

'So,' Eric said, as soon as they had the table to themselves again. 'You're probably thinking I wanted to talk to you about Jayne. I mean . . . about your mom. But that's not the case at all.'

'Oh yeah?' Jason said suspiciously.

'The thing is, Jayne and I both realise how tough this has been on you,' Eric went on. 'After all, the relationship between any mother and her son is a special one, something to be cherished. And change is always frightening for any of us. We fear change and yet, like we say back at the Healing House at home, it really is the only constant in life.'

Oh here we fecking go, Jason thought. *Yet more of this twathead and his bollockology.* He glanced down at his phone, while Eric droned on and on and on about how we shouldn't be afraid of change because, as he put it, 'we may lose something we cherish, but you know what? We may gain something even better.'

Another bloody text message, Jason thought, completely tuning Eric out. This one, even more threatening than the last.

At our last calculation, you now owe €4500, not including interest. You pay by the end of next week, or else we'll be round to
your house to sort this out once and for all.

Fuck, fuck, fuck, he thought, worry starting to put him off his
pint. Where was he going to get that kind of money by the end
of the week? This crowd didn't make idle threats either. If they
called to his front door, it would be game over as far as Irene was
concerned.

A silence fell, and even through the sunglasses, Jason could
feel Eric scanning his face up and down.

'So I do have something I wanted to talk to you about,' Eric
eventually said.

'Oh yeah?' said Jason, not sure where this weirdo was going. Just
then his phone pinged as another text came through. *Bleeding loan
sharks. Again. Christ Almighty,* he thought crossly. He'd already told
them that he didn't have the money yet, but that as soon as he got
it, he'd pay them back everything he owed. This crowd had already
robbed him of his peace of mind, so what more did they want
from him? Blood?

You'd be well advised not to ignore us, Jason. Remember, we know
where you live.

Jason twiddled distractedly with his phone, but as bad luck
would have it, Eric copped it.

'You keep looking down at your phone,' he said, calmly folding his arms. 'So you wanna tell me what's up?'

'Nothing,' Jason said sullenly.

'Sure doesn't look like nothing to me,' Eric said, glancing down at the phone in Jason's pudgy hands. The text message was still on the screen, though, and before Jason had a chance to delete it, Eric had a chance to read it.

'Something you maybe want to talk about?' Eric said slowly.

'It's a personal matter, all right?' Jason snapped. *Fecking nosey bastard*, he thought. *Why can't he just mind his own business?*

There was a long pause, as the telly in the background blared out some match between Juventus and Arsenal.

'You can take off the sunglasses,' Eric eventually said, as the rest of the bar cheered when Arsenal equalised. 'You're not fooling anyone. So tell me this: how much do you owe?'

'Excuse me?' Jason spluttered into his pint. 'What did you just say?'

'Oh, you heard me,' came the cool reply. 'Clearly you owe money to some people who aren't afraid to use violence against you, and my question is, how much? You don't need to worry,' he added. 'I'm unshockable when it comes to money. And whatever you have to tell me will stay between us. I give you my solemn word, I won't mention this to your mom.'

Jason shuffled around uncomfortably on his bar stool. The game was well and truly up, there was no question about it. Eric had guessed, so feck it anyway, he might as well know everything. If nothing else, he figured, it was a kind of a relief finally getting if off his chest after so long. Slowly, he took off the sunglasses to reveal a swollen black eye that still stung.

'Oh jeez, that's a howler,' Eric said. 'How did you explain that beauty to Irene?'

'Told her I walked into a door,' Jason muttered, mortified.

'So how much?'

'So far,' Jason sighed, 'well over eighteen grand on credit cards. And if I don't have four and a half in cash by the end of the week, chances are I'll lose me kneecaps.'

'Oh jeez,' Eric said again, smacking his hand off his head in frustration. 'Don't tell me you went to money lenders?'

A curt nod from Jason, half angry and half embarrassed.

'You know the interest rates those guys charge, right?' Eric said. 'You know it's tantamount to daylight robbery?'

Another sullen nod from Jason.

'Some kind of payday loan that got out of control is my guess,' Eric said, scanning Jason's face up and down again.

Jason looked sharply back at him. 'How the feck did you know that?'

'There are only three possible reasons why anyone would go to a money lender, in my experience: alcoholism, drug addiction or else to pay off other debts that just spiralled. Now clearly you're neither a chronic booze hound nor a drug addict, ergo . . . '

'If you ever breathe a single word of this to either my ma or Irene . . . ' Jason said warningly, to a dismissive hand wave from Eric.

'My word,' he said, 'is my bond. But the question now is, how do you propose getting out of the mess you're in?'

'I honestly don't know,' Jason sighed into his pint. 'I'm trying to build up my little business, but those bastards at the bank turned me down, didn't they?'

'Okay,' Eric said thoughtfully, taking a sip of the herbal tea in front of him. 'So what's your business model, if I may be so bold?'

'My business model?' Jason said, sounding surprised. 'Why do you want to know about that?' What was this moron droning on about now? Jason had just told him he had to come up with thousands by the end of the week or he'd be hospitalised, and now the eejit wanted to talk about business models?

'Well, as you may or may not know,' Eric went on to explain with a modest shrug, 'growing a business is something I'm pretty familiar with, as it happens. Short-term, you're in a financial mess, so what I'd like to know is how you plan to get out of it in the long-term?'

Jason didn't answer, though, just looked the other man up and down suspiciously as a distant bell rang at the back of his head. The last time the twins stayed with their granny at Primrose Square, they'd come home mouthing on about how Eric was in the property game and how he was really loaded.

'He knows the restaurant business really well too,' Holly had said, 'and he's even going to help granny to write a cookbook . . . Can you believe that?'

But then she and Molly had started squabbling about whose turn it was to clean the bathroom next and Jason had written it off.

Besides, the thought of someone like Eric rolling in it had to be a bleeding joke. For feck's sake, you only had to look at the state of him. He was dressed in white linen from head to toe, with open-toed sandals. He looked like one of those gobshites who was about to shave his head and start banging a tambourine up and down Grafton Street in a minute.

'You worked in business, then, did you?' Jason asked.

'Since the age of sixteen,' Eric replied. 'Tell me something. Are you familiar with the TV show you get here in Europe, *Dragon's Den*?'

'Course I am,' Jason said, before adding snottily, 'I'm an entrepreneur, aren't I? It's a show every entrepreneur knows all about.'

'Because you know I've been a part of that show in the United States,' Eric said. 'Or didn't your mom mention it?'

She could have done, for all Jason knew. But he couldn't swear to it. Mainly because whenever his ma started droning on about how wonderful Eric was, Jason generally told her he was mad busy with his 99s and got off the phone.

So he settled for just grunting back by way of a response.

'I was involved with the US version of that show for a grand total of five series,' Eric went on, 'and I'm real proud to say that I think we – and by that I mean my fellow Dragons and myself – did do a lot of good. We got some really great businesses started up, which otherwise might not have had the ghost of a chance.'

'Hang on a minute,' said Jason, putting his pint down and looking completely bewildered, like this conversation was five steps ahead of him. 'I thought you meant you were a contestant on the show. You know, on the scrounge for money, same as you would with a bank.'

'Oh, didn't I say?' said Eric, looking back at him with a twinkle in his eye. 'No, I was one of the Dragons on the original US show. Except, of course, over there it's got a different name. In the US, we call it *Dante's Ninth Circle of Hell*. Not the catchiest of names, granted, but like I say, we did give a lot of would-be entrepreneurs a leg up in life. People who'd had doors slammed in their faces by the banks, yet who believed in their dreams and who weren't prepared to give up. Those are the type of folk,' he added, with a knowing little nod in Jason's direction, 'that I see it as my life's goal to help. The forgotten. The underdog.'

'Is that a fact now?' said Jason suspiciously.

'Sure is,' came the cool response.

'Oh really?' Jason went on. 'Because, you know, me and Irene googled you when you first landed in on us and there was absolutely no mention of an Eric Butler who'd been linked to some big TV show in the States. None whatsoever. So what do have to say to that now, mate?'

You bleeding fantasist, he wanted to add. *Having a senior moment, are we? Did you accidently doze off in front of* Dragon's Den *and now you have it in your head that you were once a part of it?* Instead, though, he decided to take a sip of his pint and quietly savour the victory.

'That's because I did the show under my family name, which is Shapiro,' Eric explained. 'I reverted back to Butler when I set up the Healing House, because it felt like a whole new direction for me – a better direction, a true calling. And I sure as heck didn't want to put people off if they thought a place of peace and tranquility like the Healing House was run by a tough judge from a TV show where more people get turned away then actually get funding. There was absolutely no duplicity involved in this,' he went on, 'I hope you understand. The name I had on the TV show was, for me, a little like a stage name – you know? Like an actor might have.'

He'd lost his audience, though, because Jason was already on his phone, googling away. And sure enough, to his utter astonishment, the story rang true. There it was, one YouTube clip after another of Eric Shapiro, looking years younger, but sitting on a panel of Dragons, with the power of life or death over whatever gobshite happened to be pitching to them.

Fuck me, Jason thought. *He's telling the truth. He's actually telling the bleeding truth.*

'So now you believe me, huh?' Eric asked calmly.

'Jaysus,' was all Jason could mutter by way of a reply.

'Which is a lot of the reason why I wanted to meet you today,' Eric went on. 'Your mom tells me that you got a great little business going – you're in ice cream, right?'

'Mobile confectionary, yeah,' Jason managed to say, still trying to process this new information.

'So why don't you give me some details about your plans to grow your business? The more detailed you are,' he added, 'the better.'

'Well,' said Jason, softening a bit and trying his best to back-pedal on his earlier rudeness, 'I'm looking to break into . . . ' He broke off here, trying to claw back the phrase that Irene had drummed into him to use when he was dealing with bank managers. 'I want to move into the more savoury end of the market,' he said, as Eric listened intently. 'To capitalise on the growing trend for late-night snacks at sporting fixtures and big concerts,' he rattled off, like he was reading it from a brochure.

'Great,' Eric said, 'I like it. You mean burgers and fries after football matches and pizza slices at rock concerts, that kind of thing, yeah?'

'Well . . . yeah,' Jason said hesitantly.

'And you're looking for how much exactly? To finance how many mobile catering units? At what rate of interest? And what percentage of the business would you be willing to offer me, in return for a cash investment? I'd be looking for a minimum of twenty-five per cent, though, I gotta warn you.'

Eric's questions came thick and fast, like a true professional, as Jason madly tried to keep up.

'Ehh . . . ' he said, totally taken off-guard. 'I'd have to come back to you on all the nitty gritty. But only if that's okay with you?' he added placatingly.

'You take all the time you need,' Eric said calmly. 'So here's the deal. Short term, I'd pay off your debts for you, so that's one less thing you gotta stress about. Then long term, I suggest you and me talk business with my legal team, so we can agree a percentage of your company for me, in return for a cash injection. I'd really like to move forward on this sooner rather than later.'

'Well . . . yeah. Me too. Great,' said Jason, utterly stunned. 'And . . . thank you, I suppose. Thanks very much.'

'So you're interested?' Eric twinkled warmly.

'Yeah.' Jason nodded. 'Jesus, yeah! Big time!'

'Good. Because I got one condition.'

'Name it,' Jason said, suddenly terrified Eric might change his mind.

'From this day on, I want to start seeing you being nicer to your mom. A whole lot nicer. And that, my friend, is non-negotiable.'

Melissa

18 PRIMROSE SQUARE

Nancy had moved into their house and it was absolutely the best thing ever, Melissa thought happily. Everyone mucked in to help her move house: Jayne, Eric, and astonishingly Jason, who nobody liked, came to lend a hand and had even given Melissa a free 99 afterwards.

Melissa had almost fallen over in shock when he'd handed it to her, with a flake in it and everything, but for some reason Jason seemed different that day. Kinder, nicer and certainly a lot more polite to Jayne and even Eric too. Before this, Jason had bitten the face off Eric every chance he could get – he'd been so rude, it was horrible to listen to. But that sunny, warm day, he was like a totally different Jason.

Between everyone, they had the house Nancy had been renting cleared of all her stuff and empty as the day she found it in next to no time.

'So another new neighbour will soon join us on the square,' Jayne sighed, as they closed the front door of number twenty-four behind them for the very last time, taking care to put the keys back in through the letterbox. 'Let's just hope whoever moves in next turns out to be a sweetheart like you, Nancy,' she added, and Melissa could only agree.

Then everyone formed a sort of line between them and passed every single bag, backpack and suitcase belonging to Nancy from her old digs to her new one.

'You know, this is just like my grandpappy used to do.' Eric smiled, 'when he worked on a factory production line back in Idaho.'

'Idaho? Really? That's very interesting,' Jason had remarked, to raised eyebrows from Jayne and a quiet smirk from everyone else at his sudden about-turn in attitude towards Eric.

Soon after, Nancy was well and truly ensconced at number eighteen and Melissa couldn't have been happier. She'd been a bit worried at first, particularly when she had to help her mum clear a bit of wardrobe and shelf space in Ella's old bedroom for Nancy. Melissa's heart had fallen when she'd seen just how much of Ella's stuff was still there, and both she and her mum knew that throwing anything away . . . well, that was just never going to happen.

'Can I have this jumper, Mum?' Melissa asked, picking up a soft black sweatshirt that Ella used to wear day and night. It was huge, black and oversized with writing on it that read, 'Fuck the Patriarchy'.

'Of course you can, pet,' Susan told her, giving her a little squeeze around her shoulders. 'Maybe just don't wear it to school, okay? I don't want you getting into any trouble – like Ella used to, do you remember?'

Melissa nodded, smiling because she remembered so well. The school secretary had phoned the house to complain about 'your elder daughter's unsuitable choice of attire on the school premises'.

Melissa looked worriedly up at her mum, suddenly afraid that stirring up a memory like that might upset her nerves. *Please don't let her go back on those horrible purple-y pills that made her act like a zombie and sleep for days. Please, not again,* she thought.

But her mum didn't seem to mind about the jumper a bit. Instead she gave a wistful little smile and inhaled the smell of the woolly fabric deeply, before handing it over.

This is a good sign, Melissa thought hopefully. Her mother letting go of little things Ella had once owned and loved had to be a baby step forwards, didn't it?

'Take anything else you like too, while we're here,' her mum said, in her normal voice. Her best 'mammy' voice. 'Because I know what Ella would say if she were here.'

'What's that, Mum?'

'She'd tell us to shove it all into black bin liners and give everything she ever owned to the local charity shop. You know how devoted she was to that charity shop.'

Melissa smiled, because it was so true and exactly what Ella would have said if she'd been there.

'Maybe we could choose something your dad might like to keep too?' her mum offered. 'Like maybe—'

'Oh, I know,' Melissa said brightly, as her eye fell on a battered copy of *The Handmaid's Tale*, one of Ella's favourite books ever.

'Good idea,' her mum said. 'He'd love that. So what do you say we pack up as much of the rest of her stuff as we can and store everything up in the attic? That way, we can both still read Ella's books and look at her things whenever we want. Good plan?'

'Great plan.' Melissa beamed back. So they boxed away as much of Ella's stuff as they could to make space for their new lodger but, as it turned out, Nancy was about the easiest house-guest you could ever ask for. In fact, when Nancy did move in, she limited herself to using up just one single shelf in Ella's old room, and no more.

'But we made loads of room for you!' Melissa told her, proudly opening the now empty wardrobe.

'It's okay, thanks, hon,' Nancy had told her. 'I'm so used to living out of a suitcase, just the one shelf is quite enough for me.'

At first, Melissa had worried a bit about how her mum would react to someone new being in Ella's room and in the little bathroom she used, but she needn't have.

'So little trouble,' she overheard her mum say, 'and so low maintenance, you'd barely even know she was here.'

And as for Melissa herself? All of a sudden, it was like living with the coolest friend you could ever ask for. Nancy was working around the clock at the National Theatre just then, so they only ever really saw her first thing in the morning or else late in the evening.

When they did meet, though, Nancy made a big point of telling Melissa all about how the final week of rehearsals was shaping up. Then the three of them would chat and Nancy would even bring home bunches of flowers for the house, always tiger lilies, and lovely smelling scented candles to dot around the place.

It's like having a big sister again, Melissa thought, loving this sudden change in the atmosphere at home.

She didn't tell her mum that, though. She didn't dare use the word 'sister'.

Baby steps and all that.

Then something seriously weird happened. It was the week that led up the Easter holidays and there was a real end-of-term atmosphere about Melissa's school. No one was taking homework seriously and even the exam classes, like the Junior and

Leaving Certs, were acting the maggot around the place, as Miss Jenkins, Melissa's class tutor, was complaining.

It was just coming up to the end of the day, when Melissa and Hayley were strolling towards their lockers, full of chat about the holidays ahead and what they had planned. Melissa had already asked Hayley to the opening night of *Pride and Prejudice*, and both girls were beyond thrilled at the thought of getting to an actual, proper opening night.

'Do you think there'll be celebs there?' Hayley asked excitedly. 'Like . . . off the TV, I mean? And do you think we might get to meet them?'

'Well . . . Nancy did say that the President would be there,' Melissa replied, 'so maybe we'll get to see him? And there's a drinks reception for the cast and crew afterwards, and we're even invited to that too. I can't wait!'

'OMG, everyone is going to be, like, *so* jealous of us!' Hayley squealed. 'I'm so getting a new outfit for this. And a spray tan, and a Shellac on my nails, if Mum lets me.'

Just at that exact moment, Melissa felt a tap on her shoulder and turned around. Standing in front of her was Josh. Josh Andrews. He was surrounded, as ever, by his gang of merry men, as everyone called them, and Melissa just stared up at him in total shock. Even Hayley stopped nattering and stood there, gawping.

'Emm . . . can I talk to you?' Josh said to Melissa, looking directly at her.

'Ehh . . . yeah,' she answered, too surprised to say no. What would her mum say if she knew? What did he want with her?

'In private,' he added.

Hayley was rooted to the spot, having a good stare at the astonishing scene that was unfolding, before taking the hint.

'Oh! Right. Sorry,' she hissed at Melissa before walking off.

'Hey guys?' Josh said, turning back to his gang, who were, as ever, all clustered around him. 'Give me a bit of space for a sec, yeah?'

He led a terrified Melissa aside into a quiet little annex, where there was a bit more privacy to talk.

'Thing is,' he began, towering over Melissa and totally intimidating her, 'I know that it was your sister's . . . that is . . . Ella's anniversary a while back . . . '

Melissa couldn't talk. Half of her was too scared to and the other half was too intrigued. She really, really wished Hayley was with her for a bit of support.

'So . . . I got . . . well . . . this,' Josh said, clumsily reaching into the backpack he had slung around his shoulders and handing her a card. 'It's one of those . . . you know . . . in memorium cards,' he added, starting to look a bit embarrassed now. 'I didn't know what else to do. I don't even know if that's the right name for them.'

'Oh . . . right, well . . . thank you.' Melissa somehow found the words to say, automatically taking the card from him.

'It's . . . shite. Isn't it? About Ella, I mean.'

'Yeah.' Melissa nodded. That was certainly one way of putting it.

'So . . . you and me are cool then, yeah?'

'Emm . . . yeah. Absolutely.'

'All right then,' he said, turning on his heel so he could rejoin his mates, who were waiting for him over by the water cooler. Then he stopped dead in his tracks and turned back to face her.

'Just . . . maybe it's better if don't tell your mum about the card,' he said.

'If you don't want me to . . . ' Melissa said doubtfully.

Josh thought for a moment, then shook his head.

'In fact, scrap that,' he said a bit more firmly. 'Definitely don't mention the card to your mum. It's a very bad idea.'

'Emm . . . okay,' Melissa managed to say, still utterly confused by this. 'If you'd rather I didn't, then I won't.'

'I do get it, you know,' he said, sounding like he'd really given it thought. 'Sometimes people need a bad guy to shove all the blame on. And right now, as far as your mum is concerned, I'm it. But I cared about Ella, you know. I really did. She was my friend and I'd never have hurt her. I want you to know that.'

Jayne

19 PRIMROSE SQUARE

'Well, Tom, this has to be about the hardest conversation I'll probably ever have to have with you. Half of me is almost relieved you're lying there in an urn for what I'm about to say. But it's time for me, love. I really think it's time for me to finally let go of the past and "embrace my new future", as Eric says.

'The thing is, love, he and I have been getting on so famously ever since he first arrived on my doorstep, oh, it seems like such a long time ago now, doesn't it? Sure I didn't know what to make of him at all in the beginning, with his white linen gear and the way he talks about chakras and energy centres in the body. But now? Oh Tom, it feels so disloyal of me to even say it to you, but now I can't imagine my days without him.

'Best of all, though, is the absolute miracle that seems to have taken over our Jason. Well, you saw for yourself, love, how snotty and unwelcoming himself and Irene were to poor Eric when he first came here.

'But now, honestly, Jason is like a new man these days. He's all pally and full of chat with Eric and it's a joy to see. Jason has truly changed and I'd swear it's Eric's doing, I'm not imagining it. Sure, only this morning, didn't Jason call to Primrose Square and offer to wash my windows for me – without me even having to nag him into it, like I always do. Did you ever?! Not only that, but then he insisted on whisking me off to the shopping centre in his ice cream van to help me with all my grocery shopping.

He even bought a bottle of champagne, as a treat for myself and Eric, did you ever! Well, I was so shocked, I didn't have the heart to remind Jason that Eric doesn't drink, but still, though. It really did my little heart good to see my son and the man I love finally getting on so famously.

'Because that's the thing, Tom. I really do think I love Eric. I never thought I'd say those words again, not after you. But I really do think that this is love. Real, true love, just like I felt for you. So here's what I want to talk to you about, Tom – and it's a biggie, as Melissa says.

'It means so much to me that you would have liked Eric. Is it too cheeky of me to ask you for a sign? Something? Anything at all to let me know that you're okay with this from the other side. I ask so much already of you, Tom, in life and now in death too. But can I just ask you for that one last thing? If it's not too much trouble, will you send me a sign? For me? Please?'

Later that same evening, Eric encouraged Jayne to come along to what he called a Pilates Reformer class, to be held in their local yoga studio on nearby Pearce Street. Jayne readily said yes, but then that was her new mantra these days, she told herself happily. Yes to everything. Yes, all the way. Whatever life threw at her, the answer would always be a big, fat yes.

But she nearly died when she saw the actual machines you had to do the hour-long class on.

'Oh Eric, love,' she blurted out, 'are you sure this is quite safe? Those yokes look like medieval torture machines – like something out of the Tower of London.'

'Hey, just trust me, honey.' Eric smiled knowingly. 'You're gonna love this – it's all about core strengthening, you know. Like I always say, the difference between a great old age and a miserable one is our health, and I want you around fit and well for a very long time to come.'

It was little things he said, just like that, which melted Jayne's heart. The idea that Eric was really thinking long-term about their relationship. So she gamely lay down on the machine, along with the rest of their class, and joined in as best she could, bending, stretching, lunging and even doing 'tummy crunches', which hurt like hell, but which their instructor promised would drop everyone down a clothes size in no time.

Meanwhile, Eric was stretched out on the pilates bed right beside her, giving her little half winks of encouragement whenever their eyes met. Which was quite a lot, actually. What Jayne hadn't been prepared for was this. Mid-way through the class, when everyone was getting hot and sweaty, he sat forward and peeled off a lycra sports jacket he was wearing so he was just down to a simple white T-shirt with yoga pants.

It was the sight of his long, bare, tanned arms that did it for Jayne, she thought afterwards. She was so used to being around Eric physically, but the sight of those bare arms and lean, muscular legs as he did an abdominal plank beside her made her want to pull him in towards her and do all manner of things that would get the two of them arrested in a public place.

Desire is a funny thing, she thought. You think it's all but evaporated as you hit middle age, then *whoomph!* All of a sudden you know you won't be at peace till you're lying in this man's arms. Why was it, she wondered, that physical longing and attraction only ever came at you when there was nothing you could do about it? Like when Eric was stripped down to his shorts in the back garden doing her hedges? Or when he was stirring one of his delicious vegetarian sauces at the Aga in her kitchen, when she had a houseful of visitors? Or just then, as the two of them lay side by side on the weirdest-looking wooden bed slats you just ever saw, with wires and weights and pulleys hanging off their arms and feet, like prisoners back in the Dark Ages.

It was raining when they came out of the yoga centre and Eric held out a huge umbrella for them both to shelter under as they walked home. He was chatting away, making small talk about the class and the benefits of it and how Joseph Pilates said that 'if at the age of thirty, you're stiff and out of shape, you are old. If at sixty you're supple and strong, then you are young.'

Jayne let him chat away, feeling all hot and flushed with this overwhelming physical longing she felt. Somehow, they'd got as far as the square before he noticed how quiet she was being.

'You okay there?' he asked, as they stopped under a tree, rain spattering down through the leaves onto the dark, deserted street below. 'Not like you to be so tuned out.'

Send me a sign, Tom, Jayne asked one last time. Send me a sign that what I'm about to do is okay.

And that's when she saw it. Not just a single white feather, but three of them lying on the rain-soaked ground at her feet. Everything she'd asked for and more. She didn't need any further prompting – she didn't even need words.

Instead, she leaned into Eric, then turned to face up to him.

'Kiss me,' she said simply.

Nancy

18 PRIMROSE SQUARE

So another house move, but so far, this one was turning out to be magical for Nancy, with no 'ghost' landlords bombarding her with fake messages from the Far East.

The 'Far East'. She snorted, still cross at herself for being such an easily duped target. The far east of Cabra, more like. Nancy was really trying her very best, but the horrible, final words of Sam Williams Junior were still ringing in her ears. *Single women are such an easy mark.*

Well, not this single woman, she vowed to herself. *Certainly not any more.*

'I'm done trusting people and I'm particularly done trusting all the knuckle-dragging, selfish, plonkers I meet online,' she boldly told Mbeki during a break in wardrobe fittings with the cast.

'I don't blame you,' Mbeki replied, all big-eyed sympathy. 'Wow, what a rotten thing to happen – especially after, well, you know. After everything else you've had to deal with – in London, I mean.'

Nancy thought it wisest just to say nothing as the two women walked from the coffee shop across the road from the National and back into the lift that led to the very top of the building. It was just the two of them inside the lift. There was privacy, no one could overhear.

'Nancy?' Mbeki persisted, seizing her opportunity. 'Have you decided what to do yet? Because this really shouldn't go on much longer. It's not fair, for a start.'

'I know,' Nancy sighed, as they zoomed upwards.

'You have to do something,' Mbeki urged her. 'You've got to, Nancy, this is too big, too important. This is your good name and reputation we're talking about here. I'm in your corner. You can take this on and win, I know you can.'

'Just . . . just let's park it for now,' Nancy said, as the lift door slowly opened on the top floor. 'It's a work day and I have to keep my work face on.'

'Come on, Nancy!' was Mbeki's heartfelt answer. 'Where's the fight in you? I've seen you stand up to Diego when he's acting like Rumpelstiltskin. I know you can stand up to this too. You're strong. You can do it!'

'Please, Mbeki,' Nancy said, turning to face her and stopping in her tracks. 'You've no idea how much of a toll this took on me. I know it has to be dealt with but just not when I've got a show opening in less than a week. Can we just drop it till my work is done?'

'If that's what you want,' Mbeki said reluctantly. 'But you deserve a hearing. Remember, the truth is powerful. And the truth will out. It's a question of when, not if.'

The day went by in a blur for Nancy, and as she walked home much later on that night, she gave silent thanks that at least one of her worries had crumbled to dust. She had a new roof over her head, which was the biggest relief imaginable to her. Not only that, but it had turned out to be probably the easiest house move she'd ever done, mainly down to the marvellous spirit of cooperation and general 'mucking-in' that there was on Primrose Square.

Both Susan and Melissa had really bent over backwards to welcome her into their home, and she really couldn't have been more grateful to either of them. Particularly when she knew only too well the emotional cost to them of opening up Ella's old room.

It was late, well past 10 p.m., when she finally put her key in the lock and found Susan on her own with a big mug of tea in front of the TV, as Melissa had already gone to bed. It was dreary and damp outside, it had been drizzling rain all day, so it was a real treat for Nancy to come home to the warmth of a fire and the beautiful smell of something garlicky wafting in from the kitchen.

'Hey there, roomie!' Susan said, lighting up with a genuine smile as Nancy came into the living room and perched down on the sofa beside her.

She'd been reading, Nancy noticed, and was carefully putting away a book titled, *My Journey Through Grief – Honouring Your Loved One and Learning to Live Again.*

'This was a gift from Eric,' she explained, seeing Nancy noticing the title.

'Ahh,' Nancy replied. 'Any good?'

'The truth?' Susan said with a wry smile. 'Is that it's basically a diary with a fancy title, where you write down memories you have of your loved one. All the bad memories, as well as the good ones. According to Eric, the most painful memories are the ones that are never expressed or explained. Which is certainly true in my case.'

'And do you find it helps?'

'At first I didn't think it would,' Susan said drily. 'I thought this was just a big load of self-help nonsense. But actually, the more I write, the better I seem to feel. I wasn't always honest with myself, but I'm certainly seeing big changes in my life, now that I'm trying to be.'

Nancy smiled. But then the more she got to know her new housemate, the more she was coming to like and respect her. Susan was a brave soul and she was working so hard on herself to really try to heal. This world would be a far better place, Nancy thought, looking fondly at her, if there were more people like Susan Hayes in it.

'Anyway, never mind about me,' Susan said, pulling her feet up on the sofa beside her. 'How was your day? You're so late home, you must be wrecked.'

'Where do I start?' Nancy groaned exhaustedly, peeling off her coat as the full force of exhaustion really hit her. 'It's production week for us, so we finally get onto the stage and the cast and crew get to work on the actual set for the very first time. Costumes, lighting, props, scenery – this is the week where it all comes together.'

'Must be exciting.'

'It is.' Nancy nodded back. 'But it's bloody terrifying too. Generally everything that can go wrong, will – at least, that's the rule of thumb. We have to work our way through every single sound and lighting cue for the entire play and really nail them down until everything is flowing perfectly. That's just the technical end of it, though, because when that's done, we move on to doing dress rehearsals and then our first few previews, to really bring performances up to speed.'

'So a preview is a bit like a public dress rehearsal, then?' Susan asked.

'Exactly,' Nancy told her. 'But we get to gauge audience reaction, so we often do a lot of chopping and changing between the first preview and the actual opening night.'

'You poor thing – that's a gruelling week you've got ahead of you, by the sound of it.'

'That's the thing about being an assistant director,' Nancy told her. 'My job is a bit like being a plumber. When everything is ticking along nicely, no one should notice what I do – it should be invisible. But if even the slightest thing goes wrong . . . '

'Then the shit really hits the fan.' Susan nodded as Nancy smiled back at her.

'But hey! On the plus side, I get to come back to this beautiful home and spend time with you and Melissa. So I'm certainly not complaining!'

'I'm so glad you've settled in.' Susan smiled. 'Melissa loves having you here – and so do I.'

'That was one of the worst things about finding out I'd been taken for a complete ride by Sam Williams,' Nancy said, wincing a bit at the memory.

'What do you mean?'

'Well,' she went on to explain, 'when Sam Williams Senior told me to pack my bags, I wasn't upset at having to leave that gorgeous house as much as I was at having to leave all of you ladies. My tiger lilies, as I call you now. You, Melissa, Jayne – you've all been like a second family to me since I moved to Dublin and the thought of having to move far away from you . . . I love being here on Primrose Square so much, you see. Not just for the fab location, but for its sense of community. You all care deeply about each other, you look out for each other and when I first moved here from London . . . well, for various reasons, that's exactly what I was craving. A feeling like I really belonged.'

'You never really talk about your life back in London,' Susan said gently. 'In fact, you rarely mention it at all. I hope . . . well, let's just say I hope everything is okay for you over there?'

Nancy had to compose herself before she could answer. *This is the second time today*, she thought, *that I've been asked about my other life in London.*

'I had to get out of there,' she eventually said, knowing that Susan was a good listener and could be trusted. 'I just had to. It all happened so fast, but I knew I had to leave London behind, for my own sanity if nothing else.'

Then to Nancy's own surprise, she started to tear up a bit, as emotional exhaustion finally got the better of her. She could never let it show at the National, where she kept her 'work face' firmly on at all times. But here was different. Here, with Susan, she felt safe. Protected. Minded by one of her fellow tiger lilies.

'You okay?' Susan asked her.

Nancy nodded back, unable to go any further for the minute.

'You know what I think?' Susan said, getting to her feet and walking over to the drinks cabinet beside her fireplace. 'You and me need a glass of wine.'

Nancy smiled back at her.

'Now then,' Susan said, pouring two glasses of Merlot, handing one to Nancy and sitting back down again. 'At St Michael's, the one thing I learned was that talking things out is how we begin to heal. At first I thought it was a pile of bollocks, but now . . . I see the wisdom in it. So here I am, love. And I'm told I've become a good listener.'

Nancy gratefully took a sip of the wine and sat back against the lovely, plush sofa.

'Bad break-up?' Susan guessed.

A nod told her everything she needed to know.

'Very bad. *So* bad. Imagine the very worst you've ever heard of and then keep on multiplying from there,' Nancy said.

'I knew it,' Susan said. 'It never made sense to me, you know. A gorgeous, vibrant woman like you, on her own? I had a feeling something was going on, but of course, none of my business, et cetera. All I'm saying is if you want to talk, here I am.'

There was a long silence before Nancy went any further.

'His name was . . . I mean, is, Peter Wallace,' she said. 'He's a director. Older guy, onto his third marriage by the time we met, well-known around the theatre circuit for decades.'

'Go on,' said Susan supportively. 'How did you first meet?'

'On a directorship programme that I won a place on a few years ago,' Nancy told her. 'It meant two years of good, solid work at the Kensington Theatre, and of course I was thrilled, not just at that, but at the chance to be mentored by some- one like Peter Wallace, whose work I'd admired for years. And at first, it was brilliant – magic. We did four shows together, mostly classical plays, eighteenth-century comedies, that kind of thing, and audiences seemed to enjoy it, the box office was roaring and all was well. But then things began to shift a bit between Peter and me.'

'He made a move on you, you mean?' Susan asked.

Nancy nodded. 'He told me he'd separated from his wife,' she said. 'I was such a fool ever to have believed him, but I suppose a large part of me wanted to by then. We'd worked together so closely, you see, and you've no idea how claustrophobic theatre work is – you're together day and night, and all kinds of hot- house relationships develop that maybe shouldn't. But by then,

I was mad about Peter – he was so gifted and attractive and full of charm, so when he asked me out, I said yes. This, I thought, is a man I really respect and admire – I thought we made a good team. We were together for just a few months, that was all, but then . . . '

'Already I hate the sound of this gobshite, Wallace, whatever his name is,' Susan said tightly. 'Without you saying another word, I want to wring his neck.'

'What makes it all worse,' Nancy said, taking a sip of wine, 'is that all the signs were there, only of course I paid absolutely no attention. Peter would only ever meet me for dinner in out of the way places where we wouldn't meet anyone we knew. And if he stayed over, it was always at my little flat, never at his. He never even introduced me to his friends, his family. And then, not long after, I found out through a mutual pal that he wasn't separated at all. He was still very much with his wife. I'll never forget it: the Olivier Awards were on TV and I was watching it from my sofa at home. And there he was on the screen, Peter with his third wife Camilla. Looking so loved up, I could barely process what I was seeing.'

'What a complete bastard! So what did you do?'

'He called me the night after the Oliviers, but I told him I never wanted to see him again.'

'And did he keep pestering you?'

Nancy nodded. 'It went on for months. He saw no reason why we couldn't still continue "our little fling", as he so romantically put it, even though I spelled it out to him in six-foot high letters. "You're married," I kept telling him, "and you lied to me. You're unavailable and the answer is a very firm no." I thought Peter would be professional enough not to let it interfere with work, but boy, was I wrong. Because from that day on, doors that had opened for me suddenly started slamming in my face. I was supposed to start work as assistant director on a Shakespeare play at the Kensington, but I was dropped at the last minute. And I knew without being told that it was because of Peter.'

'He sounds like a very powerful man in your world.'

'He is.' Nancy nodded. 'And now I was seeing what it was like to be out in the cold. Not only that, but then he started putting out all sorts of rumours about me, that I was difficult to work with, a diva, unprofessional, a has-been.'

'Jesus, Nancy, this is horrendous!' Susan said, getting incensed.

'Worst of all,' Nancy said, taking another badly needed sip of wine, 'he took my good name down with him. All manner of horrible stories started to get back to me, through the few pals I had who believed my side of the story. Camilla, his wife, had found out about us, but Peter made it out that I was the one who'd been harassing him. That I'd thrown myself at him, and was now acting like some kind of dumped, vengeful ex from hell. All complete fiction, of course, but, you see, the theatre world is a tight-knit one and the story gained traction so fast, it terrified me. Even close pals started to ask me if it was true, that I was effectively stalking Peter – whereas the truth was, it had been the other way around.'

Nancy broke off there, too gutted to say more. Reliving it was painful beyond words for her and so many sabre-sharp memories came back. How deeply she'd cared for Peter, trusted him, believed all his lies. How he'd strung her along and messed with her mind, then cast her aside when it suited him. The emotional cost was one thing, but was it fair that she had to pay a professional cost too?

'I could kill him,' Susan said, sounding angry on her behalf. 'I could actually kill him for doing that to you.'

'Then this job in Dublin came up,' Nancy went on, 'so of course, I grabbed it with both hands.'

'And I, for one,' Susan said, 'am bloody glad that you did.'

'I am too,' Nancy said sincerely. 'You've no idea what working here has done for my confidence and self-esteem.'

'In spite of the whole Sam Williams thing?'

'Well,' Nancy said, 'in retrospect, a lot of that was my own stupid fault. The Sam I thought I was in touch with was safely in Shanghai, over five thousand miles away. Enough distance, I thought, so that he could never hurt me again, like Peter had. So I suppose I let myself fall for the idea of him, if nothing else.'

'Makes perfect sense.' Susan nodded wisely.

'I came here to Dublin to get away, little knowing that I'd never want to leave you all. But meeting and coming to live among you ladies has been better than anything. Like a kind of balm to the soul, as they say. You all took me under your wing right from the very start and you made me feel like . . . well, like family, really. I was so lonely when I first came here, you know,' she added, 'and now, the truth is, I don't know how I'll ever go back to London.'

Susan sat back, wrapped in thought.

'But you've got to go back, Nancy,' she eventually said. 'You can't hide from this forever; you've got to right it.'

'That's the whole thing, though,' Nancy said with feeling. 'I couldn't then and I can't now. It's effectively Peter's word against mine, and because he's the big marquee name, lots of people in the business are taking his side—'

'But that's crazy!' Susan interrupted. 'That Peter guy harassed you and it cost you work, and it's just wrong on so many levels. You don't have to take this lying down, Nancy. You can fight this!'

It took a long time before Nancy could answer her.

'For the longest time, though, I felt like I couldn't. Because I wasn't some ingénue actress being targeted. I was complicit. I dated Peter, actually properly dated him, when I thought he was separated. My dad wanted to wring his neck, he was so angry, but my mum was different. She and I both felt that my case was a muddy one – it's different to the ones you read about, isn't it? So when this job came along, Mum was one hundred per cent behind my taking it and putting it all behind me. "It'll be a fresh start for you," she kept saying, and I could only agree.'

'Harassment is harassment!' Susan said firmly, 'and abuse of power is just that, no matter how you dress it up. You did absolutely nothing wrong, Nancy, and the cost to you was your career in London. And you know what? It's not good enough. You were blameless in all this and you've got to do something.'

'I know,' Nancy sighed. 'Mbeki in work has been saying exactly the same thing too. But where do I even begin to right this?'

'By telling the truth,' Susan said. 'Your truth, your way. And by starting right now.'

Jayne

19 PRIMROSE SQUARE

At exactly the same time, a conversation of a very different sort was taking place in number nineteen Primrose Square. Up in Jayne's bedroom, to be exact, as Jayne lay tucked up in her own bed with Eric beside her, their limbs in a huge tangle under the duvet as he cradled her tightly into his chest.

'Oh dear God, Eric,' she said, sitting up with a sudden jolt, completely shattering the lazy, cosy spell that had held them in thrall for the past few, blissful hours.

'Hey honey?' he said through the drowsy half-darkness, looking down at her as she writhed away from him. 'What's up? You okay?'

'I'm not a bit okay,' she said. 'I'm only mortified!'

'Why is that?' he asked, genuinely worried now.

'Eric, would you look at the state of the bedlinen! If I'd known I'd be having company up here, I'd at least have put clean sheets on the bed. And hoovered up a bit. I never thought for two seconds I'd be entertaining company up here!' She could have added something about her hairy underarms and the fuzz on her legs, but prudently decided that it was probably best not to even go there.

'Aww, honey, listen to you . . . ' Eric said soothingly, wrapping his arms around her. At that, she sank back into him, loving the feel of strong arms embracing her. Loving his vitality and warmth and, if it didn't sound too mad, the rude good health emanating from the man. Just goes to show you, she thought to herself, there's a lot to be said for the teetotal, yoga-loving, organic lifestyle, no matter what anyone said.

'You think I care about stuff like your bedsheets?' Eric teased. 'You know all I care about is you.'

'And I care about you too,' she said softly. Except when she said 'care', what she really meant was 'love'. And the weird thing was, she knew exactly that that was what he had meant too.

They stretched out together. Eric nuzzled into her neck in a way that did all manner of funny things to her, and she was just about to lean even deeper into him when, out of nowhere, the phone on her bedside table began to ring.

'Oh, just let it ring,' Eric whispered hoarsely, kissing her more deeply now, and as much as Jayne was loving all the kissing, part of her still fretted that this could be important. Maybe it was Susan or Melissa or someone who needed her?

'Oh my God, it's Jason,' she said out loud, as she stretched over Eric to fumble for the ringing phone. 'What can he want?'

'Take the call, honey,' Eric said with a smile, helpfully handing the phone to her. 'I know my girl. You won't relax till you know there isn't someone somewhere who needs help.'

'Hello?' Jayne said, answering. 'Jason, love, is that you?'

She cradled the phone in between herself and Eric, so he was able to listen into both sides of the chat.

'Ehh, yeah, how are things with you, Ma?' said Jason, sounding like he was ringing from home. Jayne could clearly hear the twins in the background, fighting over a top one of them had borrowed and seemed to have got deodorant stains on.

'All well here,' Jayne said, trying not to giggle. 'Nothing strange or startling to report.'

'Ahh, great, great,' said Jason. 'Anyway, the thing is, Ma, me and Irene would like to invite you and Eric over for dinner this weekend.'

'A proper, formal dinner, tell her!' Jayne heard Irene say crisply in the background. 'In the dining room. Like a Christmas dinner, be sure to say that to her.'

'I'm telling her, will you let me talk, for feck's sake?' Jason hissed back, while Jayne and Eric tried not to smile.

'It would just be nice for us all to welcome Eric into our home, you know yourself, Ma,' Jason explained, as Irene wittered away about table centrepieces and getting out the good china for the occasion.

'Did you hear that, Ma?' Jason joked into the phone. 'Youse are even getting the good china – now don't fall over in shock, whatever you do.'

Jayne looked up at Eric, who nodded yes. In the background, Irene talked over him, unaware that both Jayne and Eric could both hear her loud and clear as they snuggled up together, with the phone still wedged in between them.

'You left out the most important part, you eejit,' she was hissing furiously. 'Which is that now you and Eric are business partners, you'd like to get to know him better. Be sure to say that, Jason! Stress the business partners bit!'

'It's all right, son,' Jayne said, terrified she'd get a fit of giggles. 'Tell Irene that's absolutely grand with us. We'll both look forward to Saturday.'

She hung up, tossed her phone aside and stretched luxuriantly back into the warmth of Eric's chest.

'Well, now, isn't that a turn up for the books?' she said.

'Amazing,' he grinned, playing with a strand of her hair, 'the attitude adjustment that just taking out my cheque book can bring about.'

'You're so good to put up with my family, you know,' Jayne said. 'You've been extraordinary. You've had the patience of Gandhi, since day one.'

'But your family are my family,' he said simply, going back to kiss her neck again, in a way that made her tingle in the strangest, loveliest way.

She couldn't hear what he said next as it all got a bit muffled, but she could have sworn it sounded like, 'Or at least, I hope someday soon, they will be.'

Melissa

18 PRIMROSE SQUARE

Living with Nancy was turning out to be the best thing ever, so much so that Melissa didn't know what she'd do when the time came for Nancy to go back to London. It was sort of one of those things that was inevitable, but something that she preferred to put to the back of her mind and not think about too much.

But till then, Nancy had brightened up her Easter holidays in the most *amazing* way imaginable. She'd invited Melissa to come along to the National Theatre with her, so she could see firsthand how they 'teched' a play, before the show eventually went in front of an actual, live audience.

'Now, it could turn out to be incredibly boring for you,' Nancy had stressed beforehand. 'Mainly because we'll be doing a lot of "topping and tailing".'

'What's that?' Melissa asked her, mystified.

'It's where we work through a scene, but instead of focusing on the performances or the flow of the piece, we concentrate on nailing all the sound and lighting cues until they're absolutely perfect. But sometimes, we have to go over all those cues again and again until we're happy they're set. So if you do get a bit bored . . . '

'As if I could ever be bored here!' Melissa said stoutly.

'So you'll be like my little PA for the day then, yeah?' Nancy said, as the two of them walked in through the main doors of the

National, all prepped for what lay ahead. Melissa had beamed, delighted with herself.

And if truth be told, delighted with the distraction from her own thoughts too. Mainly because she'd been a bit confused and puzzled ever since they'd got their school holidays.

That last day, before school broke up. She kept coming back to it time and again. Why had Josh Andrews bothered to give her the time of day? He'd been so nice to her too, giving her the little sympathy card, which Melissa still hadn't had the courage to show to her mum just yet.

Because there was so much she didn't understand. Like why her mum was so down on Josh, when he seemed as upset as everyone else about Ella? Melissa had often overheard her parents talking about Josh, and the things they both said were awful. Her mum even called him 'the spawn of the devil', back when she was still taking all those stupid purple-y pills. Yet he'd gone to all the trouble of seeking Melissa out in school to give her a card and say nice things about Ella and remember her anniversary. Why?

It didn't make sense then and it certainly didn't now either. But for the moment, at least, Melissa was happy to park her worries and instead enjoy spending time at the National.

'Oh . . . just look at it . . . it's so *beautiful*!' she gasped, when Nancy led her in through the main auditorium and she got to see the set of *Pride and Prejudice* for the very first time.

'Isn't it?' Nancy said proudly. 'I have to say, it's even more breathtaking than I ever would have hoped.'

The set was like an nineteenth-century assembly room come to life, with huge Grecian pillars that dominated the side of the stage, a proper floor like in a ballroom, and even a giant chandelier that gave the effect of being lit solely by candles. Some of the cast were already out on stage, half in costume and half not, still getting used to the space.

'Hey, Melissa! Here's our future little Olivier award-winner,' said Alan, coming over to greet her like a long lost friend. 'You're here to put manners on us today, I hope?' he added cheekily.

Melissa smiled. She'd liked Alan from the very first time she met him. He looked so funny today too, dressed in Regency white tie and tails from the waist up, and a pair of battered jeans from the waist down. He was also holding onto a paper mug from the Costa across the road, which looked all wrong against the Regency backdrop.

'Melissa is my eyes and ears for the day,' said Nancy, 'so this better go smoothly.'

'So I hear you and Nancy are housemates now?' he said lightly to her. 'You'll have to tell me what she's like to live with. A nightmare, I'm guessing!' he added jokingly.

'Now, now,' Nancy said, wagging her finger in pretend annoyance. 'No telling tales out of school, please.'

'You can fill me in later,' Alan said to Melissa, in an exaggerated stage whisper.

'D'you know, I was telling my friend Hayley in school all about you.' She grinned back at him. 'She's so excited about seeing the show – and about maybe getting to meet you afterwards too.'

'We'll make the biggest fuss of you and all your pals when they come to the show,' Alan said reassuringly. 'At the start of a tech week like this one, the opening night always seems so far away. I'm half dreading it and half just wanting to get it over with, if that makes sense.'

'Why is that?' Melissa asked.

'Critics, my daaaaahling,' he said, putting on an affected luvvie voice that made him sound just like Craig Revel Horwood from *Strictly.*

Melissa giggled, just as Mbeki bounced over to say hi, wearing the most stunning scarlet red woolly dress and beaming with smiles, as she always was. Melissa loved all the cast and crew Nancy worked with, but most especially Alan and Mbeki – they made her feel so welcome, so part of the whole show.

'Hey, there you are!' Mbeki said, giving Melissa a big bear hug. She smelt lovely too, like vanilla. Like sweets, Melissa thought. 'It's so great you're here today,' she added. 'I could really use a little helper.'

'Hands off,' Nancy teased, 'she's all mine for the day.'

'Tell you what,' Mbeki suggested, with a tiny little wink in Nancy's direction, 'how about if Melissa helps me to prompt today? Would you be up for it, honey?' she said to Melissa. 'All you'd have to do is sit out front in the auditorium with a script in your hand and prompt any unfortunate actors that dry on me. Then later on, I'll kill them, but you don't need to be here for that bit.'

'I've *love* that, thank you so much!' Melissa said, thrilled to have a proper job to do.

'Fantastic.' Mbeki grinned her lovely wide smile. 'In that case, come with me and I'll get you all set up.'

'Just go easy on me if I drop a line!' Alan laughed.

Then from behind came a voice that made everyone jump.

'*Qué es esto?* What is that? Actors standing around drinking ze café onstage? On my stage? Why are you not doing much preparations before performance? Warming up? *No professional!*'

Diego Fernandez was standing at the front row of the auditorium, and he seemed to be in a foul temper, although for the life of her, Melissa couldn't understand why. Everyone was working away and the set looked so lovely to her.

'Good morning, Diego,' Nancy said evenly, stepping off the stage and going to join him. 'If I can just go through today's schedule and running order with you?'

'*Hazlo rápido*,' Diego muttered grumpily, glowering at everyone.

'Better get cracking.' Alan winked down at Melissa. 'When he gets like this, the less the rest of us annoy him, the better.'

Mbeki guided Melissa to a great seat – 'The best in the house', as she put it – at the back of the auditorium, but with a sweeping panoramic view over the whole stage. Meanwhile, Nancy sat up in the front row beside Diego as they painstakingly worked through each and every lighting and sound cue, one by one.

It was such hard work. In less than one week, Melissa thought, an audience will come to this show, and sit in these very seats, and they'll see wonderful performances and glittering costumes and a beautiful, elegant love story played out for them. What they won't see is the blood, sweat and tears that went into making it all happen. The graft and the grit, as Nancy kept saying.

Nancy wasn't joking when she kept turning back to Melissa to ask whether she was bored off her head yet?

'No, it's brilliant, I'm loving it! Melissa hissed back at her, with a big, cheery thumbs-up sign. But the truth was that after three hours of teching the show, they were still only on Scene One, the bit where we first meet all the characters at the Meryton ball, and where Lizzy and Darcy take an instant dislike to each other. And no one had needed any prompts at all.

'No!' Diego was snapping at no one in particular. 'The harpsichord cue is *malo* . . . bad . . . terrible . . . *mierda*! Again!'

Nancy turned back to give Melissa a little eye roll and Melissa smiled sympathetically back at her, as if to say, 'God, he's so mean!' But another half hour passed and, after a whole morning of this, she was starting to get a bit twitchy with boredom.

Then she remembered that at least she had her phone to play with. Not that it was *her* phone, exactly. It was Ella's phone rightfully, but Melissa had kept it and occasionally looked through it, to see all the photos on it mainly. No one else seemed to want it, or to even notice that it was missing, so she figured, why not?

The phone had no credit on it, so making calls or going online was out of the question, but Melissa didn't mind. She just liked to look at photos of Ella, taken back in happier times. Long before she fell in with Josh Andrews and his gang, and long before those stupid drugs ever came into her life.

You'd have loved a day like today, Ella, Melissa thought, idly scrolling down through the camera roll. *You'd have loved being at the theatre and being a part of this world. You might even have liked the play too, given than Lizzy Bennet is so independent and strong*. A prototype feminist, according to Nancy, anyway.

Ella's phone was ancient and hopelessly out of date now, but the photo app still worked pretty well. So Melissa scrolled down through picture after picture, remembering Ella as she used to be, back when she was bossy and fun and full of chat and the kind of big sister you wanted to grow up to be just like.

Diego was just throwing a wobbly about a sound cue that wasn't to his liking and Nancy was frantically trying to get on top of it, when Melissa accidentally hit off another app on the phone.

The Whatsapp one, where you could message your friends and family all for free.

Well, this is weird, she thought. She'd never stumbled into this particular app before, assuming any messages would all have been wiped out long ago. It was something that had never even occurred to her to check. And yet, now that she had got into it, to her surprise she saw that there weren't just a few, but there were loads of messages both to and from Ella.

Then Melissa's eye fell on the date of some of the last messages that had been both sent and received.

And in that one moment, every single thing changed.

24 Hour Party People
Jesus, guys, that was sick last night – I've never done anything like that before. Sorry for giving you all grief about it at first, but you were right, man. That stuff got me through the night, I can tell you!
Ella

From: Josh
Ella, watch out for the munchies later on – can take you by surprise. Be warned.

And another message from someone called Marc, who was on the Whatsapp group and who'd joined in the chat.

From: Marc

Who knew that sleeping rough could turn out to be so much fun?

Melissa's blood froze. That message was dated December of the previous year. Which rang a bell with her, because that was around the same time that Ella had first gone on the charity sleep-out with Josh and his gang. When all the trouble first started, like her mum was always saying.

There was an instant response from Ella, though, that sounded far more like the kind of thing she would say.

Jesus, Marc, some people sleep rough because they have to – it's not a cocktail party for those people. Have respect.

And a response from Josh.

Well said, Ella. Party at mine this weekend, you're so coming. You don't have a choice in the matter #buddiesnow

Melissa quickly scrolled down through the next lot of messages, all of which were about a big party Josh was having, which you'd think was the Oscars the way his gang on the Whatsapp group were all going on about it. But then her eye fell on another message that stopped the breath at the back of her throat. It was dated about a month later, and it was from Marc, one of Josh's gang, to Ella directly.

From: Marc
Come on Ella, you too chicken shit to try it? This stuff is Grade A. Yours for €100 a pop. You know you want to.

Then Ella's response:

Maybe just this once . . .

From: Marc
Safe as a house. Promise.

The next batch of messages were dated about a week later.

From: Ella
More!!!! When are we doing some more? At yours again, Josh? You got a free house? My mother is down on me like a ton of bricks these days, pointless coming here.

From: Marc
Have you got the cash?

From: Ella
Not yet, but I will. Gimme time.

From: Marc
You know the rules, girlfriend. You want to play, you gotta pay. Josh, my man, you in?

Then there was a far longer message, this time sent from Josh directly to Ella, so it looked like no one else could read it.

From: Josh

Ella, I'm getting worried about you. You've gone in too deep, too soon. Come on El, is this really you? Am starting to think Marc is bad news. To be discussed later. At length. Meet you after school, the usual place.

There were a bunch more messages from Marc and Hugo, another guy who they all hung around with, about them all meeting up that weekend to 'do stuff', as the message cryptically said. Melissa wasn't too sure what 'do stuff' meant exactly, but she could hazard a fairly good guess.

The next set of messages between Josh and Ella were all a lot longer, though, and seemed to have been sent privately to each other.

From: Josh

So are we OK? You and me, El, are we good?

From: Ella

Fuck off. Best thing you could do is not contact me again.

From: Josh

Come on, am worried here. I wouldn't be a true pal unless I was worried.

From: Ella

Oh spare me your sanctimonious shite. Just listen to your-self, Josh. Never thought you could be so self-righteous.

From: Josh

If you see concern about a good friend as self-righteousness, then you need to take a good, long, hard look at yourself in the mirror, El. I'm out now and you need to do the same.

Then another message from Josh, which went ignored.

And another thing, El. Marc = very bad news. Only a matter of time before he lands himself in some seriously hot shit.

And the very last message of all. One that chilled Melissa to the bone, particularly when she realised the date it had been sent on.

I know you're going to the party tonight, El. And I've a fair idea what's planned. I'll be there too, but like I told you, clean means clean. I'm focusing on my rugby from now on and fuck anyone who tells me that's not cool. You included, El. Because this isn't the real you and you know it's not. So I'll see you tonight and I'll watch over you and I'll keep an eye out for you if you do take anything and get baked. If it goes wrong, I'll even hold your hair back while you puke your guts up.

But I won't join in with you. So are we good?

Ella?

Melissa put the phone down, feeling sick and worried, and knowing that what she'd just seen was somehow very, very big.

Nancy

Nancy called time out to the cast at 3 p.m. They looked utterly worn-out as they all exhaustedly peeled off to dressing rooms for a welcome breather.

Then she made for the back row of the auditorium to find Melissa, but instead of being her usual bubbly self, Nancy found her pale and very withdrawn. A million miles from how she'd been just a few hours ago.

'Hey, how are you doing back here?' Nancy asked, to total silence in return.

'Melissa?' Nancy gently persisted. 'You okay, honey?'

'Fine,' she replied, looking down at the floor.

'Is something upsetting you?' Nancy asked her. 'Did something happen when I was working?'

Silence from Melissa. Which was so unlike her, Nancy thought.

'Whatever it is,' she persisted, 'you can talk to me, you know that.'

'Nothing happened,' Melissa eventually said. 'At least, nothing happened to me. It's more like . . . I found out something. By accident, I mean.'

'What are you talking about, honey?' Nancy asked, growing more and more concerned about her.

'Nancy, I think I.'

Nancy looked at her little friend for a moment, at her ghostly white, worried face and made a snap decision. Seconds later, she was striding down to the cast and crew tannoy and making an announcement that went right over Diego's head. She'd be shot at dawn for this later on, no doubt, but just for the moment, she didn't care two hoots.

'Cast and crew break has been extended to one full hour,' Nancy said crisply into the tannoy. 'See you then, everyone.'

A hot, Latin glare at Nancy from Diego, which she pointedly ignored.

'Come on,' said Nancy, firmly gripping her by the hand. 'I'm taking you back to Primrose Square. Now, honey. Let them fire me for it, if they want, I don't care! Right now, you are *far* more important.'

Susan

One week later

To her surprise, he was already in the coffee shop ahead of her, waiting at a relatively quiet table for two by the window. For some reason, this pleased Susan. He automatically stood up to greet her when she came in and for a minute they talked over each other, the way you do whenever nerves take hold and you can't stop yourself.

'Thank you so much for meeting with me,' she began to say.

'It's no problem at all, I was glad to get your call,' he said at the exact same time.

A waiter appeared to take orders; both asked for Americanos.

'I shouldn't,' he said with a grimace, 'I'm in training right now, and you're supposed to cut out caffeine, but what the hell.'

Then a moment of stilted silence, while Susan regarded him from across the table. He was so physically huge, he seemed to dwarf the table, just by sitting at it.

All this time, she thought. *All along, I blamed you and you silently took it and now I somehow have to try and find words to apologise.*

'You don't have to say anything, you know,' Josh said, almost like he was reading her mind. 'It's okay. I get it. I just hope you and me are cool now, that's all.'

'No, it's not, Josh,' she said firmly. 'It's not okay. None of this is okay.'

'Oh, right, yeah,' he said, slumping back in the chair behind him. 'Sorry, I spoke before I thought there. You mean with Ella being . . . like . . . gone . . . and everything.'

'I mean Ella, of course,' she said, wincing a little at his choice of words, but reminding herself that there was actually a good heart beating underneath it all. 'But I'm talking about you, too, Josh. Because I misjudged you. God, I was so vile to you – really horrible. Then I find out, totally by chance, that instead of goading Ella on to try out even harder and harder drugs, you were actually the one trying to stop her. All along, I blamed you, when I really should have been down on my knees thanking my lucky stars she had a friend like you.'

He said nothing as their coffees arrived. Just shrugged and looked out the window, embarrassed.

'I'm sorry, Josh, she said simply. 'I really am so very sorry for all the terrible things I did to you and said about you—'

'It's okay,' he said.

'It's not okay,' she answered. 'When I think of myself, standing outside your front window night after night . . . '

'Yeah . . . that was pretty freaky all right . . . '

'Jesus, how you and your parents didn't sue the arse off me, I'll never know.'

'My dad wanted to at one point,' Josh said, starting to fidget and crack his knuckles, as if he was nervous. 'He's a barrister, you know? And he was all on about slander and assault and a whole shitload of other stuff too.'

'I can imagine,' Susan said. She'd met Josh's dad once or twice and he really was terrifying.

'But I wouldn't let him,' Josh told her.

'You wouldn't?' Susan said. 'You'd have been perfectly entitled to. No one would have blamed you.'

'I didn't sue,' Josh went on, still cracking at his knuckles, 'because I kept thinking, what would Ella do if she was here now? And you know what she'd have done, Mrs H?'

'Tell me,' said Susan, overwhelmed at what she was hearing.

'She'd have told my folks to get over it and to cop themselves on. Then, knowing her, she'd probably have reminded them that there are refugees coming from Syria who'd kill to have all of our first world problems.'

Susan nodded and smiled. Because yes, that's pretty much exactly what Ella would have said.

'I do miss her, you know,' Josh eventually said.

'I know you do – now,' Susan said, really believing it.

'No one ever got that she and I were friends,' he went on. 'But we were, you know. We really were. I loved the way she'd challenge me and get me to think about things in a different way and . . . '

'And?' Susan said, liking the way this conversation was going.

'She cared so much about everything,' Josh told her, 'and she made me care too. About stuff I never even considered before. You know, like the Gaza Strip. And Syria. And people who wear fur. Jeez, she'd give me hell for eating red meat,' he added, with a smirk. 'Even when I tried to explain to her that it was for training. She just told me to cop myself on and that there was more protein in eggs anyway.'

'That was my Ella, all right.' Susan smiled.

'In fact . . . ' he began, but he broke off before finishing.

'Go on,' Susan prompted gently.

'Well . . . everyone said she and I were such opposites and I know we were. But the way we sparked off each other was brilliant. And then we'd laugh ourselves sick . . . and . . . you remember how she used to laugh with her whole body?'

'I remember.' Susan smiled again.

'It feels weird saying this to you of all people,' he went on, sounding a lot more comfortable now, 'but I kind of fancied Ella. I did ask her out once, you know . . . '

'You did?' Susan said, surprised, but then this was news to her.

'She said we were better as friends, though. And she was right too. I'd never had a mate like her before and I never will again.'

'What matters to me now,' Susan said, leaning across the table towards him, 'is that I know you tried to help her. And there really are no words for me to say how grateful I am to you for that.'

'The drugs weren't her, you know,' he said, after a thoughtful pause. 'She was just experimenting, the way we all were, that was it. It started the night we had that charity sleep-out, do you remember?'

'Vividly,' Susan told him.

'And for Ella, it just went from there. You know how wild she was: once she'd made up her mind to do a thing, there was no stopping her. But for some reason, the night of that party last year, Ella got unlucky. It's shite, I know, and it can't bring Ella back, but I promise you, Mrs Hayes, that's all it was.'

'I know,' She said softly. 'And call me Susan, please.'

'It all was that idiot Marc Casey's doing,' he went on. 'Producing pills out of a sandwich bag and claiming that they were beans.'

Which was the street name for MDMA, Susan didn't have to be told, cut with God only knows what. She'd even heard rat poison or sometimes bath salts after the post-mortem, but a year on, that was still something she was actively trying to block out.

'You needn't tell me about Marc Casey,' Susan said. 'I have big plans to help him back on the straight and narrow.'

'You do?'

'Oh yes, you just watch this space,' Susan went on. 'I've already contacted his mother.'

'And what happened?'

'Marc's family, as you can imagine, were worried sick that the new information we now have might lead to Ella's case being reopened.'

'It won't, though, will it?' Josh asked worriedly.

'No,' Susan said sadly. 'But I know the truth and, as far as I'm concerned, that's all I ever wanted out of this.'

She did, however, make it very clear to Marc's family that she had one single condition for not pressing charges against their son. Namely, that he check himself into St Michael's Wellness Centre for immediate treatment. If they can't straighten him out there, Susan figured, then no one can. Plus the thought of Dr Ciara and Bunny and Emily and Bungalow Bill getting their paws on Marc Casey and sorting him out made her smile.

'Well, at least one good thing has come out of it,' Josh added, with a casual shrug.

'What's that?'

'I'm volunteering now. Ella was always on my case about how I came from a privileged background and that it meant I had a duty to give something back.'

Susan smiled at that. It sounded so like Ella, it was almost as if she was sitting at the table in between them.

'You know the Narcotics Anonymous group in Temple Bar?' he went on. 'Well, I've agreed to help out there once a week. My rugby coach is going apeshit about it, but . . . I think Ella would have liked it. So I'm doing it for her, really. To hell with the rest of them anyway.'

Susan gave him a warm smile. 'She'd have loved that, Josh,' she found the words to say. 'And thank you.'

'In fact, they were on at me to maybe give a talk about drugs at school,' he said. 'If that was cool with you, that is,' he added a bit warily. 'You know about how Ella was the least likely person to ever turn into a user. But that if it can happen to her, it could happen to any one of us.'

'I think that's a fantastic idea,' Susan told him, really meaning it too. 'And who knows? Maybe it's something I could help out with too, if you'd like?'

One life is gone, she thought. *But maybe, just maybe, others can be saved. Maybe you didn't die needlessly after all, my darling.*

'That would be great, thanks.' Josh grinned and, for a momentary flash, Susan could see the charm in him. The eager-to-please, sweeter side to him that Ella picked up on right away.

'And Mrs H?' he asked. 'I hope you don't mind, but I brought you something.'

'You did?'

He bent down under the table and started to fumble about a bit, then produced a slightly bashed-looking bunch of flowers.

'These are for you,' he said, looking a bit shy as he passed them over the table.

'Oh Josh, there really was no need,' Susan began to say, but then her voice caught at the back of her throat.

Tiger lilies. He'd gone and bought her tiger lilies.

'It's the weirdest thing,' Josh said. 'For some reason, I just saw them and thought of Ella. Isn't that, like, seriously *weird?*'

Melissa

'More eyeliner, or less?'

'Dopey question. More, of course – you can never have enough eyeliner! And help me with my fake tan, will you? It's starting to dribble down my arm!'

Melissa and her pal Hayley were upstairs in her bedroom, frantically getting ready for the big opening night and messing around with make-up, which neither of them really had the first clue about.

Then a text message came through to Melissa's phone.

'OMG,' she yelped, reading the message. 'You won't believe this, but it's from Abby Graham!'

'Abby Graham?' said Hayley. 'After she's been such a mean girl? What does she say?'

'*I hear you're both off to a big opening night tonight*,' Melissa read, still shocked that Abby would contact her. '*VIP tickets, the whole works. Just wanted to say enjoy and see you Monday.*'

'She's only being nice because we're in with the in-crowd now,' Hayley said. 'Just ignore her, Mel. Abby Graham is just a wagon, everyone knows that.'

'Or . . . ' Melissa said thoughtfully, playing with her phone.

'Or what?' said Hayley, momentarily abandoning her fake tan.

'Or we could be kind and take her back a programme from tonight. Maybe even one that the cast have signed. Eric always says that when you're kind to people who've been horrible to you, they turn into complete pussycats. What do you think?'

Hayley smiled fondly at her best friend. 'I think what every-one says about you is true, Melissa. You really are like an angel.'

'Girls?' Susan's voice called up the stairs. 'Come downstairs, quick! It's time to go, and wait till you see what's waiting for us outside the front door!'

Hayley and Melissa legged it down the stairs, both wearing high heels that neither of them were used to, but feeling so impossibly glamorous, the pain was well worth it.

'Well, well, well, look at these two supermodels!' said Jayne, who was over by the fireplace sipping at a glass of fizz, as Eric stood right beside her. Susan had asked them both in for a little pre-show drink and now they all gave a ripple of applause as both girls did an impromptu catwalk show for everyone.

'Amazing!' said Eric, clapping.

'The blue is stunning on you, Melissa, love,' said Jayne kindly. 'It's so your colour. And as for the pink on you, Hayley? It's to die for.'

'Blue is the colour of loyalty and wisdom.' Eric nodded and smiled. 'And pink is the colour of kindness. Great choices, ladies.'

'Now come on, everyone,' said Susan, starting to marshal everyone out the front door, 'we need to make a move or we'll be late. Imagine if Nancy had to hold the curtain just for us? And you have to see what she's organised for us outside!'

Everyone grabbed coats and bags, then scrambled out the front door, to see a giant white stretch limo waiting just for them.

'OMG!' Melissa squealed delightedly. 'You mean Nancy did all this, just for us?'

'This is turning into the *best* night ever!' Hayley screeched, as they all clambered inside, marvelling at the white leather interiors, not to mention the fact that there was a large jar of chocolates for everyone to dip into, while they drove the short distance to the National Theatre. Hayley started to do selfies from just about every angle, as Susan quietly gripped Melissa's arm.

'And you never know, love,' she said, looking utterly beautiful in a crushed wine-coloured velvet coat that she'd gone and bought specially. 'This may not be the only surprise that you're in for tonight.'

Nancy

NATIONAL THEATRE

Opening night. There was a great theatre in-gag about opening nights that was doing the rounds at the National, about George Bernard Shaw, no less. Apparently he wrote to Winston Churchill, inviting him to the premiere of *Pygmalion*. 'Bring a friend,' Shaw's invitation read. 'If you have one.'

And Churchill's pithy response? To send his apologies saying he couldn't make the opening, but that he'd attend on the second night instead. 'If you have one.'

Nancy hated opening nights. Really hated them with a passion. She was a bag of nerves and could quite happily have spent the evening with her head buried down the loo, but sadly that wasn't an option. She was backstage in the dressing rooms before the show, where everyone was in a state of heightened anxiety, dispensing good luck cards and thoughtful little gifts in each room she popped her head into, to wish everyone a cheery 'good luck'.

'Now you must remember, darling,' Lady Catherine admonished Nancy, 'it's bad luck to say good luck on opening night. Say "break a leg" instead, and then that covers us for all eventualities.'

'And I have a little something that'll bring luck to us all,' said her dressing room-mate, Mrs Bennet. 'Here!' she said, delightedly producing a bottle of fizz and putting it into the minibar conveniently tucked into the corner of the tiny, windowless room. 'A little something for after the show. To celebrate what I know will be a great success!'

'Just so long as she doesn't get at it till after the curtain comes down,' quipped Lady C, with a half-wink in Nancy's direction.

Then she rapped on the men's dressing room door, where Mr Darcy was struggling into a pair of Regency white knee breeches as Alan came over to Nancy with a little gift.

'For you,' he said, shyly handing over a little posy of roses. The cutest, neatest bouquet you ever saw. 'Just to say . . . well, you've been a joy to work with, from day one. You really have.'

Nancy caught a glimpse of the two of them reflected back at her in the dressing room mirror and it made her temporarily forget her nerves and smile. Mr Wickham in full top coat and tails, as she stood opposite him in her opening night bright red cocktail dress, which she was wearing out of superstition more than anything else, really. Her mum had bought it for her years ago and it had always brought her luck.

'Wow, thanks, Alan,' she said, genuinely touched. 'Just keep doing what you're doing and you'll knock 'em dead.'

Most astonishingly of all, even Diego was actually being nice to everyone.

'You must all keep energy up in Act Two,' he finger-wagged in the green room before curtain up, as everyone nervously paced around. 'And all will be good. Very good, even.'

Then he turned to Nancy and spoke more quietly. 'I see there are something little for you. Delivery. In the scene dock area. You need to go there – now.'

Bewildered, Nancy did as she was told and walked out of the green room to the semi-darkness of the scene dock backstage left, where the props table was laden down with fans, reticules and all manner of regency knick-knacks, all set for Scene One.

'Hey Nancy!' said Mbeki, looking as radiant as ever in a skin-tight bottle green dress. 'I guess someone has a fan club – look what just arrived for you!'

Nancy looked over to a side table, where two giant bouquets were waiting, with her name printed neatly on each one. Not, only that but, beside the flowers, was a handwritten envelope with her name scrawled across it.

'Well, go on,' Mbeki urged, 'open everything! Aren't you dying to know who they're all from?'

Nancy began with the envelope first. She felt she had to, as it looked so incongruous sitting beside such stunning bouquets of flowers.

Hi Nancy,

I'm writing to say that I'm sorry. The old man told me you really put it up to him and his solicitor buddy, insisting on an apology before you'd agree to drop the matter and not take it any further.

My apology is genuine, it really is. You were a sort of 'collateral damage' in the ongoing feud between me and my father, and for my part in that, I'm truly sorry. Meeting you that day really made me feel like a heel – and not just because you were, rightly, so annoyed with me for what I did. But because you seem like a nice woman. Normal. Friendly. You deserve better and I only hope that you find it.

Good luck, Nancy Thompson.

Sincerely,

Sam Williams, Junior

'Bloody hell,' Mbeki said, reading it over Nancy's shoulder.

'I don't believe it,' Nancy said, stunned. 'In the solicitors that day, I insisted on an apology, but I never thought I'd get one. I wanted to be sure that Sam Williams had actually learned a lesson and, with luck, that he'd never put another woman through what he'd put me through. But in a million years I didn't think he'd actually do as I asked. Wow,' she said, turning to Mbeki. 'I suppose this is what you call a result. And it feels good, it really does.'

'You want to know something?' Mbeki said, looking thoughtful.

'What's that?'

'The reason you got that apology is because you stood up for yourself. So come on, Nancy . . . if you can do that with Sam Williams, why can't you do the very same with Peter Wallace when you get back to London?'

Nancy nodded. *Why not indeed?*

'I think you're right. I think it's time,' she told Mbeki. 'Speaking to you about it, and to all the other amazing women who've come into my life lately, has really made me see that.'

'Now come on, girlfriend,' Mbeki said bossily, 'it's almost half an hour to curtain and if you're not going to see who those magnificent bouquets are from, then I am!'

'I can't believe this,' Nancy said, turning her attention to the flowers. 'No one ever send me flowers – *ever*.' Her parents had called her earlier to wish her a cheery 'good luck, darling', but they wouldn't be over to see the show till later on in the run, so she knew the bouquets couldn't be from them.

'Well, if you don't open the cards, I will,' said Mbeki. 'Quick!'

The first card read:

You have real talent, Nancy.
Maybe we work together again one day, yes? Maybe even you do
my job one day. I think so, yes?
It's been a pleasure. You did good.
Fond wishes,
Diego Fernandez

At that, Nancy almost fell over.

'And that,' said Mbeki, reading the card over her shoulder, 'is what you might call praise from Caesar. Now come on, read the other one, will you? I'm hoping you've got a secret admirer, so we can keep you here in Dublin!'

The second bouquet was ginormous, predominantly made up of tiger lilies.

To our Primrose Square star:
We're all so proud of you!
Biggest hugs from Jayne, Susan and Melissa. The ladies of Prim-
rose Square.
Your little Dublin family.

'No, these aren't from a secret admirer,' Nancy said, smiling at Mbeki and bending down to inhale the beautiful musky scent from the flowers. 'It's better than that. So, so much better.'

Melissa

NATIONAL THEATRE

Melissa and Hayley thought they'd self-combust with excitement at the pre-show champagne reception.

'Okay, so far we've seen two of the presenters from TV3, your man who plays for the Irish soccer team, Katie from *Ireland's Got Talent* and the bass player from Kodaline!' Hayley squealed. 'This is going down as the most amazing night of my whole life!'

'I know!' Melissa giggled. 'I think I might have run out of room on my phone, I've taken so many photos and selfies!'

'And right here behind you,' said Susan, gently interrupting the girls, 'is the woman we have to thank for all this.'

Everyone turned as Nancy joined them, looking stunning in what she'd told Melissa was her 'lucky' red dress, which clung to her neat little figure and made her look like one of those YouTube superstars, who work as models on the side as well. She seemed so cool and calm and unruffled, even though Melissa knew her pal was really a bag of nerves inside.

'Nancy!' Melissa said, rushing over to hug her tight. 'This is so incredible!'

'How are you feeling, Nancy, love?' Jayne asked her kindly. 'Certainly it looks as though the evening is off to a great start.'

'Oh, don't talk to me,' said Nancy, fanning her face with a programme. 'I'm just about holding it together, but believe me, I'll be a lot happier when the final curtain comes down. If all goes well, that is.'

There was a loud chorus of 'of course it will!' from Melissa, Hayley, Susan, Jayne and Eric.

'The show will go brilliantly,' said Melissa stoutly. 'I know. I've already seen it. Sort of. And it's going to knock everyone's socks off.'

'Have a glass of champagne,' Susan offered, but Nancy shook her head.

'I'd kill for a glass of fizz right now,' she said, 'but I think I'll only really enjoy it when the show is over.'

Then Susan steered Nancy to the side to whisper in her ear. Melissa couldn't catch what it was, but she did hear Nancy's reply.

'Not yet,' Nancy said under her breath. 'But soon.'

It was even stranger when they all took their seats before curtain up in the packed auditorium. Nancy had made sure that they'd got the best seats in the house, but what Melissa couldn't understand was that on a night like this, with tickets like gold dust, there was still one solitary, vacant seat in between her and Susan.

Excitement mounted as the orchestra tuned up, the National Anthem played and everyone stood up as the President of Ireland entered and took his seat, directly in front of them.

'OMG,' Hayley mouthed. 'This is like . . . sitting in the royal box! Wait till I tell everyone . . . No one will believe this!'

Then, as the lights dimmed before curtain up, Melissa was aware of someone slipping quietly into the vacant seat beside her. She turned abruptly – and there was her dad. Gripping hands with her mum, and winking sideways at her.

'Hey, princess,' he whispered. 'I told you I'd make the show, didn't I? And better late than never.'

If Melissa had thought the pre-show drinks reception glamorous and glitzy, it was nothing compared with the high-octane star wattage of the after-show party, held at the long bar in the National Theatre. Just about everywhere she looked, she was surrounded by happy friends and family, all glowing from the joy of a great show, brilliantly performed. Even Lady Catherine and Mrs Bennet, who'd been so mean to each other every time Melissa saw them in rehearsals, were actually laughing and joking and clinking champagne glasses together, side by side up at the bar.

But no one here, Melissa thought, *is as thrilled as me*. She was overjoyed to have her dad home again, and never for one second suspecting that this was a little surprise just for her that her mum had long been brewing.

'Best of all,' her dad proudly told her, 'is that I'm home for good this time. So you never know, princess. Maybe you, me and your mum will get to take that trip to the West End that I've promised you both for so long.'

'It doesn't matter about that, Dad.' Melissa beamed, gripping onto one of his hands as her mum held onto the other one. 'All that matters to me is that you're here. You're really here and Mum is here and it's . . . well, it's perfect. Tonight has been completely perfect from start to finish.'

'Hey, here's our local Primrose Square celebrity!' said Jayne, giving a spontaneous round of applause when Nancy joined their little group, clutching a neat posy of roses. 'That was amazing – the best night out I've had in years!' she added warmly.

'I'm so glad it's all over!' Nancy laughed. 'Now, for the first time in weeks, I feel like I can really breathe again.'

'Who gave you the flowers?' Susan asked, spotting the little bouquet she was carrying. 'They're so beautiful.'

'They were a good luck gift,' Nancy said, flushing just a tiny bit.

'From who?' said Jayne but, just then, Nancy was pulled to one side by someone else demanding her attention and never got to answer. Not that Melissa needed her to. Because she already knew the answer to that one, just *knew* without being told.

Later on in the evening, she made a point of finding Alan to congratulate him and to introduce him to a gushing Hayley, who insisted on using up the dregs of her phone's battery taking selfies with him. Alan smiled and grinned and gamely posed for every photo.

'You know something?' Melissa said to him, as she spotted his eye following Nancy through the crowd.

'What's that?' he twinkled down at her.

'When this is all over, I think you should ask Nancy out.'

'You do? You think she'd say yes?'

'I think you should definitely ask.'

Summer
One Year Later

Susan

PRIMROSE SQUARE

'I bind your hands in love and trust,' Eric was saying to Jayne, as a small gathering of friends and family sat around them in the tiny Remembrance Corner of Primrose Square, all looking on. Some were smiling and laughing, snapping photo after photo on their phones – like Frank, for instance, who was sitting right by Susan's side. Others were a bit teary, she noticed. Funny, she thought, the way weddings did that to people. She herself, on the other hand, was content to do nothing more than hold onto her husband's hand and remember.

'I bind your hands as a symbol of our lifelong commitment,' Jayne was saying, clearly and confidently, at the prompting of the humanist minister who was conducting the service. 'From this day forth . . .'

'And forsaking all others,' Eric finished the sentence for her, to a tiny ripple of applause as the minister pronounced them both man and wife.

Next thing, a guitarist from somewhere behind began to strum the opening chords of 'Something' by The Beatles. There was a lovely, hushed calm as everyone listened to the music, savouring the sunny, warm spring day and the wonderfully joyous atmosphere of this very special ceremony, held – at Jayne's insistence – right in the middle of Primrose Square's brand new Remembrance Corner.

So Susan looked around her, doing just that – remembering.

She glanced over at Jason and his wife Irene, who looked as pinched and sullen as ever, and remembered how horrible they'd been to Eric when he first came on the scene.

Yet when she looked at Jason and Irene now, she marvelled how far the pair of them had come in the last year. Jason was actually looking prosperous for the first time in ages. His 'mobile catering units' were doing a bomb and not only that, but he was single-handedly looking after the catering after the ceremony.

'All very posh, you know, Susan,' he'd bragged to her beforehand. 'Chicken vol au vents and sushi all the way. None of your batter burgers and fries – this is a class operation, I'll have you know. Me and Irene are going very upmarket these days. Eric says we might even start doing vegan takeaways soon. Sure all the young ones are going vegan these days, clean eating is all the rage. Might as well make a few quid of it if we can, eh?'

Then Susan's eye wandered over to Jayne herself, looking radiant in a flowing white dress with matching white trousers, with a comfy pair of sandals from M&S, the only touch that the old Jayne would have approved of.

Susan remembered only too well how lonely grief had left Jayne after her husband died. Her *first* husband, she reminded herself to say from now on. Hard to reconcile the old Jayne with the happy, glowing woman who stood at the centre of their little makeshift circle now, brimming over with joy and radiating – as she would have said herself – 'an abundance of love'. Who could have predicted that Jayne's story would have ended so happily?

Even Nancy was here too, having come all the way over from London especially for the ceremony. She was now sitting in the row beside Susan with that lovely actor guy she'd been seeing for months now – Alan what's-his-name – the guy from *Harry Potter*.

A real sweetheart and mad about Nancy too. Susan caught her eye and the two women gave each other a quick little wink as Nancy mouthed over, 'We've so much to catch up on later!'

And again, Susan remembered back to when she first met Nancy. She thought of the busy, stressed professional woman who'd first come to Primrose Square via a fraudulent Homesitter scam all that time ago, but who was as much a part of their little community now as any of them.

The fact that Nancy had moved back to London to direct a huge West End musical meant little to the ladies of Primrose Square; Nancy was and would always remain one of them. In fact, Susan herself had been the very first person Nancy had called when she went back to London, not long after *Pride and Prejudice* had wrapped. She said she had 'some pretty big news' to share and Susan was all agog to hear what it was.

'I did it!' Nancy joyfully told Susan down the phone. 'Inspired by you, I actually did it!'

'Tell me everything!' Susan had gasped.

'I took the bull by the horns,' Nancy said, the strength in her voice all too obvious. 'I formally requested a face-to-face meeting with Peter Wallace and the HR representative at the Kensington Theatre, and boy, did I say my piece or what . . . Oh Susan, you'd have been proud of me! I said abuse of power was just that, abuse, and that I wasn't prepared to see my good name and reputation and everything I'd worked for run into the ground for another moment longer.'

'And what happened?' Susan asked, on the very edge of her seat.

'Well, of course Peter denied everything and acted the bully and threw his weight around – his standard way of reacting whenever he's threatened – but I was still cool with that, because you know why? Because I'd said my piece. No more running away and hiding and behaving like a victim. I felt like a strong woman in that meeting and it was bloody wonderful.'

'Atta girl,' Susan said proudly.

'And then you know what else?' Nancy said. 'He formally apologised and the news travelled like wildfire through theatre circles. The theatre even put out a press release, can you believe it? All of a sudden, actors and directors were calling me to say sorry if they'd ever got hold of the wrong end of the stick. I even did an interview about it in the press! And since then, all sorts of doors have started opening for me again. Even the Royal Court, where I've always wanted to work, have invited me in to "have a chat about future projects"!'

Susan had been overjoyed for Nancy then, and still continued to be, with every career success she notched under her belt. Since *Pride and Prejudice*, Nancy had gone from strength to strength, and she was now directing a new musical, which was due to open in London later in the year. Frank and Susan were planning to take Melissa over to see the show as a birthday surprise for her, and Nancy had faithfully promised them backstage tours, the whole works. Not only that, but between them, they'd plotted a birthday party for Melissa – to be held in a capsule of the London Eye.

To this day, Nancy was still so incredibly kind to Melissa and was now something of a role model and big sister figure for her – it seemed that no distance could erode the bond that was there between them.

Thank God, Susan thought, closing her eyes tightly. *Thank God for sending someone like Nancy into our lives.*

She thought of all her other new friends who were now very much a part of her life now. Like Bunny and Emily from St

Michael's, who she'd grown so close to over the past year. Bunny was back home with her own family and Emily had her eye on a rental flat on Primrose Square, which Susan was madly encouraging her towards taking, loving the fact that they might end up neighbours. Poor Bungalow Bill was still at St Michael's, but Susan, Emily and Bunny made a point of visiting him regularly, always bringing freshly baked cakes for him, and taking care to let him know he had true friends in his corner who'd never desert him.

Then Susan looked over to her pride and joy, Melissa, who was standing right beside Jayne in a gorgeous new dress from Zara. She was clutching a posy of lilies and looked utterly delighted with herself, as she'd been asked to do a reading at the ceremony, which she'd preformed faultlessly.

My little pet, Susan thought, looking fondly across the garden at her, *my reason for going on, my bright, smiley child. Although not a child any more, a proper teenager now.*

Yet again, Susan remembered – this time, back to that lost, lonely, neglected girl, struggling to keep her family together at a time when everyone else was falling apart. There were no words to say how proud Susan felt as she looked at Melissa, how much she loved her, how she gave deepest thanks every day of her life for the very fact that she had a daughter like her. She and Frank had so much making up to do to their beautiful younger daughter, but they were certainly well on their way. With Frank permanently back in Dublin now, family time was what the three of them really cherished so much. They'd all sit around the kitchen table for dinner, laughing, joking and just loving the simple, ordinary pleasure of being together. For always.

As the singing went on, Susan looked around the little corner of the square, where the simple little ceremony was being held.

The Remembrance Garden had been a labour of love for Ella's old classmates, with Josh Andrews the driving force behind the whole project. They'd even raised enough money for a wooden bench, which Susan and her family often sat out on, with a simple, little brass plaque on it that read: *This is in loving memory of Ella Hayes. Always in our hearts.*

She'd even planted tiger lilies there, which had obediently come to full bloom, just in time for Jayne's special day.

I'm in a Remembrance Garden, Susan thought on that happy, sunny afternoon, *and it's only right that I remember.* So now she remembered back to that fragile, desperate, hysterical woman who kept vigil night after night outside Josh's house, somehow hoping to transfer the searing grief she felt onto someone – anyone – who she could conveniently blame. And she marvelled how she'd come full circle.

Last thing of all, Susan remembered a freckly-faced, curly-headed teenager, stretched out on that very corner of the square with a book over her face, pretending to study when she was really trying to get a tan.

A wonderfully wild, free-spirited girl, who wanted to change the world, bit by bit. Ella may not have been given enough time on this earth to do everything she wanted, but she certainly changed the lives of everyone around her.

Susan remembered.

And then, she finally let go.

Acknowledgements

Thank you, Marianne Gunn O'Connor. You're so much more than an incredible agent; you're an amazing friend too.

Thank you Eli Dryden, for taking me with you on this amazing adventure to Bonnier Zaffre. You'll never know how grateful I am to be working with you again. And I'll keep nagging you till you eventually come back to visit us in Dublin!

Thank you Pat Lynch, who works so hard and is always so positive and uplifting. See you in The Farm very soon, Chicken. Thank you to Vicki Satlow in Milan who does such an incredible job with translation rights. You're a true star, Vicki.

Thank you to the fabulous team at Bonnier Zaffre, for the warmth of your welcome and your enthusiasm, not to mention all your hard work and incredible support. I'm so lucky to be a part of Team Bonnier Zaffre. Special thanks to Tara Loder, Sarah Bauer, James Horobin, Nico Poilblanc, Angie Willocks, Victoria Hart, Stephen Dumughn, Kate Parkin, Imogen Sebba, Carla Hutchinson, Francesca Russell, Sahina Bibi, Alexandra Allden and Laura Makela. It was a real joy to meet you all at the Publishing Preview back in February. Now that's how you throw a party!

Thanks also to Natalie Braine and Sophie Buchan, whose brilliant work and forensic attention to detail was amazing.

Thanks to Simon Hess, who works so hard and does so much for all of us. And of course huge thanks to all the team here in Dublin: Declan Heeney, Helen Gleed O' Connor and, of course, the man himself, Gill Hess.

Special thanks to Mum and Dad and all my wonderful family, for everything.

Big thanks to my lovely pals from the world of publishing; Sinead Moriarty, Liz Nugent, Monica McInerney, Carmel Harrington and Patricia Scanlan. It's always such a joy to meet up with you all so we can talk books and stories and ideas.

And in case you think I've forgotten anyone – Heartfelt thanks to Clelia and Clara Belle Murphy, Karry, Caroline and Isabelle Finnegan, Susan McHugh, Marion O'Dwyer, Alison McKenna, Maria McDermottroe, Isobel Mahon, Fionnuala Murphy and Fiona Lalor.

This one is for all of you and if you want to know why, just keep reading.

Want to read
NEW BOOKS
before anyone else?

Like getting
FREE BOOKS?

Enjoy sharing your
OPINIONS?

Discover

READERS FIRST

Read. Love. Share.

Sign up today to win your first free book:
readersfirst.co.uk